B11/11

KT-407-890

A
BAND
OF STEEL

ROSIE GOODWIN

A BAND OF STEEL

headline

First published in Great Britain in 2011
by HEADLINE PUBLISHING GROUP

1

Cataloguing in Publication Data is available from the British Library

ISBN 978 0 7553 5391 0

Typeset in Calisto MT by Palimpsest Book Production Ltd,
Falkirk, Stirlingshire

Printed and bound in Great Britain by Clays Ltd, St Ives plc

Headline's policy is to use papers that are natural, renewable and recyclable products and
made from wood grown in sustainable forests. The logging and manufacturing processes
are expected to conform to the environmental regulations of the country of origin.

HEADLINE PUBLISHING GROUP
An Hachette UK Company
338 Euston Road
London NW1 3BH

www.headline.co.uk
www.hachette.co.uk

This book is for
a dear sister-in-law and brother-in-law.
Lynn Yates, who died 7 June 2010, and
Ray Yates, who died 10 September 2010.
Reunited, rest in peace.

Acknowledgements

I would like to say a very sincere thank you to Betty, Ronnie and Joan for all the advice given during the writing of this novel on Jewish customs, festivals, etc. It was invaluable!

Also a big thank you to Julie and the staff at Malpas library in Newport for making me feel so welcome on my recent visit there.

As always thank you to Jane and Tye for your support and to Penny and David for making the recent bus tour such a success, and for allowing everyone who attended access to the lovely Leathermill Grange.

Finally – a huge thank you to Lord and Lady Daventry for allowing me access to Arbury Hall and gardens whilst researching for this book.

Many waters cannot quench love. Neither can floods drown it.

Song of Solomon, 8:7

Prologue

'Come, Freyde, there is no more time for delay or we shall miss the boat.'

The woman stared at her husband from frightened eyes before taking a last look around her luxurious home. She was painfully aware that it could be the very last time she would ever see it, and the thought of the journey ahead of them struck terror into her heart. However, she knew that Ezra was only doing what had to be done. To delay could mean the death of them and their children.

Nazi troops had now entered Austria and annexed it to Germany, and already 100,000 Jews had been forced to emigrate. Kindertransport trains had been arranged to get children evacuated to England where they would be fostered until the war was over. It was heartbreaking to see the parents trudging towards the station with their children all with little nametags dangling from a string about their necks. They knew only too well that they might never be reunited.

The SS had now been put in charge of the Jews, and Ezra Schwartz feared that the persecutions would now begin in earnest. The anti-semitism that had been simmering was now flaring up into a fierce blaze. The family had no choice but to flee Germany.

'Adina, Dovid, Ariel, come.'

Her three children approached her, their eyes full of fear as Freyde tried to smile at them reassuringly. Dovid, her firstborn, was the spitting image of his father when she had first met him: tall and dark with flashing dark eyes. Now, he took her hand and squeezed it gently. At sixteen he was already head and shoulders above her and he held a special place in her heart. Next came Adina, or Dina as she was affectionately known, who at fourteen was the scholar amongst them. Adina was like a sponge when it came to learning and her father often teased her that she would one day become a professor. Like her brother she had a shock of dark hair that curled on her shoulders, and huge eyes that could change from tawny amber to black depending on her mood. Delicate and petite, Adina was at that curious age when she was neither girl nor yet woman, and was greatly loved because of her gentle nature by all that knew her. Finally came Ariel, the baby of the family at ten years old. She was like a miniature replica of her older sister and was spoiled shamelessly by all of them.

1

Now as their father gazed upon them all, his face became solemn. 'It must appear that we are doing nothing more than going for a family stroll,' he emphasised. 'Once we reach the docks, the captain will get us aboard his boat under cover of darkness. I cannot promise that it will be a comfortable passage, but you must all be brave and think yourselves lucky that we have the means to escape. Should my fears be confirmed, many of our kind will perish here. But God willing, we shall have a fresh start in a new country.'

'Shall we be staying in Italy, Papa?' Dovid asked tentatively.

Ezra shook his head. 'No, Dovi. If we can get safely to Italy I then intend to try and get us all to England, possibly to London.' Ezra would have preferred to get them all into Switzerland, but the Swiss borders were now heavily guarded. England was his second choice, and as his children had had the best education that money could buy, they could all speak English as fluently as German. He hoped that they would adapt to a new life in England reasonably well.

He patted the money belt that was buckled securely around his waist before asking his wife, 'Did you stitch the money bags into the girls' petticoats as I asked?'

'It is done.' Freyde's hand slid unconsciously to the two bulging pouches resting against her own legs beneath her skirts.

'I want to take my toys with me,' Ariel whined as she jammed her thumb in her mouth.

'We can take no unnecessary luggage,' her father explained sadly, as he stroked her dark curls. 'It would look too suspicious if we were to be seen lugging suitcases towards the docks. We must make do with what we have in our shopping bags and think ourselves lucky.'

Ariel pouted but for once remained silent, sensing that something momentous was about to happen.

Because Ezra had held a good job in a bank he was fortunate to be fleeing with enough money to give them all a new beginning – if they could get safely away, that was. But it was all in God's hands now. Many of his fellow Jews were not so fortunate and had tried to escape with nothing but the clothes they stood up in.

Since the terrible events of what had become known as 'Kristallnacht' – 9–10 November 1938 – when, in retaliation for the murder of a German official in Paris, 1,400 synagogues and 7,000 Jewish businesses had been destroyed in both Germany and Austria, and 30,000 Jews had been arrested and sent to camps, the writing had been on the wall.

Ezra looked regretfully around their comfortable sitting room in their big house in Cologne. No doubt, once it was known that he and his family had fled, the looters would take the antiques that had been lovingly collected over the years. His biggest regret, however, was having to leave his parents behind. The children would miss their Zayda and Bubba, but no amount of encouragement had persuaded them to

2

come along. The couple were elderly and set in their ways, and determined to live out their life in the home that had been theirs since their marriage. Ezra's only means of communication with them from now on would be through a non-Jewish banker friend of his, who had promised to send him word of them once he was settled. But this did nothing to quell the fear in Ezra's heart.

Now, after taking a deep breath, he ushered his family into the hallway. The parquet floor shone in the lamplight and the huge bowl of flowers on the hall table filled the air with their scent. Everything looked just as it always had, and yet everyone was aware that from this moment on, nothing would ever be the same again.

'Come, it is time to go.' Ezra shepherded his family out into the street and the first leg of the long journey ahead of them began.

Part One
A Family in Exile

Chapter One

'Come away from the window, Mama,' Adina urged from her place at the side of the hearth. 'Standing there will not make Papa return any quicker.'

'I know that, bubbeleh,' her mother sighed as she pulled her thin cardigan more tightly about her. Ezra had been gone for two whole days now and she could only pray that he would return with good news. Since managing to get to London, the family had been forced to share a single room in a large tenement in the East End. It was not an ideal situation, but even so, she knew they were fortunate, compared to many others. Every day, the newspapers were full of horror stories about the atrocities the Jews in Europe were being forced to endure. Men, women and children alike were being sent to the infamous concentration camps; it was a known fact that many of them would not survive.

For some time now, Ezra had been scouring the country for a more suitable place for his family to live. So far, he had visited many cities, hoping to find some small business with living quarters attached where he and his wife and children could live for the duration of the war. Thus far, his search had been in vain. This time, he had left to visit Birmingham, and Freyde hoped that it had been a successful trip.

As her eyes now rested on Adina, a sad smile played about her lips. The girl had been her rock since leaving Germany. The voyage to Italy had proved to be a nightmare. Freyde and Ariel had suffered from dreadful bouts of sea sickness from the second the ship had left the docks, but Adina had cared for them and cleaned up their messes without a qualm. Getting to London from Italy had also been very problematic. Many of the countries that the Jews were trying to escape to were now denying them access but thankfully, Ezra had money, and so they had been fortunate.

Dovi had found work on a market stall in Petticoat Lane, and both Freyde and Adina had earned a little from sewing in a sweatshop in the Mile End Road. Also, now that rationing was enforced, there were always people who needed things repairing or made over, since new clothes were no longer easily come by. An accomplished needlewoman, Freyde had taught Adina to sew at an early age, and so now what had once been no more than a hobby became a means of survival. It kept their savings intact, and both women were glad of the extra work to keep them busy.

The cluttered room in Stepney was a world away from their beautiful house in Cologne. Secondhand mattresses lay on the floor, and the majority of their cooking was done over the open fire. The walls were thin and they were constantly kept awake by the families on either side of them. There was only one outside toilet for all of the people who were crammed into the building, and despite their attempts to clean it, the little hut stank. It was deplorably filthy. Only the day before, Freyde had opened the door to find a large rat staring at her from red eyes, and the stench was enough to make her retch. But at least they were all alive, and every day she thanked God for the fact.

Ariel was sitting cross-legged on the floor playing with a doll that Dovi had picked up from the market for her, but now she glanced up. 'I'm hungry, Mama,' she complained, and crossing to the pot hanging above the dancing flames in the fireplace, Freyde stirred the contents before telling her, 'Not long now, bubbeleh. The stew is almost ready. I just hope your Papa is home in time to share it with us.'

Even as she spoke, the door opened and Ezra appeared looking weary but elated.

'I have good news,' he announced as everyone's eyes turned to him. 'I think I have found just the place we have been looking for.'

'*Really*?' Freyde's face lit up as she hurried to help him take his coat off.

Ezra was beaming like a Cheshire cat as he turned to the fire and held his hands out to the warmth. Again, they were fortunate; they could afford to buy coal for the fire, even if they had to lug it up the four floors to their room. Many of their neighbours were cold and hungry, and Freyde often felt guilty when she saw their sunken eyes and skinny frames.

Removing the stew now, Freyde pushed the sooty black kettle into the heart of the fire and hurried away to prepare the teapot, keeping an expectant eye on her husband all the time.

Once the tea was brewed she perched on the arm of the chair he was sitting in and asking excitedly, 'So what have you found then?'

'Well . . .' Ezra took a warming gulp of his drink, 'I went to Birmingham as planned, but I was not impressed. The city is being bombed and I wished to find somewhere a little safer for us. So, I then took the train to Coventry, but once again, the factories there are being targeted, so I went a little further afield. I ended up in a town called Nuneaton, and after walking about for a time I spotted a small empty shop. On making a few enquiries, I managed to find out that it was up for rent with living accommodation included, so I went along to the landlord who took me back to have a look at it. Very reluctantly, may I add, when he realised that I was a Jew. Until I actually showed him that I had money to pay the rent he looked at me as if I was a bad smell under his nose.' Ezra sighed and took another sip of tea. 'But

8

anyway, I believe it would serve us well. It is a little run down, but at the back of the shop is a large living room-cum-kitchen. There is an outside privy in the yard and upstairs are three good-sized bedrooms. The previous owners were elderly and let the premises get into an awful state, but there is still some stock in the shop that is salvageable. It's just shoelaces, cleaning products, stationery and so on, but after a good tidy-up we could have the business up and running again in a fairly short time.'

Freyde clapped her hands with delight. 'It sounds perfect,' she told him. 'But what about a bathroom?'

Ezra grinned ruefully. 'I'm afraid our bathing will have to be done in a tin bath in front of the fire for the foreseeable future, but at least we shall have our own space.'

'So be it. When can we go there?'

'As soon as you like. I have already paid the first month's rent, and because we don't have much to take with us, I'm sure that we could carry our belongings with us on the train. Unless you wanted to take the mattresses, that is.'

Freyde eyed them with disdain. 'No, I would prefer to get new ones when we arrive there,' she told him decisively. 'These were here when we came and I think we should leave them for the next family that inhabits the room.'

Ezra looked at his wife from tired eyes. She had lost a lot of weight and seemed to have aged over the last few months. Not that this was surprising when he thought of how she had been forced to adapt. Back in Cologne, Freyde had led a charmed life. The wife of an eminent banker, she had been used to being waited on by servants. He could barely ever remember seeing her back then without her pearls and her lipstick on, but now they were surviving any way they could, and the old days seemed a lifetime away.

He knew that she had brought the jewels he had once indulgently showered upon her, but she never wore them any more. They would have looked out of place in their present surroundings. But still, he consoled himself, the war could not last for ever, and perhaps one day things would once more be as they had been. He could only live in hope as his thoughts travelled back to his parents. He worried about them constantly and prayed daily that they might still be safe. He also worried about the new challenge ahead of him as a shopkeeper. But how hard could it be?

Ariel had wormed her way onto his lap and he kissed her affection-ately as his wife took some dishes from the small cupboard in a corner of the room and began to ladle stew into them.

'Is there any furniture in the living quarters?' she asked, excitement clear in her voice.

'A little,' her husband told her warily. 'But I am not sure how much of it we will be able to use. The place has stood empty for some time.'

She shrugged. 'It doesn't matter. There will be more in the second-hand shops. We shall only need the basic things to begin with and then we can add to them as we go along.'

Ariel scrambled down from her father's lap as her mother placed a dish of stew on the floor for her and now it was Adina who asked, 'What will you be selling in the shop, Papa?'

Ezra smiled. 'I suppose it was a sort of a general shop, from what I could make of it. You know, a bit of everything from food to shoelaces? I shall continue to trade in the same goods. It would make sense as the business is already established.'

Adina nodded in agreement, looking forward to it already. Back in Cologne, she had had her own bedroom with a beautiful four-poster bed and rosewood furniture. No doubt once they arrived in Nuneaton she would share a room with Ariel, but it would be better than having to live, sleep and eat all in one room as they were forced to do at present.

'I think we should aim to leave by the end of the week,' Freyde piped up and Ezra smiled indulgently. It was nice to see his family looking happy again.

They left the tenement building the next Thursday morning bright and early, and as they walked away from it, none of them looked back once.

Freyde had bundled up their possessions into the blankets she had bought, and each of them carried one, even Ariel. The only family member who didn't seem to be completely happy about moving was Dovid. He had quite enjoyed working on the market and had recently met an East End girl called Pearlie who had stolen his heart – not that he dare tell his father that. Although they were now in another country, his father was still trying to hold firm to his Jewish faith and customs, apart from insisting that they all speak in English at all times, whereas Dovid was more open-minded. Ezra's main concern at present was that they would no longer be living in a Jewish community. There could be no more Hebrew lessons or visits to a synagogue on Friday evenings or Saturdays, so how were his children to meet suitable partners? But over-riding this was the need to keep them safe.

As they trooped down the stairs that morning, people had stuck their heads around doors and wished them well, and they were all in a light-hearted mood as they climbed on a bus and headed for Euston station.

They changed trains twice on the way, stopping first at New Street in Birmingham, where they all gazed in awe at the great glass dome that covered the station. Steam and smoke from the trains floated upwards before being licked away by the wind that funnelled along the platforms. Coventry was the next change, and by then they were all tired and hungry, despite the smoked salmon and cream cheese beigels they had bought in Brick Lane that morning. They were greatly looking forward to seeing their new home for the first time. Due to bomb damage on

10

the tracks, they had been constantly diverted, and the journey seemed to take for ever, so when the train finally pulled into Trent Valley railway station it was already dark and bitterly cold, although it was only late afternoon.

The children followed their parents along the platform, clutching their bundles to them, and when they emerged onto the street, Freyde gasped at her first glance of Nuneaton. After the hustle and bustle of London it appeared to be like a ghost town. There were no lights visible, all the houses had blackout curtains hanging at the windows, and the streets were almost deserted. The few people who were out and about had gas masks slung across their shoulders and passed the family as if they were invisible.

'It's so quiet here,' Freyde whispered as she hitched the blanket she was carrying to a more comfortable position on her hip.

'You must remember this is only a town and not a city,' her husband pointed out as he looked along the frosted pavements.

'I'm hungry,' Ariel complained, and her father ruffled her hair. 'Never fear, little one. It won't be long now and we shall be at our new home.' He patted his pocket where the key was safely tucked away. 'Come along. The sooner we get moving, the sooner we shall be there.'

They set off, the children trailing behind, taking in their new surroundings. Not far from the train station was a bus station, but that too was in darkness, so Ezra encouraged them on.

Once they had passed through the town centre they began to walk along Coton Road.

'The house and shop is in Edmund Street,' Ezra informed them, and then almost as an afterthought he looked at Freyde sheepishly and added, 'I did warn you that it would need a little tidying up, didn't I?'

She grinned ruefully. 'After where we've been living I have no doubt this place will appear like a palace,' she assured him.

'What's that place there?' Ariel asked, pointing across the road to two huge metal gates.

'That is the entrance to Riversley Park,' her father told her, 'and if you are good, you will get to go there to play sometimes. I believe there is a museum in there too.'

The little girl's face lit up at the thought of being able to play outside again. Back home in Cologne she had had a huge garden to run about in, but since living in London she had barely set foot outside the squalid building in which they had been forced to live.

As they approached the end of Coton Road, Ezra pointed ahead to three enormous brick arches that spanned the road. 'That is what they call the Coton Arches and the trains run across it,' he informed them. Normally, his family loved to hear about things of interest, but by now they were all weary and put their efforts into lugging their bundles along rather than listening to him. A few minutes later, he led them

11

off down a street to their right and stopped in front of a shabby-looking shop.

'This is it,' he told them, dropping his blanket to the ground and flexing his aching fingers.

As he delved into his pocket for the key, Freyde eyed the building with alarm. Ezra had warned her that it needed some work doing to it, but this place looked almost derelict. The windows were so grimy that it was impossible to see through them, and paint was peeling from the sills and the door.

Still, it's probably better inside, she thought to herself as Ezra inserted the key in the lock. Once the door was open he ushered them all inside and they stood there, their eyes adjusting to the inky darkness.

'The kitchen is through this way,' Ezra told them, as excited as a child. 'And once we're in there we should be able to put the light on. The landlord assured me that he would have the electricity and the water connected by today.'

They groped their way along the wall until they came to a door at the back of the shop – and sure enough, they found themselves in a fair-sized room.

'Don't turn the light on just yet,' Freyde warned him as she looked towards the window. 'There are no curtains up so we shall have to dangle one of the blankets over the curtain pole for tonight to stop the light being seen from outside.'

Ezra instantly untied the blanket containing some of their belongings and tipped them out unceremoniously onto the floor before standing on a chair and draping the blanket across the window as Freyde had requested.

'*Now* we can put the light on,' he said with a measure of satisfaction as his hand fumbled along the wall for the light switch.

When the bare bulb dangling from the centre of the room came on, Freyde looked about her with dismay. The inside was even worse than the outside. The floor was littered with rubbish and the smell . . . she sniffed, trying to distinguish what it was. It was certainly damp but there was another smell that she did not wish to think too much about.

'Well,' she said, trying to keep her voice light. She knew how hard Ezra had worked to find this place and had no wish to upset him. 'Just as you explained, there is work to be done but it's nothing that a little elbow grease can't put right.'

Seeing the look of relief that washed across her husband's face she turned to her son and took control as she told him. 'Dovi, go out into the yard and see if there is any coal in the coal house. If we can get a fire going, I can make a broth from some of the food I brought with us. And you, Adina, would you check that there is water at the sink? I think we could all do with a wash and a nice warm drink.'

As her son and daughter scuttled away to do as she asked, Freyde looked around the room. In one corner was a table, leaning drunkenly to one side with three mismatched chairs placed around it, and next to the sink was a cooker that was so thick with grease that she almost retched at the sight of it. That would certainly need a good scrub before it was used, she decided, and there was no time like the present. As she took off her coat and rolled up her sleeves, the back door opened, letting in an icy blast of air, and Dovi appeared with a bucket almost full of coal.

'This is all I could find,' he told her.

She clucked with satisfaction. 'That will be more than enough to keep us going until morning and then we can get some more. Will you light the fire, Ezra? There are some old newspapers you could use over in that corner – look.'

Ezra obligingly did as he was told and within an hour there was an enormous fire roaring in the grate and the room didn't look quite so bleak.

Soon the broth was simmering in one of the cooking pots that Freyde had brought with them.

'Now,' she said, looking around thoughtfully, 'if the rest of the house is anything to go by I think we shall have to sleep in here tonight. At least we shall be warm. We can sleep on the blankets we have brought and tomorrow I shall scrub the bedrooms while you and Dovid go and find us some mattresses.'

Pride shone from Ezra as he looked at his wife. Sometimes she amazed him. His Freyde was taking all this in her stride. She really was a remarkable woman!

Ariel's head was drooping now, and seeing this, Freyde broke off a chunk of bread from the loaf she had brought with her and pressed it into hand, fearing that the child would fall asleep before the broth was ready.

'Come, little one,' she said softly. 'Eat this up and then Mama will make you comfortable.'

While Ariel did as she was told, Freyde spread a blanket at the side of the fire and settled the child onto it before rushing away to fill a bowl with soapy water. She then set about scrubbing the table.

'Do you know, I think with a little work this could be a good solid piece of furniture,' she commented to her husband as she scrubbed it within an inch of its life.

He grinned. It seemed that he was going to be very busy tomorrow, as the list of jobs that Freyde had lined up for him was growing by the minute. Not that he was complaining. They were here in their new home and, *Gott sei Dank*, they would all now be safe for the duration of this terrifying conflict.

Chapter Two

It was mid-morning the following day when Freyde met her neighbour for the first time. Freyde was outside sweeping up the rubbish in the small paved yard when a head clad in metal curlers with a headscarf wrapped turban-style around them appeared over the fence.

''Ello, love. Settlin' in, are you?' The woman flashed her a cheery smile, then before Freyde could answer her she rambled on, 'I were wonderin' how long it would be afore this place got taken on again. The Harpers used to run the shop an' a right thrivin' little business it were an' all, but their lad were killed in an accident a year ago an' it sent the old woman a bit doolally, if you know what I mean. The poor old sod's in a mental 'ome now an' the old man's gone to live wi' their daughter in Attleborough. Eeh, it were a rum do, an' no mistake.' She wrapped her arms about her gaily flowered apron. 'Lovely young man, Geoffrey were. Engaged to be married to a lass from Coton an' all. He had his whole life ahead o' him. But there you go. It's no use cryin' over spilt milk, is it? What's done is done.' Cocking her head to one side, she studied Freyde solemnly. The woman was a looker, there was no doubt about it, even if she was a bit on the skinny side.

Freyde straightened and smiled at the woman before saying, 'It is very nice to meet you. How do you do?'

The woman's eyes almost popped out of her head as she heard Freyde's accent and she said cautiously, 'You ain't from around these parts, are you?'

'No. My family and I have travelled here from Cologne.' Freyde saw no reason to lie as she waited for the woman's reaction.

'I see.' There was a frown on her new neighbour's face and her voice was stiff. 'So you're German then?'

'No, we are Jewish,' Freyde informed her. 'But it was no longer safe to stay in Germany so my husband arranged for us to come here for the duration of the war.'

'Oh.' The woman visibly relaxed. She couldn't blame her neighbour for coming here, although Jews were somewhat of a rarity in this area. As far as she knew, there was only one other Jewish family in the whole of the town, although she had heard that some of the Jewish evacuee children had filtered into the town from the Kindertransport trains that had enabled them to escape from their homelands. They were having a hard time of it, by all accounts, as the majority of them could only speak German.

'Well, I'm Mrs Haynes,' she now informed her, holding her hand out, and Freyde leaned across the fence and politely shook it. Mrs Haynes wasn't too sure how she felt about living next door to Jews, but then she had always been a great believer in 'live and let live' so she supposed she should give them a chance at least.

'I am Freyde Schwartz.'

The two women surveyed each other solemnly until Ariel skipped into the yard. Seeing the stranger she hastily snuggled into her mother's skirts.

'This is my youngest daughter, Ariel,' Freyde introduced her as the child smiled shyly.

'Pleased to meet you, I'm sure.' Her neighbour smiled back, but then a piercing cry came from behind her and she hastily turned away. 'That'll be our Freddie,' she apologised. 'He's twelve an' still don't know his arse from his elbow 'alf the time.' She grinned as Freyde's eyebrows disappeared into her hairline. 'See you later, love.' With that she was gone, leaving Freyde and Ariel to stare at the place where she had been standing.

'Why does that lady talk so strangely, Mama?' Ariel asked innocently.

'I think you will find that is the local dialect,' her mother informed her with a grin. 'And if we are to live here I am sure we shall get to hear a great deal of it in the future.' She then turned to continue sweeping the yard as Ariel shrugged and disappeared off back indoors.

Ezra and Dovi had been gone since early morning in search of essentials for their new home. First on the list were beds and mattresses and a settee for the small lounge behind the shop. They had also been told to look out for a secondhand sewing machine so that Freyde could make new curtains. Sadly, they had been forced to sell the one they had purchased in London since it was too heavy to carry. Now as Freyde glanced towards the house she felt a little overwhelmed at the amount of work that needed doing. She was determined to get the living quarters clean first, and then they would have to think about restocking the shop, ready for it to open – which would be no easy task, with rationing in place.

Adina was inside attacking the cooker again, since it had turned out to be even filthier than Freyde had first thought in daylight. Still, it seemed to be in working order, so that was one blessing at least. Shivering, Freyde entered the kitchen and Adina looked up to smile at her. Freyde then filled a bowl with water and vinegar and began to scrub the windows, and shortly afterwards, Ezra and Dovi staggered in carrying a sturdy brass bedstead.

'I thought this would be good for our bedroom.' Ezra informed his wife. Drying her hands on her apron, Freyde beamed. There were a few minor dents in it and it needed a good polish, but otherwise it looked to be a good solid bed. 'I managed to get beds for the children too, and mattresses.' Ezra was feeling pleased with himself. 'There is an excellent secondhand shop just down the road. They even have a Singer sewing machine there so I've bought that too, but I haven't managed to find us a settee as yet.'

Freyde had already scrubbed the bedrooms, and now as Ezra and Dovi lugged their prize up the stairs she sighed with satisfaction. At least they would all sleep comfortably tonight.

By teatime the house looked a lot more habitable although they still had no curtains to hang at the windows.

'I shall go into town and try to get some material tomorrow,' Freyde declared as she straightened the counterpane on Ariel's bed. The little girl and Adina would be sharing a room and Dovi would be sleeping in the small box room that overlooked the yard.

Ezra had filled the coal house and now, with a fire blazing in the grate and the room shining, the place looked warm and cosy even if it was still a little bare.

Freyde had cooked them a chicken, which Ezra had managed to buy from a gentleman who kept fowl, and that evening they all sat cross-legged in front of the fire, tired but content with their day's work.

The following day, Freyde white-washed the walls whilst Ezra went in search of a settee and some chairs, then after lunch she tidied herself up and she, Adina and Ariel went into town to purchase curtain material. By lucky chance, there was a market on in the town centre, and although the choice was sorely limited, she arrived home a few hours later with enough black-out material to cover all the windows.

The first things she saw when she entered the kitchen were two wing chairs on either side of the fireplace and a rather overstuffed settee. It was nothing like the quality of the furniture she had owned in Germany but even so it looked reasonably clean and comfortable, and suddenly the place was beginning to look more like a home.

In less than a week, Freyde had the whole place glistening from top to bottom and Mrs Haynes, her neighbour, could not fail but to be impressed. She had called around with a pot of her homemade jam as a house-welcoming present and when she stepped into the kitchen she was shocked at the transformation.

'My God, you've worked hard,' she declared, thinking of her own rather untidy kitchen next door. 'I'd never 'ave believed you could have got so much done in such a short time.'

'It is surprising what you can do when you set your mind to it,' Freyde told her with a twinkle in her eye. 'Now, would you like a cup of tea?'

She had been told that the English loved their tea. She herself much preferred coffee, but as it was in very short supply she supposed she would have to develop a taste for tea instead.

'I wouldn't say no, luv.' Mrs Haynes perched her considerable bottom on one of the chairs Ezra had purchased to go around the table as Freyde hurried away to put the kettle on.

'I dare say you'll be lookin' to get the little 'un into school, won't you?' the woman asked as Freyde carefully measured three spoonfuls of tea into a heavy brown teapot.

'Yes, and as soon as possible. Would you be able to recommend one?'

'Well, the nearest one is just around the corner,' Mrs Haynes told her obligingly. 'I could show you where it is, if you like, an' I'd recommend it. All my brood went there an' you shouldn't have any trouble gettin' her in. Some o' the kids from hereabouts have been evacuated, so it's half-empty at present.'

'That would be very helpful. Thank you.' Freyde poured the boiling water over the tea leaves and after giving them a stir she placed the tea cosy on the pot and left it to mash while she prepared the cups.

It was as they were drinking that Dovi appeared wheeling a borrowed trolley on which was a chest of drawers that he had found in yet another secondhand shop. Their neighbour looked at him approvingly, thinking what a handsome young man he was.

'Ooh, he'll have the girls 'ereabouts fallin' at his feet.' Mrs Haynes chuckled at the shocked look on Freyde's face.

'I sincerely hope not unless they are Jewish girls,' Freyde retorted primly.

Placing her cup on its saucer, Mrs Haynes said solemnly, 'I reckon you'll find there's a shortage o' them round here. An' you know the sayin', luv – when in Rome, do as the Romans do.'

Understanding her meaning, Freyde blushed hotly. She supposed the woman was right. There was not even a synagogue in the area as far as she knew, so they would have to practise their faith as best they could.

'I'm sorry,' she muttered. 'I was not trying to imply that English girls are not good enough for my son.'

Mrs Haynes smiled goodnaturedly. 'No offence taken. I realise that everythin' must seem strange to you, comin' to a new country an' all that. But I dare say you'll be safer 'ere than you would have been back home, wi' the way things are goin'.'

'There is no doubt about that,' Freyde agreed. Her thoughts turned to Ezra's parents and she prayed that they were safe.

That night, when the children had retired to bed, Ezra sat in the wing chair that he had adopted at the side of the fireplace, reading the newspaper.

'They have begun to call up young British men between the ages of twenty and twenty-seven,' he told Freyde. 'It states that by the end of this month, two million of them will be gone to fight for their country.'

Freyde looked up from the sock she was darning. She desperately missed their home in Cologne and had suffered agonies of guilt about leaving Ezra's parents behind, but now more than ever she realised that Ezra had done the right thing by getting them away.

'Then may God go with them.'

They both bowed their heads in prayer and fell silent.

The following day, Freyde enrolled Ariel in the school that Mrs Haynes had recommended in Coton and it was decided that she would start there the following Monday.

On the way home, Ariel was distraught. 'I don't *want* to go to school,' she whined.

Freyde laughed as she held fast to her hand. 'But why not, bubbeleh?'

'Because all the children there speak English *all* the time.'

'But of course they do! They *are* English, and you can speak the language as well as they can – in fact, you have been doing so since we arrived in England,' Freyde patiently pointed out. In that moment she realised that she would have to speak to Ezra that very evening. Since coming to England they had sometimes lapsed into their native tongue when they were alone, but now she knew that they must adopt English as their first language at all times if they were to be accepted by the townspeople.

Ariel sulked but said no more on the subject as they hurried on their way.

Adina was stitching a new skirt for herself with scraps of material left over from the curtains when they arrived home, and she smiled brightly as her sister entered the cosy kitchen.

'So, how was your new school?' she asked.

Ariel scowled as Freyde hung her coat up and gave her eldest daughter a warning look.

'Ariel is feeling a little nervous about starting there, which is to be expected,' she said, hoping to sound positive. 'But I'm sure she will be happy there when she has made some new friends.'

'Of course you will,' Adina agreed, keeping her smile firmly fixed in place as she looked at her younger sister. 'So when will you start there?'

'On Monday,' Ariel muttered peevishly.

'Good, then in the meantime you can come through to the shop with me and help me white-wash the walls.' Adina took her foot from the treadle of the Singer sewing machine and grinned. She knew how much Ariel liked to be involved with what they were doing and hoped to take her mind off things.

Sure enough, in no time at all, the little girl was her usual cheery self as she splashed white-wash haphazardly on the walls and chattered away fifteen to the dozen.

'Papa and Dovi have gone for some wood to make the new shelves,' she told Adina. 'And Papa is going to keep a shelf just for sweets. Great big glass jars full of them . . . if he can get them.' Suddenly pausing, she asked unhappily, 'Adina, when can we go home?'

'We *are* home, little one,' Adina said softly, and then they both continued with what they were doing as their thoughts drifted back to how things had once been.

Later that afternoon, Adina decided to take a stroll. Since moving in she had barely left the house but now she felt the need for some fresh air.

'*Must* you go?' Freyde asked. The sky was leaden and grey, and she suspected that it might snow. It was certainly cold enough.

'I shan't go far,' Adina promised as she slipped her arms into her warm coat and wrapped a scarf about her neck. 'I'd just like to get to know my way about a little.'

'Very well, but be careful,' Freyde warned.

At the end of the road, Adina turned right and walked beneath the Coton Arches; within seconds she came to Chilvers Coton parish church. It looked so pretty that she found herself walking through the church-yard admiring the beautiful stained-glass windows. She paused at the big wooden doors and then, taking a deep breath, she stepped inside and allowed her eyes to adjust to the gloomy interior. She had never been inside a church before. The ceiling was high and carved pews were spaced all along the length of it on either side of a long aisle. On the altar was a large brass cross and a bowl of flowers, and it was as she stood there thinking how peaceful it was that she suddenly became aware of someone standing behind her.

Whirling about, she came face to face with a man dressed in long vestments.

'I . . . I am so sorry,' she mumbled. 'I was just curious and wanted to see what it was like inside.'

'Please don't apologise,' the kindly priest told her. 'The house of God is always open to everyone.'

'I usually pray in a synagogue,' she told him, her eyes solemn, but he merely shrugged.

'A church, a synagogue – what does it matter? We still worship the same God and you are welcome here any time.'

Adina relaxed a little. What the man said made sense, although she wondered if her father would see it that way. He still tried to keep their faith alive and they had celebrated Chanukah as best they could.

'Have you just moved into the area?' he asked now, noting her accent.

Adina nodded. 'Yes. My father is renting a shop in Edmund Street but it isn't open yet. We've been too busy getting the living quarters up to my mother's standards.'

'All in good time. I'm sure that you will be ready to open the shop soon.'

Edging towards the door, Adina smiled nervously. 'Goodbye then.'

'Goodbye, and don't forget, you are always welcome.'

Back in the biting cold again, she wandered about the Pingles Fields for half an hour before heading back the way she had come. Despite the fact that she had put a brave face on since coming to Nuneaton, she too missed her real home and wondered how long it would be before she could return to it.

19

Chapter Three

On 9 April 1940 the Nazis invaded Norway and Denmark, and a month later they took the Lowlands and Holland. Ezra bought newspapers daily and read of Hitler's conquests with fear in his heart. By then the shop was as fully stocked as he could make it and he had opened its doors – but it was not doing well. The people of the town were friendly enough when they met the family in the street, but seemed to be avoiding using the shop. Ezra was gravely concerned. He knew that his savings could not last for ever and wondered what he should do to encourage people to come into the shop, which he had named 'Coton General Store'. He knew he must avoid using the word 'Schwartz', unfortunately, because of its German origins.

Freyde had become quite friendly with her new neighbour, Mrs Haynes, to the point that she and the family were now allowed to use the woman's Anderson shelter, should the need arise. And the need was arising more and more of late, which was terrifying for the townspeople. Coventry was the main target for the Germans because of the many industrial factories there, but Nuneaton had not gone unnoticed.

Now as Ezra laid his newspaper aside he sighed and looked towards his wife who was chopping vegetables on the kitchen table. She smiled at him, knowing how worried he was. There had been no word from his parents in Cologne for months now and they were beginning to fear the worst. The door leading into the shop was open but the bell heralding a customer's arrival remained stubbornly silent.

Ariel was at school and Adina was sewing at the side of the fire.

'I'll go and fetch Ariel home for her lunch, if you like,' she offered.

'That would be wonderful, bubbeleh, thank you,' her mother said gratefully.

Laying her sewing aside, the girl rose and put on her coat. A thick fog hung over the yard and it was bitterly cold.

'I just hope your sister will settle soon,' Freyde fretted as she scraped the chopped vegetables into a saucepan and set it on the cooker.

'Of course she will' Adina told her, with a conviction that she was far from feeling. 'She just needs a little longer to make some friends.' She set off then with her coat collar turned up about her ears. It was only a short distance to the school, and once she reached the railings that surrounded it she stuck her hands into her coat pockets and stamped her feet to keep warm until the school bell rang.

Seconds later, children began to pour out of the doors closely watched by a teacher who was trying to keep them in some sort of order. When she spotted Adina she crossed the playground to her and said, 'It's Adina, isn't it? Ariel speaks of you often.' She held out her hand and shook Adina's as she introduced herself. 'I am Miss Millington and I was wondering if I might have a word with you when it is convenient?'

'Of course,' Adina spluttered, slightly taken aback. She wondered if Ariel was in some sort of trouble, in which case her mother should be told. 'Shall I come in to see you when I bring Ariel back to school after lunch?'

'That would be ideal,' the woman beamed, and turning, she hurried back into the school.

Minutes later, Ariel appeared with her head down.

'So what's wrong with you?' Adina teased as she took her hand.

Ariel kicked at a stone. 'I don't like it here. I want to go home and back to my old school.'

'I know you do. We would *all* like to go home but it wouldn't be safe for us,' Adina pointed out. 'As soon as you make some friends you will be happier, but you'll never make friends if you don't try.'

'I *do* try,' Ariel retorted pettishly, 'but the other children make fun of the way that I speak. The only people who don't are the ones that are Jewish like me, and they can only speak in German.'

Not quite knowing how to answer, her sister hauled her along as she wondered why the teacher would wish to speak to her.

After lunch, she tidied Ariel's plaits and took her back to school, to find the teacher waiting for her on the steps.

'Come into my office,' she invited, and after hastily kissing Ariel, Adina followed her down a long corridor to a small office, noting as they went that Miss Millington was quite attractive. Adina thought that she looked to be in her late twenties to early thirties; she had short fair hair and was slim and graceful. She also noticed that there was a small diamond ring on the third finger of her left hand.

When they reached the office and Adina was seated the teacher began, 'As I am sure you will be aware, we have a number of German-Jewish children here and they are struggling with the language. I have been very impressed by your sister's use of English and wondered . . . I know this is a great imposition, but I wondered if you would be prepared to come into the school on certain days and help the Jewish evacuees with their English? If your parents have no objection, of course! I couldn't pay you a great deal, unfortunately, but I really feel that if they could master the basics of our language they would be much happier here.'

'I would love to,' Adina replied without hesitation. She had become increasingly bored now that the work on the house and the shop was finished, and she was sure that her parents would approve of the idea. She skipped home; excited at the prospect of doing something useful.

She had just turned the corner of Edmund Street when she saw Dovi walking a short way ahead of her. His head was down and his hands were thrust deep in his pockets. All in all, he looked the picture of misery.

'What's wrong?' Adina asked when she caught up with him.

'There is nothing wrong exactly,' he replied, 'it's just that I feel so useless now. While I was helping Papa to put the house and the shop to rights I felt as if I was doing something worthwhile, but now . . .' His voice trailed away.

Adina knew exactly what he meant. Hadn't she herself just jumped at the chance of working part-time at Ariel's school?

'Perhaps you could find a job?' she suggested tentatively.

He smirked. 'Oh yes – doing *what*? Had I stayed in Cologne I would be in university by now, but as it is I have no qualifications yet. Who would want to employ me and what would I do?'

Adina chewed on her lip as they moved along. Dovi was bright and hoped to be a lawyer one day. The chances of that looked very remote now, at least for the foreseeable future.

'Well, there must be *something* you could do; this war can't go on for ever.'

He laughed wryly but then caught her arm as they approached the shop-front. 'You won't say anything to Mama and Papa about what I have just told you, will you?' he pleaded. 'I know they are already concerned enough about the shop, without them having to worry about me as well.'

'Of course I won't,' she assured him. 'And try to stay optimistic. Something is bound to turn up.' She would have loved to tell him about the little job that she had just been offered but felt that now wasn't the right time. She didn't want to make him feel any worse than he already did. He had so much to miss, far more than she did. Because he was slightly older than her, he had enjoyed a busy social life in Cologne. He was young and extraordinarily handsome, and he had been very popular amongst the Jewish girls in their community. Eventually their parents would have arranged a marriage for him, probably with a girl of his choice, but that was unlikely to happen now. Adina had noticed more than the odd English girl attracted by his dark good looks, but Dovi was wise enough to know that a marriage outside his faith would be frowned upon. No wonder he is feeling so glum, she thought to herself.

They set off up the long entry that divided their shop from the neighbours, and as they entered the warm kitchen their mother looked up and smiled at them both.

'So what did Ariel's teacher want to see you about?' she asked Adina.

'Oh, I'll tell you about it later,' Adina said as she shrugged off her coat and went to fill the kettle at the sink.

Dovi hovered by the door. 'I think I'll pop into town and get some books from the library.'

His mother nodded approvingly. Dovi had always loved to read, everything and anything he could get his hands on, much like Adina. Back in Cologne their home had had a wonderful library, full of books from floor to ceiling, with everything from Aristotle and Plato to Shakespeare, Goethe and Chekhov. Now he had to rely on whatever the local library could provide.

Once he had gone, Adina told her mother about the proposition that Ariel's teacher had put to her.

Freyde approved. 'I can see that you could be a great help to the Jewish children who attend the school, and it will give you something to keep you occupied too,' she said. 'When will you start?'

'On Monday.' Glancing around the kitchen, Adina asked, 'Where is Papa?'

'Oh, he heard about these socks that are available without coupons and he has gone to try and purchase some for the shop. The nickname for them is "oily socks" – apparently they are very popular with the soldiers because the oil in the wool helps to prevent them from getting blisters. I'm not sure that they will attract any more customers though. We have everything in there from dustpans and brushes to sweets, but it doesn't seem to do any good.'

'Things will improve. I bet most people don't even realise that the shop has re-opened yet,' Adina said gently.

'We shall see,' her mother sighed, and as she bent her head back to the skirt she was sewing, Adina quietly slipped away.

The following Monday morning, Adina set off to school with Ariel. She was wearing a plain white blouse that she had teamed with her best black skirt, and she was looking forward to her new job enormously.

'I don't know why *I* can't be in your class. *I* am Jewish,' Ariel whined.

'It's because you can already speak good English,' her sister said patiently. 'What good would it do you to be with me? You are far better off learning arithmetic and writing in another class.'

Ariel looked glum but said nothing more on the subject, and soon they arrived at the school gates where Miss Millington was waiting for them.

'Ah, Adina, I have the children ready for you in a separate classroom,' she beamed. 'I thought it would be easier for you if there were no interruptions from the other children. But come along to the staff room first and have a cup of tea before you start and meet the other teachers. Ariel, you run along to your class, there's a good girl.'

Ariel glared at her before trudging off to do as she was told while Adina followed the teacher into the school.

'This is Adina Schwartz who will working with the German children to improve their English,' she told the other members of staff as Adina blushed hotly, and they all smiled at her.

Miss Millington poured her out a cup of tea and showed her where to hang her coat as the other teachers began to drift off to their class-rooms. Very aware that the children were already waiting for her, Adina swallowed her drink as quickly as she could and followed the teacher to a small classroom overlooking the playground at the far end of the school.

Eleven children ranging from five to nine years of age stared solemnly at her as she entered the room.

'*Guten Morgen, Kinder,*' she addressed them once Miss Millington had left, and crossing to the blackboard she then wrote the greeting in English: *Good morning, children.*

They looked back at her blankly for a moment but then as they grasped what she was doing, they began to roll the words around their tongues.

'*Wie geht es euch heute?*' Adina asked them next, and then she again wrote the question in English, *How are you today?*

The children began to smile as they realised that she could under-stand them, and very soon their first lesson was well under way and Adina was thoroughly enjoying herself.

Chapter Four

On 10 May 1940, Winston Churchill was summoned to Buckingham Palace and appointed the new Prime Minister, becoming the head of a coalition government. He assured King George VI that he would build an all-party team to achieve victory against Hitler. Chamberlain, his predecessor, had sought peace but Churchill informed the King that he had no intentions of seeking peace now, only victory.

The week before, the Allied attempt to force the German invaders out of Norway had gone badly. The Allied Forces had been ill-equipped to fight in Arctic conditions and had found themselves up against highly trained mountain troops. as well as under constant attack from enemy dive bombers operating out of Norwegian airfields. But now that the pugnacious Winston Churchill had taken over from Chamberlain, the country was heartened.

Rationing was now firmly in place. In Nuneaton, a few more people were now venturing into the shop in Edmund Street to obtain their measly rations of bacon, butter and sugar, but Ezra knew that trade would have to improve substantially if he was to keep the wolf from the door.

Adina had been working at the school for one month now and was loving every minute she spent with her young pupils. Even Ariel seemed to be finally adapting to her new way of life. But sadly, the same could not be said for Dovi, who seemed to have lost some of his old sparkle.

This morning as she looked across to where he was hunched in the chair at the side of the fire, Freyde asked, 'And what do you plan to do with yourself today, son?'

'The same as I do every day,' he replied sulkily. 'Get the coal in, run errands for you. What else is there for me to do?'

'But you help out in the shop too,' Freyde said, as she lifted some of the washing down from the drying rack that was suspended from the ceiling, ready to iron it.

'Huh! Papa hardly needs me to do that. There are barely enough customers to keep one person busy, let alone two.'

'But they will come in time. We just have to be patient,' Freyde told him gently, keeping an eye on the door that led into the shop. Ezra was out and as yet she had not had a single customer since opening the shop that morning.

Rising from the chair, Dovi suddenly snatched his coat from the hook on the back of the door. 'I am going for a walk,' he snapped, and with that he marched from the room, slamming the door behind him so hard that it danced on its hinges.

Freyde frowned as she listened to his footsteps in the entry. It wasn't like Dovi to be churlish. He had always been the joker of the family. But then they had all had a lot of adjusting to do, and she knew he was bored.

Spitting on the bottom of the iron to check that it was hot enough, she then attacked the pile of ironing as she sought in her mind for a way to make him feel worthwhile again.

Ezra arrived home at eleven thirty, delighted with the purchases he had managed to acquire for the shop at a very fair price.

After placing three enormous glass jars full of sweets on the edge of the table he glanced about and asked, 'Where is Dovi?'

'I think he's gone off to the library again.' Freyde added two starched sheets to the pile of ironing. 'I am very concerned about him. I think he's feeling at a loose end.'

Ezra nodded. 'It isn't so bad for the girls; they have things to keep them occupied. Ariel is at school and now Adina is helping out there, she seems to be blossoming. But Dovi . . . well, there is so little for him to do. I was hoping that he would become more involved in the shop. But first, of course, we need trade to pick up before that can happen.'

'All in God's good time,' his wife told him, and sighing, Ezra went through to the shop, leaving her to put the neat pile of ironing away.

When Dovi arrived home later that afternoon he was still somewhat subdued and remained that way throughout the evening meal. When it was over, Freyde and Adina cleared the table and washed up, then they all settled down whilst Ezra read them passages from the *Torah*, as was usual.

It wasn't until everyone else had retired to bed and they were finally alone that Adina asked her brother, 'Is everything all right, Dovi? You seemed very preoccupied tonight.'

Glancing towards the stairs door to make sure that they were truly alone, Dovi edged closer to her before whispering, 'I have something to tell you, but first you must *swear* that you will not tell Mama or Papa.'

Adina frowned, filled with a sense of foreboding, Even so, she nodded. Dovi was her big brother and she had always looked up to him.

He took her hand and smiled at her tenderly. 'The thing is,' he said, 'I have signed up.'

Adina's eyes almost popped out of her head. 'B . . . but why? And *how?*' she stuttered. 'You are not quite eighteen yet. Surely you need Mama and Papa's permission?'

'I lied about my age,' he admitted sheepishly, and then seeing the tears welling in her eyes he hurried on, 'You *must* see it my way, Dina. So many of the young men from the town have already gone and I couldn't bear to be looked upon as a coward. The chances are I would have been called up in a few months anyway. I need to feel that I am doing something towards this war, and this was the only way I could think of. You know as well as I do that Mama and Papa would have refused to give their permission had I asked them.'

Dina blinked as she tried to take in what he had just told her. 'So when will you be going?' she asked, still shocked.

'First light tomorrow morning. I shall already be gone by the time you get up, and I shall leave a letter for our parents explaining everything. *Please* try to understand. You are doing your bit helping at the school, but I feel so useless. You must be strong for me, to comfort Mama and Papa when I am gone.'

'I will,' she promised, although she felt as if her heart was breaking. It was hard to imagine life without Dovi around – and what about the dangers he might face? 'Where will you go?'

He shrugged. 'All I know is I am to report to the Town Hall and from there I shall be transported to a training camp on Lake Windermere before being shipped abroad.'

'But you could be killed,' she objected.

'And so could the thousands of other young men who are already out there fighting.'

They fell silent for a while until she asked, 'Would you like me to help you pack?'

He grinned ruefully. 'There will be no need to take more than one change of clothes. Once I arrive at the training camp I shall be issued with a uniform, and who knows how long it will be before I get to wear civilian clothes again. Please, tell me you will stay strong and not think badly of me. I could not bear that.'

'I could *never* think badly of you and I believe you are very brave,' his sister told him solemnly. 'Just promise me that you will take no unnecessary risks. I don't know how I would cope if anything happened to you.'

'I promise.' He put his arm about her shoulders and they sat content in each other's company, Dina knowing that this might well be the very last time she ever saw him. There was nothing to be heard but the roar of the flames up the chimney and the room was cosy and warm, and as they sat there she locked every second of the time away in her memory.

When they finally rose to go to bed, she asked, 'Will you write?'

'Whenever I can,' he said, planting a gentle kiss on her nose. She then went upstairs, leaving him to write the letter that their parents would find when they rose the next morning.

Once upstairs, Dina crept into the bedroom she shared with Ariel, undressed silently then slid into bed, listening to her little sister's snores echoing around the room. Sleep refused to come as she imagined how her parents would react when they found Dovi's message in the morning.

She had no doubt in her mind that they would be as devastated as she felt right now. And yet she could understand why her brother had chosen to do this. Dovi was a proud young man and he needed to feel useful. Adina began to send up prayers that God would keep him safe and end the war quickly, and finally as the first colours of dawn streaked the sky she fell into a restless doze.

A sound akin to a wounded animal brought her wide awake, early the next morning.

'NO . . . nooo . . . nooo!'

Recognising her mother's voice, Dina sprang from the bed, shuddering as her feet came into contact with the cold wooden floorboards. Shoving her arms into her dressing-gown, she sprinted towards the door and raced downstairs to the kitchen, where she found Freyde clutching the letter that Dovi had left, tears spurting from her eyes.

'He's gone,' she gasped as she waved the letter in Adina's face. 'Dovi has signed up.'

Above, Dina could hear her father running along the landing and seconds later he burst into the room.

'Whatever is wrong?' he asked his wife, staring at her aghast.

She thrust the letter into his hand and as his eyes scanned the page, she watched him expectantly as if he could somehow stop what Dovi was doing.

Dina saw the colour drain from her father's face.

'We must stop him!' Freyde cried, but he merely shook his head.

'It is too late.' His voice was, heavy with pain. 'He will already have left for Lake Windermere. I am afraid we shall have to stand by his decision.'

'No!' Freyde thumped the table so hard that the sugar bowl standing in the centre of it danced at least six inches across the chenille tablecloth. 'He is only a child. He should never have done such a thing without our permission.'

'Ah, but that is exactly why he has done it as he has. He knew that we would never have allowed him to go.'

Freyde began to sob now, and Dina bowed her head in shame. Perhaps she should have told them of his intentions, after all? But then she would have been betraying her brother. She had been caught between them, although her father seemed to be taking it far better than she had anticipated. He was upset, admittedly, but she thought she also detected a look of pride in his eyes.

'God will keep him safe,' he said stoically. 'And in the meantime we shall hold our heads high and be proud of the brave thing he has done. Come. Let us pray for his safe return.' And bowing their heads, that is exactly what they did.

*   *   *

Three weeks later, they received their first letter from Dovid. In it, he wrote that he was well and now in France, although they had no idea which part. He apologised for leaving the way he had, and said he hoped they had forgiven him.

Freyde sobbed with relief to discover that he was well, and even Ezra's eyes filled with tears as his wife read the letter aloud to them.

Since Dovid's departure the shop had started to do much better, as news spread of the Schwartzes' underaged son enlisting. Many of the townspeople's husbands, sons and brothers were also away at war, and now they slowly began to accept the family. Each day the little bell above the shop-door would tinkle within minutes of Ezra turning the sign to Open, and now it barely stopped until late at night, when he finally turned off the lights and locked the door.

'Well, we really have something, in common now,' Mrs Haynes declared when she heard what Dovid had done. 'Let's just 'ope as 'im an' our Anthony stay safe.'

Her own son, who was a year older than Dovid, had enlisted shortly before him – and although she fretted constantly about him, the woman was very proud that he had gone off to fight for his country.

Adina continued to teach each morning at the school Ariel attended and loved every minute of it. The children she taught had now got a rudimentary grasp of the English language and Miss Millington was full of praise for her.

'She has all the makings of a wonderful teacher,' she would tell Freyde each time she saw her, and Freyde's chest would puff with pride. Even Ariel seemed a little more settled now, although she still tended to keep herself to herself at school. So, all in all, Freyde felt that things were looking up, until one morning in June, she noted her husband's expression as he sat reading the paper after breakfast.

The moment the girls had set off for school and the first rush in the shop was over, she asked him, 'What is it? I can see by your face that something is wrong.'

'German forces have invaded France,' he said heavily.

Freyde's heart leaped into her mouth. 'But Dovi is in France,' she whispered.

'So are thousands of other young men,' her husband replied, and they both then fell silent. Each day, word reached some poor family in the town, that their loved one was dead or missing, and now all the Schwartzes could do was pray that their son would not be amongst them.

When Adina entered the staff room that morning, the teachers were all talking about the dramatic turn of events. Like her parents, she was terrified that Dovi would be amongst the dead or injured, but there was nothing that she or anyone else could do but go about their daily business as best they could.

As well as teaching at the school, word had spread about how skilled she was at sewing, and each afternoon Adina spent working on the Singer sewing machine that her father had put in the corner of her bedroom for her. At present she was making a wedding dress for a young girl from Stockingford. Fabric, like so many other things since rationing had been enforced, was hard to come by now and so Adina had taken apart the bride's mother's wedding dress and painstakingly remade it in a more modern style. The girl was coming for her final fitting that very afternoon and Adina could only hope that she would approve of what she had done to it. All that remained to be done now was the hem, but that couldn't be finished until the bride had tried it on.

The young woman arrived at three o'clock in the afternoon with her mother, all starry-eyed and excited about seeing her gown, and Freyde politely showed them upstairs.

'I believe it is almost finished now,' she assured them with a smile as she tapped on Adina's bedroom door. The gown was on a mannequin that Ezra had managed to find on one of his frequent visits to the second-hand shop, and when the girl stepped into Adina's room she gasped with delight.

'Oh, it's absolutely *beautiful*,' she breathed. 'It looks brand new.'

'I washed and pressed the material once I had taken the original gown to pieces before I started to remake it,' Adina explained, blushing with pleasure. In actual fact she herself was more than pleased with how the gown had turned out. The weight of the heavy satin ensured that it hung beautifully and the girl could hardly wait to try it on.

Once she was in it, she twirled this way and that as her mother looked on with a proud smile on her face. There was no doubt about it, she was going to make a beautiful bride.

'If you could just climb up onto this chair I'll pin the hem up and then I can have it ready for tomorrow for you,' Adina told her through a mouthful of pins.

When the bride and her mother had departed, she set to and within an hour the dress was finished.

'Why, you've excelled yourself,' Freyde told her when she came back to check on how Adina was progressing. 'The Queen herself could wear such a dress. What with your sewing and teaching, I think I've ended up with a very talented daughter. No wonder you are in such demand.' It was she who had taught Adina to sew almost from as soon as she could hold a needle, but Freyde was happy to admit that her daughter was a much better seamstress than herself now.

'Then I hope I shall never be out of work,' the girl retorted teasingly, and when her mother grinned she stood back to admire her work with a satisfied smile on her face. It was nice to be able to make people happy.

Chapter Five

Come along, you must drink it,' Freyde urged as she pushed a cup of chicken soup towards her daughter. Ariel had developed a bad case of whooping cough, which had already caused her to lose three weeks off school, although thankfully she did seem to be on the mend now.

Ariel grudgingly did as she was told as Ezra threw some more coal onto the fire and shuddered. He had just been out to the coal-house to fill the scuttle and it was bitterly cold.

'I'm glad we don't have to venture out tonight,' he commented as he prepared to settle down in the chair at the side of the fire. The words had barely left his lips when the air-raid siren wailed.

'Oh no.' Freyde always panicked whenever this happened, but tonight she was even more frightened than usual. Normally they would all huddle together in Mrs Haynes's Anderson shelter, but tonight she knew that Ariel was not well enough to go out into the cold air.

As if reading her mind, Ezra ushered her and Ariel towards the heavy oak table at the side of the room, and as Adina spilled out of the stairs doorway white-faced, he told her, 'Run upstairs and bring as many pillows and blankets as you can carry. We shall all have to shelter beneath the table tonight.'

'But you and Adina could go out into the shelter,' Freyde argued, terrified of putting them at risk.

'We are a family and we shall stay together,' Ezra told her grimly as he dragged the settee in front of the table. 'It won't be very comfortable under here, but at least we shall be in the warm.'

Knowing that it would be useless to argue with him, she ushered Ariel beneath the table, and when Adina appeared with her arms full of pillows and blankets she began to make them as comfortable as she could. In the meantime, Ezra collected their gas masks and checked that the blackout curtains were in place before scrambling down to join them. Within seconds the drone of enemy planes sounded overhead and they all looked at each other fearfully. Minutes later, they heard the first distant explosions, and inching out from beneath the table with firm instructions to his family to stay where they were, Ezra crossed to the window and carefully tweaked the curtain aside. Parachute flares hung in the sky like great white iridescent chandeliers to mark the targets for the ordinary

31

bombers that were soon to follow, and in the distance multi-coloured incendiary bombs were dropping from the sky like fairy lights. Searchlights were sweeping the sky and the sound of heavier bombs falling was deafening. The ack-ack guns and Bofors burst into life, but the sky was dark with enemy planes and Ezra feared that they were wasting their time.

'It sounds as if they are targeting Coventry, may God help them,' he told his family, and then they all fell silent as the terrible attack continued.

The raid went on and on, but thankfully none of the bombs seemed to be falling near them. Adina and Ariel eventually fell asleep, but Freyde and Ezra sat on listening to the deafening crashes and praying for the people who were being attacked. It was 6.15 the following morning before the all-clear finally sounded, and by then Ezra and Freyde were dropping with exhaustion. Even so, Ezra ventured out into the street to speak to people who were finally emerging from the shelters.

'They say Coventry city centre is flattened, Saint Michael's Cathedral along wi' it,' one man told him. 'My brother is in the Home Guard an' he were there till a couple of hours gone. He said the place is like an inferno, whole streets o' houses flattened just like that and God knows how many dead. The Army were already there diggin' the bodies out o' the rubble when he left, the poor sods. They reckon there were over five hundred German bombers in all. They were after the factories, but there have been a lot o' civilians killed too, by all accounts. Nearly six hundred, if what they're sayin' is true.' The man wiped his face in a gesture of despair. 'They knocked out the water mains, the electric and the gas in most areas, an' the roads are so bad that the fire engines couldn't even get through to some areas.'

As Ezra shuffled back inside, all he could do was thank God that his own family was safe and pray that his son was too, wherever he might be.

The newspapers were full of the story. It was reported that the Luftwaffe had christened the raid 'Moonlight Sonata', which Ezra considered was too beautiful a name for such a murderous attack.

The people of Coventry were heartbroken at the fall of their once fine city, but on Saturday 16 November, King George visited them – and the sight of him walking amongst the ruins of the Cathedral with tears on his cheeks gave them the courage to go on.

On 20 November, the first mass burial of the people who had been killed took place at the London Road Cemetery, but as workers continued to dig amongst the rubble, yet more bodies were found, and the following week a second mass burial took place. It seemed that there would be no end to the tragedy.

The following week Mrs Haynes was outside scrubbing her front step and chatting to Freyde who was cleaning the front window of the shop when they both suddenly heard the sound that every mother and wife

32

had come to dread. Mrs Haynes straightened as the telegram boy came hurtling down the street towards them on his bicycle. Hitching her ample bosom beneath her wraparound pinny, she prayed for him to ride past. But just as both women had feared, he slowed down as he approached them, peering at the numbers on the doors.

'Mrs Haynes?' he asked, and Freyde's hand flew to her mouth.

'Y-yes . . . that's me.'

He handed her an official-looking envelope before cycling away, and for a moment the woman stood there staring at it as if she couldn't believe it was real.

'Why don't you come in and open it while I make you a hot drink?' Freyde suggested quickly. She knew that Bert, Mrs Haynes's husband, was at work and didn't want her to be alone if it contained bad news.

'I er . . . reckon I might take yer up on that offer, luv,' the woman replied as Freyde gently took her elbow and guided her into the shop. Ezra looked up as they entered and frowned when he saw their neighbour's face. She was holding an envelope at arm's length as if she was afraid it might bite her.

'Mrs Haynes has received a telegram and I thought she might like to open it in here, seeing as her husband isn't at home,' Freyde said quietly.

'Oh yes – yes of course. Let me close the shop for a moment and I'll come through to the back with you,' Ezra offered.

On entering the kitchen, Freyde looked at Ariel, who was curled up in the chair at the side of the fire reading a comic, and said firmly, 'Go upstairs and read that, would you, there's a good girl.'

Ariel, who was normally wilful, took one look at Mrs Haynes's stricken face and rushed away like a frightened rabbit to do as she was told for once.

Seconds later, Mrs Haynes was seated at the kitchen table whilst Freyde quickly filled the kettle and placed it on the stove to boil, but still she did not attempt to open the envelope.

It wasn't until there was a steaming cup of tea in front of her that Ezra suggested gently, 'Don't you think you should read it, Mrs Haynes?'

'No – you do it,' she told him, pushing it into his hand.

He glanced towards Freyde and when she nodded encouragingly he began to open it. The way he saw it, there was no use delaying the agony, and maybe it wouldn't be bad news, after all.

But Freyde instantly knew that it *was* bad news as the colour slid out of his cheeks too.

'Would you like me to read it to you?' His voice was little more than a whisper.

Mrs Haynes shook her head as she took a scalding gulp of her tea. 'You've no need to. I already know what it says. It's our Anthony, ain't it? He's dead.'

'I-I'm afraid he is.' Ezra wished he was anywhere but there at that

33

moment, but he could not lie to her. 'He was shot. He died a hero and you should be proud of him.'

She nodded, appearing to be outwardly calm, while tears slid unchecked down Freyde's cheeks, for she knew that it could quite easily have been her receiving a telegram about Dovid, and the thought was unbearable.

'He were just nineteen years old,' the woman muttered as she stared off into space. 'He had his whole life ahead o' him an' he were bright as a button at school, yer know. He could 'ave been anythin' he wanted to be but that ain't goin' to 'appen now, is it? An' the worst of it is, we probably won't even know where he's buried till after the war. We can't even give 'im a decent send-off.'

Feeling her pain, Freyde and Ezra hung their heads. Words of comfort could only sound inadequate, so they remained silent.

And then at last they came – great gulping sobs that shook the woman's body and threatened to choke her as Freyde sprang forward to wrap her in her arms.

'Ask the neighbours the other side of us where Bert works and go and fetch him,' Freyda ordered urgently and Ezra shot off like a bullet from a gun, glad to escape the heartrending sight of a mother who had just lost a much-loved son.

Adina was devastated when she came home at lunchtime and heard the news. Mrs Haynes was back in her own kitchen by then with her husband, who was even more griefstricken than she was. She made them a large meat and potato pie for their evening meal and took it round to them, guessing that her neighbour would be in no mood to cook, and then she hastily retreated, leaving them to the endless stream of visitors who were calling to pay their respects as word spread of the tragedy.

'This war is so senseless,' she raged to her parents once she was back in her own kitchen and they both nodded in agreement. But they didn't make a comment. There was nothing they could say.

Six months later, on 8 and 9 April 1941, Coventry again came under attack when 237 bombers dropped 315 high explosive bombs and 710 incendiary canisters on the city. Two days later they were back and a further 475 people were killed and more than 700 people were seriously injured. By then the spirits of the people were very low as all the work they had done to rebuild their city was undone again.

'Thank God we live in Nuneaton and not in Coventry,' Ezra told his wife, and although Freyde nodded, she lived in fear, wondering how long it would be before the town they had chosen to live in was targeted too.

* * *

34

The following month, as the family sat down to supper, the air-raid sirens sounded once again and Freyde sighed with fear and frustration. It was getting to be a regular occurrence now, and she often opted to hide beneath the table rather than join the Haynes family in their shelter. It was a dark dismal place, despite Mrs Haynes's attempts to cheer it up. Bert had erected a makeshift bunk bed to one side of it, which the children slept in, and she always kept a good supply of candles in there, but still it was damp and cold and Freyde always felt panic build in her as soon as she set foot in the place.

'Fetch the pillows and the blankets, Adina,' she said regretfully as she looked at the lovely meal she had prepared for them.

'I think we should go into the shelter tonight,' Ezra frowned.

'But why?' Freyde asked. 'No doubt they will be aiming for Coventry again so we shall be quite safe in here.'

Ezra had a bad feeling, but knowing Freyde's fear of the Anderson shelter he decided against his better judgement to comply with her wishes. They had barely settled beneath the table when the drone of the planes approaching sounded high above them. And then there was a deafening explosion and the windows imploded as Ariel began to scream.

'Quickly, we must go to the shelter now,' Ezra shouted as he hauled the child from her hidingplace. She was crying and clung to her father as she buried her head in his shoulder, and then as they ran towards the door there was another explosion, closer still this time, and a fall of soot from the chimney extinguished the fire and covered them all in dirty black ash. The ornaments on the mantelshelf danced along the polished wood before crashing into the hearth as Ezra yanked the back door open. Heedless of the carpet of glass beneath his slippered feet, he struggled with the catch on the back gate, and then Mrs Haynes was there in the doorway of the shelter urging them on and he breathlessly pushed his family inside ahead of him.

'It sounds like they're aimin' fer the train lines on the Coton Arches,' she told them as she took Ariel from her father and cuddled the terrified child against her. And then another terrible bang shook the shelter and Ariel began to sob with fear.

'It's all right, luvvie,' the woman soothed her as she rocked her to and fro.

The first air raid on Nuneaton had been back in August when the Germans had targeted Weddington. One person had been killed then, but if the sounds reaching them now were anything to go by, they guessed that the death rate would be much higher tonight. And so they sat in silence as the ground shook around them with the sheer force of the raid and they could do nothing but wait and wonder if they would have homes to go to – if and when they got out of the shelter. At one point, Mrs Haynes attempted to light some candles as Freddie and Ariel wailed pitiably, but the matches were damp, so in the end they resigned themselves to being in darkness until the raid ended.

The women closed their eyes and silently prayed as the roar of bombs crashing about them obliterated every other sound. At last, after what seemed like a lifetime, the all-clear finally sounded and the adults rose, stretching their aching limbs as they looked apprehensively towards the door of the shelter. Amazingly, the children had fallen into a doze, and not wishing to disturb them, Mrs Haynes whispered, 'D'yer reckon our houses will still be standin'?'

'There is only one way to find out,' Ezra replied as they stepped out into the damp night air. The first thing they saw was the silhouettes of their homes in the darkness and they all sighed with relief before heading towards the entry. The rattle of bombs dropping had been replaced by the clanging of fire engines' bells as they emerged onto the street – where they all stopped dead in their tracks as they saw the devastation that had been caused.

To their right, flames were licking into the sky and there were great smouldering craters in the road.

'Looks like the church has been hit,' Ezra stated as he gazed towards the Coton Arches which miraculously were still standing.

As they rounded the end of the road they saw ambulances trying to deal with the wounded. Many of the houses there had been flattened and already people were frantically digging in the rubble for signs of those who had not been able to get to the shelters. The whole area was shrouded in a cloak of smoke and water was spurting into the air from the mains that had been hit.

'My dear God,' Mrs Haynes mumbled as she gazed about in horror. Even from here they could see that the church had been destroyed and headstones flattened. Home Guards were rushing about in tin helmets and as one of them raced past, covered in blood, he shouted, 'Get back to your homes if you still have one! Unless you can help, you're in the way. Better still, get back to the shelters. They could come back!'

Taking a firm hold of Adina's hand, Ezra hauled her back the way they had come, ushering Freyde ahead of him.

'He's right,' he told them. 'Let's go back and see if Ariel is still asleep. We can do nothing here. We will just be in the way.'

When they entered the kitchen minutes later, Freyde stared about her in dismay. She had worked tirelessly to make the house into a home, but a lot of the work she had done had been ruined. Even so, she was well aware that she and her family were fortunate. At least they still *had* a home and they were all alive, unlike many others.

'Can you manage here?' Ezra asked as he tugged his warm coat on. 'I'm going to go back and see if there is anything I can do to help.'

'Of course.' She hurried away to fetch the broom and began the task of sweeping all the broken glass into a corner. 'But please be careful.'

When Ariel returned with Adina, they worked together to put the room back into some sort of order. Adina taped large pieces of cardboard up over the windows and set the kettle on the fire to boil as there was no gas.

Ezra returned three hours later, bleary-eyed and looking immensely sad.

'I was just speaking to one of the Home Guards. It seems that the damage is extensive in the town centre. Saint Nicholas Church took a hit too and Vicarage Street School has been virtually destroyed. He told me that the death count is up to a hundred already and God alone knows how many have been injured.'

'Then may God have mercy on them,' Freyde muttered, and as she hung her head and clasped her hands together, they all began to pray.

Chapter Six

1942

'I wish we could have some word from Dovi,' Freyde sighed as she kneaded a large lump of dough at the table.

Adina knew how much her mother fretted about him. 'It is hard for mail to get through, Mama. No doubt when we do hear we shall get three or four letters all come together,' she said optimistically.

Every day, word of the atrocities of war reached them on the wireless, but at present the whole town was in a state of great excitement about the proposed visit from King George and Queen Elizabeth. Adina was busily stitching costumes for a play that the children at school were planning to put on for their parents at Easter. The play was going to be about the animals on Noah's Ark and she had already stitched her way through two elephants, two tigers and two giraffes; now she was just putting the finishing touches to the second monkey costume. She was content with her life at present – or at least, she would have been, had it not been for the nagging worry about Dovi. It seemed like a lifetime ago since he had enlisted in the Army.

She was now eighteen years old and her father always teased her that she was turning into a beauty although Adina did not agree with him. To her mind her eyes were a little too large and her long dark hair a little too unruly to be classed as beautiful by modern-day standards.

She had recently been befriended by Beryl Tait, a girl her own age who lived just down the road and who often popped into the shop on errands for her mother. Adina and Beryl had hit it off straight away, and since then a whole new life had opened up to Adina. Sometimes they went to the cinema or for a stroll in the park, and whilst Adina was aware that her father wasn't wholly approving of her new friend, she could see no harm in getting out and about a little. Tall and slender with sparkling blue eyes, Beryl was a larger-than-life character, she had to admit, but Adina found her highly amusing and loved every minute of the time they spent together. Beryl was the youngest of four children but the other three had flown the nest to get married and so now her parents spoiled her shamelessly – a fact of which Beryl took full advantage.

This Thursday, the girls were planning on going to see *Gone With the Wind* at the Palace Cinema, and Adina was looking forward to it. She was actually planning in her mind what she would wear when her father came through from the shop.

'The postman has just been,' he informed them as he flicked through a handful of mail. 'I swear he gets later every day and no doubt it will be nothing but bills.'

He suddenly stopped talking and drew one envelope out to stare at the postmark. It was from Cologne and was no doubt from his banker friend, who had promised to keep an eye out for his parents when they left.

Tearing it open, Ezra read it, then dropped unsteadily onto the nearest chair.

'What is wrong?' Freyde asked.

'It is from Abram Kaufmann, as I thought,' he muttered. 'He is sending me news of my parents, but it is not good, I am afraid.'

Freyde quickly took off her floury apron and hurried across to rest a comforting hand upon his shoulder.

'The letter is postmarked early February,' he told her gravely, 'and Abram tells me that Mama and Papa were sent to a concentration camp that very week. He says that I must not expect any more correspondence from him for a while as it is too dangerous.'

Freyde paled to the colour of putty as she stared into her husband's stricken face. *A concentration camp!* The mere name was enough to strike terror into any Jew's heart.

'But what can we do?' she asked anxiously.

Her husband answered with a tremor in his voice. 'Absolutely nothing. They are in God's hands now. They were both old and frail, and it is highly unlikely they would even have survived the journey to the camp. It may be as well if they did not.'

Adina began to cry as she thought of the beloved Bubba and Zayda who had chosen to stay behind in Cologne when she and the rest of the family had fled. If only the old people had come with them. But it was too late for if onlys now.

'I'm so sorry, Papa,' she whispered as tears streamed down her cheeks and nodding, he quietly stood up and left the room to grieve in private.

That evening, when the family were all together, Ezra read out the Prayers for the Dead and lit candles for his parents. They then sat shiva throughout the night and the next day he gravely wrote their names in the family Book of the Dead.

The following evening, Beryl knocked on the back door and when Adina opened it she said, 'I were wonderin' if yer fancied a stroll round Riversley Park?'

Adina glanced nervously towards her parents who were listening to the wireless, and was just about to refuse when Freyde piped up, 'Why don't you go, bubbeleh? A little fresh air will do you good and there is nothing to be gained by sitting here.'

'Are you sure?' she asked, seeing the disapproval flit across her father's face.

'Quite sure,' her mother replied firmly. 'But put your coat on. There is a nip in the air.'

Adina did as she was told, and once she had stepped into the yard after closing the door behind her, Beryl hissed, 'What's up? You've got a face like a smacked arse on you.'

'We had word from Cologne yesterday that my grandparents have been sent to a concentration camp,' she told her friend.

Beryl looked horrified. 'Christ almighty,' she gulped. 'I'm so sorry, Dina.' She tucked her arm into her friend's and they set off down the entry.

'Thank you,' Adina said sadly. 'They will be a great loss to our family. We have all missed them dreadfully . . . and now this.'

At the bottom of the entry they turned right and were soon strolling along the banks of the River Anker in the park. A couple of young men in Army uniform wolf-whistled at them as they passed by and Beryl giggled self-consciously as she raised her hand to check that her bleached blonde hair was in place. She was a terrible flirt, which was one of the things Adina found amusing about her.

'How are your parents taking it?' she asked, once the men had passed by, and when Adina stopped to stare into the water, Beryl took a lipstick from her handbag and slicked yet another layer onto her already scarlet lips.

'As you would expect,' Adina replied dully. 'I just wish that we had forced them to come with us when we fled from Cologne.'

'You can't *force* anyone to do sommat they don't want to do,' Beryl said wisely. 'So there's no use whippin' yourself about it now.'

'I suppose you are right,' Adina admitted, and they moved on towards the museum in silence.

'Are you still up for the pictures on Thursday?'

Adina shrugged. 'It will all depend how my parents are. I would not wish to leave them if they are upset.'

'Nearly everyone yer talk to 'as got sommat to be upset about nowadays,' Beryl sighed. 'The Matthews family at the end o' the road got word yesterday that their Timmy had copped it. What a waste, eh? Timmy were a right looker an' all.'

Just then it began to spit with rain and Beryl quickly inspected the back of her legs where she had drawn two straight lines with her eyebrow pencil to resemble stocking seams. It never failed to amaze Adina, how she could get them so regimentally straight. The only time she herself had attempted to do it, they had ended up all over the place and Ariel had fallen about laughing.

'Come on,' Beryl urged, hooking her arm through her friend's. 'We'd best shelter in the museum for a time else I'll have to put the pipe cleaners in me 'air again tonight an' I only did it this mornin'.'

With a wry grin, Adina hurried along at the side of her, glad that she had come. There was one thing that could be said for Beryl: she was certainly never boring.

Later that week, Freyde took Ariel and Adina into town and to Ariel's delight she was able to catch sight of the King and Queen as they passed by.

'Fancy being a *real* Queen,' she sighed as she stared dreamily at Queen Elizabeth. 'If she was my mama I'd be a princess, wouldn't I?'

'You already *are* a princess – to us,' Freyde told her fondly.

Adina smiled. It had been a difficult week as they all tried to come to terms with the news of their grandparents' fate, but today had lifted their spirits considerably and now she had this evening to look forward to when she was going to the cinema with Beryl. Life wasn't all bad news.

When Beryl turned up on Thursday evening, Ezra put down his newspaper and gave her a disapproving glare. Tonight she wore a crimson dress that was cinched in tight at the waist with a wide black belt, and her hair was curled in the Veronica Lake style that she tended to favour. Her face was thickly plastered in Max Factor pancake foundation and her lips were scarlet. Adina felt quite plain at the side of her. She herself was wearing a white blouse that she had made out of one of her mother's best pillowcases and then trimmed with lace, and a plain black pencil skirt that reached just below her knees.

'Would you like me to come and meet you when the film is finished?' Ezra enquired. He was not at all happy about young women walking about unaccompanied after dark. But then he had had to adapt to a lot of different customs since coming to live in England. Had they still lived in Cologne he would have been searching about for a nice Jewish boy for Adina to marry by now, and they would have sat Shiva properly for his parents, which was too impractical with the shop to keep open.

Beryl looked horrified at the very idea. 'Thanks, Mr Schwartz, but we'll be fine,' she assured him. 'I'll get your lass back safe and sound, just you see.'

'Hmm.' Ezra sniffed disapprovingly before shaking the newspaper and burying his head in it again.

Once outside, Beryl told her, 'There's some German prisoners o' war been shipped into the grounds of Astley Hall an' my mate reckons there's some right tasty blokes amongst 'em.'

'Beryl!' Adina was appalled. 'But they are *Germans*!'

'So?' Beryl retorted huffily. 'They're still blokes, ain't they? An' we could certainly do wi' a few more o' them about. All our lads are off fightin' in the war.'

They moved along in silence for a time but Adina could never stay annoyed with Beryl for long. 'So how long will the prisoners of war be stationed here?' she asked eventually as curiosity got the better of her.

Beryl shrugged nonchalantly. 'Fer the duration o' the war, I expect. Me dad got wind that they're goin' to be set on repairin' the railway lines an' the places that 'ave been bombed, but I don't know if that's right. They reckon the grounds of Astley Hall is covered in Nissen huts to accommodate 'em, but I don't know how true that is neither.'

By now they were approaching the end of Edmund Street and there they turned right towards the Palace Cinema.

'Come on,' she said as she saw the queue outside. 'If we don't get a shufty on there'll be a full 'ouse an' we won't be able to get in.'

Grinning, Adina allowed herself to be tugged along. It looked set to be a good night.

When they came out some time later, Beryl sighed as she thought of Clark Gable. 'Ain't he just the most 'andsome bloke you've ever seen?' she asked, and then before Adina had a chance to answer her she went on, 'So what we doin' tomorrow then?'

'Oh, I can't come out tomorrow,' Adina told her apologetically. 'I always spend the Shabbat eve with my family.'

'What the 'ell is the Shabbat?'

Adina tried to think of the best way to explain. 'I suppose it is like your Sabbath on a Sunday,' she told her friend eventually, 'But our Shabbat begins on a Friday at sunset and lasts until sunset on a Saturday. Back in Cologne we observed it fully, but since coming to England we have had to restrict the hours because of the shop. We are not allowed to work on Saturday but spend it in prayer, study and holy songs. We have had to forego many of our religious ceremonies since coming here because there isn't a synagogue close by, which means that Ariel may have to miss her Bat Mitzvah.'

'An' what exactly is one o' them?'

'A Bat Mitzvah is celebrated when a girl reaches the age of twelve. She is then a daughter of the Commandment. A Bar Mitzvah is cele-brated for a boy when he reaches the age of thirteen, and he is then the son of the Commandment, and from then on we have to keep the Ten Commandments.'

'Sounds a bit borin' to me,' Beryl commented. 'But then I suppose it's each to 'is own.'

And with that, the two girls began to talk about the film they had just watched as they hurried homeward in the dark.

Chapter Seven

Later that month, as she was making her way to school with Ariel, Adina got her first glimpse of the German prisoners of war who were stationed within the grounds of Astley Hall.

The men were walking in a procession along Coton Road, making for the railway lines. She wasn't altogether surprised as her father had told her some time ago that they had actually volunteered to do any necessary repairs about the town. It was even rumoured that they had offered to rebuild Coton Church, although Adina had no idea if that was true. The townspeople, despite their initial disapproval at having the prisoners there, were slowly beginning to accept them. In fact, the people who had actually spoken to them said that they were a very well-mannered group of men.

They bowed their heads politely as they passed Adina and Ariel, and one man in particular caught Adina's eye. He was a head taller than most of the other men and ridiculously handsome, with golden-blond hair and the bluest eyes she had ever seen. When he saw her looking at him he flashed a friendly smile in her direction and Adina blushed to the very roots of her hair.

'That man smiled at you,' Ariel stated. 'Do you fancy him, Dina?'

'Of course I *don't*!' her sister snapped, more sharply than she should have. 'Whatever are you thinking of, to say such a thing?'

'Well, he *did* smile at you, and you were looking at him too,' Ariel retorted indignantly.

Not sure of how to answer, Adina quickened her footsteps. 'Come along or we shall be late,' she scolded, and secretly amused, Ariel did as she was told and the subject was dropped.

Adina arrived home for lunch in a light-hearted mood on her own that day, as Ariel had starting staying at school to eat with her friends. As Adina passed the shop-front, she saw that the Closed sign was on the door. It wasn't like her father to close the shop unnecessarily, and she hurried up the entry wondering what was wrong.

The first thing she saw when she entered the kitchen was Mrs Haynes from next door leaning over her mother who was sitting at the kitchen table sobbing uncontrollably. Her father was seated at the side of the fire, staring unseeing into the flames.

Seeing Adina, Mrs Haynes lifted a telegram from the table and handed it to her without a word.

The girl hastily began to read it.

It is with great regret . . . Corporal Dovid Schwartz . . . missing in action. Presumed dead . . .

Adina felt her legs buckle and dropped into the nearest chair. Shock mingled with disbelief was coursing through her. It couldn't be true. Dovid *couldn't* be dead. He was her big brother. And then she reread it and began to clutch at straws.

'It says he is missing, *presumed* dead!' she said. 'So that means he is probably still alive somewhere. He could be in a prisoner-of-war camp. We mustn't give up on him until we know for sure. We *have* to believe that he will come home.'

'That's the best way to look at it, luv,' Mrs Haynes told her sympathetically. 'At least yer have hope to hang on to, which is more than I got wi' my Anthony, God rest his soul.'

'I would *know* if he was dead,' Adina went on. 'I would feel it . . .*in here.*' She thumped her chest as if to add emphasis to her words as her mother looked at her from red-rimmed eyes.

'You can't give up on him this easily,' Adina scolded her. 'We will get in touch with the Red Cross – they will help us, I'm sure.'

Her mother nodded, but deep inside she had a terrible feeling that her beloved boy was gone from them for good.

In May 1942, more than 1,000 aircraft were sent aloft by the RAF to devastate the city of Cologne, which had once been the Schwartzes' home. Within 90 minutes, 1,455 bombs had been dropped and over 2,300 fires were started. Vital machine tool and chemical plants were crippled and 3,000 buildings were destroyed, leaving 45,000 civilians homeless. Every available plane was used from the new Lancasters to the ancient Whitleys, and among the 6,500 crewmen who flew them there were many who had not even completed their training.

Later that day, Winston Churchill told the people of England, 'This proof of the growing power of Britain's Bomber Force is also a herald of what Germany will receive, city by city, from now on!'

'Perhaps this will be the turning-point,' Ezra muttered to his family and they could only pray that he might be right.

Adina got her second glimpse of the handsome prisoner of war one hot July day. Beryl had called round for her on Sunday afternoon and they had decided to go for a walk which led them to the imposing gates of Astley Hall on the outskirts of the town.

Many of the young women from the town had taken to congregating there although Adina was not aware of the fact as Beryl led her there like a lamb to slaughter.

'Who are all those girls talking to?' she asked as the high walls topped with vicious rolls of barbed wire drew closer.

'Oh, probably the Germans,' Beryl replied innocently. 'They get to go pretty much where they please nowadays, so long as they're in fer a certain time at night. Seven o'clock's their curfew time, I believe.'

Adina blushed as Beryl made a bee-line for two young men who were standing slightly apart from the rest, and then blushed an even deeper shade of red when she realised that one of them was the handsome blond man she had seen one day on the way to school with Ariel.

'Got a light?' Beryl asked coquettishly as she held a cigarette to her scarlet lips. The soldier standing next to the blond man almost fell over himself in his haste to light it for her as his eyes looked her up and down appreciatively.

'Thank you,' she said with a flutter of her thickly mascara-coated eyelashes as he blew the match out.

'It is my pleasure, Fräulein,' he assured her with a cheeky smile.

Adina shuffled from foot to foot wishing that the ground would just open up and swallow her as her friend began to flirt shamelessly. It was as she was standing there not quite knowing what to do with herself that the fair-haired man came to join her.

'It is a beautiful day, is it not?' he asked politely.

Not trusting herself to speak, Adina nodded. He was so tall that she found herself having to look up at him, and she couldn't help but think how handsome he was. She guessed that he was slightly older than her, at least in his mid-twenties. She also saw that he had dimples when he smiled and deep blue eyes, and when he looked at her admiringly her heart fluttered.

Beryl and the other German were deep in conversation now and as Adina glanced towards them the stranger asked, 'Would you like to walk for a while? It seems that our friends have forgotten all about us.'

A refusal hovered on Adina's lips. She had never walked unchaper-oned with a young man before, but then what was the option? She had no wish to stay there and play gooseberry to Beryl, and what could be the harm in a stroll?

'All right then,' she agreed in her native tongue, making him raise an eyebrow. Turning to Beryl she told her in English, 'I'm going for a walk, I won't be gone for long.'

Beryl flapped her hand towards her, never taking her eyes from the young man she had targeted, so they fell into step as they headed away from the tall imposing gates. The man at her side actually spoke very good English although he had a distinct German accent.

They wandered along the leafy country lane in silence for a time until eventually they came to Seeswood Pool, where he paused.

'Shall we stroll around the lake?' he asked, and again Adina nodded as they turned off the lane and headed for the water.

45

Eventually they stopped and sat down at the edge of the lake, enjoying the feel of the warm sunshine on their faces.

The young man had said barely a word since they had left the gates of the Hall, and curious now, Adina asked, 'What is your name?'

'Karl Stolzenbach,' he answered.

When he offered no more information she went on, 'And where are you from?'

'My home is – or was – in Hitzacker near Bremen before the war.'

'Oh.' Adina became quiet for a while before asking, 'And what was your job?'

'I was a blacksmith,' he informed her, and when he saw her blink in surprise he smiled, showing a beautiful set of straight white teeth. 'A blacksmith does do other things than shoe horses,' he grinned. 'I worked with metal and I made many things – cooking utensils, gates, tools; anything that was made from metal basically. And the metals were varied. I worked with steel, brass, iron, copper and bronze mainly.'

'How interesting,' Adina remarked. 'Was your father a blacksmith?'

'Actually no, my parents owned a farm. I had a wonderful childhood but . . . I do not know where they are now. Apparently the farm has been burned down and my grandparents were killed. I can only pray that my parents managed to escape and are safe somewhere.' He looked so sad that Adina had to resist the urge to reach out and touch him. She knew how awful it felt to lose a brother and leave her own grandparents behind, so could only imagine how heartbreaking it would be not to know if your parents were dead or alive as well.

'I had no choice but to join the war,' he went on now. 'One day I was happily working in the forge, and then before I knew it I was crewing anti-aircraft guns. And then after more training I was issued with a rifle and sent to the front. But now what about you? You are not English, are you?'

Adina shook her head. 'No, I too am from Germany, although I am Jewish. My family fled from Cologne and came here when the Nazis started to persecute the Jews. Had we stayed there we would no doubt have perished in a camp by now.'

He nodded in sad understanding. It seemed that both of them were deeply embroiled in a war they wished to have no part of.

'And what are your family doing now?' he asked.

'My father has opened a small shop,' Adina informed him. 'And we are fortunate to have our own living quarters at the back and above it. Before the war, my father was a banker and we had a beautiful house, so we were lucky to have enough savings to escape whilst there was still time. My brother, Dovid, joined the British Army not too not long ago, but we recently received a telegram to say that he is missing, presumed dead. We also heard that my grandparents, who had refused to come with us, had been sent to a concentration camp.'

46

Seeing the tears that had started to her eyes, Karl's heart went out to her. She was yet another victim of the war, just as he was, but worse still was the knowledge that he might have faced her brother on the battlefield as an enemy. Two young men who were forced into fighting for a war they did not believe in. It was unthinkable.

Suddenly they were at ease in each other's company and standing, he held out his hand and pulled her to her feet. 'Come,' he urged with a gentle smile. 'Our friends will think we have forgotten them.'

'I doubt they will even have noticed we have been gone, if I know Beryl.' Adina hastily took her hand from his, confused at the feelings that were coursing through her.

'You have not told me yet what your name is,' Karl now remarked.

'It's Adina Schwartz, but my friends call me Dina,' she told him shyly, suddenly reluctant to look him in the eye. She could only imagine what her father would say if he ever found out she had been speaking to a German prisoner of war, let alone going for a walk with one. He would most probably lock her in her bedroom and throw away the key. He would not approve of her lapsing into her native language again, either.

Karl matched his steps to hers as they set off back up the lane to Astley Hall, and when it finally came into sight, Beryl and Karl's friend were still there chatting animatedly.

'Hadn't we better start back?' Adina asked Beryl when they drew abreast of her.

Beryl clucked with disappointment. 'But we've only just got here, haven't we?' she answered waspishly.

'Actually, it's almost six o'clock. You've been standing here for nearly two hours.'

'Never!' Beryl glanced at the cheap watch on her wrist. 'Well, it just goes to show 'ow times flies when yer havin' fun, don't it?' She gave the man she had been speaking to a cheeky wink and then linking her arm through Adina's, she began to lead her away, saying over her shoulder, 'I'll see you around then. Another time, eh?'

Adina smiled shyly at Karl who gave her a polite little bow and then they rounded a corner and the entrance to the Hall was lost from sight.

'I gather from the smile on your face that you've had a good time,' Adina remarked.

'Huh! Not on yer nelly,' Beryl retorted churlishly. 'The German geezer were all right but you should 'ave seen some o' the Americans that passed us as is stayin' in the Hall. Phew, I wouldn't mind sinking me teeth into one o' them, I don't mind tellin' yer.'

'I didn't know any Americans were staying there,' Adina answered.

'Oh yes. They're actually in the Hall itself an' most of 'em are offi-cers,' Beryl told her. 'The Germans are in Nissen huts in the grounds. Phyllis from work is goin' out wi' one o' the Americans an' she ain't never short o' stockin's, jammy devil. I'm goin' to hook me one if it's the last thing I do – you just see if I don't. By all accounts they go down the Co-op Club on a Friday an' Saturday. Are you up fer it, one Saturday night?'

'I suppose so,' Adina said uncertainly, wondering if her father would allow her to go and whether she really wanted to. She doubted that any of the American officers would be as nice as Karl. He had been a true gentleman and had kept his hands to himself, apart from helping her up from the grass. But then it was no good thinking about it now. She would probably never see him again. She was shocked to discover that the thought made her feel sad and gave herself a mental shake. What was she thinking of? Karl was a German and she was a Jew. It was just about the worst combination you could get. She decided that it would be better to forget all about him – but over the next few weeks she found that it was much easier said than done.

Chapter Eight

'I tell you it's the best job I've ever had,' Beryl chattered happily as she plastered some Pond's cold cream onto her face. She and Adina were sitting in Beryl's little bedroom in Deacon Street, and downstairs they could hear the hum of the wireless set her parents were listening to in the scullery.

Beryl had recently got herself a new job at Woolworth's and was loving every minute of it. She had just washed her hair and now Adina was twisting pipe cleaners into it so that, come morning, it would be a mass of waves. Adina was secretly glad that her own hair had a tendency to curl as she couldn't begin to imagine how uncomfortable it must be to sleep in the things. Not that it seemed to bother Beryl; she was so used to them that she had become oblivious to the discomfort.

Rationing was now stricter than ever, but since working in her new job, Beryl was getting more than a few perks, make-up being one of them. A few treats were also coming her way from her new American boyfriend – if the silk stockings laid across the back of her bedroom chair were anything to go by.

She had been courting Captain Tyrone Hughes for three months now and was totally besotted with him. Adina could understand why. Tyrone was a very attractive man and although the courtship had severely curtailed the time she got to spend with Beryl, still she didn't begrudge her friend her happiness. And Beryl *was* happy. Anyone with half an eye could see that. She was positively glowing.

'Tye's takin' me out dancin' to the Locarno in Coventry on Saturday,' Beryl now told her as she stared at her reflection in the dressing-table mirror. 'Do you reckon you could have that dress you're makin' me finished by then?'

'I don't see why not,' Adina replied amicably as she twined the last pipe cleaner into the back of Beryl's hair. 'I've only got an hour or so's work to do on it and I'm sure I could fit that in somewhere.'

Suddenly feeling guilty, Beryl stared at her friend in the mirror. 'An' what will you be doin' wi' yourself Saturday night?'

'Oh, reading I dare say,' Adina told her airily. 'I went to the library yesterday so I'm well stocked up.'

'*Readin*' . . . on a Saturday night?' Beryl was horrified. 'Why would you want to sit in *readin*'? Wi' your looks you could have any bloke you fancied.

I can't understand why you never saw that German bloke we met up at Astley Hall again. It was more than obvious that you liked him.'

'Don't be so silly,' Adina scolded, dropping her eyes. 'I *have* seen him out and about in the streets a few times on his way to jobs and he always waves to me. But we just kept each other company for a while that afternoon, that's all there was to it.'

'Well, it's a damn shame if you was to ask me,' Beryl huffed. 'He were a nice bit o' stuff, he were.'

'Yes, he probably was, but he was also a *German*,' Adina pointed out. 'And in case you've forgotten, I am a *Jew*. Can you even begin to imagine what my father would say if I were to start seeing him? He'd probably lock me away for ever.'

Beryl chuckled. 'I still say it's a shame. I reckon you've got a soft spot fer him.'

'Oh rubbish! And now if you'll excuse me, it's time I was off. If I'm going to get that dress finished for you for Saturday night I'd better get a move on. My father doesn't like me out after dark on my own anyway.'

She pecked Beryl on the cheek and she descended the steep staircase.

'Goodnight, Mrs Tait. Goodnight, Mr Tait,' she shouted politely through the open door leading into the scullery.

'Goodnight, luv,' the couple chorused as Adina let herself out into the entry. There was a sharp wind whistling up it and she felt her way along the clammy walls until she came to the darkened street. She had gone no more than a few steps when a voice hailed her.

'Hey there. It is Adina, isn't it?'

As she peered into the gloom behind her, a shape approached – and she was shocked to see that it was Karl Stolzenbach. It seemed uncanny for him suddenly to be there when Beryl had mentioned him only minutes before.

'Hello, Karl,' she greeted him as he drew alongside her. 'What are you doing here? I thought you had to be back at the Hall for seven.'

'I do normally, but they sent me out to do a job at an old folk's home and I've only just finished it,' he confided.

'Oh I see.' She was glad of the darkness that would hide her confusion. She would have loved to invite him to her parents' home for a cup of tea – just as a friend, she told herself – but of course, she didn't dare. She shuddered to think what her father would say if she were to turn up with a German in tow, so instead they walked on in silence for a time as she struggled to think of something to say to him. It seemed that he had the power to make her tongue-tied each time she met him.

It was he who eventually broke the silence when he asked pleasantly. 'Off somewhere nice, are you?'

'No. I've just been round to see Beryl and now I'm on my way home.' She then hastily added, 'Not that my house isn't nice, of course. I just meant . . .'

He laughed as her voice trailed away. 'I think I know what you meant. It's got to be nicer than the Nissen hut I live in. It's freezing in there in this weather and the blankets they issue us with are so thin that they're neither use nor ornament.'

As she glanced down at the pavements sparkling with frost she felt sorry for him but she didn't say anything, and after a while he took her completely by surprise when he asked, 'Would you like to go for a walk again on Sunday afternoon?'

She was further surprised when she heard herself say, 'Yes, I'd like that. Shall I meet you at the gates of the Hall at two o'clock?'

He nodded, and when they came to the corner of Edmund Street he took her cold hand in his and raised it gently to his lips.

'Until Sunday then. I shall look forward to it.'

As he walked abruptly away she stroked the hand he had kissed and gazed after him in open-mouthed amazement. Why on earth had she agreed to meet him? And what on earth would she tell her parents? They always asked her where she was going, and now she would have to lie to them. But then she decided she would just not turn up, and if ever she bumped into him again, she would apologise and tell him that something had come up and she had been unable to go. That would be best all round. After all, what sort of future could they have if they got involved with each other? With her mind made up, she went on her way.

The warmth of the cosy room at the back of the shop wrapped itself around her like a blanket when she stepped through the door to find her mother and father sitting at either side of the fireplace. Her father had his head buried in a newspaper and her mother was busy darning socks but they both looked up and smiled at her as she entered.

'Goodness, you must be frozen through!' Freyde exclaimed. 'Why don't I put the kettle on and make you a nice hot drink to warm you up?'

'I'm fine,' Adina assured her. 'And if you don't mind, I'm going to go up and finish the dress I've been making for Beryl. She'd like to wear it this weekend.'

'Hmm, no doubt she's off out with that fancy American again, is she?'

Hearing the note of disapproval in her mother's voice, Adina said in her friend's defence. 'She is, as a matter of fact, and actually Tyrone seems really nice.'

'*Most* of them *seem* nice,' her mother pointed out. 'But one of our customers was telling your father only this morning that a young girl in her street is expecting a baby by one of the GIs, and he's cleared off. I just hope the same doesn't happen to Beryl. It's so easy for young girls like her to have their heads turned.'

'I think Beryl has a little more sense than to let that happen,' Adina said quietly, and she hurried away upstairs.

Ariel was fast asleep in the bed they shared, but Adina knew that the sewing machine would not disturb her. It was a family joke that the other girl could sleep through anything. Even so, Adina wondered if her mother might let her use Dovid's room. She hadn't dared to ask her yet for fear of upsetting her, but it would certainly make sense. The room was so cold that Adina could see her breath hanging on the air in front of her, but even so she sat down at the machine and within minutes was busily treadling as she put the finishing touches to Beryl's dress. It was a lovely shade of blue in a heavy satin, and Adina knew that Beryl had saved her clothing coupons for months to buy the material, so she wanted to make an especially good job of it.

At last she held it up to examine it and sighed with satisfaction. She was sure that Beryl would be pleased with it, and now at last she could wash and get ready for bed. It wasn't until she was tucked in at the side of her sister that she recalled her encounter with Karl. He was a nice man, but she knew that it would be foolish to meet him, so, turning on her side, she snuggled deeper into the bed and tried to put all thoughts of him out of her mind.

Chapter Nine

On Sunday afternoon, Adina set off for a walk after dinner and before she knew it she was within sight of the gates of Astley Hall where she saw Karl waiting for her as he stamped his feet and blew into his hands to try and keep warm. She had no idea what had led her there, as she had promised herself that she wasn't going to come. But she was here now and she knew that he had seen her, so she had no choice but to join him.

'I wasn't sure that you would come,' he told her as she approached, and she bit her lip guiltily. She briefly wondered if perhaps he could read her mind and had realised that she had had no intention of keeping their date.

Taking her elbow, he led her away from the gates where some of the local girls were laughing and chatting with other men from the camp. Once more they strolled along Arbury Road before taking the lane that led down to Seeswood Pool. The sky overhead was a curious grey colour, and as they turned to walk around the edge of the lake the first flakes of snow began to fall.

'Come on, we can shelter under those trees.' Briskly, he led her towards them. Once there they settled down to sit on the carpet of fallen pine needles, and Adina wrapped her arms about her knees as she stared out across the vast expanse of water. It was so quiet that all that could be heard was the sound of the birds in the trees and she felt herself beginning to relax.

'So tell me,' she said after a while. 'How did you come to be here?'

Karl sighed as memories flooded back.

'When I was captured, to be truthful it was almost a relief. I never wanted to be part of this terrible war in the first place, but back in Bremen, I and other young men my age had no choice. When I was taken captive I was held at gunpoint whilst the injured were loaded into jeeps, and then I and the rest of the men were placed upon cross-country trucks. As we travelled through the villages people shouted obscenities at us and threw stones.'

Adina saw the frown on his forehead as he remembered but he seemed willing to continue so she let him go on.

'GI's in steel helmets and leather-padded vests walked in front of us and we just had to protect ourselves by ducking down in the trucks as best we could. Eventually we got to the coast near Dieppe. It was a terrible sight. Everything was flattened but soon I saw an enormous barbed-wire enclosure and I guessed that we must be nearing the camp. There was not a plant to be seen anywhere, the endless tramp of soldiers' boots had turned the whole area into a sea of mud, and streams of prisoners were lined up outside. The noise of the nearby surf made it difficult to hear anything else and I couldn't at that point envisage just how enormous the camp was. Later I was to discover that there were more than a hundred thousand prisoners of war already incarcerated there.' He ran a hand across his eyes.

'Once I got inside I saw that there were enormous tents full of straw erected on the side of the hillside. I was led to a separate area where tea was being made beneath a roughly constructed metal roof on open fires in huge tin kettles. We were each given a mug.' He grimaced as he remembered. 'It was very sweet and finished off with condensed milk, but we were all very thirsty so we drank it. Then we were given a white loaf of bread to share amongst four of us. There was a round tent with a pointed roof where the injured were treated. Prisoners with severe injuries were transported from there to military hospitals outside the camp. The rest of us bedded down in the ordinary tents and I remember wondering that first night if I would ever get away from there. It was a frightening experience . . .

'The next morning we were led to a deep trench that an American construction crew had dug out with a large bulldozer. This too was covered by a corrugated roof, and this was to be our latrine. All along the side of it were sacks full of chlorinated lime that would be thrown into the trench to cover the contents and mask the smell – not that it was too successful. We were then led to yet another shed where we were all treated with DDT powder for vermin. Infection was rife.'

Karl glanced at Adina, suddenly embarrassed to have mentioned such things in front of a lady, but Adina was a good listener and didn't appear to have taken offence so he went on, 'Our main diet consisted of pea soup cooked in jerry cans with bits of bacon floating in it, although we also sometimes got milk soup made from condensed milk, oatmeal, and for a real treat a handful of raisins. Within weeks of being there, the death count had reached four hundred, and many more were fatally ill. It was whilst I was there that I met Hans, a former schoolfriend of mine from Bremen who had been called up after me, and it was he who was able to tell me that my grandparents had been killed and almost the whole of the residential area of Bremen had been flattened during a raid.'

Here Karl paused and bowed his head. He took a shuddering breath before continuing. 'The worst thing I remember about that camp was the cold. It seemed to seep into your bones, and the sound of the waves pounding on the beach day and night became like a torture. Even so, things could have been worse and the guards were decent to us. In fact, many of the prisoners soon realised that gold wedding bands could be exchanged for treats . . . cigarettes and such, and they took full advantage of the fact. Within a few months, I and some other camp inmates were selected for transportation to England and within twenty-four hours we were taken to Dieppe Harbour and loaded into a boat. We set sail for Folkestone and I don't mind admitting I was sick all the way.' He grinned at her ruefully. 'Once there we travelled in a passenger train to the stadium at Wimbledon where we were again deloused and given a medical. We were then each assigned a registration number and everything of our own that we had managed to hang on to was confiscated. I was told that I was to go to POW Camp 196 in Nuneaton. Next they herded us all into lorries and we were taken to an area where military personnel were waiting for us. They demanded our pay books and identity discs, and officials filled in extensive forms on our behalf before searching us to make sure that we had given up all our personal possessions, although I was allowed to keep my wallet containing my family photos.'

'Oh, Karl,' Adina interrupted with tears in her eyes. 'It must have been so awful for you.'

'No more so than for anyone else,' he answered stoically. 'Do you want me to go on?'

She nodded numbly and so he continued. 'Next we were sent across a large sports field to a barracks where we were issued with two sets of underwear, socks and an English military uniform which was covered with brightly coloured patches. We also got a German military coat and a duffel bag each, but we wcrc not allowed to keep any of our own clothes apart from our shoes. Finally we were given a toothbrush, a clothes brush and a piece of soap and a towel. Before we knew it we were then placed on another train with a British officer in charge who had a list of prisoners he was responsible for during the journey. Everything had happened so fast that I barely had time to take it all in. We travelled through the night with the officer continually doing a headcount to make sure that none of us had escaped, although where he thought we might go, I have no idea.'

Karl grinned at her. 'Once we arrived in Nuneaton we were shepherded onto a coach and soon I got my first glimpse of Astley Hall. I saw that we were in what appeared to be a large park, with Nissen huts dotted all about. Later, I was to find that there are at least two thousand five hundred prisoners stationed there at any one time. The British Commandant and his staff stay in the Hall itself along with a number of American officers, but you probably already know that?'

When Adina nodded he resumed, 'We were issued with a palliasse and two blankets and then I was installed in one of the Nissen huts. They are incredibly ugly buildings that sleep up to twenty-four men, but after being used to sleeping in a tent it felt quite luxurious. We were allowed to fill the palliasses with wheat straw and then we had to choose our beds. Two rows of bunk beds are set against the walls on either side of the hut, and it made sense for the taller of the men to take the top ones. Before we retired for our first night here we were then each given a tin bowl full of strong milk soup from the camp kitchen. When we had finished that we were served with strong sweet tea from the same bowl and I was so hungry by then that I don't think a meal has ever tasted so good. It revived our flagging spirits and now we were ready to settle down for our first night's sleep in our new home. In the middle of each hut is a small cast-iron stove; its vent leads vertically out through the roof. Of course, we are only allowed enough coal to use it when it is very cold, so the rest of the time we rely on wood we can find lying about. The only other furniture in each hut, apart from the bunk beds, is two small tables and some long benches. I slept like a log the first night here, completely exhausted from my long journey but the next morning when I emerged from the hut I was pleasantly surprised to find myself in beautifully maintained gardens. We have contests amongst ourselves to see which group can keep the area around their hut the tidiest.'

'And who does your laundry?' Adina asked.

He chuckled. 'We have washing rooms with cold running water in long half-cylindrical channels. We wash our socks and our second set of underwear there once a week and we can boil our linen in our jerry cans on the cylindrical stove in the huts. Mind you, with twenty-four of us queuing up to do it, that doesn't get to happen too often.'

Adina wrinkled her nose in distaste. She had thought she was hard done by, having to leave her beautiful home back in Cologne, but compared to what Karl was forced to endure, her living quarters at the back of the little shop in Edmund Street suddenly seemed quite luxurious.

'There's also a larger barracks in the grounds that serves as a medical station and a church,' he went on, aware that Adina was listening to him raptly. 'And opposite the main camp entrance is the kitchen hut and this is manned purely by prisoners of war. Every six months a British military dentist visits us, and if anyone needs a tooth removing he will pull it out, outside in the open. Thankfully, I have not needed that service yet and pray that I never will.' There was a twinkle in his eye and Adina found herself smiling with him.

'We have a weekly roll call in front of our respective barracks, so that the British officers can check to see that we are all still present and correct. If the weather is bad we each have to stand beside our bed whilst he does the head-count.

'No later than twilight each evening, a trumpet call will finish the day, and then a British Corporal checks whether all the lights have been switched off. In the morning at seven o'clock the trumpeter blows the Reveille signal again.'

Adina sighed at the picture he had conjured up. She had been so intent on listening to him that she was shocked to see that the field in front of them was slowly turning white and the snow was coming down faster than ever.

'Goodness, I could listen to you all day, but I think we ought to be heading back,' she said.

He nodded in agreement as he rose and held his hand out to her. She took it and he helped her to her feet but then he stood aside and did not offer to touch her again as they made their way across the field.

'Everywhere looks so pretty with the snow coming down, doesn't it?' she commented.

'It does . . . but not as pretty as you.' Karl immediately looked as if he could have bitten his tongue off when Adina became embarrassed. 'I'm so sorry, I should not have said that,' he apologised.

By the time they reached the gates to the Hall, the pavements were white over.

'Will you be all right walking home alone?' Karl asked considerately. 'I would be quite happy to accompany you.'

'You'd better not,' Adina answered, and again he looked uncomfortable. She was a Jewish girl and he could just imagine the gossip that would be spread if she were to be seen walking with him.

'I er . . . I've enjoyed talking to you very much,' she told him shyly, and he clicked his heels together and bowed from the waist.

'The pleasure has been all mine, I assure you, Fräulein,' he answered. 'Perhaps we could do the same again. Shall we say at the same time next week?'

Uncertainly flitted across her face. 'I'm not sure – but if I can make it I will.'

And with that she turned and walked sedately away as Karl watched her go with a troubled look on his face.

Chapter Ten

'Ah, bubbeleh, *here* you are,' Freyde said as Adina entered the kitchen some time later. 'Wherever have you been in such weather? Look at you, you are covered with snow and no doubt will have caught a chill.'

'I'm fine, I just fancied a walk,' Adina replied guiltily as she took off her coat and hung it on a clothes-horse to dry.

'Well, come and sit by the fire and let me get you some hot soup,' her mother fussed.

Ariel was sitting cross-legged on the hearthrug with her nose stuck in a book, and she was so engrossed in it that she didn't even appear to have noticed that Adina had come into the room. Miss Millington had allowed her to bring it home from school and they had barely heard a peep out of her all weekend. The book was *Heidi*, and Adina could understand why she loved it so much as it had been one of her own particular favourites when she was a child.

Her father, as was usual for this time of day, was reading the newspaper, and as she sat down he glanced at her across the top of his glasses and commented, 'The RAF made their first bombing raid on Berlin today.' He shook his head in disgust. 'The Germans are evil, the whole lot of them, and one day, God willing, they will get their comeuppance – each and every last one of them.'

Adina felt colour seep into her cheeks as she thought of Karl. 'Papa, like our boys, many of them may not even want to be in the war,' she said quietly.

'Huh! I doubt that very much.' His hatred of the enemy was loud in his voice. 'They are a wicked race and *nothing* you say could convince me otherwise.'

Realising that it would be pointless to try and persuade him otherwise, Adina took the cup of soup her mother held out to her and sipped it in silence.

That night as she lay in bed listening to the sounds of her parents' snores coming through the thin wall, Adina's mind was in turmoil. Since living in England she had been asked out by quite a few English boys. It had been easy to refuse them as none of them had particularly appealed to her. Adina knew that her parents would never accept her marrying someone of another faith. But there was *something* about Karl . . . she tried to put her finger on exactly what it was but could come up with no answer. He was ridiculously good-looking, of course, but it was something more than that which attracted her to him. He seemed like a very kind and caring person and had behaved like a perfect gentleman whenever she was in his presence. It appeared that he had been forced to join the war and hated what was happening as much as she did. So why should he be pilloried for being born in Germany? He had lost his grandparents, just as they had lost their Zayda and Bubba, and the pain in his expression when he spoke to her about them had been plain to see.

Even now, her mother was hounding the Red Cross to try and find what had become of her son. Freyde flatly refused to believe that he was dead, preferring to hope that he was in a prisoner of war camp somewhere, and Adina prayed daily that she was right, although as time went on her hopes were dying.

Snuggling further down into her blankets she tried to empty her mind and lay there waiting for sleep to claim her.

'Tye has *proposed*?' Adina said in astonishment the next evening as she sat with Beryl in the girl's bedroom.

'Yep!' Beryl looked like the cat that had got the cream. 'He asked me last night when he dropped me off. I can hardly believe it an' next weekend he's takin' me shoppin' to buy me a ring.'

'Why, that's wonderful. I'm really happy for you, but I have to say it's unexpected.'

Beryl giggled. 'Well, let's just say Tye is a redblooded man and I made it clear that if he wants any hanky-panky he has to put a ring on me finger first, know what I mean?'

Adina gulped. 'Yes, I think I do, but where will you live when you get married?'

'To tell the truth we ain't talked about that yet, but no doubt I'll go back to America with him when this bloody war is finally over.'

'Oh.' Adina lowered her eyes. She was happy for her friend but knew that she would miss her when she left.

'Don't look like that,' Beryl said with a bright smile. 'You'll be able to come an' see us. We won't lose touch, I promise.'

'And what do your parents think about it?'

'I ain't actually got round to tellin' 'em yet,' Beryl admitted. 'But I reckon they'll be pleased. If truth be told, they'll most likely be glad to see the back o' me.'

'And are you going to have an engagement party?' Adina now asked.

Beryl shook her head. 'I very much doubt it. As Tye pointed out, wi' rationin' the way it is I doubt we'd be able to get our hands on enough food. Me mam queued up for two hours yesterday for a bit o' beef, an' when she finally got served it were scarcely big enough to make one good meal for us all. An' she was one o' the lucky ones! Not long after she'd been served they ran out o' meat altogether an' a lot o' people went away empty-handed. I tell you, it's goin' from bad to worse, though Tye keeps us supplied wi' sugar an' coffee.'

'I know what you mean,' Adina agreed. 'My father is finding it harder to keep the shop well-stocked now. There's very little left on the shelves each week by the time people have had their rations. But then I suppose we should look on the bright side. This war can't go on for ever, can it?' Suddenly leaning forward, she confided, 'I went for a walk again with Karl yesterday.'

Beryl whistled through her teeth. 'Christ Almighty, do your mam an' dad know?'

'Of course they don't,' Adina replied. 'Can you imagine what they'd say if they did?'

'All hell would be let loose,' Beryl responded. 'Though I can see what you see in him. He's a good-lookin' bloke, ain't he? So . . . do you really like him then?'

Adina shrugged. 'Yes, I do like him, but there's nothing between us. What I mean is, he hasn't even attempted to hold my hand. We just seem to enjoy each other's company, that's all. That isn't so wrong, is it?'

'Depends on how you look at it,' Beryl pointed out sensibly. 'It ain't exactly a match made in heaven, is it?'

'I know,' Adina mumbled. 'But as I said, I just like talking to him. There's absolutely nothing going on between us.'

'Yet!' Beryl remarked caustically. 'Why, gel, a blind man on a gallopin' hoss could see you've got the hots for the bloke. It ain't my place to tell you what to do, but all I'm sayin' is, go careful like, eh?'

Adina nodded as she stared at Beryl's cluttered dressing-table. There wasn't a single inch that wasn't covered in cosmetics of some sort or another. And the worst part about what her friend was saying was that deep down, Adina knew that it was true. Nothing could ever happen between her and Karl, so why, she asked herself for the hundredth time, had she ever turned up to meet him in the first place?

With a new resolve she looked Beryl in the eye. 'You're absolutely right,' she told her. 'And from now I shall avoid him. There are plenty more fish in the sea, aren't there? That's saying if and when I decide I *want* a boyfriend.'

Beryl nodded understandingly. 'I think it might be for the best if you did give him a wide berth,' she told her gently. 'But come on now, cheer up. Help me decide what sort of ring I should have. I can't decide whether I'd prefer a diamond solitaire or a cluster.' After twisting her hair high onto the back of her head, she pushed it into a knitted snood which would have to suffice until she had time to pop in her pipe cleaners again. She then applied a layer of lipstick before embarking on yet another explanation of how just how wonderful her soon-to-be fiancé was.

Adina listened to her friend's excited chatter and for now all thoughts of Karl were put aside.

Adina was kept busy for the rest of the week. She was now working every morning at the school and in the afternoons she sewed and helped her father in the shop.

It was during one Thursday afternoon that Mrs Thompson, a large lady who lived in Cheverel Street, entered and plonked her food coupons on the counter.

'Huh!' she said gloomily as Adina weighed out her two ounces of tea. 'Just 'ow the 'ell do they expect us to make that piddlin' amount stretch fer a week, eh? My Ronnie needs at least three cuppas afore he can get hisself out of bed of a mornin'.'

Adina agreed that it didn't look much, but unfortunately there was nothing she could do about it. Everyone was in the same boat. Not that Mrs Thompson looked bad on it. She was the size of a doubledecker bus.

Next she weighed out the allotted eight ounces of bacon and again the woman grumbled. ''T' ain't even enough fer one good fry-up,' she said, and then suddenly remembering something, she asked, 'Have you had a visit from the Red Cross today?'

'Not that I'm aware of,' Adina answered. 'Why do you ask?'

'Well, I were just comin' under the Coton Arches about half an' 'our since when this bloke stopped me. He said he were from the Red Cross an' asked if I knew where the Schwartzes' shop were. I pointed 'im in the right direction, o' course, an' I'm surprised he ain't paid yer a visit by now.'

'I wonder what he could want with us?' Adina said musingly, and then as a thought occurred to her, her heart began to pound. Could it be that they had some news of Dovid?

Hurrying now, she finished serving the disgruntled customer at top speed, and the second the woman set foot out of the shop she turned the sign to Closed and hastily locked the door before rushing through to the kitchen.

'Molly Thompson was just in the shop and she said—'

Before she had a chance to say another word, there was a loud rapping on the back door.

Ezra immediately rose from the table and went to answer it.

Half an hour later they all sat in shock, scarcely daring to believe what the stranger had told them before going on his way. The Red Cross had been working tirelessly trying to discover what had become of Dovid, as well as hundreds of other young men who were missing, and the gentleman had brought them some news. He couldn't be 100 per cent sure, he had warned them, but it appeared that someone answering Dovid's description had been located in a prisoner-of-war camp in France.

Freyde was almost beside herself with joy, while Ezra looked on with a mixture of delight and apprehension flitting across his drawn features. He so wanted to believe that what the man had told them was true, but there would be no way of knowing for sure until this confounded war was over. Unless Dovid was seriously injured in which case he might be shipped to a military hospital in England. But that didn't even bear thinking about. All they could do now was wait and pray that he would come home to them safe and sound.

At that moment Ariel came in from school and seeing the shocked faces instantly asked, 'So what's going on then? You all look as if you've seen a ghost.'

When Freyde told her what had happened, the girl was joyful; she had missed her big brother so much and hoped that he was still alive somewhere.

'Couldn't we write to him?' she asked with the innocence of youth.

Ezra smiled as he stroked her shining hair. 'I'm afraid it isn't quite as simple as that, bubbeleh. We must wait now and trust God to keep him safe until he can come home.'

'All right. So what's for dinner then?' Ariel asked, losing interest. Adina frowned. Ariel was now almost fourteen years old and was far too used to being spoiled by all of them. Especially by her mother since Dovid had gone missing.

Freyde was in such a state that she could barely concentrate on anything apart from the wonderful news they had just received, but she hurried across to the oven anyway to check on the cottage pie that was cooking in there.

'It will be ready in another half-hour or so,' she told the girl, and then turning her attention back to Adina she asked, 'Don't you think you should go and open up now? Our customers will not be happy if we just close the shop without warning.'

'Of course,' Adina said guiltily, but as she made to rise from her seat her father placed his hand on her shoulder.

'It's all right,' he told her. 'You stay here and make your mama a cup of tea. She looks like she could do with one. I shall go and serve in the shop.' And with that he left the room, closing the kitchen door softly behind him.

That night after prayers, Adina wrapped up warmly and hurried around to Beryl's house, bursting to tell her friend the good news. She knew that Beryl would be in. This was her hair-washing night.

Mrs Tait answered the door and smiled at her. She liked this little friend of Beryl's, Jew or no Jew. She was polite and pretty, and sometimes the woman wished her wayward daughter was more like her. Mr Tait was sitting at the side of the fire listening to Flanagan and Allen singing 'Run Rabbit Run' on the wireless. His foot was tapping in time to the music but he grinned at Adina as she passed him on her way to Beryl's room.

She found her friend twisting pipe cleaners into her still damp hair, and as Adina entered she sighed with relief.

'Ah, I'm glad you've come,' she grinned. 'The ones at the back are buggers to get in. Can yer give me an' 'and, Dina?'

'Of course I will.' Adina hung her coat on the back of the bedroom door, sending a flurry of snow onto the lino.

'So what you lookin' so happy about, all of a sudden?' Beryl studied her friend in the mirror. 'It's nice to see yer all smiles again.'

Adina told her about the visit they had had from the Red Cross man earlier in the day, and Beryl grinned.

'Well, bugger me, an' just when you were beginnin' to lose hope, eh? That's wonderful news. Your mam an' dad must be dead chuffed. 'An' just when you'd persuaded them to let you sleep in his room an' all!'

Adina was still struggling to understand some of Beryl's expressions but she beamed back at her.

'The trouble is, we have no way of knowing for sure that it *is* Dovid,' she explained. 'But as Papa said, it's extremely doubtful that they would tell us unless they were fairly sure.'

'Too bloody right. That would be just too cruel,' Beryl quipped, and then grinning widely she changed the subject. 'I told me mam an' dad that me an' Tye were goin' to get engaged an' they're tickled pink about it. I reckon they quite like the idea o' me being married to an American airman.' She sighed dreamily at the thought of it. 'I made him come round an' ask me dad, all official-like, an' me dad didn't 'alf give 'im a grillin'. I reckon he put the fear o' God into the poor chap. The long an' the short of it is though, that I reckon I've dropped on me feet. It turns out that Tyrone is loaded! His mam an' dad own a massive stud ranch where they breed horses in Texas, an' they've got servants an' everything. *Imagine* that, eh? *Me* with me own maid. I allus knew I were cut out for better than staying around here.'

'Oh dear, should I start curtseying to you now?' Adina teased.

Beryl punched her playfully in the arm. 'No, I don't think there'll be any cause for that. We just need to find *you* somebody 'alf-decent now. God knows, you get enough offers an' it's hardly surprisin', wi' your looks. Keep on the way you are though, an' you'll end up an old maid – an' you don't want that, do you?'

Adina laughed but then suddenly felt sad. Beryl was like no one she had ever met before and she would miss her when she left. But then that could be a long way away yet, and now she had hope that Dovi was still alive, things were looking up. Suddenly a picture of Karl flashed in front of her eyes and she pushed it away as she tried to concentrate on what her friend was saying.

Chapter Eleven

Sunday dawned, and after lunch Adina found herself staring at the clock. She had promised herself she would not go and see Karl, but it was hard to keep away.

'Are you feeling unwell?' Freyde gazed with concern at her daughter's pinched face.

'Oh, I've just got a bit of a headache, that's all,' Adina lied, and reaching for her coat, she started to shrug her arms into it. Her mother had bought a wonderfully bright red blanket from a rummage sale recently and Adina had transformed it into this very fashionable garment. It set off her dark hair to perfection and she loved it. Her father, who was busy with his accounts, didn't even register the fact that she was going.

'I think I might go and get a bit of fresh air and call in to see Beryl's engagement ring,' she told her mother as she pulled on her boots. The snow had stopped falling some days ago and what remained looked slushy and dirty from the many feet that had tramped through it.

'Then don't forget your gas mask,' her mother advised, and sighing, Adina unhooked that from the back of the door too and slung it across her shoulder. She hated the damned thing and having to carry it about with her.

It was a cold overcast day with a slight drizzle falling, and as Adina headed for Beryl's house her mood matched the weather. She could picture Karl standing at the gates of Astley Hall waiting for her and felt awful for letting him down. But then commonsense told her that as nothing could ever come of it if a relationship developed between them, she was doing the right thing by staying away.

She had gone no more than a few yards down the street when she noticed Ariel, some way ahead of her, talking to a boy. They had their heads together and were laughing at something. Adina frowned. Ariel was getting a little out of hand lately – not that her parents would accept the fact. In their eyes, she could do no wrong. She was now almost as tall as her sister and was very pretty, something of which she had recently become very aware.

When she glanced up and saw her older sister marching towards her she flushed guiltily.

'Hello.' Adina deliberately kept her voice light as she drew abreast of them. 'And who is this then? I thought you were going round to Sylvia's house.'

'This is Michael,' Ariel muttered. 'He's my friend from school and we just stopped to have a word.'

'That's fine then, but don't stay outside too long, will you? This drizzle soaks you through before you know it.' Adina marched away as her sister glared at her resentfully, and soon she was lost to sight as she turned a corner.

What a hypocrite I am, Adina thought. Here I am scolding Ariel for talking to a schoolfriend when I've made arrangements to meet one of the enemy. Biting her lip, she hurried on.

In no time at all she was knocking on the door of the Taits' little terraced house in Deacon Street. Mrs Tait ushered her inside. 'Come on in out o' this rain,' she urged. 'We've just made a brew. Would yer like one?'

'I wouldn't mind,' Adina told her as she took off her woollen mittens and rubbed her hands together. She then joined Mr Tait at the table and he told her, 'Beryl should be down in a tick. She's upstairs makin' herelf look beautiful for her fiancé. He's takin' her to the flicks later on.'

'Oh, perhaps I should leave then,' Adina said, but Beryl's father waved her back into her seat as she made to rise.

'You'll do no such thing,' he warned her. 'Our gel'd have me guts for garters if I let you go before she'd had time to flash her ring at you. Tyrone took her shoppin' for it yesterday an' she ain't stopped showin' it off ever since.' Then his tone becoming serious, he leaned towards her and asked, 'He is a decent enough bloke, ain't he? I mean, I know I must sound like an old-fashioned dad, but if he's goin' to whip my girl off to the other side o' the world, I need to know he's half-right for her, don't I?'

'To be truthful, Mr Tait, I've only met Tyrone a few times,' Adina admitted. 'But he seems nice enough to me and Beryl obviously adores him. I can understand you worrying about her – you're bound to be concerned, with her going so far away. But I'm sure she'll be just fine. Beryl is actually quite sensible and she certainly knows what she wants.'

'Well, you got that bit right,' he chuckled, his normal cheery self again. 'Trust her to go an' fall for a Yank! She's always been a stubborn little cuss, has our Beryl.'

At that moment, Beryl herself walked through the stairs door. 'What's goin' on in here then? Me ears are burnin',' she said. Then, without waiting for an answer, she hurried over to Adina and flashed her hand at her.

'So what do you think of it then?' she asked as Adina took her hand to examine the ring. It was a small square-cut sapphire surrounded by tiny diamonds, and nowhere near as showy as Adina had been expecting – if Tyrone was as rich as he had told Beryl's parents he was. However, she wouldn't have hurt her friend's feelings for the world so she quickly assured her, 'Why, it's absolutely beautiful.'

Drawing a package from her coat pocket, she handed it to Beryl self-consciously. 'Here's a little something I made for you as an engagement present. I hope you'll like it.'

Beryl carefully undid the string tied around the brown paper and then sighed happily as she saw two snow-white lace-trimmed pillowcases.

'They're really lovely.' Beryl held them up to show her parents. 'Thanks, Dina. I shall treasure them, an' these will be the first thing in me bottom drawer.'

Adina saw that her friend was positively glowing and hoped that her American would continue to make her happy.

'We just need to get *you* fitted up wi' a decent lad now, Dina luv,' Mr Tait teased gently. 'But I dare say yer dad has his sights set on you marryin' a Jewish chap, an' sadly there's a shortage o' them hereabouts.'

Seeing her friend's embarrassment, Beryl hastily pushed a mug of tea towards her and a pressed-glass bowl full of sugar.

'Help yourself,' she said. 'That's one o' the perks o' bein' engaged to an American. We ain't never short o' sugar, thank goodness. Me dad has to have at least three spoonfuls in every cup else he reckons he can't taste it.'

Adina sipped gratefully at her tea as her eyes slid towards the clock standing on the mantelshelf. She should be meeting Karl now and she wondered how he would feel when she didn't show up. She hoped he wouldn't mind too much. After all, they hardly knew each other, did they?

Half an hour later, Adina stood up and pulled her coat on again. 'I ought to be off now so you can get ready to see Tyrone,' she told her friend. 'Bye, Mr and Mrs Tait. Thanks for the tea.'

Beryl saw her to the door where they hugged each other and then Adina set off for home. It was only three o'clock in the afternoon, but already the light was fading. She knew that she ought to go home and work on the skirt she was making for one of the teachers at school, but instead, feeling restless, she headed for Riversley Park where she wandered along the banks of the River Anker. Because of the miserable weather the place was almost deserted, which suited her mood, just fine. Large weeping willow trees were trailing their branches into the sluggishly moving water and she watched a family of ducks swimming along, seemingly without a care in the world.

Eventually, when it got too dark, she set off once more for home.

Ezra had received no word from his friend, Abram Kaufmann, since the latter had written to tell him that his parents had been transported to a camp, and he could only hope that Abram and his family were alive and well. Like everyone else in this war, the Schwartzes had no choice but to get on with their lives as best they could, to listen to the news bulletins on the wireless, and to hope and pray that this inhuman war would soon be over.

In the autumn of 1943 it had been many months since Adina had seen Karl, yet still she thought of him and wondered how he was faring.

It was Molly Thompson who provided them with news of the German prisoners of war when she came into the shop one day.

'Heard about that lot up at Astley Hall have yer?' she asked, sliding her ration book onto the counter. 'Seems they've formed a work party to start repairin' Coton Church.'

'Really?' Ezra was surprised.

'Yes. Apparently there are some very skilled men amongst them – builders, carpenters an' all sorts. I suppose they were their jobs afore they got called up. Anyway, they volunteered to do it, an' now they've had the go-ahead. It's funny when you think about it, ain't it? What I mean is, it was their lot that bombed us an' now they're goin' to make good some o' the damage.'

'I suppose it does make sense,' Ezra said musingly. 'And you have to give them credit for offering.'

'Huh! As far as I'm concerned they should stand the whole bloody lot of 'em against a wall an' shoot 'em,' the big woman said indignantly.

Perhaps at one time Ezra would have agreed with her, but now he was very aware that his own son was somewhere in a prison camp in a strange country, and he prayed daily that Dovid was being treated fairly. In truth, the German prisoners were now a familiar sight about the town and the townsfolk had come to accept them. From what he had heard, they were a very polite bunch of men who were only too happy to help whenever they could. Some of them had taken on the job of tending old folk's gardens and were now being invited into people's homes to share their Sunday dinners.

As the conversation progressed Adina slipped away to her room where she stood at the window staring down at the roof of Mrs Haynes's Anderson shelter. She had spent far more nights in that dark cold place than she cared to remember, and still the war showed no signs of ceasing. And now Karl Stolzenbach could well be working just around the corner from her if he was in the party that intended to rebuild the church, and she wondered how she would be able to avoid seeing him. She had to pass the church each day on her way to the school where she worked. As the Christian Christmas approached, she was teaching the Jewish children Chanukah songs and they were loving it.

As she thought of Karl's open honest face she bit her lip, but then she told herself that he probably wouldn't even remember her by now, and tried to stop worrying.

Chapter Twelve

February 1944

On a chilly day in February as Adina walked to the school with Ariel she saw lorries laden with building materials at the gates of Coton churchyard and guessed that the rebuilding work was about to start. Men were swarming about like ants carrying steel girders and bricks up the path and she kept her head down as they hurried past.

Ariel on the other hand slowed her steps and watched curiously.

'Some of those German men are quite handsome, aren't they?' she commented saucily.

Adina glared at her but said nothing. That morning she found it hard to concentrate and dreaded the time when she would have to walk past the church again on her way home. But she needn't have worried. By then, the lorries had gone and although the men were still there they were too far away to take much notice of her.

She was surprised to see the Closed sign on the shop door once more, and her heart sank. On entering the kitchen she found her parents sobbing unrestrainedly, and her mother immediately waved a letter in front of her nose.

'It is good news, bubbeleh,' she cried. 'Look – here is a letter from the Red Cross. Dovi is to come back to England.'

Shock registered on Adina's face. 'What? You mean he's coming home?'

'Not exactly,' her father told her. 'He is being transferred from the POW camp in France to a military hospital in Portsmouth.'

'Why, is he ill?'

'We do not know,' Ezra admitted. 'All the letter says is that he should be there by the end of the month. Once he is, they will give us the address of the hospital and then we will be allowed to visit him.'

'Oh.' Adina's joy was edged with fear. She knew that only injured soldiers were released from prisoner-of-war camps, and she wondered how serious Dovid's injuries might be. Would they find him missing a limb, or worse still, two limbs? But then, she consoled herself, at least he is still alive and whatever is wrong we will nurse him through it when he is allowed to come home.

She hugged her mother fiercely, shocked at how thin Freyde felt beneath the neat knitted twinset she wore. Adina had noticed her losing a lot of weight over the last few months and had put it down to the fact that she was fretting about Dovi. But now she wasn't so sure. Her mother's skin was sallow and her eyes looked dull despite the good news she had just received.

'Are you feeling all right, Mama?' she asked.

Freyde laughed joyously. 'I am feeling wonderful,' she assured her. 'And I will feel better still when I finally see my son again. I have felt that a part of me is missing.'

And then the three of them began to make plans for her brother's homecoming, as Freyde set the lunch out on the table.

It was two weeks later as she was returning home after her morning's work at the school that Adina literally almost bumped into Karl. She was approaching the church gates and was about to hurry past them as she always did, when he walked through them and they nearly collided.

'Adina,' he said, putting his arms out to steady her.

'Hello, Karl.' As she stared up into his bright blue eyes, her heart skipped a beat. He was every bit as handsome as she had remembered him being.

'How are you?' he asked.

'I . . . I'm fine, thank you. And yourself?'

'Busy.' He cocked his head towards the church. 'And glad to be so. This is such a beautiful old church and it is nice to see it rising from the ashes again.'

'I heard that you were all going to start work on it.' She forced a smile before saying hesitantly, 'I . . . I'm sorry I didn't come to meet you that Sunday.'

'It is quite all right. I understand.'

They stood there for a moment solemnly regarding one another.

'How is your friend – Beryl, isn't it?' he asked eventually.

Adina grinned. 'Organising her wedding, as it so happens. She's engaged to one of the American officers up at the Hall and they are planning to go back to the United States once the war is over.'

'That still feels like a long way away,' he said quietly, and she nodded in agreement before hurrying on to tell him the exciting news they had received about Dovi.

Karl seemed genuinely pleased to hear it, although just as she herself had, he wondered what might be wrong with him.

'Will you be going to see him once he is in the hospital in Portsmouth?' he asked.

She nodded eagerly. 'Yes, but we have already been warned that it might not be for some time yet. The worst of it is not knowing what's wrong with him. Mama and Papa go from being deliriously happy to being deeply depressed.'

'I can quite understand that,' he responded, and glancing across his shoulder he told her reluctantly, 'I should be getting back to work. They will be wondering where I have got to.'

'Of course. Goodbye, it was nice to see you again.'

'And you too. Perhaps we shall see each other again if you walk this way each day?'

Adina nodded shyly, suddenly hoping that they would, despite what her parents might think. And then she hastily moved on as he stood there and watched her go with a sad smile on his face.

The letter they had all been waiting for finally arrived, telling them that Dovi was now in a hospital in Portsmouth and that they would be contacted in due course about when they were allowed to visit him.

'But why can we not see him *now*?' Freyde wailed. 'If he is ill or injured he will need us.'

'Be patient,' her husband advised. 'There must be a reason for the delay and these doctors know what they are doing. Dovi will be receiving the best of care. At least we know he is safe now, and when they wish us to visit him they will tell us.'

'I suppose you are right,' Freyde sighed, and from then on she began to mark off the days on the calendar.

Adina saw Karl almost every day on her way home from the school at lunchtime and she looked forward to their little chats. If Freyde noticed that she was suddenly taking special care of her appearance before setting off each morning she put it down to the fact that her daughter had been perked up by the good news about her brother.

Karl was in charge of all the steel works that needed doing on the church, but every day he would find an excuse to wander down to the gates around lunchtime. In those few snatched moments, he and Adina would talk of everything from politics to the war, and they soon discovered that they had a lot in common. Like Adina, Karl loved to read and she began to slip him books from the library, which he would return to her when he had read them.

It was the middle of March when the letter from the military hospital arrived saying that they could now visit Dovi.

'We shall go tomorrow,' Freyde told her husband in a voice that brooked no argument. 'I shall go to the station right now and see what time the earliest train is.'

Knowing that it would be useless to argue, Ezra agreed. 'Very well – but who will mind the shop?'

Freyde flapped her hands in the air. 'We shall shut it if we have to. What is more important to you?'

'That is a silly question to ask,' he retorted as he watched his wife pulling her coat on, and without another word she was gone to find out the time of the trains.

When Adina arrived home that day, her father immediately told her of the latest developments, and she listened wide-eyed.

'Will I be allowed to come?' she asked. 'I'm sure Mrs Haynes would cook a meal for Ariel after school and we can be home by bedtime. I know that the school would allow me to have a day off for such an occasion. I have already asked them.'

'I do not see why not,' Ezra agreed, and so it was decided.

It was almost lunchtime the next day when their train arrived in Portsmouth, and the second they had left the platform, Freyde approached a policeman and showed him the name of the hospital. 'Could you please direct us to this address?' she asked politely.

He stroked his chin. 'I could, but it's a long walk and the chances are you'll get lost. My advice to you would be to take a cab there. Would you like me to call one for you, sir, madam?'

'That would be most kind of you,' Ezra answered.

Half an hour later, after driving some distance along the coast road, the cab pulled up outside a picturesque house that spoke of bygone times.

'This is it, folks,' the driver told them obligingly. 'An' that'll be half a crown, if you please. Would you like me to wait for you?'

Ezra quickly paid him. 'No, thank you. We do not know how long we shall be.'

'No problem, guv'nor.' The man tipped his cap and pulled away, leaving them to stare up at the house. It really was a beautiful place, with ivy growing up its walls in thick profusion and its many windows winking in the early-afternoon sunshine. It was surrounded by well-kept gardens and now they saw men being pushed about in wheelchairs by nurses in crisp white caps and navy uniforms, warmly wrapped up against the chilly March air. Tall chimneys stretched up into the sky, wisps of smoke lazily drifting from them, and after a moment Ezra asked, 'Are we all ready then?'

Suddenly nervous, Freyde nodded as she clutched her handbag. They marched into the reception foyer, which might easily have been that of a first-class hotel, and approached a desk where a nurse with a friendly face smiled at them.

'May I help you?'

'Er . . . yes. We are here to see our son, Dovid Schwartz.'

'Dovid Schwartz,' she repeated as she ran her finger down a large register in front of her and then she stabbed it at his name. 'Dovid is Doctor Sawyer's patient,' she told them. 'If you wouldn't mind waiting here I shall fetch him for you, and then you can have a chat before you go to see Dovid.'

They stood nervously looking about until the nurse reappeared some minutes later with a surprisingly young-looking doctor at the side of her.

'Mr and Mrs Schwartz?' he asked, holding his hand out welcomingly, and when they had shaken it he asked the nurse, 'Could you bring a tray of tea into the waiting room please, Nurse?'

They followed him down a long corridor, looking from left to right as they went. The atmosphere was pleasant and the sound of patients laughing reached them as they passed what was obviously some sort of recreation room. The sun was streaming through the windows and the patients all seemed cheerful enough, but it broke Freyde's heart to see so many young men in wheelchairs. Both she and Adina had tears in their eyes by the time they were shown into a small comfortable room that overlooked the gardens. Easy chairs were dotted here and there, and after asking them all to sit down the young doctor sat opposite them.

'My name is Richard Sawyer,' he told them, 'and I have been looking after your son since he arrived here.'

At that moment the door opened and a plump nurse with a pleasant smile bustled in and placed a laden tray on a small table. The question that Freyde had been about to ask died on her lips until the woman had left the room, and then she burst out, 'So what exactly is wrong with our son, Doctor Sawyer?'

'Oh, call me Richard, please. We try to be as informal as possible here.' He lifted the tea pot and began to strain the tea into delicate china cups and saucers before going on. 'Dovid was shot in the left arm whilst fighting at the front, and sadly, the wound became infected. That's why he was shipped home, because the surgeon in France feared that gangrene might set in. Had that happened, he would have been in grave danger of losing his arm, if not his life.'

Seeing the fear in Freyde's eyes, he held his hand up. 'Don't worry. We caught the infection in time and it's healing well now, although we did have to remove two of the fingers from his hand. But the thing is . . .' When Freyde sucked her breath in, he repeated, 'The thing is . . . Dovid has had a complete break down and may not be as you remember him.'

'What exactly do you mean?' Ezra asked.

Dr Sawyer sighed. 'We keep the men who are suffering from the same complaint as Dovid in a separate wing, as they can be . . . shall I say prone to violent mood swings?'

Ezra and Freyde exchanged a concerned glance.

'And what can you do for him? Will he recover?' Ezra breathed fearfully.

'I would like to think so, but I must be honest and tell you that I think it will take a very long time. And there is no guarantee,' the doctor told him truthfully. There was no point in lying to these people; they would soon see for themselves how the war had affected their son.

Freyde looked on the verge of tears as her husband squeezed her hand

72

reassuringly. 'He *will* recover,' Ezra said with determination. 'Once he is allowed to come home we shall make sure of it. He will receive the best care we can give him.'

'I don't doubt it,' the young man answered. 'But I'm afraid it isn't just down to the care he will receive. Before Dovid was shot himself he saw a friend step onto a landmine right in front of him. The poor chap was blown into pieces and Dovid was shot trying to get to him to help him. Not that there was much of his friend left to help, from what I can make of it.' Richard Sawyer cleared his throat. 'Dovid crawled in stinking mud for days and went without food and water. When they found him he was clutching his friend's dismembered hand. Such things affect the mind – and the mind is a funny thing.'

Adina was so appalled at the things she was hearing that it took all her willpower to stop herself from bursting into tears. It sounded as if her brother had been to hell and back, and if what the doctor was telling them was true, it was no wonder his mind was affected. How could he have lived through all that and remain unchanged?

'Are you ready to see him now?' the doctor asked quietly. 'Or would you like me to give you a few moments to prepare yourselves?'

'We are ready,' Ezra said resolutely as he rose to his feet and so, nodding, the doctor led them all out into the long corridor again and back towards the foyer. Once there he took them up a magnificent sweeping staircase that led to a galleried landing. At the top of the stairs was an enormous stained-glass window, and all the colours of the rainbow were reflected in it. It was hard to believe that they were in a hospital, but then no doubt this place would have been someone's home and commissioned to become a military hospital for the duration of the war.

They moved on past open doors through which they glimpsed rows of comfortable beds until at last they came to a door at the very end of the corridor, where the doctor paused to knock. They noticed that it was securely locked, but after a second they heard the sound of a key being turned and a middle-aged nurse peeped out at them.

'Ah, good morning, Richard. Staff Nurse informed me that Dovid's family were here.' As she spoke she flashed them a warm smile, but they were all too apprehensive to respond.

'Come in,' she invited, holding the door wide, and once they had done as they were told she again locked it securely behind them.

'Dovid's room is along here, but I ought to warn you that we are keeping him heavily sedated for now.'

Ezra nodded silently, and they began to follow her along yet another corridor. They passed one open door where some poor soul was thrashing about on his bed, his hands held out in front of him as if he was fighting off some imaginary foe. The sight was sickening and Adina averted her eyes.

73

At last the nurse paused in front of another door before telling them, 'Dovid is in here. Would you like me to come in with you?'

'No, thank you. We would prefer to go in alone,' Ezra told her solemnly.

'Of course – in your own time then, and should you need me, just call. I shall be at my desk down there.'

They all looked at each other and the same thought was in each of their minds. What were they going to find on the other side of the door? Would it be their beloved son and brother, or some stranger they could not recognise?

Ezra took a deep breath and opened the door cautiously and then they all sidled into the room. It was large and airy, with a huge sash-cord window draped with soft green velvet curtains, giving far-reaching views over open countryside. A neatly made bed was positioned against one wall, next to which stood a highly polished mahogany bedside table. On the other wall was a matching wardrobe and chest of drawers.

But it was the wing chair standing in the bay window to which their eyes were drawn. Someone was sitting in it. Ezra was the first to stride across the bedroom, closely followed by the women, and when his eyes first rested on his son he sucked in his breath painfully.

It was Dovid who sat there – and yet it wasn't. His son had been vibrant and full of life, whereas the person he was looking at now had had all the life drained out of him. His lovely thick dark hair, which Freyde had always sworn had a life of its own, was now clipped close to his scalp. He was skeletally thin and his once twinkling dark eyes were now dull and lifeless. His mouth was hanging slackly open and saliva dribbled from the corner of it to pool on the shirt that looked to be at least three sizes too big for him.

'Dovid . . . we here are here, son,' Ezra choked, but his words brought forth no response.

It was Freyde's turn to try to reach him now as she gently took his hand in hers. 'Have faith, child,' she breathed gently. 'You will soon be back at home with us where you belong.'

Adina hung back, trying to recognise this stranger sitting in front of her. She wanted to speak to him but the words stuck in her throat.

Ezra now crouched to Dovid's level, his eyes brimming with tears as he searched for some sign of recognition from him – but there was nothing.

'The doctor did warn us we would have to be patient,' he said, looking at his wife's stricken face. He then fetched some chairs from against the wall and they all sat down as close to Dovid as they could get, content for now just to be in his company. Some fifteen minutes later, the door opened and a nurse appeared pushing a trolley.

'Hello,' she greeted them brightly. 'I was told you were here. It's time for Dovid's medication now.'

74

For the first time since entering the room, Dovid reacted. He turned to look at the nurse and then as he saw her lift a syringe from a dish on the trolley, his arms began to flail wildly.

'No! Get away from me, do you hear!'

'Now, Dovid, don't let's start that again,' she said patiently as if she were speaking to an errant child. 'You know I'm not going to hurt you and this will make you feel better.'

His head began to thrash against the back of the chair and tears poured down his cheeks as cold sweat stood out on his forehead.

She advanced on him, and the closer she got, the more agitated he became. It took her no more than a second to roll his sleeve up, but just as she was about to administer the injection his arm came out and sent the syringe skidding across the floor.

'Oh, Dovid. Now I shall have to go and fetch another one,' she scolded, and with a nod at his family she quietly left the room. A few moments later she returned with another syringe and two men in white coats.

They each calmly took one of Dovid's arms as the nurse slid the needle into his vein and all the time he was shouting obscenities and baring his teeth at them as his parents and sister looked helplessly on.

'He'll be all right in a few minutes when that starts to work,' the nurse assured them as she rolled his sleeve back down, and she and the two men then left the room.

Sure enough, Dovid was soon calm again and the same blank expression settled over his face. They sat for another half an hour but when they still got no response from him, Ezra said, 'I think we should leave him in peace now. We shall come again very soon and next time, God willing, he might know us.'

Freyde was sobbing into her handkerchief as she sniffed her agreement. The women then kissed Dovid's hollow cheek before stealing quietly from the room, praying that Ezra might be proved to be right.

Chapter Thirteen

As the summer of 1944 approached, Adina continued to see Karl for a few moments each day. They were completely at ease in each other's company now, and sometimes of an evening when the prisoners had returned to the camp, Adina would take a stroll around the church to see what progress was being made. The fine stained-glass windows had been shattered in the bombing, but the plain glass ones that the men had replaced them with looked elegant and in keeping with the lines of the building. It had been agreed before the job was started that the building should be rebuilt as closely to how it had been originally as was possible, and Adina thought they were doing an excellent job of it. Already she could see the massive steel girders in place that would eventually hold up the new roof. The men had painstakingly sorted through the rubble, reclaiming and cleaning every piece of the original stone they could before re-using it. Now their efforts were becoming apparent and the people of Coton were delighted. So much so, in fact, that even more of the men working on the church were now being invited into the townsfolk's homes for Sunday dinner.

Ezra and Freyde now visited Dovid at least once a month, but as yet there were no signs of improvement although Dr Sawyer urged them not to give up hope.

'At least your lad is alive,' Mrs Haynes said enviously one day as she sat sharing a morning cup of tea with Freyde. The woman instantly felt guilt sharp as a knife. Her kindly neighbour was quite right; where there was life there was hope, and Freyde forced herself to believe that some day soon Dovid would turn the corner and start to recover.

By now, Ariel was also giving her parents cause for concern; the girl seemed to grow more wilful with every month that passed. She now flatly refused to join them for family prayers and had taken to sneaking out with her friends whenever she could. One night in early June she had come downstairs with her face heavily made-up. Her eyebrows were pencilled and her lips scarlet, and Ezra had almost hit the roof. She looked at least eighteen and she knew it.

'You are *not* walking out of this house looking like *that*,' he had raged. 'You look like a common street girl!'

'Oh Papa, *why* do you always have to be so old-fashioned,' she said in exasperation. 'All the girls my age dress like this and they are allowed to go to dances and have friends, so why aren't I?'

'Because you are a *child*,' he had raged as Freyde looked fearfully on. 'Now get back up those stairs and wash that muck off your face *right now!*'

Ariel had stamped away in a rage and ever since then things had been very strained between them.

'She is growing up,' Freyde placated him. 'You should make allowances for that and try to be more lenient with her. Compromise a little.'

Ezra had snorted in disgust. 'Whilst she lives under my roof she will obey my rules,' he thundered. 'I will *not* have her bringing shame upon our family.' And that had been the end of the argument. Freyde knew her husband better than to try and change his mind.

The dispute had put the fear of God into Adina. What would happen if her father were to discover that she was having anything to do with a German? But she could not stop it now, even if she had wished to. She lived for the few short moments they stole together, and his smile could light up her day. She knew now that she was falling in love with Karl, and there was not a single thing she could do about it.

On 6 June 1944, just before dawn, 24,000 British, American, Canadian and Free French airborne troops landed in Normandy for what was to become known as the D-Day Invasion. They seized bridges and disrupted German communications, and as their progress was reported on the radio, the English people rejoiced. Darkness gave way to a dull grey morning as 1,000 RAF planes dropped 5,000 tons of bombs on German batteries, causing absolute chaos. Meantime, a vast armada of more than 5,000 ships, including merchantmen, men of war, landing crafts and barges were rolling and heaving offshore in heavy seas waiting to go ashore. The operation was named Overlord and saw the long-awaited Allied assault against Nazi Germany. The attack had not come a day too soon, and for the first time, the people of England began to hope that at last, the end of the war might be in sight.

Hitler's scientists, however, hit back with their latest weapons, and by the middle of July, V1 rocket attacks on London were causing yet another wave of destruction. Mothers and children were once more being evacuated. But even so, nothing could stop people feeling optimistic that the end was on its way. The Allies had now established a firm foothold in Normandy, and Germany was under assault from Italy, Russia and France. The whispers that certain German people were not happy were rife as they questioned why their Führer was placing the Reich in crisis – but those brave enough to speak out were instantly shipped off to concentration camps or executed. Now it was more than obvious that not everyone in Germany was pro-Nazi and pro-SS, including certain German generals. Hitler had cowed his nation, and their disquiet filtered through to England via British Intelligence.

Many trainlines across England were still being targeted by enemy bombers, and sometimes Freyde and Ezra were unable to get to see Dovi because of damage to the tracks.

One morning as they set off, Ezra warned Adina, 'Expect us when you see us. Who knows how long it might take us to get there and back. Will you and Ariel be all right?'

'Of course we shall.' The young woman pecked her father on the cheek. 'I shall make sure that everything is fine until you return. Please give my love to Dovi and tell him that I am thinking of him.'

Once her parents had departed she finished getting ready for her teaching session at the school. Ariel had already left and she followed shortly afterwards.

As usual at lunchtime she met Karl, and it was as they were standing at the church gate that an idea occurred to her. Ariel was going to a friend's for lunch so she would have the house to herself.

'Why don't you come back with me for a break?' she invited, and when he frowned she explained, 'I shall have the house to myself. My parents have gone to visit Dovi and Ariel is going to her friend's for lunch.'

'But your parents would be most unhappy if they were to find out I had been there.'

'Who is going to tell them?' she said coyly. Adina was not normally sly but she was tired of only having a few minutes to talk to him. And who would they be hurting? She was only going to make him a sand-wich and a cup of tea, after all.

He stood there uncertainly for a moment but then told her, 'I will just go and inform the men that I am taking a short break, and then I would be delighted to take you up on your offer – if you are sure it will not be an imposition.'

Adina stood there whilst he strode away, suddenly wondering if she had done the right thing. But then he was back and it was too late to retract her invitation.

Thankfully the entry and Mrs Haynes's back yard were deserted as Adina led Karl to the back door, and once they had slipped into the kitchen unobserved she let out a sigh of relief before hurrying across to the sink to fill the kettle. She made them both cheese and chutney sand-wiches, which they washed down with two cups of tea, and all the way through the meal they chatted easily as if they had known each other for years.

Once she had cleared the pots into the sink they sat together on the sofa and it was then that Karl became serious. 'Adina,' he said, 'there is something I have been meaning to talk to you about.'

'Oh yes, and what is that then?' They were inches apart and now as she looked deep into his eyes she found that she could not look away.

'The thing is I . . .' Suddenly he leaned down mid-sentence and pressed his lips to hers and a thousand fireworks seemed to explode behind her closed eyes. When they finally broke apart they stared at each other as she sighed, 'Oh Karl, I have wanted you to do that for such a long time.'

Without another word he kissed her again and suddenly all the things that stood between them just melted away. They were simply a man and a woman in love and it didn't matter if she was a Jew and he was a German – to them, at least.

The next time they broke apart he hotched along the sofa away from her, looking guilty.

'I am sorry. I should not have done that,' he whispered.

'Why not? You didn't force yourself on me and I wanted you to,' Adina said bluntly. He shook his head. 'It is wrong. We should stop this now before it goes any further.'

'But I *can't* stop it, Karl,' she told him. 'I love you. I think I have loved you since the very first second I set eyes on you, and I can't help how I feel. It just happened.'

'Ach, mein Liebling,' he groaned, slipping into their native tongue. 'I love you too. I have tried not to, but I cannot stop thinking about you. What are we to do? There can be no future together for us.'

'Then we will just take what we can for now and worry about the future another day,' she told him softly.

He took her in his arms again, and as their lips joined they gave themselves up to the pure pleasure of being together.

'I should be going. The men will be wondering where I have got to,' Karl said breathlessly. He kissed her tenderly one last time. 'No regrets?' he murmured.

She shook her head, her eyes sparkling.

'Until tomorrow then?'

She nodded, and once he had left, she went to open up the shop, leaning against the door and wondering where this might lead.

Her parents arrived home late that night just as Adina was preparing to go to bed. Ariel had gone up some time ago, but now she hurriedly placed the kettle on the stove to boil as she asked them, 'How was he?'

Her mother looked unnaturally pale but then Adina supposed that was to be expected after the exhausting day she had had.

'I think he is a little better,' Freyde told her. 'At least he is speaking now, although the doctor informed us he still has a long way to go. He gets the shakes and suffers from terrible nightmares. He is still quite violent too, if they don't keep him on his medication.'

'But we have always known that he wasn't going to recover overnight,' Adina pointed out as she spooned tea leaves into the tea pot.

Her mother nodded. 'Even so, it is painful to see him as he is when I remember back to how he used to be. Back in Cologne, Dovi was the life and soul of every party. He could have had his pick of any girl he wanted, and now he cannot even feed himself.'

Adina's heart went out to her as she saw the look of despair in her mother's weary eyes.

'We must stay strong for him. He *will* come out of this,' Ezra stated with conviction, and Adina could only hope that he was right.

Much later, as she lay in bed staring at the cracks on the ceiling, her mother's sobs came to her through the wall and Adina sighed as she thought back to the time she had spent with Karl. Her parents already had so much to contend with. How would they feel if they found out about her blossoming relationship with him? To have anything to do with a man other than one of her own faith before marriage was unthinkable for a Jewish girl, and should it ever become known, no decent Jewish boy would ever look at her twice. But then she didn't want a Jewish boy. She wanted Karl, so what was she to do?

As she lay there she found no answers to her question.

Chapter Fourteen

For the next week Adina and Karl had no chance of any time alone together apart from the few moments at midday when they would stand and gaze at each other with starry eyes at the gates to the church.

Adina thought about him every waking minute and longed to be in his arms again, but she knew they would have to choose their moments carefully.

After the evening meal one night when she had helped her mother to wash and dry up, she told her, 'I think I might go for a walk round to Beryl's. I haven't seen her for a week or so.'

'All right, bubbeleh.' Her mother sat down at the side of the empty grate and took up her knitting. 'But don't be too late in, will you?'

As Adina let herself into the back yard, she sighed. Ariel had already slipped off somewhere, so no doubt there would be another blazing row later on when she got back in. She had just left school and started work in Woolworth's in the town, a fact her father was none too pleased about.

'It is not right for young women to go out to paid work,' he complained to his wife, but she shook her head.

'Times are changing, Ezra, whether we like it or not. And Adina is paid for the work she does at the school. Where is the difference?'

'But that is to teach children of our own culture the English language,' he argued stubbornly. 'That is acceptable.'

Freyde decided not to disagree with him. There had been enough arguments in the house lately.

Now, as Adina set off down the entry, Molly Thompson's voice wafted towards her and she grinned. She and Mrs Haynes were a familiar sight, standing over the latter's gate with their heads bent together as they put the world to rights.

She was just about to open the gate when a name made her hand stop in mid-air.

'Yep, it was her all right,' she heard Mrs Thompson say. 'Young Ariel from the shop here wi' her tongue stuck just about as far down young Brian Rowley's throat as it 'ud go. Her dad would have had a dickey fit if he'd have caught her. But then I doubt it were the first time. I've heard on the grapevine that she's a right hot-arse little bugger.'

'*Never!*' Mrs Haynes responded, scandalised. 'Well, I knew Ezra were havin' a few problems wi' her but I didn't realise she were like that. An' him so religious, an' all. It just goes to show, don't it? There are skeletons in every closet.'

Not wishing to be caught eavesdropping, Adina coughed before swinging the gate open.

'Hello,' she said politely to the two women as they flushed guiltily. 'It's a lovely evening, isn't it?'

'It is that, luv,' Mrs Haynes said hastily. 'Where you off to – somewhere nice?'

'Oh, I'm just going to pop round to see Beryl for half an hour. Goodbye now.'

'Now *there's* a lovely girl for yer if ever I've seen one,' she heard Mrs Haynes confide. 'Never gives her parents a moment o' worry, that one don't. She'll make someone a lovely wife one o' these days. Her an' Ariel are as different as chalk from cheese.'

Adina cringed inwardly. Oh, if only they knew, she thought, and she hurried on with Mrs Thompson's words ringing in her ears. She was still reeling from what she had heard when something else just as shocking occurred. She was just about to turn into Deacon Street when she saw a U.S. Army jeep coming towards her, and thinking that it looked like the one that Tyrone drove, she peered towards it. If it was Tyrone on his way to see Beryl, she would go back home rather than disturb them.

As it drew closer her mouth gaped open when she saw an attractive dark-haired girl sitting in the passenger seat. She was laughing at something the driver had said – and as it drove by, Adina saw that it was Tyrone. But who was the girl? And why wasn't he with Beryl? They were engaged to be married, after all. She forced herself to move on, sure that there must be some logical explanation for it. Beryl would probably tell her all about it when she got there.

'Hello, love,' Mrs Tait greeted her at the door. 'Our Beryl is upstairs wi' her head stuck in one o' them bridal magazines, if you want to go up to her.'

Adina squeezed her way up the steep narrow staircase and seconds later she knocked at Beryl's door.

'I wasn't sure if you would be in or out with Tye,' she said, as her friend greeted her.

'Oh, Tye is at some sort of military meeting tonight up at the Hall,' Beryl informed her. 'But I did see him last night. We went dancin' an' I did so much jitterbuggin' that I thought me feet were goin' to drop off . . . But what are you looking' so glum for?'

Adina felt as if someone had smacked her in the face, but keen to save her friend from any hurt she told her, 'I just heard Mrs Haynes and Mrs Thompson talking about our Ariel over the gate. Mrs Thompson reckons Ariel is seeing one of the local boys.'

'It wouldn't surprise me,' Beryl replied. 'But it'll be God help 'er if your dad gets to hear about it. He's very strict, ain't he, an' the shit will hit the fan bigtime then. But never mind about that for now. What do you think o' this wedding dress? Ain't it just the best you've ever seen?' When she pointed a long scarlet fingernail at the page, Adina had to admit that the dress was truly beautiful.

'Not that I could get anything like it around here,' Beryl complained. 'Even if I could buy it, it would be more than I could afford, an' I'd never be able to get me hands on that much silk. There must be yards o' the stuff in the train alone.'

Adina stared at the dress thoughtfully. 'Leave it with me,' she told her friend. 'I just might be able to come up with something.'

'Really?' Beryl's face lit up.

'Let me take the magazine with me when I go and I'll see what I can do', Adina said. 'But I'm not making any promises, mind.'

'You are just about the *best* friend anyone could wish for!' Beryl flung her arms about her and kissed her soundly on the cheek. 'But now tell me what *you've* been up to since I last saw you.'

When Adina blushed a deep brick-red, Beryl laughed knowingly. 'Mmm, is there somethin' you want to tell me about?'

In truth, Adina was longing to talk to someone about Karl, and as Beryl was about the only one she could trust with her secret, she told her what had happened.

When she had finished, Beryl let out a long breath. 'Phew, you don't believe in doin' things by halves, do you, gel?' she muttered. 'But what's goin' to happen if your mam an' dad find out about him?'

'I don't know.' Adina bowed her head in misery. 'But what can I do? We can't *choose* who we're going to fall in love with. It just sort of happens, doesn't it?'

'I suppose it does,' Beryl admitted, but no matter how much she thought about it she just couldn't picture a happy ending for her friend in this scenario. She was no fool and had guessed on the very first day when they had met outside the gates of Astley Hall that Karl and Adina were attracted to each other. But she had thought that her friend had more sense than to pursue it. From where she was standing Adina was up the creek without a paddle now and she couldn't think of a single thing that she could do to help her.

'Couldn't you just sort of stop seein' him before it goes any further?' she asked with concern.

Adina shook her head. 'I could just as easily give up breathing.'

'Then from where I'm standin' you're in deep trouble,' Beryl stated flatly, and as much as she hated to hear it, Adina knew that she was right. But what about the girl she had seen Tyrone with, earlier in the night? He had told Beryl that he would be attending some military meeting up at the Hall but it was definitely him Adina had seen: she would have staked her life on it. She wondered again if she should tell Beryl, but couldn't bring herself to do so. There might have been some perfectly plausible explanation as to why he was with the girl. She could have been a secretary or someone he was simply transporting to the meeting. Deciding that she preferred to believe that, Adina held her tongue.

The next day when she saw Karl she said shyly, 'Would you mind very much if I asked you a favour?'

'Ask away,' he answered with a grin.

'Well, the thing is, Beryl has seen this picture of a wedding gown in a magazine but we aren't able to get hold of the silk to make it, what with all the rationing. So I was wondering . . . would you happen to know if any of your friends might have a spare parachute tucked away somewhere? The silk they are made of is lovely quality and I'd be able to make two wedding gowns out of one parachute.'

'Hmm.' He tapped his chin thoughtfully. 'Leave it with me and I'll see what I can do.'

She flushed with pleasure when his fingers closed briefly around hers.

Two days later when she met him, Karl was clutching a large parcel wrapped in brown paper.

'Here,' he grinned. 'I think this might be what you were after.'

As Adina tore a corner of the paper and saw the smooth white silk folded inside she squealed with delight. 'Oh Karl, this is wonderful! Thank you *so* much. Beryl will be thrilled and I'll be able to start making her wedding dress now. But what do we owe you?'

'Not a thing,' he assured her. 'I was just happy to help.'

Adina had to resist the urge to kiss him there and then. As she was discovering, Karl was a very caring man, always happy to help anyone when he could. If only my father could see that, she found herself thinking, but she knew that the chances of that happening were remote. Karl was a German and a non-Jew, and because of that, her father would never accept him.

As soon as she got home, Adina went to her room and began to study the picture of the wedding dress that Beryl had admired in the magazine.

It was actually quite a simple design, and Adina was sure that she could copy it. The bodice was fitted tight into the waist, and came to a point, with tiny pearl buttons running all the way up the back and front to the sweetheart neckline. The sleeves were long and tapered to a point on the back of each hand, and the front of the skirt then fell away into an A-line shape. The back stretched away into a pretty train.

Adina could almost picture Beryl floating down the aisle in it and determined to make a start on it straight away. She decided she wouldn't tell her friend about it yet though, until she was sure that she could get it just right. Thankfully they were almost the same size, apart from the fact that Beryl was taller than her, and Adina had her measurements, so she knew that she could get quite a fair way with it before having to ask Beryl to try it on.

Untying the brown paper, she lifted the parachute from the parcel and sighed happily as it drifted onto the bed in a swish of silk. It was just perfect for the design that Beryl had chosen, and already Adina could imagine her face when she first got a glimpse of it.

By teatime she had the pattern cut out. She had taped old newspapers together and cut them into the different sections that would make up the dress. Next she would have to start cutting the fabric, which was slightly more nervewracking.

When her mother eventually called her down for her evening meal Freyde glanced at her curiously. 'So what have you been doing, shut away in your room all afternoon then?' she asked.

Adina took a seat at the table with a wide smile on her face. 'Can you keep a secret?'

'It all depends what the secret is,' her mother responded, so Adina began to tell her how she was hoping to surprise Beryl.

'And just where did you manage to get the parachute from?' her mother asked when Adina paused for breath.

The girl said vaguely, 'Oh, some friend of her fiancé's managed to get hold of it.' Once again she hated lying, but how could she tell her mother the truth?

Thankfully, Freyde seemed quite happy with the explanation and the rest of the meal passed without another mention of it.

Within a week, Adina had the dress tacked together and she was thrilled with how it was beginning to look. Now the more intricate work would begin as she machined all the hems. She was humming softly to herself as she walked to her friend's house one night when she once again saw Tyrone in his US Army jeep with the same woman she had spotted him with the week before. Adina's heart sank into her shoes as she watched the tail-lights of the vehicle disappearing off down the road. What if he was two-timing Beryl? The girl would be broken-hearted. Suddenly unable to face her, she turned and went back home whilst she tried to put her thoughts into some sort of order.

She entered the kitchen to find herself in the midst of yet another blazing row between Ariel and her father. Her parents were going to see Dovi the next day and Ariel had informed them that she would not be accompanying them as she was intending to go to a dance in the town that evening.

'You are telling me that you would put a *dance* before going to see your own brother?' Ezra raged, red in the face.

'Yes, I am,' Ariel retorted boldly. 'He doesn't even know we're there anyway, so what's the point in going?'

'How could you be so *heartless*,' Freyde wept. Sometimes she didn't even recognise this selfish young woman as her daughter any more.

'Oh, I'm not going to stand here arguing about it,' Ariel spat peevishly and with that she turned on her heel and stormed away upstairs.

'Try to be patient with her,' Adina muttered, hoping to ease the tension. 'She's only young. She's just going through a stage.'

'A *stage*!' Ezra stormed. 'She doesn't seem to care about anyone but herself any more and I'm sick of it!'

Not knowing what else to say, Adina too slipped away upstairs where she sat on her bed with her mind in turmoil. What with one thing and another, she felt as if she had the weight of the world on her shoulders. There was Beryl, totally besotted with her fiancé – but was he besotted with her? And then there was Ariel, who seemed to have gone completely off the rails over the last few months. And Dovi, poor Dovi – it broke her heart just to think of him, and sometimes she could scarcely remember him as he had been before he went away to war. And finally there was Karl. Just the thought of him made her break out in goosebumps, but her parents would never accept him in a million years, which left her with only one solution. Once the war was over and he was a free man again, she would have to go away with him.

But do I love him enough to cut all ties with my family? she asked herself. And the answer came back loud and clear. *Yes I do, and if need be I shall follow him to the ends of the earth.*

Part Two

Loving and Leaving

Chapter Fifteen

The war raged on, taking a terrible turn for the worse in September when the new V2 rockets were aimed at London. Silent until the last moment, these deadly weapons dropped from the sky without warning, causing widespread devastation.

Ezra listened to the radio reports with a heavy heart. It was now almost two months since he had seen his son, as the last time he and Freyde had set out to do so they had been unable to get trains to Portsmouth because of widespread damage to the railway tracks.

'I'm sure you will manage it tomorrow,' Adina soothed as she saw him studying the train timetables.

'I hope so.' Freyde looked towards the fire. 'He will think we have forsaken him.'

'Never.' Adina was adamant. Thankfully, her brother was now showing signs of recovery – and had even recognised his parents on their last visit – but they were well aware that he still had an awful long way to go.

If they did manage their journey the next day, she intended to bring Karl back to the shop at lunchtime. She was so besotted with him now that she didn't even feel guilty about their secret rendezvous any more.

Yawning now, she asked her father, 'Do you think they'll drop any of those rockets on us?'

'Who can say what the Nazis are capable of?' he said. 'But now, bubbeleh, you get yourself off to bed and try not to worry about it. I shall be up too shortly, when your sister finally decides to come in.'

After planting a kiss on his thinning hair, Adina then embraced her mother and went upstairs to Dovi's room, where she still slept, and stood surveying Beryl's wedding dress. It stood in the corner of the room on the dressmaker's dummy, completely finished now all but for the hem – and that could not be turned up until Beryl had tried it on. In truth, it had been finished for weeks now, and Adina wondered why she hadn't shown it to her friend before. She supposed it was because she still had doubts about Tyrone's commitment to Beryl after seeing him with the girl in his jeep those couple of times. Admittedly she hadn't seen him with her since then, but still the niggles of unease were there deep in the pit of her stomach each time she thought of him.

Recently, some of the officers stationed at the Hall had been shipped back to the States, and Adina knew that Beryl was wondering when it would be Tyrone's turn. The girl was secretly hoping that it would be soon because she felt sure that as soon as he knew he was going home, they would be married. Adina wasn't so sure but wisely held her tongue. She knew how much Beryl loved the American and hoped that things would turn out well for her.

It was as she was slipping her nightdress over her head that she heard the back door open and close. No doubt it was Ariel returning from her date – which meant yet another row with her father.

Sighing, she snuggled down into the cold cotton sheets and as sleep came to claim her she wondered why life had to be so complicated.

The next morning, Ezra and Freyde left early for the station, closely followed by Ariel when she went off to her job at Woolworth's. After washing and drying the breakfast pots, Adina set off for school with a million butterflies flitting about in her stomach. Ezra and Freyde had not returned, which meant that they must have been able to get a train to Portsmouth. It also meant that she would be able to bring Karl home during his lunch-break – and the thought of spending time with him lent speed to her feet.

The morning passed interminably slowly but at last the bell for the lunch-hour rang and Adina tidied her hair in the staff room before setting off for Coton Church. Karl was waiting for her as usual at the lychgate and her heart sang at the sight of him.

'My parents have gone to visit Dovi,' she told him shyly, as he fell into step beside her.

'Then we must not waste a single second of the precious time we have,' he told her, and as they moved along, he delved into his coat pocket. 'I have something for you,' he told her looking slightly embarrassed. He pressed something into her hand, and when Adina glanced down, a band of steel winked up at her in the sunlight.

'It is not much,' Karl told her hurriedly. 'It is just something I made when I was at the forge. I would like you to have it as a keepsake.'

'A keepsake?' The thrill of the gift was lost for the minute as fear flooded through her. Was Karl trying to tell her that he was going away?

'Are you leaving?' she managed to ask.

He shook his head. 'No no – at least not for the foreseeable future. But one day when the war is over . . .'

'But I thought . . .'

When her voice trailed away he smiled at her sadly. 'One day I shall have to return to Germany mein Liebling, and the ring is just something to remind you of me.'

'But I . . . I thought we would be together,' she said falteringly.

Karl pursed his lips. 'There is nothing I would like more, but there are things . . . But come – do not let us spoil our time together. Take the gift and think of me when you wear it.'

90

As Adina stared down at the steel band it was more precious to her than platinum. She slid it onto her finger and sighed happily as it shone in the sunshine.

'I shall treasure it always,' she murmured as they turned the corner leading to the shop. Mrs Haynes was standing outside her gate, chatting to the neighbour from the house on the other side of her, and Adina was suddenly unsure what she should do. But then an idea occured to her.

'Wait there,' she told Karl. 'I shall go and unlock the shop and then you can come in as if you were just a customer. Mrs Haynes won't think anything of that.'

'I do not wish to cause any trouble for you,' he said uncertainly, but Adina waved her hand at him.

'Just give me two minutes.' And then she was hurrying away as he stood there watching her.

'You all right, are you, luv? Just finished at the school for the day?' Mrs Haynes asked good-naturedly as Adina approached.

'Yes, I have, and if you'll excuse me I ought to get the shop open now,' Adina replied with a smile.

'Yes, an' I ought to go in an' get my Bert's dinner on the go – otherwise he'll have me guts for garters!' Mrs Haynes exclaimed as she nodded towards her neighbour. 'See you, Gertie.' With that she pottered away up the entry ahead of Adina as the girl sighed with relief.

After hurrying through the shop she admitted Karl and they went through to the kitchen. Each time she glanced at the shining band of steel on her finger she found herself smiling. Surely this was Karl's way of telling her that he was committing himself to her. Why else would he have made her a ring? And yet her joy was tinged with sorrow as she thought of the sacrifices she would have to make to be with him. Her family would disown her once they knew that she was going to marry a Nazi – but what choice did she have, if she was to be with the man she loved? Glancing across at him now, she noticed that Karl seemed strangely distracted. 'Is everything all right?' she asked.

'Yes, it is, but there is something I must talk to you about,' he told her.

'Of course.' She sat down next to him on the couch. 'Now – what is it you want to tell me?'

He opened his mouth to answer, but at that moment the bell on the shop door began to tinkle.

'Ignore it,' Adina urged. 'They will go away in a moment.' But when the noise continued she sighed with frustration. 'I won't be long,' she told him as she hurried away into the shop. She hastily served the customer and then went back into the kitchen, only to find no sign of Karl. He had probably gone outside to the lavatory, she told herself. The minutes on the clock ticked away until eventually she crept into the yard where she whispered, 'Karl . . . are you there?'

When no answer came she inched the privy door open, only to find that it was empty. It was then she saw that the gate was also slightly ajar, and she frowned. Why would Karl have shot off like that without a word? Deciding that he had probably gone in case whoever was ringing the shop bell might find him there, she sighed with disappointment. It was just like him to be so considerate, she decided. But what had he been about to tell her? There could be no way of knowing now until she saw him the next day, so she put the latch on the gate and went through to open the shop. There wasn't much else she could do for now.

When her parents arrived home late that evening they were weary but excited.

'Dovi may be able to come home soon,' her mother told her as she took the hat pin from the back of her hat and patted her hair into place. 'He knew us immediately today when we arrived at the hospital and the doctors are pleased with his progress.'

'That's wonderful news,' Adina told her with genuine pleasure.

'He is still far from well, of course,' her father continued in a more cautious manner, 'and he will be on heavy medication for some time, but at least he will be home again and that is the main thing.'

'How soon?' Adina asked.

Ezra shrugged. 'They did not give us a definite date but perhaps a couple more months.'

'I shall feed him up with my chicken soup.' Freyde beamed. She believed that chicken soup was the cure for all ills. 'He will have meat on his bones again in no time, once I can have him back with us.'

Adina did not doubt it and began to look forward to having her brother home.

The following evening there was a knock at the back door and when Ezra went to open it he found Beryl standing on the doorstep.

'Good evening, Mr Schwartz. Is Adina in?' she asked politely. Adina's father always made her feel nervous.

'Yes, she is,' he answered as he held the door wide. 'She is sewing up in her room. Perhaps you would like to go up to her?'

'Thank you.' She slid past him and nodded at Freyde and Ariel who smiled at her as she headed for the stairs door.

'Beryl was looking a little pale, didn't you think?' Freyde commented when the girl had gone; she then turned her attention back to the sock she was darning as Ezra shrugged and settled back into his chair. He had never wholly approved of his daughter's friendship with Beryl but he supposed it was up to Adina who she chose to mix with. Up to a point, of course.

Upstairs, Beryl tapped on Adina's bedroom door before entering to find her friend busily at work on the old Singer sewing machine.

'Beryl, what are *you* doing here?' Adina took her foot off the treadle as she smiled a welcome. 'Don't you usually see Tyrone on Wednesday nights?'

Beryl plonked herself down on the edge of Adina's bed. 'Yes, I do, but he said he was going to be busy tonight. He seems to be busy a lot just lately.'

A picture of him sitting next to the dark-haired girl in the jeep flashed into Adina's mind but she pushed it away as she looked at her friend's downcast face.

'Well, he does have a job to do and he can't be in two places at once, can he?' she said kindly.

Beryl shook her head. 'It's now that they're shipping some of the officers back home to America,' she said glumly. 'Tyrone has to organise everything so I don't get to see so much of him any more.'

Adina crossed to sit beside her friend and draped her arm around her shoulders. 'And is that all that's bothering you?'

Beryl suddenly burst into tears, which wasn't like her friend at all. She was usually such a happy-go-lucky sort of person. Adina remained silent as Beryl sobbed until eventually the girl took a deep breath and mopped at her eyes with the handkerchief Adina had passed her.

'Now, is it something you want to talk about?' Adina asked.

For a moment it appeared that Beryl wasn't going to answer her, but then she suddenly blurted out, 'I'm in real trouble, mate.'

'What sort of trouble?' Adina probed gently. 'Is it something I can help you with?'

'No one can help me,' Beryl wailed. 'You see, I'm pregnant.'

Adina gulped before asking, 'Are you quite sure?'

'Well, I ain't been to the doctor's yet but my monthlies are usually as regular as clockwork an' I've missed two now. Added to that I keep bein' sick in the mornin' an' me boobs are killing me, so I reckon I can safely say I am, don't you?'

'It certainly sounds like it,' Adina admitted. 'What has Tyrone had to say about it?'

'I ain't told him yet. I wanted to talk to you first. What do you reckon I should do, Dina?'

'I think you should tell him,' Adina advised without hesitation. 'And it isn't the end of the world, you know. You are engaged, after all. This just means that you'll have to get married slightly sooner than you'd planned. Tyrone might even be pleased to know that he's going to be a father.'

'Do you *really* think so?' Beryl looked slightly happier. 'But what are me mam an' dad goin' to say?' she said after a while. 'Me dad will bloody slay 'im alive.'

'Your parents needn't know straight away,' Adina soothed. 'Just say that with the war on you don't want to wait, and get the wedding organised as soon as you can. Lots of couples are doing it nowadays. Ruth Connor from Riversley Road married her boyfriend last week while he was on two days' leave.'

'An' just what am I supposed to wear?' Beryl grumbled.

Adina hopped off the bed and chuckled. 'Now there I *can* help you,' she told her with a twinkle in her eye, and crossing to the mannequin in the corner of the room, she whipped the white sheet off it.

Beryl's jaw dropped with amazement as she saw the beautiful dress beneath it. 'Why, that's like the one I showed you in me magazine,' she choked.

Adina grinned from ear to ear. 'I copied the pattern and now all I need you to do is try it on so that I can turn the hem up.'

'But where did you manage to get the material from?'

Adina tapped the side of her nose. 'Let's just say I have friends,' she chuckled. 'Now come and try it on, and let's see if we can't cheer you up a bit.'

Within minutes Beryl was twirling delightedly in front of the cheval mirror. 'It's the most beautiful dress I've ever seen,' she breathed as she sashayed this way and that.

'Good, then hurry and decide when you're going to wear it, otherwise I shall have to be letting the seams out,' Adina teased.

'I'll tell him tomorrow,' Beryl promised. 'But now help me out of it, would you, afore I muck it up.'

Within minutes the dress was safely back on the mannequin and as Beryl got dressed she told Adina, 'Thanks fer listenin', Dina. I didn't know who else to turn to.'

'That's what friends are for,' Adina told her with a warm hug, but once Beryl had left in a slightly happier frame of mind she frowned. She could only pray now that Tyrone would stand by her friend and marry her. The alternative was just too awful to contemplate.

Her hand rose to finger the steel band that Karl had given her and that was now suspended on a silver chain about her neck. She dare not risk wearing it on her hand in front of her parents for fear of any questions they might ask about it. But why had he rushed off as he had? She pushed her fears aside. Karl was an honourable man, she would have staked her life on it, and he would stand by her no matter what, just as, hopefully, Tyrone would stand by Beryl.

Her eyes settled on the white silk on the sewing machine. She had already begun to make her own wedding gown, and one day she would wear it when she married Karl. As far as she was concerned, the day could not come soon enough.

Chapter Sixteen

'Be sure an' have her in at a decent time now, do y'hear, son?'

'Yes, sir.' Tyrone told Beryl's father respectfully as he steered her towards the door. Once outside he let out a sigh of relief. Beryl's parents had always made him welcome in their home, but he had a feeling that Mr Tait would not be a man to cross. Not that he ever intended to, if he could help it.

'So, how are ya, honey?' he asked now as he helped Beryl into the jeep. She seemed a little subdued tonight, which wasn't like her at all. Usually Beryl was the life and soul of the party.

'I'm fine,' she muttered as he closed the door and strode round to the driver's seat. Soon they were cruising along Queen's Road and he asked her, 'So what did you have in mind for tonight?'

'Actually, I'd quite like us to go somewhere quiet. There's somethin' I need to talk to you about.'

'In that case we'll head out into the country and find us a quaint little pub, eh? How about the Cock at Sibson? They do a nice pint of ale there.'

Beryl nodded absently as Tyrone glanced at her from the corner of his eye. She was looking a bit peaky – perhaps she was sickening for something? There seemed to be an awful lot of bugs flying around. They drove through Weddington and Fenny Drayton in silence until the pub came into view, and Tyrone pulled the jeep into the car park and switched off the engine. He loved this inn; it was reputed to be the oldest in England, and legend had it that it had once been the haunt of Dick Turpin, the notorious highwayman. He loved anything with an English history attached to it, but after staring at it for a while he slid his arm across the back of the seat and asked, 'You feelin' ill, honey?'

'Not *ill* exactly,' she told him as she squirmed in her seat. 'But . . . look – I may as well get it over with and tell you. I'm pregnant, Tye. I'm going to have your baby.'

The look of horror that swept across his face brought tears stinging to her eyes. She had expected him to be shocked, but he looked as if she had just told him that the world was coming to an end.

'It'll be all right,' she gulped, grasping his hand as panic flooded through her. 'It just means that we'll have to get married a little sooner than we'd planned.'

'B-but I might be flyin' home next month,' he mumbled.

'You didn't tell me that before, but that's fine.' Alarm bells started to clang in her head but she rushed on, 'We can get married and then I can fly home with you. We'll be in America before I even start to show, an' no one here need ever be any the wiser.' Her eyes were full of hope as she smiled at him, and swallowing, he looked away and stared across the fields. His mind was working overtime. This was the last thing he had wanted. Beryl was a nice enough girl but he had never intended to marry her. He had just bought her a ring to string her along and get her to allow him to use her until he was tired of her. She was just one of several, could she have known it, and if this hadn't happened he could have just discreetly disappeared off the scene without telling her, but now what was he to do?

'Do your folks know?' he asked eventually.

Beryl shook her head. 'No, I wanted to tell you before I told them. The only other person who knows is Dina, and guess what? She's made me the most *wonderful* wedding gown you've ever seen. It's fit for a queen, although I didn't think I'd be wearin' it quite so soon.'

'Now hold on, honey.' Tye ran his hand distractedly through his thick thatch of hair. This was his worst nightmare come true. *Wedding gown, wedding!* 'We need to think this through. Marriage isn't somethin' you go into lightly.'

'Lightly!' Beryl frowned. 'In case you'd forgotten, we *are* already engaged to be married.'

'Yes, yes, of course we are,' he said in a placating tone of voice. 'All I'm sayin' is we need to think what's best to do.'

'Don't you think it's a bit late for that?' Beryl said acidly.

'There are er . . . things you can do if you don't want a child.'

When she stared at him in horror he rushed on, 'One of the guys up at the Hall found himself in a similar predicament not long ago and he took his girl to see this woman who lives in the town. She fixed it for them – at a price, of course. But money ain't a problem if you feel that's best.'

'Y-you're telling me you want me to go to some seedy place and have a back-street abortion?' she stuttered as she recoiled from him.

'*No, no,* honey. I'm just saying we have to think what's best.' He tried to take her hand but she thrust him away from her as she swiped at the tears that were streaming down her cheeks.

'How could you even think o' doin' that to our baby?' she choked and then slowly her distress was replaced by cold hard rage.

'I know what happens to blokes like you if their Commanding Officer gets to hear about situations like this,' she threatened, and now it was his turn to tremble.

'They don't look too well on unwanted pregnancies,' she went on with venom in her voice. 'An' neither will my dad. It will be God help you if you don't do the right thing by me, Tyrone. I'm warning you, I ain't some floozy who you can just use an' abuse an' then cast away.'

'I never thought you were, honey,' he lied as panic engulfed him.

'Good! Then in that case I suggest we start to plan the weddin'.' Her voice was colder than any snow he had ever stepped in, and his mind raced as he tried to think of a way out of this nightmare.

Suddenly his shoulders sagged. 'So how do we go about it then? Are you going to tell your folks?'

'No,' she said with determination. 'There's no point in upsettin' them unless we have to. I'll just tell them that you have the chance to fly home sooner than expected so we're bringin' the weddin' forward so that I can fly back with you.'

He nodded as resignation settled around him like a cold damp cloud.

'I'll see to all the arrangements,' she went on. 'All you'll have to do is turn up at the church. We'll apply for a special licence an' you can arrange for me to fly home with you.'

She sidled across the seat and stroked his cheek, surprised to feel that it was damp with sweat.

He nodded numbly. There didn't seem to be any point in arguing; whatever happened now, he felt he was up the creek without a paddle.

'So how did he take the news then?' Adina asked the next evening as she took her coat off and curled up on the end of Beryl's bed.

'Well, he was quite shocked when I first told him,' Beryl replied cautiously as she twisted another pipe cleaner into her damp hair. 'But once he'd got used to the idea he agreed that the best thing we could do was to get married as soon as we can.'

Adina had expected to find Beryl jumping with joy at the prospect of the forthcoming wedding, but if anything she seemed a little subdued. But then, getting married was a big step so she supposed her friend was bound to have mixed feelings, particularly as she would be leaving with Tye to live in America.

'How did your parents take the news?' Adina babbled on. 'Did you tell them about the baby?'

'Of course I didn't,' Beryl snapped. 'There won't be any need for them to know about that. You see, shortly after the wedding, Tye will be going home, so I just told them that we plan to get married sooner than we'd expected to so that I can fly back with him.'

'*How* shortly?'

'Next month,' Beryl admitted, and her face softened as she caught sight of her friend's stricken expression in the mirror.

'B . . . but you never said before that it would be so soon,' Adina mumbled.

'I didn't know myself until Tye told me last night.'

'Oh!' Adina found it quite strange that Tyrone was being flown back so soon, and stranger still that he hadn't told Beryl before, but then she gave him the benefit of the doubt. After all, he might only just have been told himself.

'I shall miss you.' As tears shimmered in her eyes Beryl turned to give her a hug.

'We'll keep in touch,' she said gently. 'I'll write to you every single week and after the war is over we'll meet again. I'll come back to see you and Mum an' Dad, I promise.'

'Of course you will.' Adina returned the hug but her heart was heavy.

Beryl sat down beside her. 'Me an' Tye are goin' see the vicar at Saint Nicholas Church on Saturday an' we're goin' to get married as soon as possible. I'd have liked to get married at Coton, but it ain't quite finished yet. Mam's in a right old flap, I don't mind tellin' you. She's insistin' that we have a proper do even if it is a rushed affair. She's already ordered a cake from the baker's shop in town but they've told her that she's got to supply the eggs, flour an' fruit for it herself. She's been buyin' ration coupons off the neighbours left right an' centre, but the shop is still chargin' her six pounds six shillin's to make it. Then me bouquet is costin' another three quid. It's daylight robbery, ain't it? I told her about the lovely dress you've made me an' she were thrilled to bits that that's one thing she won't have to worry about, but on Friday she's takin' me over to Husselby's in Primrose Hill Street in Coventry to get me a headdress.' Beryl gave her friend's hand a squeeze. 'I'd have loved to have you as a bridesmaid, Dina, but they're askin' seven clothin' coupons each for a bridesmaid dress, an' I don't think we'll have enough time to rustle that many up on top of everythin' else.'

'Oh, don't get worrying about that,' Adina assured her quickly. In actual fact, it was a blessing in disguise. She couldn't see her father approving of her taking part in a Christian service, and if he were ever to discover that her friend was pregnant to boot . . .

'Will you be having a reception?' she asked now.

Beryl sighed. 'Well, we'll just be havin' a *little* one,' she said. 'The Rose Inn have told me mam they'll put a spread on for six shillin's an' fourpence per head, though Lord knows what they'll manage to rustle up, wi' rationin' bein' as it is.'

'You don't look very excited,' Adina said quietly as she studied Beryl's sombre face.

Beryl instantly forced a smile to her lips. 'I suppose I'm just feelin' a bit nervous about leavin' everyone I know behind, now that it's actually goin' to happen.'

'I dare say you are,' Adina agreed, but something deep down told her that there was more to Beryl's mood than she was letting on.

As she hurried home through the darkened strees later that evening, her own heart was heavy. Karl had avoided her yet again that lunchtime. Adina couldn't understand it. His ring lay in the cleft of her breasts, warm against her heart, so why was he suddenly choosing to ignore her? On her way home that day she had seen him in the distance heaving a great metal girder from the back of an Army jeep, but he had studiously kept his eyes fixed on what he was doing and had not even acknowledged her. The rest of the day had passed in a blur of depression, made no better by her visit to Beryl's.

Adina's own wedding gown was well under way, but she was beginning to wonder now if she would ever get the chance to wear it – and even if she did, wouldn't her own feelings be much as Beryl's were now? If anything, they would be even worse because she knew that if she did marry Karl, her family would disown her for ever. Glancing up and down the deserted streets, she shuddered. Not a glimmer of light showed through the blackout curtains and she might have been walking through a ghost town. But at least it was quiet, and she hoped that she might get to spend a night in her own bed rather than in the inky darkness of the neighbour's air-raid shelter.

Chapter Seventeen

On 14 October 1944, as British troops were returning to Greece intent on liberating Athens, Beryl and Tyrone were married in St Nicholas parish church. Behind her smile, the bride seemed to be somewhat subdued, Adina thought, and the groom, too, seemed strangely on edge, but then she supposed it was to be expected. The wedding had been a rushed affair, to say the least, and Beryl was no doubt fretting about the fact that she was soon to fly out to a new life in America. She had confided to Adina that the thought of going on an aeroplane filled her with dread.

In fact, unbeknownst to Adina, Tyrone had been intending to travel back to the USA alone, until all of Beryl's necessary travelling visas were in place. However, he had soon abandoned that idea, following a tantrum from his fiancée, who had told him in no uncertain terms that if he even attempted to go without her she would tell her father and his superior about the baby. And now here they were leaving the church as husband and wife as Adina showered them with rice.

'How does it feel to be an old married woman Mrs Hughes?' she whispered in Beryl's ear as she slipped her a horseshoe made of silver paper suspended from a white satin ribbon.

'Ask me in about another fifty years,' Beryl answered as she looked up at her new husband. Tyrone was dressed in full uniform and Beryl was convinced he was the most handsome man she had ever set eyes on. She just wished that he could have shown a little more enthusiasm in the lead-up to the wedding. But then, she tried to convince herself that he was merely nervous. Far better to believe that, than consider the alternative – that he felt he was being trapped into marriage, which in truth he had been. Deep down she had a terrible suspicion that, had she not allowed him to have sex with her after she had insisted he put a ring on her finger, he would have been long gone, but she had loved him so much she would have done anything to keep him – and this was the consequence.

Mrs Tait was sniffing into her handkerchief and Adina gave her a reassuring hug.

'Your daughter looks truly beautiful,' she told her with a gentle smile.

'Well, luvvie, I reckon we have you to thank for that,' the woman replied. 'That dress is stunnin'. Lord knows what we'd have done if you hadn't made that for her. I reckon she'd have had to get wed in a two-piece.'

Adina watched Tyrone guide her friend to the taxi that was waiting for them at the church gates. She herself had trimmed it with ribbons, and now she set off on foot to follow the couple to the Rose Inn.

When she arrived she found about fifteen people present and Beryl and Tyrone waiting at the door of the back room to greet them. A buffet of sorts had been set out on a long trestle table that was covered in a snow-white damask tablecloth, and Adina thought the landlady of the pub had done them proud, considering the shortages.

There were paste and cucumber sandwiches, sausage rolls and pork pies and a number of small fancy cakes. On a separate table the wedding cake took pride of place and after everyone had eaten their fill and raised their glasses in a toast to the newlyweds, they duly cut it.

'I notice you steered clear o' the pork pies, love,' Mr Tait said teasingly to Adina as he raised yet another glass of ale to his lips. It wasn't every day his youngest child got wed and he intended to make the most of every second of it.

'If my father thought I'd so much as looked at anything containing pork, I think he'd keel over in horror,' Adina rejoined with a twinkle in her eye, and then she followed her friend who was heading for the ladies. Once inside, Beryl let out a relieved breath and leaned back against the sink.

'Phew, I'm glad that bit's over,' she muttered as she fumbled in her bag for her lipstick. 'What time is it? We'll have to be off to catch our train soon – if they're runnin', that is. It would be just my luck to have to miss me honeymoon – not that three nights in Stratford-on-Avon is much o' one.'

'It's better than nothing and there *is* a war on,' Adina pointed out.

Beryl looked suitably shamefaced. 'I know, I shouldn't grumble should I? I mean, most girls 'ud snap me hand off to be in my shoes, wouldn't they?' Chewing on her lip she suddenly blurted out, 'Tyrone *does* love me, doesn't he?'

'Why . . . what a question to ask on your wedding day! Of *course* he does, you silly goose. He wouldn't have married you if he didn't, would he? It stands to reason.'

'No, o' course he wouldn't. Just ignore me, eh? I'm bein' daft. Me an' Tyrone are goin' to live happily ever after.' Beryl quickly applied a layer of lipstick before catching Adina to her in a bear hug. 'I'm really goin' to miss you,' she said, her voice thick with unshed tears.

'Now don't start that or you'll set me off as well,' Adina warned as she returned the hug.

'An' what about you an' Karl? Seen anythin' of him, have you?'

'I've seen him as I've passed the church but I haven't really spoken to him,' Adina answered guardedly. She had no wish to get into a conversation about him, today of all days. It hurt too much to talk about it and she didn't want to spoil Beryl's day. It was then that a noisy rendition of 'Roll Out the Barrel' floated from the back room and Beryl sighed.

'Oh dear, it sounds like me dad's gettin' into his stride,' she grinned.

'There'll be no stoppin' him now. I suppose we'd better go back an' join 'em, eh? Otherwise Tyrone will think I've run out on him already.'

Arm in arm, the two young women made their way back to the party until it was time for Beryl to leave to get changed back at her mother's home. She and Tyrone would be living there for the next few weeks until they flew to America.

When she finally departed Adina watched her go with a lump in her throat. She was pleased that her friend had married the man of her dreams, but wondered if it would ever happen to her. Karl was still going out of his way to avoid her, and his sudden coldness had hurt her far more than she could say.

When the bride and groom had left, Adina said goodbye to Mr and Mrs Tait and slowly walked along Coton Road. She was so engrossed in her thoughts that when a familiar voice spoke her name, she almost jumped out of her skin. Her head snapped up and she found Karl not an arm's length away, staring at her.

'Wh . . . what are *you* doing here?' she stuttered.

He bowed his head, unable to look her in the eye. 'I knew that Beryl was getting married today and guessed that I would find you on the way home from the reception if I hung about for long enough.'

'Well, you certainly haven't been so eager to see me for the last few weeks,' she retorted haughtily, as all the hurt he had caused her bubbled up inside. 'I had made my mind up that you didn't wish to see me again.'

'I *didn't*,' he told her, stunning her into silence. 'But I can't keep away from you – that is the trouble. I told myself that for your sake I should end it, have no more to do with you. But you see I can't. You are here in my heart and I can't stop thinking about you. I'm so sorry if I have caused you pain but I was doing it with the best of intentions.'

Adina's anger melted like an icicle in the sunshine. She wanted to stay angry with him but it was impossible. She knew that what he had said was true, but was no more able to end it than he was, even if it meant losing her family.

'What are we going to do?' she asked miserably, and now he looked her straight in the eye.

'I do not know, mein Liebling. All I *do* know is that we were meant to be together. When the war is over I shall have to return to Germany, but as soon as it is humanly possible I shall return and then somehow we will be together. We will go somewhere far away where no one knows us and we will get by. That is, if you can forgive me for the way I have treated you.'

'Of course I forgive you,' she gasped, strongly resisting the urge to throw herself into his arms there and then.

'So when can I see you again?'

'Well, we could go for a stroll in the park right now if you don't have to get back to the camp,' she suggested. It was only five o'clock in the afternoon but it was already getting dark so there was little chance of them being seen.

He nodded and strode ahead of her, and without another word she followed at a discreet distance until they came to the tunnel that would lead them into Riversley Park.

It was pitch black inside and Adina had to feel her way along the cold damp walls until he suddenly stopped and drew her into his arms. And then as he kissed her, all the pain of the last weeks fell away and she gave herself up to the pleasure of being in his arms again. Nothing else mattered. She was back where she felt she was destined to be.

An hour later, she let herself into the cosy kitchen at the back of the shop, only to stop abruptly when she found herself walking into what appeared to be a battle zone.

Ariel was facing her father, her eyes blazing and her hands clenched into fists. 'I *love* him, do you hear?' she shouted. 'And we're going to be together whether you give us your blessing or not!'

'You cannot be with him. You are too young to marry without my consent and you will *never* have that,' Ezra roared. 'We have brought you up to be a good Jewish girl. How could you even *consider* marrying an English boy – and a Catholic at that!'

'Oh Papa, you are *so* old-fashioned,' Ariel groaned as her mother looked on, wringing her hands in despair. 'Times are changing and there is a war on. What difference does it make, what nationality he is, or what religion? I love Brian and that's an end to it . . . and if you won't give us your blessing then I will live in sin with him!'

Ezra clutched at his heart. 'You would do such a thing and bring shame on our family?'

'Yes, I *would*!' Ariel tossed her head defiantly and banged away upstairs as her father gazed after her in stunned disbelief.

'What's going on?' Adina asked as she glanced from one to the other.

'Ariel has met a young man called Brian. He is going into the Army in four weeks' time and she is saying that she wishes to marry him before he leaves,' her mother told her tearfully.

'Oh.' Shock coursed through Adina's veins. If they were reacting like this about Ariel having a relationship with an *English* boy, what would they say if they were to find out that she was in love with Karl? She shuddered at the thought. Her father was stamping up and down the kitchen like a man obsessed, with profanities in German and Yiddish spewing out of his mouth. Adina had never heard him swear before, and for the first time she felt afraid of him although he had never so much as raised a finger to her or her siblings in his whole life. This was a side of him that she didn't like, and she felt as if she had been doused in cold water. Her lips were still tender from Karl's kisses, and should her father find out, she wondered what he might be capable of.

'I'll go up and talk to her, shall I?' Adina scuttled towards the door and, not waiting for a reply, she shot off up the stairs. On the landing she tapped lightly on the bedroom door but only the sound of muffled sobs answered, so she cautiously pushed it open. Ariel was curled into a tight ball on her bed sobbing uncontrollably and Adina's heart went out to her. How could she be annoyed with her, when she herself was no better?

'Come on, bubbeleh,' she said soothingly, closing the door behind her. 'Things cannot be that bad. I'm sure we'll find a way around this.'

'*How*?' Ariel shot back scathingly. 'I can't help it if I've fallen in love, can I? I never planned it, but we can't choose who we fall in love with, can we? It just happens.'

'Yes, it does,' Ariel agreed as she took her sister in her arms and rocked her to and fro. She of all people knew that. It suddenly felt as if the whole family was falling apart. Not so long ago they had been united. Now, Dovi was in hospital, which had turned her mother into a nervous wreck with worry, Ariel was threatening to run away with her English boyfriend, and she herself was in love with a German prisoner of war. She wondered if things could get any worse but seriously doubted it.

The following morning, as the family sat at breakfast, Ezra tried to be reasonable.

'Ariel,' he said solemnly as he laid his knife and fork down in a regimentally straight line. 'Your mother and I have talked about this issue and think we may have come up with a solution. We realise that you *think* you are in love with this young man, but we do not wish you to jump into anything that you might later regret.' When Ariel opened her mouth to protest he held his hand up. 'Please . . . hear me out. We realise that we cannot forcibly stop you from seeing him, but what we are going to suggest is that you allow him to go off to war, and if you still feel the same about him in one year's time, we will reconsider the position.'

Ariel glared at him as if he had lost his senses. 'In case you hadn't noticed, Papa,' she said rudely, 'a lot of the young men that go away to fight never come back. If I don't go to Brian now before he leaves, I might never get the chance to – and I would rather spend one week with him than a whole lifetime with somebody else.'

'I fear that you have been watching too many romantic films,' Ezra told her, as if he was talking to a two year old. 'And that, I am afraid, is all I am willing to say on the subject. The discussion is closed.'

Without another word, Ariel got up from the table, her breakfast untouched, and then she snatched up her coat and slammed out of the door.

Ezra lifted his knife and fork and continued to eat as if nothing untoward had happened, and as Adina silently watched him, a cold hand closed around her heart.

Chapter Eighteen

It was almost a week later when Ariel didn't come down to breakfast one morning.

'Run up and fetch her, would you, bubbeleh?' her mother asked.

'I thought she was already up,' said Adina taking the stairs two at a time. She was running late this morning, and needed to get a move on.

'Ariel, hurry up, your porridge is going cold!' she shouted as she tapped at the door before flinging it open. She then stopped dead in her tracks as she spotted the empty wardrobe. The bed hadn't been slept in and the suitcase they had used when they moved from London was missing from under the window. If Adina had still been sleeping in their room she would have known that Ariel was missing.

Her sister must have sneaked off in the early hours, whilst they were all asleep. What on earth was she going to tell her mother? Freyde had been living on her nerves ever since the day they had received the telegram telling them that Dovi was missing – and Adina was afraid that this latest blow might just tip her over the edge. Not that she could blame Ariel for making a stand to be with the boy she loved; she herself might have to do exactly the same thing very shortly.

'Come on, girls, *do* hurry up,' her mother called, and Adina braced herself. There was no point in delaying and she wanted to get it over and done with.

'Ariel isn't in her room,' she announced, the second she set foot back in the kitchen. 'And her suitcase and all her clothes have gone.'

Freyde's face turned white. 'Perhaps she's just gone off to visit someone,' she said desperately to her husband, ever the peacemaker.

'Yes, and I think we all know who she has gone to visit,' he said harshly.

Untying her apron, Freyde rose from her seat. 'I'll go and see if I can find her,' she declared, but Ezra's voice sliced through the air between them.

'You will do no such thing! She has gone of her own accord, and if she is not back in this house within one week, that will be an end to it. I will not have her name mentioned in my presence again. Is that understood?'

'B-but Ezra, she's only—'

'*Enough!*' He held his hand up to silence her and Freyde dropped back into her chair, her shoulders sagging with despair.

'I'm going to get off to work now.' Adina shot from the room, glad to escape the atmosphere. As she trudged along the road, tears pricked at the back of her eyes. Everything was going wrong and she knew that she too would soon be causing her parents yet more heartache.

The morning dragged interminably, but at last the bell sounded heralding the lunch-hour. Adina smiled at her pupils. 'You may close your books now, children, and make your way to the dinner hall,' she told them.

'Yes, miss,' they chorused as they slammed their work into their desks and then there was a mad clamour for the door. Most of the Jewish children could speak English fluently now and Adina was proud of them.

Within seconds the classroom was silent. Adina quickly cleaned the blackboard and went to collect her coat from the staff room. Karl was waiting for her at the gates to the churchyard and the instant she saw him, she began to feel better. She had been battling with her conscience all morning, but now once again she knew that any sacrifice was worth making if it meant they could be together.

'Is everything all right?' He gazed into her troubled eyes. 'You look a little pale.'

'Ariel has left home,' she told him bluntly.

'Oh, and how have your parents taken that?'

'About as you would expect.' She glanced towards the church. The roof was more than half-tiled now, and it looked like a church once more.

'You are worried about how they will react when you leave also? Is this so?'

'Naturally I am,' she said, 'but it doesn't change my mind. We will go somewhere where no one knows us as soon as the war is over – if you still want to.'

'Of *course* I want to,' he assured her, and his voice was so genuine that she could not doubt him. 'But it is not quite as simple as that. First I must return to Germany and then I will come back for you.'

'But why can't I just come with you?'

He averted his eyes. 'There are things that I have to attend to before we can be together properly,' he muttered.

Adina wanted to question him but guessed that this was not the time or the place, so instead she turned the conversation towards the progress of the church until it was time for Karl to return to his work.

It had turned bitterly cold and on her way home she shuddered as she pulled the collar of her coat up. The sky was a curious grey colour and she wondered if they were in for some snow. She also wondered what sort of battle zone she would be walking into when she arrived, but having nowhere else to go she resolutely strode on.

Thankfully, everything was quiet. Her mother was kneading dough on the scrubbed table in the kitchen, her father was serving in the shop – and apart from Freyde's red-rimmed eyes, it might have been any ordinary day.

Adina asked casually, 'When were you and Papa thinking of going to see Dovi again?' It felt strange without Ariel but she did not dare even mention her name for fear of her mother bursting into tears again.

'We have to phone the hospital tomorrow,' Freyde said dully, and then placing a damp cloth over the dough and leaving it to rise, she lapsed into silence again. Adina tried to think of a way to start a conversation but eventually gave up and went to her own room. It was very cold up there, and she would much rather have been in the cosy warmth of the kitchen, but even so, the cold was preferable to the frosty atmosphere down there. Putting another cardigan over the one she was already wearing, she approached her sewing machine. Her wedding gown was draped across it, and as she fingered the silk a sad smile twitched at the corners of her lips. She had always dreamed of standing beneath the *chuppah*, the bridal arch, in a synagogue, with her family looking on, but the chances of that happening were non-existent now if she was to marry the man she loved. Her thoughts turned to Ariel. Her sister had confided in her that she was seeing Brian Rowley some time ago, but Adina had not realised how serious their relationship had become. Brian was just eighteen years old, a likeable, happy-go-lucky sort of lad, but that would gain no points with her father.

Adina stared unseeingly out of the window. She had a vague idea what area Brian lived in, so tonight after the evening meal she decided she would go for a walk round there and see if she could catch sight of Ariel. It would be nice to know that she was all right. Meantime she turned her attention back to the dress she was sewing and soon, as she treadled away, she was humming softly to herself.

It was bitterly cold that evening, and as Adina traipsed along Fife Street for the fifth time, she was forced to admit that she was on a fruitless errand. All the curtains were firmly drawn together and the streets were all but deserted. She was just about to turn and head for home when the front door of one of the terraced houses further along the street opened and a young woman appeared, hastily closing the door behind her. Adina began to hurry towards the figure.

'Ariel, is that you?'

The figure turned and then crossed her arms defiantly across her chest. 'If you've come to try and persuade me to come home, you can forget it,' she told her sister ungraciously.

'I haven't,' Adina said. 'I just needed to know that you were all right.'

'Well, I am, so you can stop worrying about me now.' Ariel was standing as if she was about to do battle but as Adina drew to a halt in front of her, her tone softened. 'I'm sorry for all the trouble I've

107

caused,' she sighed, 'but I won't go back. We don't live in Cologne any more. Things are different here and I'm sick of Papa being so strict.'

'He only wants what's best for you. I suppose he thinks that by being strict he is keeping us safe.'

'I know that, Adina, but I'm a grown-up now. Loads of girls my age are getting married. They're having to, because they don't know if their boyfriends will come back once they're called up.'

'But you're not old enough to get married without Papa's permission,' Adina pointed out.

Ariel nodded. 'I know that too, but I'm going to stay here with Brian's parents until I am old enough. They've made me really welcome, and then when I am of age we'll get married on one of his leaves – if the war doesn't end before that. It doesn't matter to them, you see, what religion I am so long as Brian and I are happy together – and we *are* happy. Try and understand, please. I'm sick of all the readings from the *Torah* and not being able to wear modern clothes; of having to be in for nine o'clock at night. They treat me as if I'm still at school and I'm a young woman now. Surely you feel the same?'

'It's different for me,' Adina said. 'You're the youngest and I suppose to them you will always be the baby.'

Ariel snorted and tossed her head, but then her shoulders sagged and she spread her hands in a helpless gesture. 'As I said, I'm so sorry for all the hurt I've caused, but I hope you won't turn your back on me too.'

'Never.' Adina stepped forward and then before they knew it, the sisters were hugging each other.

'I know I've gone off the rails a bit since I left school,' Ariel admitted tearfully. 'I suppose it was a bit of rebellion. But then I met Brian and everything was different. Right from the start I knew he was the one for me and I'm not going to change my mind on that. One day you'll understand, when you meet the right person.'

Adina could have told her that she already had, but wisely held her tongue. Things were complicated enough as it was.

'Just promise me that if you need me, you won't be too proud to come and ask for help?' she said.

'I promise,' Ariel told her, and the two sisters stepped apart.

'Take care of yourself,' Adina whispered.

'And you.'

Tears ran unchecked down her cheeks as Adina watched Ariel walk away. When she got home, she decided, she'd transfer all her things back into the room she and Ariel had once shared, and then at least Dovi would have his own room back when he eventually returned home.

By early November 1944, renewed German assaults on London led to a fresh exodus of the capital's children that was even greater than in the early years of the war. Some of the children arrived in Nuneaton pale-faced and fearful of what was going to happen to them – and this time, the townsfolk welcomed them with open arms.

Mrs Haynes agreed to take in a six-year-old girl, and in no time at all she was a firm favourite with the neighbours. Her name was Sarah and she was a skinny little thing with ginger hair that she wore in two pigtails, and a scattering of freckles across her nose. Within days of arriving she had settled in and was attending the school that Ariel had once gone to, where her cockney accent delighted the other children. Sarah and young Freddie Haynes hit it off instantly, and for the first time since the death of her beloved son Anthony, the sound of Mrs Haynes's laughter could be heard ringing across the garden fence and she seemed to have a purpose in life again.

'She's lookin' good, ain't she?' she said proudly one day in the shop as Sarah gazed wide-eyed from one of the enormous glass jars of sweets to another.

'She certainly is,' Freyde told her sincerely. It was nice to see her neighbour so happy again. She just wished there could be a little more happiness in her own home.

'O' course, as you know, she didn't look like that when she arrived,' Mrs Haynes whispered across the counter. 'Poor little mite were crawlin' wi' nits – an' some o' the buggers were nearly as long as me fingernail. I tell you, I reckon I've nearly wore that nit comb out, but I reckon we've shifted 'em all now. An' eat! As God is me witness I ain't never seen a child put away what she can. I sometimes think she must have hollow legs. But then I've got a funny feelin' she didn't get regular meals where she came from – not like my Freddie.'

'Well, she is certainly a credit to you now,' Freyde said and meant it.

'A lot o' that is down to your Adina,' Mrs Haynes went on. 'Those little dresses she run up for her on her sewin' machine fit her a treat. They're far nicer than the clothes she brought with her. Not that she brought that many, mind.' She sniffed disapprovingly as she leaned even further across the counter. 'From what the poor little sod has told me, her mam is a bit of a one. You know . . . for the men, like. She ain't got a dad and her mam often went out at night to the pub an' left her in, all on her own. It's a disgrace, if you were to ask me. I mean, what sort of a woman would do that, wi' all them air raids goin' on? *Anythin'* could have happened to the lass. I sent her mam a postcard wi' my address on when young Sarah first arrived, so that she'd know where she was, but she ain't even bothered to write to her yet. Too busy off out wi' her fancy men, I dare say.'

Mrs Haynes was well into her stride now and would have said a lot more, but at that moment the shop-door bell tinkled and another customer came in.

'Right, well, this ain't buyin' the baby a new bonnet, is it?' she said, as she took Sarah hand. 'Come on, luvvie, I'm gonna make you some stew an' dumplin's for your tea. You like that, don't you?'

Sarah nodded vigorously and broke into a wide gappy grin as Freyde pressed a big gobstopper into her hand.

'For after your dinner,' she said kindly. 'And here's one for Freddie.'

'Cor, *ta*, missus,' Sarah gasped, and she left the shop clutching the paper bag as if it contained the Crown Jewels.

At that precise moment, the loud ringing of the phone reached them from the back room, and with an apologetic glance towards her husband, Freyde hurried away to answer it.

When Adina arrived home from work early in the afternoon, she stared at her mother cautiously. She was actually smiling – something she hadn't done since Ariel left home.

'You look happy, Mama,' Adina said. 'What's happened to put you in such a good mood?'

Freyde patted the side of her nose conspiratorially.

'You'll see soon enough,' she promised, as she bustled about the kitchen preparing the evening meal, and with that her daughter had to be content.

Chapter Nineteen

It was almost a week later when Adina discovered the reason for her mother's lift in spirits. There had been a sharp frost the night before, and after spending her customary precious few minutes talking to Karl at the churchyard gates, she headed for home blowing into her hands, which were blue with cold despite her woollen gloves.

As she passed the shop she saw the Closed sign on the door. Her father usually kept the shop open from dawn till dusk nowadays, so she wondered what could have happened to make him close it. Hurrying up the entry, she let herself into the yard and pushed the back door open. Her eyes almost popped out of her head when she saw her mother leaning over someone who was swaddled in a warm blanket in the fireside chair.

'Come in, my darling – see, we have a wonderful surprise for you,' her father boomed in a rare good humour.

At that moment her mother straightened and Adina's face broke into a rapturous smile. '*Dovi!*' she shouted as she stepped towards him with her arms outstretched, but then she halted in mid-stride.

The young man sitting in the chair was undoubtedly her brother, but a mere shell of his old self. His eyes were sunk deep into their sockets, and his shirt still seemed to be hanging off his emaciated frame. Of course, having already seen him once in the hospital she had realised then how ill he was. But to see him like this in his own surroundings was somehow ten times worse.

Blinking away her tears, she sank to her knees beside him.

'How are you feeling?' she asked softly, as she took his two warm hands in her cold ones. 'It's so wonderful to have you home.'

He stared back at her with no signs of recognition.

'He isn't always like this,' Freyde told her reassuringly. 'Sometimes he can be quite lucid. We just have to be patient, that's all. The doctors have warned us that it could be a long time before he is properly well again. They have done all they can to make his arm and body heal. Now his mind has to heal. But now that we have him home I'm sure he'll start to improve in no time at all.'

'Of course.' Adina nodded, but inside she was crying and had very grave doubts. She stroked his hair, and after a moment stood up and took off her coat as she asked, 'Why didn't you tell me he was coming home?'

'Because I wanted to surprise you. Goodness knows I think it's time this family had something to be pleased about.'

Guilt, sharp as a knife, stabbed at Adina's heart. How would her parents react when she too left home? Perhaps it was a blessing in disguise that Dovi was back. At least they would have him to focus their attentions on, and they would *never* be ashamed of him. Dovi was a hero, and even if he never fully recovered he would remain so.

'Let me help you dish the dinner out,' she offered now as her mother lifted a chicken from the oven. Freyde had been determined that Dovi should have his favourite meal on his first day home and had gone to endless trouble preparing it. First off she placed a steaming tureen of lokshen soup in the middle of the table. It contained chicken, noodles, celery, carrots and onion. She then started carving the chicken, which would be served with carrots, potatoes and leeks. For dessert she had made her son's favourite – apple strudel.

Ezra and Adina helped Dovi to the table and Ezra said a blessing – but within minutes of them all being seated, it was obvious that the sick man wasn't interested in the meal. He ignored the soup, and just stared blankly at his plate until in the end, Adina began to feed him tiny pieces of chicken. The urge to cry came upon Adina again as he opened and shut his mouth like a bewildered bird. He had taken no more than half a dozen mouthfuls when he pushed the loaded fork away and began to rock backwards and forwards in his chair.

'He is tired from his long journey here in the ambulance,' Ezra said, standing up and leaving his own dinner to go cold. 'Shall I take him upstairs to his room for a lie-down?'

'No.' Freyde too rose from the table. 'It's cold up there. Settle him back in the chair by the fire. He can doze there and he will not feel all alone. It's important that we talk to him as much as we can.'

Ezra did as he was told and thankfully, once he was back by the fire, Dovi stopped rocking and fixed his gaze on the flames licking up the sooty chimney.

Suddenly, Adina's appetite had gone too. Dovi's first meal back within the walls of his own home clearly hadn't been much of a success, but then Adina supposed that this was to be expected. She made a solemn vow to herself to be as patient with him as she could in the weeks that lay ahead.

In no time at all Christmas was almost upon them, although for the Schwartz family it made little difference. There would be no Christmas tree or celebrating the Christian festival for them.

On certain days, Dovi seemed a little better and would even hold short conversations with them. At other times he would retreat back into his own world and there was no getting through to him. Adina had become accustomed to being woken at night by his terrified screams as he lay trapped in some unspeakable nightmare. She would then hear her mother and father rush along the landing to Dovi's room to soothe him, and then after a time all would be peaceful once more.

Strangely enough, it was little Sarah from next door who seemed to get the first positive reaction from Dovi. She knocked on the door one day in the first week of December after school, and when Freyde opened it there she stood on the doorstep clutching a snowman that she had made of cottonwool.

'Mrs Haynes said your boy was poorly so I made this for 'im for Christmas,' she said, solemnly holding her present out in front of her.

'Why, that is very kind of you, Sarah,' Freyde told her with a smile. 'Why don't you bring it in and give it to him? I'm sure he will like it.'

Sarah stepped into the room and instantly her eyes fell on Dovi, who was huddled in his normal position by the fire. Without a moment's hesitation, she marched across to him and held out her offering.

'I made this for yer, mate. I like snowmen, don't you?'

At first it seemed that Dovi hadn't heard her, but then he slowly raised his head to look at her and his eyes fastened with hers. He slowly reached out to take the snowman from her as if it was an enormous effort.

'So what's wrong wiv yer than?', the child asked bluntly. 'Mrs Haynes said yer were poorly, but yer look awight to me.'

Dovi really smiled then, for the first time since coming home. 'I . . . I was shot in France,' he managed to tell her, his voice rasping from lack of use.

Sarah's eyes grew round as saucers, and when Freyde pushed a small stool towards her she sank down onto it, studying Dovi intently. 'So you must be an 'ero then,' she stated matter-of-factly. 'Mrs Haynes's big son were an 'ero an' all. He got killed in the war, yer know? Sometimes she cries when she talks about 'im. It's sad, ain't it? But you're lucky 'cos at least yer got to come 'ome, didn't yer?'

'I . . . I suppose I am,' Dovi said, and before he could say another word, she then launched into an explanation of how the snowman had been made.

'First of all I 'ad to make a sort of cone out of cardboard,' she told him. 'An' then I got to stick all the cottonwool on – like this, see? Then I made 'is 'at out of cardboard an' all, an' painted it black, an' then that got glued on the top like this. Next we stuck 'is eyes an' 'is mouf on. They're made out of silver paper. An' then last of all, miss let us make 'is scarf out of scraps of material. He looks really luvly, don't 'e?'

'H . . . he looks fine,' Dovi assured her.

As Freyde and Adina watched this interchange taking place they smiled at each other. It was the first time Dovi had really shown any interest in anything since coming home, and they hoped it was a good sign. However, Adina was still feeling sad. Shortly she would be going to say goodbye to Beryl, who would be leaving for the States the following day. Since the wedding the couple had been staying with Beryl's parents and Adina had a sneaky feeling that Tyrone would not be sorry to leave. With Sarah chatting happily away to Dovi, she sneaked away to her room and began to get ready, missing her friend before she had even gone.

The Taits' house had suitcases piled everywhere when Adina arrived there about an hour later.

'Eeh, luvvie,' Mrs Tait sighed. 'I swear that gel o' mine has taken everything bar the kitchen sink. She'll need an aircraft all to herself at this rate.'

Adina chuckled. 'Upstairs, is she?'

Mrs Tait nodded. 'That she is, prettyin' herself up, no doubt. Tyrone is up at the Hall.'

With a friendly nod, Adina bustled upstairs into Beryl's bedroom to find her friend packing a few last-minute things.

'I'm glad you managed to get round here,' she told Adina. 'I wouldn't have wanted to leave without saying goodbye.'

'As if I would have let that happen,' Adina retorted. 'Are you excited?'

'Wouldn't you be?' Beryl laughed. 'I can't believe I'm really going at last. Tyrone has hardly mentioned where we'll be living since we got married, but if what he told me when we first got together is anything to go by, I'll be living in the lap o' luxury from now on. Who would have thought it, eh? A girl from a small town in the Midlands ending up on a posh ranch in Texas, eh? It's like something you read about, ain't it? Mind you, I don't intend us to stay living with Tye's folks for ever. As soon as this damn war is over I shall expect him to buy us our own place and keep me in the manner to which I will have become accustomed. I wonder if I'll have servants?' she went on dreamily.

Adina punched her playfully in the arm. 'With an imagination like that, you should have been a writer,' she teased.

'And how are Dovi and Ariel?' Beryl now asked.

Adina shrugged. 'I've seen Ariel a couple of times. She seems happy enough living with Brian's folks, and Dovi . . . well, what can I say? He is off in a world of his own half the time. We just have to be patient for now.'

Beryl nodded and the mood suddenly became sombre when she said wistfully, 'I wish you were coming with me. I mean, I know I'm lucky to have such a chance but I'm going to miss you and me mam and dad so much. Between you an' me, I reckon me mum has a sneaking suspicion that I'm pregnant. She commented the other day that she hadn't noticed me have a period for a while, so perhaps it's as well we're goin'!'

'You'll be fine,' Adina assured her, 'And as soon as the war is over you can come back and see us. You'll have the baby by then and I'll be longing to see it.'

Beryl stroked her stomach before asking, 'And what about you and Karl? I suppose you're still seeing him.'

Adina nodded. She knew that Beryl worried about her relationship with the German prisoner of war, but it had gone too far to stop it now. She couldn't imagine a world without Karl in it any more.

Beryl sighed, 'You know your family will kick you out on your arse if they get wind of it, don't you?'

'I've always known that,' Adina acknowledged. 'But just like you couldn't help falling in love with Tyrone, I can't help how I feel about Karl.'

Beryl couldn't argue with that. After a moment, her hand found its way into her friend's. 'You will write to me, won't you?'

'Of course – every single week, although I can't promise how quickly the letters will get to you with this war on.'

'Well, it can't go on for much longer now. We were listening to the wireless the other day when the King took the salute as the Home Guard gathered for its final parade. King George is certain that victory is close, which is why they've disbanded.'

'Then let us pray he is right,' Adina muttered.

'Do you think your family will go back to Cologne when the war is over?'

'I doubt it very much. Our family is already divided, and there is no saying our home would still be there. Our grandparents are gone too, so what is there to go back to? Things could never be the same again.'

The two young women lapsed into a thoughtful silence until Beryl sighed, saying, 'Well, I suppose I ought to get on. This sitting about won't get the rest of the packing done, will it, and we're leaving really early in the morning.'

When Adina stood up, the girls hugged each other with tears in their eyes, knowing that this might be the last they would see of each other for a very, very long time.

'Take care an' be happy now, do y'hear me?'

Adina sniffed loudly. 'Yes, I hear you, and the same to you, eh?'

'Of course.'

They hugged each other one last time and then Adina slipped away to leave her friend to her last-minute preparations.

Chapter Twenty

The two weeks' holiday that Adina had off over the Christmas period that year was the loneliest that she could ever remember spending. Work on the church was almost finished, which meant that she now only got to see Karl for a few moments each week, as he had been assigned to another job.

Ariel was still keeping her distance and Dovi was still nothing like the brother she remembered before he went away to war, although he did venture out for short walks now sometimes. Freyde wasn't at all happy about it, but Ezra encouraged him to go. He must learn to live again, he told his wife and so she bit her lip, wrapped him up warmly and said nothing as she sent him on his way. Adina knew that her mother still missed Ariel terribly, but as her husband had banned their daughter from the house, as a good wife she knew better than to go against his wishes.

Rumours had been rife that some of Hitler's right-hand men had tried to assassinate him, to stop his rule of terror, but as yet nothing had happened and people could only pray that the rumours would come true. The man was a tyrant and needed to be toppled. The Allied forces were still doing wonderfully well, and in January 1945 the German counter-offensive in the Ardennes was defeated.

Ezra had now been able to afford a Morrison shelter, just in case Nuneaton should come under attack again. A sturdy steel-framed structure with a solid top which could also serve as a table, it had been designed for indoor use by Herbert Morrison, the Home Secretary. Theirs now stood in the far corner of the kitchen. Adina had to admit that on the few times they had been forced to use it, it had been far preferable to sitting outside in Mrs Haynes's damp Anderson shelter. Dovi was still quite slow on his feet and so it was much easier for him to get inside it, and at least it was warm in the kitchen.

It was a cold Saturday evening after Ezra had said his prayers that he finally got to read his newspaper. Suddenly, he frowned and peered at his wife over his spectacles.

'My goodness me, have you read this, Freyde?' he asked.

His wife, who was darning in the chair opposite, shook her head. 'I haven't had time to even look at the paper today,' she answered truthfully.

Adina was sitting at the kitchen table trying without much success to get interested in the book she was currently reading, which was *Far From the Madding Crowd*. Hearing this, she glanced up.

'It seems that a young man was found brutally beaten this morning in the tunnel leading into Riversley Park,' he told them. 'The police are asking for witnesses.'

'How bad is he?' Adina asked with a tremor in her voice.

'It does not say – only that he is stable in hospital. But how terrible!' Ezra exclaimed. 'It is only up the road from us. Be careful in future, If a young man is not safe to walk the streets after dark, then a young lady certainly isn't. Let us just hope that whoever did this is caught soon.'

The two women in the room nodded in agreement as Dovi stared dully into the fire.

The following afternoon after lunch, Adina slipped away to meet Karl. The entrance to the tunnel leading into Riversley Park was cordoned off and crawling with policemen, who were investigating the attack that had taken place late on Friday night. Adina walked on underneath the Coton Arches, taking the longer route to meet Karl. He was waiting for her near the paddling pool in the Pingles Fields as usual.

His face lit up at the sight of her, and quickly leading her into the shelter of a nearby copse, he kissed her as if he had not seen her for a whole month.

'Have you heard about the attack?' he asked after a few moments.

Adina nodded. 'Yes, Papa read it in the newspaper last night.' She shuddered. 'You can hardly believe that such an awful thing could happen right on your own doorstep, can you?'

'You must be very careful now,' Karl warned her solemnly, much as her father had. 'It is not safe for you to walk about alone whilst there is a such a bad person on the loose.'

'They'll soon catch whoever did it,' Adina replied confidently. 'But let's change the subject, eh? How are things up at the Hall?'

'The Americans are still being shipped back to their homeland, a few each week,' he informed her. 'But other than that, things go on as normal. I miss working on the church although I have to say we are all very proud of our efforts. Have you been to see it yet?'

'Yes, I have, and I have to admit it looks as good as new.' Adina beamed at him. 'You and your friends did a really fine job of it. I hear the vicar is thrilled to have it open again.'

She suddenly shivered as an icy draught blew amongst the trees, and quick as a flash Karl took his coat off and wrapped it around the top of hers.

'But *you'll* be cold now,' she protested.

He shook his head, 'I could never be cold when I am with you, mein Liebling. But I think it is time we had a talk. You see . . .'

Once again, just as he had been about to tell her something, he was interrupted. The sound of someone thudding through the undergrowth made them glance behind them. Seconds later, Sarah, Mrs Haynes's little evacuee, skidded to a halt in front of them.

117

'Why, 'ello Dina,' she grinned. Her cheeks were rosy from the cold and her nose was running but now she stared curiously at Karl. 'Who's this 'ere then? Is he yer boyfriend?'

Adina felt colour flame into her cheeks as she hastily handed Karl his jacket. 'Oh no,' she assured her. 'He is just a friend.'

As Sarah looked towards the giant stranger, Karl clicked his heels together and bowed slightly, making the little girl's eyes almost pop from her head.

'Cor, are you a *Jerry*?' she croaked.

Deeply embarrassed, Adina tried to change the subject. 'Are you with your friends?' she asked, peering back into the trees.

'Naw, I'm wiv your Dovi,' the child informed her, never taking her eyes off Karl, who was thrusting his long arms back into the sleeves of his coat. 'I went round your 'ouse just after you'd gone out an' asked if 'e fancied a walk. We was playin' 'ide an' seek in the trees. Your mum fought you'd gone to see one o' yer mates. I didn't fink I'd find you 'ere.'

'I er . . . was just about to go,' Adina stuttered, wishing that the ground would open up and swallow her. If Sarah were to tell her father that she had caught her talking to a man, there would be hell to pay.

Nodding towards Karl as if he was little more than a stranger, Adina took Sarah's shoulder and led her back into the trees, leaving Karl to stare after them.

'So, who was 'e then?' Sarah asked as they spotted Dovi staggering drunkenly towards them. His movements were still very uncoordinated although he was slowly improving.

'Oh, he is my friend's friend,' Adina lied glibly. 'She asked me to pass on a message for her. But the thing is, I'd rather you didn't mention you'd seen me with him, if you don't mind. Her parents don't approve of him, you see.'

At that moment, Sarah spotted Dovi, and Karl suddenly forgotten, she raced towards him, seizing his hand in hers.

Sighing, Adina went on her way leaving them to it. Dovi seemed to have more in common with Sarah nowadays than he did with her, and she knew that she would not be missed. The afternoon was ruined, so miserably she made her way back home.

When she arrived, she found her parents listening to Flanagan and Allen on the radio so she made her way upstairs to her room. Taking a small suitcase from beneath her bed she withdrew her wedding dress from the layers of brown paper in which it was wrapped. It was finished now, and as Adina eyed it critically, a mixture of emotions raced through her. It was easily the most beautiful dress she had ever made, but on the day she wore it, she was painfully aware that she would lose the rest of her family, or what was left of it, for ever. Blinking away tears, she refolded it and placed it carefully back into the case.

* * *

118

The following evening as they all sat listening to the wireless, a loud bang from outside, which turned out to be the dustbin lid blowing off, echoed around the room and Dovi leaped from his chair with his eyes starting from his head.

'It is all right, son,' Ezra soothed. 'It is nothing to alarm yourself about.' But the damage was done and before any of them could stop him, Dovi began to scream and hurl anything he could get his hands on about the room.

Ezra and Freyde ran to restrain him but when this happened, which it had on a number of occasions before, Dovi seemed to have the strength of ten and it took them all their efforts to force him back into his chair. It seemed that he could be relatively calm one moment and ready to take on the world the next.

'Get his medication, Freyde, we need to calm him down,' Ezra gasped.

Adina was used to Dovi's terrible and unexpected outbursts of rage by now, but they never failed to upset her and she wondered again if he would ever be back to his old self – the carefree young man he had once been.

It was on a blustery market day in the centre of town when Adina next bumped into her sister, and she knew at once that something was wrong. Ariel looked very pale and fragile.

'Hello,' Adina said brightly. 'How are you? Not sickening for this new flu bug that's flying around, are you? You look a bit peaky.'

Taking her sister's arm, Ariel led her through the mass of stalls that lined the streets. 'Let's go and have a cup of coffee,' she suggested. 'I've only got half an hour of my dinner-break left and I really need to speak to you.'

Ariel was still working in Woolworth's and as far as Adina knew, was still enjoying it.

Eventually they ordered two cups of coffee in a local café and sat together in a windowseat as Adina asked, 'So what's wrong then? You and Brian haven't fallen out, have you?'

'Oh no, it's nothing like that,' Ariel hastily assured her. 'Brian was on leave last month and it was wonderful to get to spend some time together. It was awful when he left. But the thing is . . .'

'Well, come on then and spit it out,' Adina said impatiently. Ariel was looking so wretched that she wanted to give her a hug there and then, but not until her sister had told her what was wrong.

At that moment a waitress appeared and placed two steaming mugs of Camp Coffee in front of them. Adina smiled her thanks before turning her attention back to Ariel.

'So, out with it then,' she ordered bossily, as she spooned sugar into her drink.

'Well, the thing is . . . I've missed a period,' Adina mumbled, keeping her eyes downcast.

Adina gasped as the implications of what Ariel had just told her sunk in. Surely Ariel couldn't be pregnant too? It seemed like only two minutes since Beryl had found herself in the same predicament.

'It's probably just worry,' she gabbled. 'You know, about Brian and whatnot. You're probably just late.'

'I'm usually very regular,' Ariel reminded her miserably.

'Even so, you've been through a difficult time.' Adina refused to let herself believe that Ariel could be pregnant. 'There's no point fretting about it just yet.'

'But what if you are wrong? What if I *am* having a baby? Do you think Papa will let me marry Brian then?'

Adina sighed. All she knew was that he would really disown Ariel for good if she was pregnant. Up until now, Adina had prayed that he would have a change of heart – but she knew him well enough to know that he would see this as his youngest daughter's final betrayal. A Jewish girl pregnant outside of marriage was something that he would never countenance. She deliberately turned the conversation to other matters, hoping to distract Ariel, and eventually they wandered back through the marketplace to Woolworth's where they hugged and parted after promising to meet up again the following week.

As Adina made her way home she felt as if she had the worries of the whole world on her shoulders. She missed Beryl and Ariel every single day, and the fact that she was seeing Karl behind her father's back was weighing on her mind. Her father had always been a kind, if somewhat strict parent, and Adina loved both him and the rest of the family unconditionally. But they were living in changing times and she knew that if she was to have any sort of life at all with Karl, she would soon have to say goodbye to all of them. The war was finally going in the Allies' favour. In fact, some people were saying that it could all be over soon. When that happened, she would return to Germany with Karl and she would probably never see her family again.

Adina could scarcely begin to imagine what sort of an effect this would have on her mother. Both of her daughters would be lost to her for ever, and now they were also slowly having to accept that Dovi might never be the same again. He had taken to roaming the streets at the most ungodly hours, and for most of the time seemed oblivious to them. The only time he seemed to be truly happy was when he was in the company of the little cockney evacuee next door.

Lately, Adina had got the impression that Mrs Haynes wasn't too happy about the amount of time Sarah and Dovi spent together. She could understand it. Many of the people hereabouts gave Dovi a wide berth, and she knew that it was whispered that he wasn't quite right in the head since he had returned from the war. But then after what he had gone through, how could he be? War was a truly terrible thing.

Chapter Twenty-One

When Ariel had missed three periods, Adina finally persuaded her to go to the doctor's with her. She had now confided her fears to Brian's parents and they had promised to stand by her no matter what, although they were not pleased with her father's attitude, and considered he was being unreasonable. And so on a frosty February morning in 1945 Ariel and Adina both took a morning off work and set off for the surgery in Riversley Road.

'What am I going to do if I *am* pregnant?' Ariel wailed as she clung to her sister's arm.

'If you are, then Papa must allow you to get married,' Adina replied matter-of-factly. 'But let us cross that bridge when we come to it, eh? You don't even know that you *are* pregnant yet.'

They were finally shown in to see an harassed grey-haired doctor after sitting on hard wooden seats in the waiting room for over half an hour, by which time Ariel had almost chewed her fingernails down to the quick.

He peered at Ariel over the top of horn-rimmed glasses before asking, 'So what seems to be the trouble, Miss Schwartz?'

Ariel bowed her head in shame as she mumbled, 'I think I might be having a baby, sir.'

'Hm, do you now? Well, jump up on the couch and we'll have a little look at you, shall we?'

To her surprise there was no reproach in his voice. He had seen so much during the years of the war that another unplanned pregnancy was nothing to him.

'Do your breasts feel tender?' he asked as he examined her.

Ariel nodded, blinking back tears.

His fingers gently probed her stomach and then he told her, 'You can do your blouse and skirt up now. I'm fairly sure that you're about three months or so.'

'Oh!' A whirl of emotions were sweeping through her as she fiddled with the buttons on her blouse. Half of her was thrilled to think that Brian's child was growing inside her. The other half was terrified of how her parents would react to the news.

'What am I going to do?' she asked later, as she and Adina strolled through Riversley Park.

Adina had been very quiet but now she told her, 'I think we ought to just go and tell our parents and get it over with.'

'*I can't!*' Panic laced Ariel's voice. 'I am too frightened.'

'Well, they will have to find out sooner or later,' Adina sensibly pointed out. 'And far better that they hear it from you, than from someone else. I shall be there to speak up for you, so what do you say?'

Ariel gulped. 'All right then. I suppose you're right but . . . would you tell them for me?'

'If you think it will help,' Adina said bravely, already fearing what lay ahead. 'Come on then. Let's go and get it over and done with, eh?'

Ariel gripped her sister's hand, much as she had used to do when she was a little girl, and they turned in the direction of home.

The closer they got to the shop, the more nervous Ariel became. This would be the first time she had seen her parents since the day she had left home, and although she had missed them far more than she had thought possible, she dreaded this encounter.

It was a dark overcast day and as they approached, the light from the shop window spilled out onto the pavement.

'Best go in through the back way,' Adina advised as she saw her father serving a customer.

Ariel nodded in silent agreement and they scurried towards the entry. They had just started up it when the gate opened and Mrs Haynes appeared, wrapped up in a warm coat and scarf.

'Why, bless my soul!' she exclaimed as she looked towards the two girls. 'Ariel, it's lovely to see you again, luv. Are you coming home?'

When Ariel gazed back at her tongue-tied, the woman squeezed past them and continued down the entry. It seemed that the cat had got the girl's tongue but then she supposed it was none of her business why Ariel had suddenly turned up like a bad penny again. No doubt she would get to hear of the visit in due course anyway. She and Freyde had become quite close now and she knew how much her neighbour had missed her daughter.

'I'll see you later then, girls,' she trilled with a cheery smile. 'If I don't get a shufty on, all the best pork will be gone from the butcher's an' we'll be havin' scrag end fer tea again.'

The girls waited until she had disappeared from sight and then Adina asked, 'Are you ready?'

'As I'll ever be,' Ariel murmured as her heart began to pound. She followed her sister through the gate and across the yard, and then they were entering the kitchen – and as Freyde looked up from the pastry she was rolling on the kitchen table, her mouth dropped open.

'*Ariel!*' she gasped as she slammed the rolling pin down. 'Whatever are you doing here, bubbeleh?'

When Ariel burst into tears, Freyde quickly wiped her floury hands on her apron and wrapped her daughter in her arms. Ariel sobbed on her mother's shoulder until the shop door suddenly opened and her father appeared in the doorway.

'What's this then?' he asked sternly. 'I thought I had made it clear that you were never to darken our door again.'

'Ezra, stop it! Can't you see that she is distressed?' Freyde pleaded, then turning her attention back to Ariel she asked gently, 'What is wrong? Has Brian hurt you?'

'No, it's nothing like that.' Ariel looked helplessly at her sister, and as their parents' eyes turned towards her, Adina took a deep breath.

'The thing is, Ariel is in trouble.'

'What sort of trouble?' Her father's eyebrows had almost disappeared into his hairline, so she hastily went on, 'We just came from the doctor's, who informed us that Ariel is going to have a baby.'

The silence in the room was deafening, and Adina could have bitten her tongue out. Surely I could have put it more gently to them? she thought, but it was too late for whipping herself now. It was said and there was no going back.

Her father became so red in the face that for a moment, Adina was scared that he was going to burst a blood vessel. He seemed to have swelled to twice his size too but then suddenly he raised a trembling finger and pointing it at Ariel, he growled, 'Get out now and let this be the last time I ever have to set eyes on you. You have brought shame onto our family.'

For the first time in her life Adina stretched to her full height and confronted her father.

'She *can't* just go like that!' she exploded. 'She's made a mistake but she wants to put it right and marry the child's father. For her to do that, she will need your permission and I think that's the least you could give if you're not prepared to stand by her, Papa!'

Shock registered on her father's face. Adina had never given him a day's worry in her whole life, but now here she was squaring up to him as if they were facing each other in a boxing ring.

'How *dare* you,' he ground out, his voice quivering with rage. 'This is between your sister and me. You just keep out of it.'

'But it *isn't*,' Adina defied him, as angry as he was now. 'This concerns all of us. You say she has brought shame on the family, but how much more shameful will it be if she gives birth to a child out of wedlock? Brian is away fighting for his country – doesn't that count for *anything*?'

Ezra hesitated as his wife stared at him from teary eyes. He was a fair man and had always done the best for his family, but old habits were hard to break and his religion was still important to him. Had Ariel fallen in love with a Jewish boy it would have been a different matter entirely, but the way he saw it, she had betrayed everything that he stood for.

'Could you not consider it?' Freyde now implored him. 'We cannot choose who we fall in love with, Ezra, and had we been able to stay in our own country, no doubt this situation would never have arisen. But it has, and now we must do what we can to make the best of it. We are living in difficult times.'

Just for a moment it appeared that Ezra was weakening, but then with his hands clenched into fists he strode back into the shop, slamming the door behind him.

'So now what shall I do?' Ariel sobbed.

Dovi had witnessed all this from the depths of the armchair at the side of the fire, and now Ariel noticed him for the first time. She took a step towards him with her hands outstretched and her face full of love, but he simply stared through her as if she was a stranger.

Her hands dropped limply to her side as her mother gently turned her towards the door. 'Go now, bubbeleh,' she implored her. 'At least he hasn't definitely said no yet. He may come round and grant permission for you to marry. I shall send word of his decision with Adina and meantime we shall work on him.'

Once she had gone, Freyde ran a hand wearily across her forehead. 'Where is all this going to end?' she groaned. 'Not so very long ago we were a united family, and now look at us.'

Adina patted her arm sympathetically. 'It isn't the end of the world,' she said wisely, 'and as Bubba always used to tell us, "there is always light at the end of the tunnel".'

Freyde nodded but her heart was heavy, for she knew that whatever Ezra decided, her youngest daughter was lost to her for ever.

Their conversation was stopped from going any further when Dovi suddenly rose from his seat and shuffled over to put on his coat.

'Where are you going?' Freyde asked. She hated Dovi to go off on his own but was powerless to stop him.

'Out,' he mumbled, and seconds later he was gone. Freyde sighed before returning to her baking. Adina headed for the stairs door, glad of a chance to escape the gloomy atmosphere when her mother said, 'Oh, I forgot to tell you with everything going on. A letter came for you this morning. It's behind the clock on the mantelpiece.'

Curious, Adina went and lifted the letter, and as she saw the foreign stamps, her face lit up. 'I think it's from Beryl,' she told her mother excitedly. 'I'll just go up to my room and read it and then I'll come down and help you with the baking.'

Freyde smiled indulgently. At least Adina never let her down. Little did she know.

Once upstairs in the privacy of her room, Adina eagerly tore the letter open and began to read, but the further she went down the page the faster her smile disappeared. Beryl didn't sound her normal bubbly self at all. Oh, she told her that she was settled with Tyrone's parents and that they were kind to her, but other than that it was very uninformative. Adina frowned. She had been expecting Beryl's first letter to be full of praise about her new life in America, but it might have been written by a stranger and was very formal.

Deeply disappointed, she pushed it back into the envelope and stared off into space. Perhaps Beryl was finding it difficult to adapt to her new life? After all, she was far away from friends and family. Feeling slightly better, Adina nodded to herself. Yes, that must be it. The next letter would probably be more forthcoming, once she had had time to get used to everything.

Humming softly to herself, she slipped back downstairs to help her mother, her head full of Karl, whom she would be meeting that evening.

He was waiting for her in the tunnel that led into Riversley Park, which had now reopened, and Adina's heart raced at the sight of him. She had been glad to escape from the tense atmosphere back at home and had told her mother that she was going to meet one of the young teachers from the school where she still worked. She hated lying to her but knew that she had no option. Her mother and father had barely spoken to each other since Ariel had left, and when Dovi had returned from his walk he too had seemed nervy and tense.

'Adina.' Karl hurried to meet her and she wrapped her arms about him as she snuggled her head into his broad chest. She could hear his heartbeat and wished that they could just stay that way for ever.

'Come, let us walk,' he said. He was very aware that they might be seen, and that was the last thing they needed at present.

Walking a safe distance apart they emerged from the tunnel and began to cross the fields towards the brook, glad of the darkness that hid them from prying eyes.

She began to tell him of Ariel's predicament and he listened sympathetically. He knew how much she loved her family and hated what their relationship might do to them, but it had gone too far for them to stop it now.

'I had a letter from Beryl today,' she told him and he smiled.

'Is she well and happy?'

'Well . . .' Adina chewed thoughtfully on her lip. 'It was very brief, to be honest. I expected it to be full of Tyrone's parents' ranch, but she didn't even mention it. She just said that all was well with the baby and that she was fine.'

He shrugged. 'Perhaps it is taking her some time to adjust to being away from home.'

'That's what I am hoping,' she agreed and they wandered on, their breath flowing out in front of them like fine lace in the light of the moon that was filtering through the leafless trees.

'I have a feeling that the war will soon be over now,' he told her as stroked her hand tenderly.

'Yes, Papa has said the same,' Adina replied. 'We were listening to the wireless tonight and it said that Winston Churchill, Joseph Stalin and Franklin Roosevelt are meeting in Yalta to redraw the map of postwar Europe as the Red Army advances into Germany. Papa has said that Adolf Hitler is running scared now.'

'And so he should be,' Karl spat bitterly. 'The British troops have been sickened by what they discovered at the Belsen camp. It is a crime against humanity to treat people so. And many hundreds of thousands have been sent to the gas chambers at Auschwitz and elsewhere. The man is a monster and must die for his sins! He has made me ashamed to be German!'

Adina could not reply. The scale of the atrocities committed by the Nazis against the Jews was something that would take a lifetime to comprehend; an eternity to forgive.

Karl cleared his throat, then ploughed on: 'What I told you before still stands. I must return to Germany alone, but as soon as it is possible I will return for you and then we will never have to be apart again.'

Adina longed to ask him why, but refrained from doing so. She knew Karl well enough to know that he would not leave her if it was not absolutely necessary, and he was worth waiting for. And then he laid his coat down on the frozen earth, and she forgot all her worries as she gave herself up to the sheer joy of his kisses.

Chapter Twenty-Two

Two days later, Adina arrived home after lunch one day to find her mother comforting Mrs Haynes in their kitchen.

'What's wrong?' she asked at once.

Their neighbour blew her nose noisily on a huge cotton handkerchief as she waved a letter in the air.

'It's our little Sarah,' she gulped.

Adina's forehead creased with concern. 'What about her?'

'Well, it ain't her exactly.' Mrs Haynes dabbed at her streaming eyes. 'It's her mother, God rest her soul. I got word that she's gone. Poof, just like that, took out by one o' them bleedin' doodlebugs. Poor bugger – poor Sarah an' all. I can't pretend I ever had much time fer that mother o' hers, but she didn't deserve to go like that. An' what am I supposed to tell the little mite, eh?'

'Why – how awful.' Adina sank into a chair before asking, 'But what will happen to Sarah now if she has no other family to go home to?'

'Ah, well, me an' the old man were just discussin' that afore he left fer work an' we've decided that we'll keep her. After all, she ain't no trouble, is she? An' at the end o' the day, I dare say stayin' wi' us will be better than her bein' carted off to some bloody orphanage. I know everyone will say we're mad, but what else can we do?'

'I think you're doing exactly right,' Adina said and Freyde nodded in agreement.

'So do I, and I think it's wonderful of you,' she assured her kindly neighbour. 'This is going to be hard for the child, but at least she still has you willing to stand by her.'

Dovi, who had been listening to the conversation, nodded in agreement too and they all looked towards him with surprise. Dovi never seemed to have much interest in anything, but because they were speaking of Sarah his ears had pricked up. 'S-Sarah stay?' he stammered.

Freyde smiled at him sadly. 'Yes, Dovi. Sarah will be staying. That will be nice for you, won't it?'

He turned back to the dancing flames in the grate and became silent again as the women contemplated how the child would take the news. The whole country was praying that the end of the war was in sight now, but unfortunately, it had not come soon enough for Sarah's mother.

The following day the papers were full of yet another vicious attack on

127

a second young man in Nuneaton and the shop was alive with gossip as the customers surmised who might be the culprit.

'I'll bet yer any money it's one o' them bleedin' Jerries from up at the Hall,' one man commented when he came in for his daily packet of Woodbines.

'Don't talk out o' yer arse,' said an indignant lady who was rifling through a barrel of apples. 'Them blokes are as polite as can be. Why, they've even rebuilt the church, ain't they? 'Tain't their fault as they were sent off to fight the war, no more than it were fer our lads. There's good an' bad in every race, that's what I say.'

'What yer forgettin' is it were them buggers that bombed the church in the first place,' the man retorted, and Adina felt her cheeks grow hot. No matter what the German prisoners of war who were stationed at the Hall did, there were still those in the town who were ready to condemn them.

'They come here,' the man ranted on, 'rapin' our women an' leavin' 'em with their bellies swollen. It's a bloody disgrace, if you were to ask me. Trouble is, it was too dark fer either o' the poor souls to see their attacker so the police are no nearer to catching 'em!'

'Huh! There are certain girls who don't need rapin' from what I've seen of it,' the woman said. 'Practically thrown themselves at the GIs an' the Jerries, so they have, so it ain't all one-sided.'

Adina and her father exchanged an uncomfortable glance as they both thought of Ariel, but they said nothing until the customers had left the shop and then Adina plucked up the courage to ask, 'Have you given any more thought to Ariel's plight, Papa?'

'I have, as it so happens.' Her father busied himself in straightening up the sweet jars as he carefully avoided her gaze. 'And you can tell her that when the young man next has leave, I shall give them my permission to get married. But don't expect me or your mother to be there. As far as I am concerned, once she is wed she will be dead to us.'

'But Papa, this is your *grandchild* that Ariel is carrying!' Adina cried.

Now he turned to glare at her and the hurt in his eyes silenced her instantly.

'I shall say no more on the subject,' he barked. 'I cannot prevent you from seeing your sister, but I have said my last word about it.'

Blinking back tears, Adina flew blindly past him and upstairs to her room. She had a skirt to finish making by teatime for a lady who lived just along the street, and she was glad. At the moment, sitting in her room sewing was preferable to being in her father's company – although she was relieved that he had at least agreed to Ariel getting married. She knew her sister would be delighted with the news and could hardly wait to tell her.

She met Ariel out of work the following lunchtime and when she passed on their father's decision, her sister sighed with relief.

'Thank God for that,' she said chokily. 'Though I haven't a clue when Brian will be home again or what I will wear. I certainly don't have enough clothing coupons saved up for a new blouse, let alone a wedding dress. And I don't even know where Brian is.'

'I'm sure he is safe.' Adina squeezed her arm reassuringly. 'And you won't have to worry about a dress. I can sort you out with one.'

'How would you just happen to have a spare wedding dress hanging about?' Ariel asked suspiciously.

'I had some parachute silk left over from the one I made for Beryl so I made another one up.' Adina refrained from telling her sister that she had actually made the dress for herself. At the moment, her sister's need was greater than her own and she reasoned that it wouldn't matter if it had already been worn by the time she got to wear it, especially if the bride was Ariel.

'I'll bring it round to Brian's for you to try on,' she promised. 'It will probably need a few alterations but I'm sure we can make it fit.'

Ariel hugged her and really smiled for the first time in weeks. 'Oh, this is wonderful. Will Mama and Papa be coming to the wedding?'

'I'm afraid not,' Adina told her regretfully. 'But at least you can get married now and that's the most important thing. We'll face all the other problems as we come to them, eh?'

Ariel nodded and they then spent the rest of Ariel's dinner-hour searching the shops for some fine netting so that Adina could make her a veil to go with the dress.

After they had parted, Adina hurried home with the netting they had managed to find. She was keen to make a start on it but it seemed that her parents had other ideas.

'Would you mind helping your father out in the shop for a couple of hours?' her mother asked, the second she set foot through the door. 'I have the most awful headache and would like to lie down for a while.'

'Of course.' Adina glanced towards Dovi who was eyeing her with that vacant look she had come to dread. Sometimes she felt that she didn't know him at all any more. He had kept them all awake for most of the two previous nights, screaming and crying with nightmares, and Adina wasn't surprised that her mother was feeling unwell. Caring for Dovi was proving to be a challenge for all of them, and sometimes she wondered if he would ever be truly well again. But only time would tell, and for now she was happy to help out.

Beckoning her mother over to the table she whispered, 'I just saw Ariel and told her that Papa has agreed she can marry Brian.'

'Oh!' Tears filled Freyde's eyes and then she wiped them away. 'Who would ever have thought it would come to this. My youngest daughter planning her wedding and me being no part of it.'

'You could be,' Adina told her stoutly. 'If you were prepared to stand up to Papa.'

Freyde stroked her daughter's smooth cheek and smiled wistfully. 'It is hard to break the habits of a lifetime, bubbeleh. Your father has always been the head of the family, and I could not go against his wishes, even for Ariel.'

Adina's heart sank. She knew all too well that the same reasoning would apply to her when her parents discovered that she was going to marry Karl. But she would not think of that for now. It was too painful.

She gave a deep sigh before going off to help her father in the shop.

Later in February 1945, over 50,000 Germans died in an RAF raid which devastated Dresden, and the jubilant Allied troops began to prepare to cross the Rhine. The British people's spirits were high as they dared to hope that the end of the war really was in sight.

Karl, along with some of the other prisoners of war who were stationed at the Hall, was now busily working in the park dredging the River Anker, and just as she had when he had been helping to rebuild the church, Adina took to walking home that way when she finished her job at the school.

It was on one particular day when he had been allowed to have a lunch-break that they sat together in the bandstand.

'Is there any news of your sister's boyfriend yet?' he asked as he offered her a sandwich.

'No, nothing as far as I know,' Adina replied, taking one. 'Ariel is beside herself with worry. The last she heard of him, Brian was preparing to cross the Rhine.'

'He could well be on the front line then,' Karl commented – and they both knew all too well what that could mean.

Rumour had it that Adolf Hitler was running scared although he was still fighting back and refusing to accept that defeat could be in sight.

'Have you heard anything from your family?' Adina asked.

Karl shook his head. 'Nothing at all, but then letters are scarce up at the camp. My family were informed that I had been taken prisoner, so they will know that I am safe – *if* the letter ever reached them, that is. I am more concerned about them, to be honest.'

'Well, let's just hope that the rumours are true and that it will soon be over.' Adina stood now and straightened her coat over her slim hips. 'I ought to be getting back now otherwise my parents will be wondering where I am. Ever since the second attack that was reported in the papers they seem to hate me even going out alone to the school.'

'I can understand that. My comrades told me that the man is still in a bad way in the Manor Hospital. If he dies, the police will be searching for a murderer. What madman could commit such evil crimes? But will you still be able to meet me this evening?'

Adina smiled. 'Yes. I have some sewing to deliver to a customer, but I won't be able to be out for too long.'

'Of course.' Karl glanced about to make sure that no one was watching them before raising her fingers to his lips and kissing them; then she left him and hurried home through the drizzly overcast day.

'Where is Dovi?' she asked her mother when she entered the kitchen.

'Out walking again,' Freyde answered. She was busily chopping vegetables on the table and looked at Adina curiously. 'You're rather late again, aren't you?'

'Oh, I er . . . got caught up at the school.' Adina went to hang her coat up. It was then that a knock sounded on the kitchen door and before they could answer it Ariel stepped into the room. Her mother opened her mouth to protest but clamped it shut again when she noticed her daughter's red-rimmed eyes.

'What is it?' she asked instantly.

'It's Brian.' Ariel held out a crumpled telegram and as her mother's eyes scanned it her face creased with sympathy.

'He was injured in action last month,' Ariel told her sister. 'And now he is on his way home.'

'What's wrong with him?' Adina asked, but the girl could only shrug helplessly. 'I don't know. He's being transported to a hospital in Portsmouth and they have said that they will let me know more when he gets there.'

Adina shivered involuntarily as she thought of Dovi. How would Ariel cope if he returned as a shell of the man he had once been, as their brother had? But she knew that she mustn't voice this concern. She had to be strong for Ariel now.

'Well, at least you know that he is still alive,' she told her optimistically.

Ariel wiped her eyes with a handkerchief that her mother had handed her. 'Yes, I suppose there is that to it.'

At that moment the door leading from the shop opened and her father appeared, his face set in grim lines.

'What are *you* doing here again?' he ground out. 'Did I not make myself clear the last time you visited? You are no longer welcome here.'

'But Ezra, she has received some very bad news. She had a telegram to say that Brian has been injured in action and—'

'Be quiet.' Ezra glared sternly at his wife. 'It is no longer any of our concern. I am sorry to hear that the man you turned your back on the family for is hurt, but you made your decision. Now please leave.'

Ariel rose from her seat with what dignity she could muster and with a last glance towards her mother and sister she silently left the room, closing the door quietly behind her.

'Have you no heart?' Freyde admonished.

'Oh yes, I have a heart, and our daughter broke it the day she chose that boy over us. So now if you will excuse me I must return to work. I think I just heard a customer come into the shop.' And with that, Ezra turned and left them without another word as mother and daughter looked helplessly at each other.

It was five weeks later when Brian was returned to his parents' home in an ambulance. Unlike Dovi, his mind was intact but he had lost one of his legs from below the knee. More worrying still, he felt obliged to inform his nearest and dearest that there was still a piece of shrapnel in his body that the doctors had considered too dangerous to try and remove.

Ariel was devastated at the loss of his limb but did not seem to understand the implications of his other injury.

'Will it just stay there?' she asked innocently as she fussed over him.

Brian looked towards his mother, who was trying her best to put a brave face on. He was still reeling from the shock of discovering that he was to become a father, and was only too happy to make an honest woman of the girl he loved.

'Well, there is a possibility that it will move one day,' he told her cautiously. He omitted to mention that the surgeon at the hospital had warned him that if the shrapnel moved towards his heart, it could be fatal. He felt that Ariel had more than enough to come to terms with at present, and wanted to take one day at a time. He was furious to hear of the way Ezra had turned his back on her, and determined to make her happy with or without her father's blessing.

Ariel was content with that answer. It had been a shock to see Brian as he was now, but she was just grateful that he was alive and home with them. And of course, she could now start to plan the wedding which they all agreed should take place as soon as possible.

Ariel and Brian were married in Coton Church on 26 March 1945 – on the same day that David Lloyd George, the Prime Minister in the First World War, died at the age of eighty-two. Ariel was painfully aware that Ezra would frown on her marrying in a Christian church, but she was past caring now.

There were few people present at the wedding. Brian's brother, John, gave the bride away, and although Adina felt the absence of the rest of her family, Ariel seemed to have a glow about her as she made her vows to the man she loved. She looked beautiful in the dress that her sister had made, even though it was a little tight across the stomach now and Adina cried as the newlyweds kissed when the ceremony was over.

It was a blustery day, and as they left the church with Brian leaning heavily on his crutches, the veil that Adina had so lovingly sewn floated about Ariel's face. There was to be no reception but Ariel seemed content to just be married.

'You be happy now,' Adina sniffed as she kissed her sister.

'Oh, I will be,' Ariel assured her as she looked lovingly towards her husband. He might be a little gaunt and crippled now, but he was still the man she loved.

'I'll get the dress back to you as soon as I can,' Ariel promised. 'Thank you for letting me wear it. Who did you make it for anyway?'

'Oh, for someone who doesn't need it just yet,' Adina told her blandly, and then the young couple turned and as she watched them go she fingered the ring that she still wore on a chain about her neck and wondered when it would be her turn.

Chapter Twenty-Three

The war raged on, but on 27 April 1945, as Allied forces closed in on Milan, the Italian dictator Benito Mussolini was captured by Italian partisans as he tried to flee Italy. He had been travelling with a German anti-aircraft battalion in an attempt to reach Switzerland. The following day, he and his henchmen were taken to the village of Dongo and executed and then their bodies were hung on public display. On 29 April the rest of the Fascist Italian armed forces surrendered at Caserta, and the English people rejoiced as they listened to the news on their wirelesses. It was another victory for their armed forces.

'It won't be long now,' Ezra prophesied as the family sat in the kitchen that evening. 'That pig Hitler is running scared now and – so he should be.'

'Pray God you are right,' Freyde muttered as she turned her attention back to the pair of socks she was darning.

Without another word being said, they each knew that they were thinking of Ezra's parents and the terrible fate they had probably endured in one of Hitler's camps. The end of the war might be close, but for them and many others, life would never be the same again. Their hearts were permanently scarred.

Adina looked forward to the end of the war with mixed feelings; part of her longed for it to be over, so that she and Karl could make a life together. Yet the other part of her dreaded having to be estranged from her family, which she knew would be inevitable once they learned that she had fallen in love with a German.

She was still seeing Ariel once a week. Her sister was blossoming now and would soon be finishing work to prepare for the birth of her baby. She seemed content and happy, although Adina knew that she desperately missed her family. She had tentatively tried to tell her father as much one day when they were working in the shop together, but he had pointedly changed the subject. Now all Adina could do was hope that once he had a grandchild, he would also have a change of heart.

Adina knew that her mother fretted about Ariel. She had taken to occasionally strolling through Woolworth's just so that she could catch a glimpse of her. But she never approached her; her loyalty to her husband was stronger even than her need to speak to her own child.

Dovi was still giving them cause for grave concern. He would sit for hours rocking to and fro as he stared into the fire, mumbling incoherently and playing with the stumps where his fingers had once been. His night-mares seemed to be getting worse if anything, and they were all tired following a procession of disturbed nights.

'He just doesn't seem to be showing any signs of improvement,' Adina sobbed to Karl that evening as they sat in their favourite place beneath the trees in the copse.

'These things take a long time,' Karl told her compassionately. 'Your brother saw terrible sights, and they are not easily forgotten. Be patient. God will bring him through this.'

'But how will my mother cope when I leave too?' Adina questioned as guilt settled around her.

'God never sends us more than we are able to bear, and we will face that when the time comes. For now you should try not to fret about it.'

'I know you are right,' she admitted. 'But sometimes it's so hard.'

Karl had long ago discovered that Adina adored her family and he too felt guilty that he would be the means of taking her away from them. He slipped his arm around her shoulder and soon the guilt and the worry disappeared just as it always did when they gave themselves up to the pleasure of being together.

The following day, 30 April, the second letter from Beryl arrived and Adina tore it open eagerly. She had written asking Beryl to tell her all about the ranch and Tyrone's parents, but again she was disappointed. Beryl informed her that she was due to give birth any day now and that she was well, but little more.

'I'm worried about Beryl. I don't think she's happy,' Adina said to her mother.

Freyde was down on her hands and knees sweeping the tiled hearth and she looked up to ask, 'What makes you think that?'

'I'm not sure, to be honest. She doesn't say that she's unhappy but I expected her letters to be full of her new life in America.'

Freyde chuckled. 'Could it be that you are looking for problems that aren't there?'

Adina returned the all too short letter to the envelope. 'I suppose I could be,' she said. 'But all the same, I think I might pop round and see her mother later on. Perhaps Beryl has said a little more to them?'

'It certainly wouldn't hurt if it is going to make you feel better,' Freyde answered as she disappeared out of the back door with a shovelful of ashes in her hand.

Two hours later, Adina tapped on Mr and Mrs Tait's front door. The woman opened it, wearing a bright, wraparound pinafore and a turban on her head, from which peeped a metal curler.

'Eeh, you've caught me in me working clobber,' she chuckled as she held the door wide. 'I've been up to me neck in washin' and was just

135

puttin' it through the mangle but I'm glad you've called round, luv. It's a good excuse fer a tea-break. Come on in.'

Soon they were seated in the cosy kitchen facing each other across the dropleaf table with a steaming mug on a mat in front of them.

'So, how are things then?' Mrs Tait asked pleasantly. 'An' how are yer brother an' sister doin'?'

Adina quickly updated her before asking, 'Have you heard from Beryl lately?'

'Just this mornin', as a matter of fact,' the woman said. 'She didn't say much though. I feel bad, I don't mind tellin' yer, what wi' her first sprog due an' me so far away from her.'

Adina had been about to voice her concerns but now she decided against it. Mrs Tait was obviously worried enough as it was, without her adding to her worries.

'I'm sure she'll be absolutely fine,' she said instead.

'I dare say you're right. But what about you, miss? When are you going to find yourself a nice young man? A lovely-lookin' girl like you – why, I'm shocked some chap ain't snapped yer up before now. But then I dare say yer father wants yer to marry a nice Jewish boy – an' there ain't many o' them around here, is there? Though I heard from a woman down the street the other day what marvels you've done wi' them little Jewish evacuees at the school. She reckons you've got 'em talkin' better English than us now.'

Adina blushed at the compliment. 'Well, I wouldn't go quite that far,' she said modestly, 'but I will say I'm very proud of them all, the way they've all adapted.'

'Mm, problem is, once this war is over many of 'em might not have families to go home to,' Mrs Tait said. 'An' then what's goin' to happen to the poor little mites?'

'I don't know,' Adina admitted. 'I dare say they'll ask the foster families they're with if they'll keep them, and if they're not able to I dare say they'll put them into orphanages.'

'Poor little buggers,' Mrs Tait sniffed as she slurped at the scalding tea. 'That Adolf has a lot to answer for, don't he? Still, I reckon our lads have got him on the run now. My old man reckons it's only a matter o' time now an' then hopefully he'll get his comeuppance. An' it won't be a second too soon, from where I'm standin'. The lousy cruel bugger should rot in 'ell.'

'I've no doubt he will,' Adina agreed, and they then chatted of this and that until Adina returned home to finish a dress she was making for a lady in Weddington.

That evening, as the family sat listening to the wireless in the kitchen, the news that everyone had been praying for reached them. Adolf Hitler was dead. Sensing that all was lost as the Battle of Berlin raged about him, and not wishing to be captured alive and share Mussolini's fate, he had committed suicide with his lover Eva Braun, whom he had married just hours before. The joint suicide took place in his bunker, and in his Will he named Joseph Goebbels as the new Reichskanzler, or Chancellor (of Germany). He also named Karl Dönitz as the new President of Germany.

The following day, however, Goebbels also committed suicide, and on 1 May in unauthorised secret negotiations nicknamed 'Operation Sunrise' between Germany and the Western Allies, General Heinrich von Vietinghoff, the German Commander-in-Chief, ordered all German armed forces in Italy to cease hostilities and signed a surrender document stipulating that the German forces in Italy were to surrender unconditionally on 2 May. On the same day, the German forces in Berlin surrendered, followed by the German forces in north-west Germany, Denmark and the Netherlands.

Suddenly everyone Adina saw was smiling as the English prayed for a final end to the war, and their prayers were answered on 7 May in Reims in France, and 8 May in Berlin in Germany, when Dönitz signed the Act of Military Surrender. Sir Winston Churchill then solemnly broadcast to his people that the war in Europe was finally over.

Chapter Twenty-Four

Suddenly, everyone was celebrating. In London, crowds gathered in Trafalgar Square and all the way up the Mall to Buckingham Palace. King George V1 and Queen Elizabeth appeared on the balcony of the Palace, accompanied by Sir Winston Churchill before cheering crowds, whilst Princess Elizabeth and Princess Margaret mingled freely with the people assembled there.

In the United States, the new President Harry Truman, who was also celebrating his sixty-first birthday on 8 May, dedicated the victory to the memory of his predecessor, Franklin D. Roosevelt, who had died less than a month earlier. Celebrations were also taking place in Chicago, Los Angeles, Miami and in New York City's Times Square.

In Nuneaton, street parties were in full swing and the atmosphere was joyous. Large trestle tables were erected up the centre of the roads and soon everyone was piling their contributions of food onto them. Banners were hung from bedroom windows and red white and blue bunting adorned the streets. Men were happily helping themselves from large barrels of ale that had been rolled into the streets. Bonfires were lit and Adina was sure she had never seen such happiness in her whole life before. On this special day everyone was friends, and even the German prisoners of war from Astley Hall were included in the party. The street outside the shop was teeming with people and children, who craftily sneaked treats from the tables before they were even properly loaded.

Ezra gave generously of his stock in the shop and even agreed to close for the day to join in the celebrations.

It was mid-afternoon before Adina managed to snatch a moment alone with Karl. He had been mingling with the crowds but now he inched close to her and whispered, 'Do you think we would be missed if we slipped away?'

'I doubt it,' she chuckled as she looked towards her father who was deep in conversation with Bert Haynes. Someone had dragged an old piano into the street and was banging out the tune 'Roll Out the Barrel', accompanied by numerous voices that were singing along, all totally out of tune. It didn't seem to matter. Everyone was enjoying themselves and today everyone was happy.

Once they were in the tunnel that led into the Pingle Fields, Karl stopped and took Adina's hands in his. 'So at last it is really over, mein Liebling.'

'Yes.' She stared up into his face. 'But what will happen to you all up at the Hall now?'

'We were told this morning that over the next few months we will be shipped back to our countries, so many at a time. It seems that I will leave sometime next month.'

'So soon?' Adina's face clouded.

'You must not think of it like that,' he urged, shaking her hands gently. 'You must think the sooner I leave and do what has to be done, the sooner I can return and then we can begin our new life together.'

She nodded numbly. 'I suppose you are right but I hate the thought of you leaving without me. Is there no way at all that I could come with you?'

Just for a moment it appeared that he was going to tell her something, but then he seemed to change his mind again.

'You must trust me,' he told her. 'If what I had to do was not important I would not be going.'

They moved on to the other side of the tunnel, blinking as the bright sunshine momentarily blinded them, and then without a word they headed towards the copse where they hoped they would find some privacy. They were not disappointed, and in no time at all everything else was forgotten as they sat with their arms entwined as if for the very last time.

The street party went on well into the night, with no signs of abating. By then Mr Haynes was more than a little tiddly, much to his wife's disgust.

'Just look at the silly old bugger,' she griped to Freyde. 'He can barely keep hisself upright. An' where is our Sarah?'

'The last I saw of her, she was standing outside the shop with Dovi,' Freyde commented as she glanced up and down the street. There was no sign of them now, but she supposed that Dovi would have gone back indoors. He was never very comfortable amongst people any more and had only ventured outside in the first place because Sarah had persuaded him to.

'I'll just pop inside and see if she's in there with him,' Freyde told the woman, as she saw that Mrs Haynes was getting anxious. She was back in no time. 'They're not in there, but they can't be far away,' she said soothingly. 'Come on, we'll have a wander down the street and see if we can spot them.'

Side-by-side the two women set off amidst laughter and cheering from the people assembled in the street. It was dark now but the party was still in full swing. Half an hour later they were back where they had started without sighting either Dovi or Sarah.

'It ain't like her to go off wi'out tellin' me,' Mrs Haynes fretted.

Freyde patted her arm reassuringly. 'I'm sure they'll be back before you know it. They probably just lost track of time. You know what those two are like when they get together. Sarah is about the only person Dovi shows any interest in any more. She'll be safe with him.'

Mrs Haynes wasn't so sure. From what she had seen of it, Dovi was incapable of looking after himself, let alone anyone else – and his mood swings were frightening. However, she supposed it was a little early to be panicking just yet. This was a special day, after all, and Sarah was probably just making the most of it.

The people in the street, were finally beginning to disperse. Adina had been helping the women to clear away as most of the men were incapable of doing anything and had been sent home to sleep off the effects of the beer they had swigged.

It was as she was walking towards the entry, loaded down with a plateful of half-eaten sandwiches, that Adina saw Dovi coming towards her. His hands were sunk deep into his coat pockets and his head was down.

'Dovi.' Adina looked behind him with a worried expression on her face. 'Where is Sarah? I thought she was with you.'

Clearly agitated, he shook his head from side to side. It was at that moment that Mrs Haynes spotted him too and she rushed towards him, demanding, 'Where's my lass then?'

Again he shook his head and then before she could say another word he shuffled past them and disappeared off up the narrow entry.

Mrs Haynes looked up and down the street. 'It's well after eleven now,' she mumbled. 'Where can she be? She ain't *never* been out this late before.'

Adina was feeling concerned too now but she kept her voice calm as she told the kindly neighbour, 'Look, let me just go and put these plates in the kitchen and then we'll go and look for her, eh? What with all the excitement she's probably just lost track of time.'

When she entered the kitchen she instantly looked towards the fire-side chair that Dovi had claimed as his own. It was empty and she frowned. Usually her parents had to practically frogmarch him to bed. Still, she supposed that he was probably tired out, so snatching her coat off the back of the door she rushed back outside to join Mrs Haynes.

'Let's walk up towards the Pingles Fields first, shall we?' she suggested as she slipped her arms through the older woman's. 'Sarah loves to play there. I'll bet you that's where we'll find her.'

'I hope yer right,' Mrs Haynes muttered as she fell into step beside her. An hour later when they had walked the entire perimeter of the field, they had caught not so much as a glance of the missing child and now they were both seriously concerned. It was now well after midnight.

'What do yer think we should do?'

Adina could see the fear reflected in the woman's eyes from the light of the streetlamp. 'I think we should get a few more of the neighbours to join in the search and then if we still can't find her, I'm afraid we shall have to call the police,' she replied sensibly. And so they hurried back to the street and in no time at all people were scattering in all directions calling the child's name.

By two o'clock in the morning they were all exhausted, and when they had all gathered once again in front of Ezra's shop he told them, 'I think it's time someone went to report her missing to the police.'

'I'll go,' Adina offered.

Ezra shook his head. 'You most certainly will *not*, young lady. There have been two serious attacks around here over the last few months and the attacker is still at large somewhere. It isn't safe for a young woman to be abroad in the dark. I shall go and fetch the police myself.'

Freyde placed a comforting arm around Mrs Haynes, who had started to cry.

As Ezra set off for the police station, Freyde guided her neighbour into their kitchen. 'I'm going to make a nice hot cup of cocoa,' she told her.

Ezra arrived back with two tall policemen in tow almost half an hour later. They instantly took a statement and a description of Sarah from Mrs Haynes before standing up to leave.

'There's not much we can do before daylight,' the stouter of the two warned her. 'But rest assured we shall have a search-party out looking for her at first light. Meantime, I suggest you go home and try to get some sleep.'

'An' just 'ow the bloody *'ell* am I supposed to do that?' she barked. 'Knowin' that the little 'un is out there. She could be lyin' somewhere hurt.'

The policeman shrugged sympathetically. 'I shall inform all the bobbies on foot to keep their eyes open for her,' he promised. 'And as I said, first thing in the morning we'll all be out in force. We'll find her, I'm sure.'

Mrs Haynes glared at them as they left the room and once they had gone, she exploded. 'Well, a fat lot o' good them pair were! A little 'un is missin' an' they ain't even goin' to start lookin' fer her till mornin'.'

Ezra and Freyde exchanged a glance. They could understand how worried and frustrated she was, but they could also see things from the policeman's point of view.

'Why don't I get you round to your house and wait with you in case there's any news,' Freyde offered.

Sighing, Mrs Haynes nodded and once they had left, Ezra told Adina, 'You might as well go to bed, bubbeleh. There is no point in all of us staying up.'

'Will you wake me if she turns up?' Adina asked.

Her father wearily ran a hand through his hair. 'Of course I will. Now off you go. I shall be up shortly when I have locked up down here.'

Adina reluctantly made her way to her bedroom where she quickly undressed and slipped into bed. But she tossed and turned and sleep evaded her as she thought of Sarah somewhere all alone. The little cockney girl had wormed her way into all of their hearts without them even realising it, and Adina prayed that she would turn up safe and well. Eventually her eyes grew heavy, but before she could drop off, a heartbreaking scream floated along the landing. Dovi was having another of his nightmares, by the sound of it. Knowing that her mother was next door with Mrs Haynes, Adina put her dressing-gown on and almost collided with her father on the landing as she left her room.

'You go back to bed,' he told her. 'I will settle him.'

Adina turned to do as she was told. It was hard to believe that a day that had started out so wonderfully could have turned out so badly.

Chapter Twenty-Five

The police arrived at Mrs Haynes's home as dawn was breaking to find Mr and Mrs Haynes, along with Freyde, sitting in the kitchen, dry-eyed and fearful. Throughout the long night Freyde had made them numerous cups of tea, and now they all felt as if they were drowning in it. The police took yet another statement and asked endless questions: what time had they last seen Sarah? Who had she been with? Did she normally wander off?

Mrs Haynes answered them all with what patience she could muster until eventually they went away to begin the search. There were pitifully few police officers. The majority of them had been called up when the war started, and for years the local police force had been surviving on a skeleton staff. Even so, as the morning progressed and news spread of Sarah's disappearance the local men joined in the search and fanned out over every square foot of the local area in the hope of finding her.

Adina joined in too. It was too painful just sitting at home waiting for news. The police assured Mrs Haynes that a child wandering off was far more common than she might think. She had probably just stayed at a friend's house. They also told her that the majority of children who went missing usually turned up within twenty-four hours. Mrs Haynes desperately wanted to believe them. The alternative was too terrible to contemplate.

The day before, the whole street had been celebrating the end of the war, but now it was as if a dark cloud was hanging over it and those not searching for Sarah scuttled past the house with their heads bent.

Once again the shop remained closed. Ezra was out with the other men searching. At lunchtime Adina returned home to make them all a meal to find Dovi cowering in his usual seat. He started when she walked into the room and as she moved towards him he jerked away.

Adina bent to his level to ask, 'Dovi, you were with Sarah last night. Do you know where she went?'

His head wagged from side-to-side and not wishing to agitate him further, she sighed and set about making platefuls of sandwiches for anyone that wanted them.

The afternoon dragged on and soon darkness streaked the sky but still there was no sign of the little girl: it was as if she had dropped off the face of the earth. Adina had arranged to meet Karl but she stood him up and hoped that he would understand why. She had an inkling that he might already know about Sarah being missing as the police had informed them that the prisoners of war up at the Hall had been given permission to join in the search. Even now they were combing the town with the rest of the volunteers, fruitlessly it seemed.

Adina carried two platefuls of food round to the Haynes' house after trying without success to tempt Dovi to eat something, but the sandwiches remained on the table untouched as the vigil continued.

The search was finally called off at ten o'clock and another long night followed, during which none of them slept again. Adina heard two policemen speaking in the entry as she returned to check on Dovi earlier in the evening, and what they were saying struck terror into her heart.

'If you was to ask me, time is running out,' she heard one of them say in a low voice to his colleague. 'In my experience, if a kid isn't found alive within the first twenty-four hours of going missing, it's usually a body we find.'

Adina shuddered but said nothing, who already seemed to be living on their nerves as it was. Mr Haynes spent most of the time in the small backyard smoking one Park Drive after another as he waited for news, whilst Mrs Haynes flitted from the kitchen table to the window like a butterfly.

At midnight, Freyde and Adina returned to their home. They were all exhausted but yet again, none of them managed to get much sleep.

Adina was the first up the following morning, just in time to see Dovi putting his coat on.

'You're an early bird,' she smiled, trying to keep her voice light. 'Where are you off to at this time of the morning?'

Dovi almost jumped out of his skin as he swung around to face her, and she was shocked to see how pale he was.

'Are you feeling ill?' she asked, taking a step towards him. He flinched away from her as if he had been burned and despair washed through her as she thought back to how he had been before he went away to war. This poor wreck standing in front of her was just a parody of the handsome, jolly young man she remembered. He flapped his hands at her now as if to ward her off, and then before she could stop him he threw the door open and disappeared outside at a shambling run. Adina sighed then filled the kettle at the stone sink before setting it on the stove. Striking a Vesta match she lit the gas ring beneath it. Upstairs she could hear her parents pottering about and no doubt they would want yet another cup of tea when they came downstairs. At the moment it felt as if that was all they were surviving on.

Once breakfast was over, Ezra again went out to join in the search while Freyde hurried around to the Haynes' to wait with them for news.

Adina attempted to work on the blouse she was making for one of her regular customers, but it was impossible to concentrate, so she went back downstairs and looked for something to do that would pass a little time. Noting that the washing basket was overflowing she decided to fill the copper and get some of it done out of the way. It would save her mother a job when things had settled down.

Whilst the copper was heating up, Adina filled the dolly tub in the yard and began to wash some of the coloured clothing that she had separated into a neat pile. It was as she lifted the shirt that Dovi had worn the day before that she saw a stain down the front of it which she hadn't noticed the night before. Holding it up to the light, she examined it more closely, gasping when she realised that it was dried blood. But where could it have come from? Dovi had shown no signs of being hurt in any way.

Plunging it into the water to soak, she dried her hands on her apron and slowly went back into the kitchen. She then went upstairs and cautiously pushed Dovi's door open. The bed was unmade as yet, so crossing to it she threw back the sheets. It was then that a scream rose in her throat. The pillow and bottom sheet were stained a brilliant red. The stains stood out in stark contrast to the snow-white linen, and for a while hysteria gripped her. She was vaguely aware of someone thundering up the stairs and then there was her mother standing in the doorway struggling to get her breath back.

'Whatever is wrong?' she demanded. 'We could hear you next door. I thought you were being strangled, at the very least.'

Now other footsteps were heard and within seconds Mr and Mrs Haynes appeared too. Adina was gesturing towards the discovery with a trembling hand, and as their eyes looked upon it, Mrs Haynes gasped.

'Oh, dear God above.' She hastily crossed herself. 'Do you think that could be . . . Sarah's blood?'

Mr Haynes turned without a word, his lips set in a grim line, and they all knew that he had gone to get the police. They also knew that if it was Sarah's blood, it could only mean one thing: Dovi must be responsible for her disappearance. But *why?* Adina asked herself. Her brother had always been so gentle with the child, and it was more than obvious that he loved Sarah.

Within minutes a policeman panted up the stairs close on the heels of Mr Haynes, and when he saw the bloodstains he visibly blanched. 'We need to find your son,' he told Freyde before rushing off the way he had come.

A silence settled on the room, broken by Freyde who muttered miserably, 'I cannot believe that my son could be responsible for hurting a child. Perhaps it is his own blood. He could have hurt himself.'

And then suddenly there were police everywhere, ushering them all out of the room and closing the bedroom door firmly behind them.

As yet, Mrs Haynes had not shed a tear, but now suddenly they erupted from her in great shuddering sobs that shook her ample frame.

'We'd best get back round home, luv,' her husband told her as he placed a comforting arm about her shoulder. 'The police will deal with this.'

As Freyde watched them go, she bowed her head in shame and clung to Adina as if her very life depended on it.

Three hours later, the police came to inform them that Dovi had been found wandering and was now being questioned down at the police station. Freyde felt as if she was caught in the grip of a nightmare and could not believe that her son was capable of such a crime.

'Why would he hurt Sarah?' she asked over and over again as she rocked to and fro in Dovi's chair. 'And where is she?' But no one could answer and the minutes on the clock continued to pass painfully slowly.

When Ezra returned home he went straight to the police station, but when he eventually returned he could tell them very little.

'Dovi is with a doctor,' he informed them. 'But they were not able to question him. He seems locked away in a world of his own.'

'And is there any news of Sarah?' Adina asked,

Her father shook his head. 'Not as yet. The police are still scouring the area though. It can only be a matter of time now.'

And so once again they all sat down to wait.

Sarah was found at five o'clock that evening by a man who was walking his little mongrel dog. Her small body was lying beneath a tree in the copse in Riversley Park that Adina and Karl had adopted as their own. It was said that the man who found her could be heard shouting and screaming from over half a mile away, and when the police arrived he was inconsolable. The ambulancemen who were called thought at first glance that the child was dead, and a cheer went up when one of them detected a faint pulse.

'We've got to get her to the hospital and quick,' the man barked. 'She's in a really bad way. If she survives this, it will be a miracle.'

The child was whipped away into the ambulance as the police hurried off to inform the Haynes family that she had been found.

Sarah's life hung in the balance. She had taken such a severe beating that her little face was unrecognisable, and she was in a deep coma. She had a broken arm, a broken leg and three cracked ribs, and once Mrs Haynes was shown in to see her, she nearly fainted at the sight.

'Is she goin' to live, Doctor?'

The doctor shook his head gravely. 'It could go either way at the moment,' he told her truthfully. 'We have set her broken arm and leg, and her ribs will heal with time – but the coma is the most worrying, along with exposure and dehydration. We have no way of knowing if she will come out of it or whether she will just slip away from us. All we can do is wait now.'

As word spread of what had happened, the whole town went into shock. They had long since grown used to the news that one of their sons, lovers, husbands, brothers or fathers had been killed in the war, but this senseless attack on a child was unforgivable.

'What will become of Dovid now?' Freyde asked the Police Constable who brought them the terrible news.

He removed his helmet and coughed. 'I can't rightly say, ma'am, but I do know that the doctor who is with your son at the station reckons he wasn't responsible for his actions – if that makes you feel any better.' He felt sorry for these people who seemed decent and law-abiding.

'So when will we know?' Ezra asked.

'I should think within the next few days. Meantime I should try not to blame him too much. The poor chap hardly knows his head from his elbow at present, and he doesn't seem like the type who would do this knowingly.'

It was like being caught in the grip of a nightmare, Freyde thought, but she was all too aware that this particular nightmare might never end.

Four days later they were informed that Dovid was being transferred from the police station to Hatton Mental Hospital, where he would be properly assessed. Several doctors had already examined him and had decided that he was insane and dangerous.

It was possible that there would be no court hearings for Dovi, but those who heard of the transfer knew that he could suffer a far worse fate than prison. Few people ever left Hatton after being incarcerated there.

Sarah opened her eyes the following week and Mrs Haynes, who had scarcely left her bedside for the whole time, burst into a fresh fit of sobbing, but this time these were tears of relief. She had come to love Sarah dearly, and had been blaming herself for not watching her more closely on the night of the party.

'I think she's going to pull through,' the doctor told them after examining her yet again, and her foster family rejoiced.

The burden of guilt that Ezra and Freyde bore for their son's crime was weighing heavily upon them, although the Haynes family bore them no ill-feeling.

'Your lad weren't of his right mind,' Mrs Haynes told them kindly. 'I dare say he never set out to hurt her, nor them other two poor buggers that he attacked. Sarah will be able to tell us what happened soon when she's a bit better. Let's just thank God that she came through it an' stop whippin' yourselves.'

Sarah was able to speak to the police three days later, and she told them that she and Dovi had been playing hide and seek in the copse. Everything had been fine until they suddenly heard a loud bang, and then Dovi had suddenly turned on her. That was the last she could remember. The doctors could only assume that the noise had startled Dovi and he had perhaps thought it was a gunshot – and once more in his mind returned to the terrible conditions of the battlefield, where it was kill or be killed.

But no one would ever know for sure now unless he chose to tell them – and the chances of that seemed remote.

Chapter Twenty-Six

Ezra and Freyde were allowed to visit Dovid two weeks later. Hatton Hospital was almost twenty miles away from them and they had to catch three buses to get there, so it was mid-afternoon by the time they finally arrived at the gates which were unlocked by a solemn-faced man who was sitting in a small hut to one side of the drive.

Set in over 377 acres, Hatton was a huge Victorian asylum built in the Gothic style. It dated back to 1846, and since it had been erected on a site purchased from the Earl of Warwick, it had originally been known as the Warwick County Lunatic Asylum. However, from 1930 onwards, it had been renamed the Warwickshire County Mental Hospital, although everyone referred to it as simply, 'Hatton'. Patients there received electric shock treatment amongst other things, and many of the rooms were reputed to be haunted which Freyde could well believe as she stared at the bleak façade.

'I cannot believe that our son has ended up in such a place,' she breathed to her husband.

He glanced at her sympathetically. The change in her over the last three weeks had been dramatic. She had lost yet more weight and found it hard to sleep, for when she did she was tormented by pictures of Dovi beating Sarah mercilessly. Sometimes now, Ezra wondered if she would ever be the same again. He had reopened the shop – after all, he still had to make a living – but trade had dropped off dramatically as word spread of the horrendous things that their son had done.

Thankfully, Sarah was now safely back at home, but her recovery would take a long time and she would bear the mental scars of Dovi's attack for ever. Many people had offered condolences but others avoided the whole family like the plague now. At present Ezra was barely taking enough money to meet their bills, but this was not the right time to worry about that and he pushed his concerns to the back of his mind.

'Come,' he coaxed as he took her elbow. 'There is nothing to be gained by us standing here. Let us go in.'

Freyde nodded as they began to walk along the endless drive.

They were met at the enormous double doors by a nurse who led them into a small side room to wait for a doctor. It was a small room, but clean and comfortable with five easy chairs positioned around a shining mahogany table. As Freyde stood looking out across the grounds it was hard to believe that they were in a mental institution – but she knew that they were.

The doctor when he arrived was a small stout man with a bald head and huge, gold-framed glasses perched on the end of his enormous nose. He held his hand out and smiled welcomingly.

'Ah, Mr and Mrs Schwartz,' he greeted them. 'I have been expecting you. Do take a seat.' Flicking the back of his white coat aside, he sat down as Freyde and Ezra perched nervously on the edge of two chairs.

'How is my son?' Ezra asked without preamble and now the doctor's smile faded.

'I am afraid he is not good,' he told them truthfully. 'We have him in the high security area. I fear that in his present state of mind he could be a risk to himself and to others.'

'But . . . he will get better, won't he?' Freyde asked.

The doctor steepled his fingers and seemed to consider her question for a time before saying quietly, 'If you are asking for my *personal* opinion, Mrs Schwartz, I would have to say no, I do not believe that Dovid will *ever* recover. In fact, I think he is now totally insane. It's so sad. We have many like him here. Young men who have seen things in the war that should never be seen. It tips the balance of their minds. Some recover, some do not, but none of them will ever be the same again. But never fear; we shall take good care of him. It is a blessing really that he does not even realise that he is in a hospital. But I should warn you, you must prepare yourselves, for the son you see will not be the son you remember. Are there any more questions you would like to ask?'

When the couple shook their heads, the doctor rose and rang a small bell to the side of the door. Within seconds a nurse dressed in a navy-blue uniform topped by a crisp white apron appeared and the doctor asked her, 'Would you take Mr and Mrs Schwartz along to the high security unit please, Nurse? The staff there are expecting them.'

'Of course, Doctor.' The nurse smiled at them and they followed her out into the corridor with their hearts thundering in their chests as they each wondered what they were about to see. It was hard to imagine Dovi being even worse than he had been.

The enormous entrance foyer was in actual fact quite presentable if somewhat plain. They followed the nurse up a huge sweeping staircase and along a corridor, and when they came to the end of it she paused in front of a door and knocked on it. A small hole in the top half of it instantly popped open as someone peered out at them, and then it slammed shut again and they heard a key turning in the lock.

The nurse who appeared now was wrapped in a voluminous calico apron with a large bunch of keys dangling from her thick leather belt. She nodded at them curtly to follow her, after hastily locking the door behind her. They found themselves in yet another long corridor, with locked doors leading off either side of it. Cries and groans issued from within each one as they passed and Freyde had to take a deep breath to hold herself together.

Towards the end of the corridor the nurse stopped to tell them, 'Dovid is in here. Would you like me to come in with you? He can be quite aggressive although he should be all right for now; he had his medication not long ago.'

Freyde drew herself up to her full height and stared at the woman with disdain. 'Dovi is our *son*,' she told her imperiously. 'And so we won't need anyone to come in with us, thank you.'

'Suit yourself.' The woman selected a key from the bunch and unlocked the door before telling them, 'There's a buzzer at the side of the door. Just ring it when you want to come out.'

Freyde and Ezra stepped silently past her and they were scarcely in the room when they heard the key turn behind them.

The room they found themselves in was little more than a cell and very sparsely furnished. There was a narrow bed against one wall and an easy chair beneath the window that was set high up in the wall and covered by thick iron bars. The floor consisted of unpolished wooden floorboards and the walls were bare with no pictures or adornments of any kind. But it was not these things that Freyde was looking at now. It was the poor pathetic soul who was huddled in the chair with his arms wrapped tightly around himself.

Suddenly she felt as if her feet had been glued to the floor and it was Ezra who first took a tentative step forward.

'Dovi? Hello, son. It's me, Papa. How are you?'

Dovi showed no sign of having heard him. His head was lolling to one side and saliva was dribbling from his mouth onto what appeared to be some sort of bib that was fastened about his throat. Beneath the undignified bib he was dressed in old grey trousers and a grey jumper that hung from his thin frame. His hands and fingers were twitching convulsively, and as Ezra took one in his own the young man snatched it away and began to make terrible mewling noises.

'It is all right, Dovi. We are here now,' his father soothed, but the sound of his voice only seemed to agitate the young man further.

Freyde longed to go to him, to comfort him, but somehow her legs would not do as they were told.

'Look, your mother is here,' Ezra told him as he struggled to catch Dovi's hand again, but it was flailing wildly in the air now as if he was trying to knock away some unknown enemy.

'It's going to be fine.' There was a note of desperation in Ezra's voice now and he glanced at Freyde, silently pleading for help. She took a step forward and forced herself to say, 'Come along, Dovi. Do not distress yourself so, please.'

Now he suddenly lunged forward and Freyde flattened herself against the wall as he started to hammer his fists into the hard mattress on the bed. He then turned, and before either of them could stop him he began to bang his head repeatedly against the wall, keening loudly.

'*Ring the bell!*' Ezra barked urgently as he tried to stop him. Freyde turned and quickly did as she was told. Within seconds the door exploded open and two burly men, accompanied by the sour-faced nurse who had admitted them, charged into the room.

The two men wrestled Dovi into the chair and once he was trapped they held him as the nurse plunged a loaded syringe into his arm. Within seconds Dovi began to calm down and soon his head lolled to the side again and he seemed oblivious to everyone as the nurse strapped him into a straitjacket.

'I think you should be leaving now,' she told his parents. 'He doesn't know anyone anyway.'

On feet that felt like lead, Freyde and Ezra stepped out into the corridor and Freyde knew that she would never set foot in this place again. The young man she had just seen was not her son. Her Dovi had been so handsome, with a ready smile and a kind word for everyone. She could picture him now on the day he had been born and the proud way Ezra had looked on as their son snuggled into her warm full breasts. She could see him taking his first steps and remembered the day he had lost his first tooth. She still had it somewhere. It was one of the treasures she had insisted on bringing with them from Cologne.

Shortly before she and Ezra had left to come here, a solemn-faced policemen had visited the house to inform them that Dovi would not have to stand trial for the three attacks he had committed.

It was official now. The psychiatrists who had examined him at Hatton had declared that he was not responsible for his actions. Dovi would escape hanging: his punishment was to be far worse. He was to stay at Hatton for the rest of his life. It had been decided: their son was a danger to the public. Freyde had been appalled at their decision – until she had seen him, and now she knew that it made no difference where he was. That empty drooling shell was not her son. Dovid Schwartz was gone from her for ever.

They waited patiently at the end of the corridor until the nurse came to unlock the door, and then they strode away without so much as a backward glance.

It was late evening by the time they arrived home looking unbelievably tired and strained.

'I'll make you a hot drink,' Adina offered the second they set foot through the door. 'And have you had anything to eat? You must be starving.'

Freyde flung her coat over the back of the chair. 'I'm not hungry,' she told her and swept up the stairs before Adina had a chance to say another word.

When Adina looked questioningly towards her father, he sighed heavily. 'Give your mother a bit of peace,' he muttered. 'This is very difficult for her.'

Adina felt like saying it was difficult for all of them, especially little Sarah, but wisely held her tongue. Her father was obviously as wound up as a spring and she didn't wish to say anything that might upset him further.

Instead she asked cautiously, 'How was he?'

Ezra looked at her before saying, 'From this moment on, your brother shall not be mentioned in this house again.'

'But that's so *unfair!*' Adina cried, before she could stop herself. 'He wasn't responsible for what he did. He's ill and—'

'*Silence!*' Her father's voice rocketed across the room, stopping her mid-sentence.

She stared at him for a moment before quietly walking past him and making her way to her bedroom with tears streaming down her face. It seemed that now she had lost a brother as well as a sister, and it was almost more than she could bear.

Unknown to her parents she had spent the afternoon with Karl making the most of her parents' absence. But soon he would be gone too – and then it would be just her and her mother and father. Until Karl came back for her, that was. And then they would be completely alone. She bowed her head at the thought.

On a sunny June day, Karl and Adina stood together in the gloom of the copse in Riversley Park to say their goodbyes. Adina was sobbing unashamedly and Karl was greatly distressed.

'Please do not cry,' he implored her. 'I shall be back before you know it, and then nothing and no one will ever part us again. Just keep the beautiful dress you made ready to be worn.'

Ariel had returned the wedding dress some time ago and now it was back in the suitcase under Adina's bed.

She clung fiercely to him and listened to his heartbeat, unable to imagine what her life was going to be like without him. She knew without a doubt that he was the only man she would ever love. He was her soulmate and she would willingly have died for him.

'Can you not give me any idea at all how long you might be gone?' she asked again for the tenth time in as many minutes.

'No, I cannot,' he said regretfully. 'But before I go, I must be honest with you or I could not live with myself. I have been trying to tell you for some time, but now I can put it off no longer.'

Drawing her down onto the grass, Karl sat beside her, then staring over her head he composed himself before beginning, 'Before I joined the war I was engaged to be married to a girl back home.'

Seeing the hurt that instantly flared in Adina's eyes, he hurried on.

'It was not what you think. It was to be an arranged marriage between her family and mine. That is how things were done in my parents' circle. It had been expected of us since we were children. The girl and I were friends, but I cannot pretend that we were in love. Even so, I would have gone ahead with the marriage had I not met you. But now . . .' He sighed wearily. 'I am a man of honour, and before you and I can come together, I must go back and see if my parents are still alive. I will then free myself from the engagement and come back to you as soon as I can.'

He cupped Adina's chin and stared into her eyes. 'All I can tell you is I will not be gone for a second longer than is necessary. Meantime, wear my ring and each time you touch it, know that I will be thinking of you.'

She nodded as she fingered the band of steel suspended on the fine chain about her neck and then they were in each other's arms and Adina wondered how she would bear to be parted from him. Now, as their lips joined, their passion mounted and soon they were lying side by side on the grass as his large hands played across her body. Adina knew that what they were doing was wrong, but she was powerless to stop it.

Scarcely before she knew what was happening they were both naked, and she rejoiced at the feel of his firm skin beneath her fingertips. He stroked and sucked at her pert nipples until they stood to attention with desire, and she arched her body into his – and when he finally rolled across her and took her virginity, she gave herself to him gladly. There was one moment of intense pain but then she was lost in ecstasy as she called out his name. And then it was over and he lay at her side panting as she snuggled into him, fingering the silky blond hairs on his chest.

She clung to him as if she would never let him go. It was unforgivable for a Jewish girl to give herself to a man before marriage, but in her mind they already were married and she needed to belong to him in every way.

Eventually he pushed her away from him and stood up looking repentant. 'I am so sorry,' he muttered. 'I should not have let my feelings get the better of me.'

'Don't be sorry,' she whispered, as all the love she felt for him shone in her eyes. 'I wanted it to happen, I am truly yours now.'

They dressed hastily and then he was holding her hands again and gazing into her eyes.

'I must go now. The jeeps will be waiting up at the Hall ready to take us to the plane.'

He kissed her one last time and as he strode away without looking back she covered her eyes and wept.

154

Chapter Twenty-Seven

At the beginning of July Adina received another letter from Beryl informing her that she had given birth to a baby girl. She had called her Catherine and for the first time she admitted how much she was missing home. Adina's heart ached for her. She could only imagine how hard it must be, to be far away from home with a new baby and a new family to adapt to. She was still delighted that mother and baby were doing well though, and hoped that Beryl would be slightly happier and a little more settled when she next wrote to her.

The weeks since Karl had left had passed painfully slowly, with each day seeming like a week. As yet she had received no word from him, although that was not giving her cause for concern yet. Letters were still taking a long time to be delivered and she knew that she would have to be patient.

She had been very busy at the school, which she supposed was a blessing, as whilst she was busy she wasn't moping over Karl. The Headmistress, Mrs Downes, had her busily writing letters to the evac- uees' families, and the Red Cross were trying to locate them too, to see if it was possible for them to return home. Karl had agreed to address his letters to the school, as they had decided that Adina's parents might wonder who was writing to her from Germany if he should send them to Edmund Street. Not that her mother seemed to notice much any more. Since the day she had visited Dovi in the asylum she had said barely more than two words to either of them. She was giving Adina serious cause for concern, and as well as the extra work at the school, the girl was also now almost running the house single-handed. She still tried to find time to see Ariel once a week, and her sister was distraught to hear how sad her mother was.

'It's not right,' she told Adina one day as they strolled through the marketplace. 'If only Papa would let me visit, I could help you. You have enough to do with the work at the school and all the sewing you take on. You're as pale as a ghost. Are you sure it isn't too much for you?'

'I'm fine,' Adina assured her. 'I'm just a little tired, that's all. And anyway, you have enough to do, waiting for the baby to arrive. It won't be long now, eh? I can hardly wait to meet my niece or nephew.'

Ariel grinned as she stroked her swollen stomach. The baby was due any day now and she was waddling like a duck and hugely uncomfort- able.

'I shall be glad when it's here now,' she admitted ruefully. 'Lugging this lot around in this heat isn't much fun, I don't mind telling you. And Brian is so excited. I think he's going to make a lovely father. Did I tell you that he had managed to get a job? He's working part-time at the post office sorting mail now. It's done him the world of good. I think he feels useful again, if you know what I mean.'

'That's wonderful.' Adina was genuinely pleased to hear the news. On the few occasions she had met her new brother-in-law he had seemed like a thoroughly nice young man, and it was obvious that he loved Ariel dearly.

'You know, I'm *so* lucky,' Ariel went on. 'If only I wasn't estranged from Mama and Papa, and if our brother had been well, everything would be perfect. But then I suppose we can't have everything. And who knows, perhaps when the baby is born Papa will have a change of heart and want to meet his grandchild.'

Adina nodded, although she thought there was very little chance of that. Ezra too had changed almost beyond recognition since Dovi had been locked away. He seemed bitter and angry all the time, and it had got to the stage where Adina was almost afraid to open her mouth in case he snapped her head off. On top of everything else she was helping out in the shop more now too, as Freyde just sat for hours in the chair that Dovi had once adopted, staring into the fire-grate as he had.

Sometimes when she dropped into bed each night, Adina was so exhausted that she was asleep almost before her head hit the pillow. She was feeling tired and unwell all the time, but guessed that this was because she was missing Karl so much. Every morning when she arrived at the school she would look through the mail hoping to see a letter addressed to her from Germany, but up to now she had been sadly disappointed.

She and Ariel had reached the end of Queens Road now where they kissed and said goodbye.

'Be sure and let me know if anything happens with the baby before next week,' Adina told her sister.

Ariel grinned. 'Don't worry. Brian will get word to you one way or another. Goodbye.'

Adina set off towards home, and as she was approaching the shop she saw an ambulance parked at the kerb. Suddenly she was running and as she neared the entry she saw Mrs Haynes standing there in her turban and her pinny.

'What's happened?' she cried as she sucked air into lungs which felt as if they were bursting.

'It's yer mam, luv,' the woman told her tearfully. 'Yer dad come runnin' round an' asked us to phone fer an ambulance. Apparently he popped out the back an' she were in the chair. He couldn't wake her. The ambu-lancemen are in there with her now.'

156

Without bothering to answer Adina shot up the entry. She ran through the yard and the open door just in time to see two tall men loading her mother onto a stretcher. Her father was looking on with tears streaming down his cheeks.

'What's happened?' Adina addressed the question to him but when he didn't reply she looked towards the men. 'She's my mother,' she gabbled. 'Can't you tell me what's wrong with her?'

The two men glanced at each other and then one cleared his throat before telling her quietly, 'I'm so sorry, but I'm afraid she's gone.'

'What do you mean . . . she's *gone*?' Adina felt as if someone had slapped her in the face.

'We can't be sure yet, but it looks as if she had a massive heart-attack. She was already dead when we got here, although we did everything we could, I promise you.'

'*NO!*' Adina's head wagged from side-to-side as shock coursed through her veins like ice cold water. 'She *can't* be gone!'

Ezra placed his arm about her trembling shoulders as the men silently pulled a thin blanket across her mother's pale face. They then lifted the stretcher and headed towards the door as she looked on in stunned disbelief. This couldn't be happening. It just *couldn't*! First Ariel had been sent away in disgrace, then they had lost Dovi, and now this!

Freyde Schwartz was buried forty-eight hours later in Witton Cemetery in Birmingham. It was the nearest Jewish cemetery that the undertaker they appointed could find for them and the earliest that the undertaker could arrange for the burial and appoint a rabbi to perform the service for them. Freyde had been returned home to them within hours of her being taken to the hospital, and Adina had washed her mother's body from head to foot in warm water and dressed her in a *tachrichim*, a plain white shroud as was their custom. Freyde was then placed in a plain pine coffin and the night before she was buried Adina never left her side. This practice was known as *Shemira*, honouring the dead, and whilst Adina sat there her father watched over her, reciting Psalms.

The cemetery was a huge sprawling place that covered a hundred and three acres, but only two of these were used for Jewish burials and it was there that Freyde was laid to rest with no one but her daughter and husband present. Before the simple ceremony began, the rabbi tore black ribbons into strips, which Ezra and Adina pinned to their clothes to symbolise their loss. The rabbi then recited Psalms, followed by a short eulogy and a memorial prayer. The coffin was then taken to the grave that stood open, and as Ezra and Adina followed it they stopped seven times to recite Psalm 91. And then it was over, and as the funeral car drove them home, Adina sat in deep shock staring blindly from the window.

Her father had confessed to her the day before that he had known for some time that Freyde had a heart problem, but they had decided to keep it from their daughter so as not to worry her. And now she was gone and Adina felt cheated because she had not even had the chance to say a proper goodbye, or tell her Mama how much she loved her. It seemed so unfair. But then as she was discovering, life *was* unfair. Now, more than ever, she needed to feel Karl's strong arms about her, but still there had been no word from him. During the burial service Adina had glanced up to see Brian standing on his crutches some way away, and she wondered how he had managed to get there, and why Ariel was not with him. Surely she could have come to their mother's funeral even if she had not been invited?

Her father was deeply distressed because the Jewish custom of the dead being buried within twenty-four hours had not been adhered to. But the police and the doctor had insisted on a hurried post mortem being carried out because of the suddenness of the death, and as they were not in their own country they could not argue their religious beliefs.

That morning before leaving for the service, Ezra had written Freyde's name in the Book of the Dead.

There had been no flowers or wreaths. The Jewish faith did not recognise flowers at funerals and now it was over and Adina could barely take it in. Life would never be the same again.

Part Three

Mothers and Daughters

Chapter Twenty-Eight

The day after his wife's funeral, Ezra opened the shop again, and for the first time since Dovi had been sent to Hatton, people began to pour in again, wishing to offer their condolences at Freyde's passing. The customers were all eager to tell Ezra what a wonderfully kind woman she had been, and while he was coping with this, Adina took the first opportunity to go round to her sister's home.

'Where is Ariel?' she demanded, when Brian opened the door. 'I cannot believe that she chose not to attend her own mother's funeral!'

'She didn't *choose* not to come, Dina. She *couldn't* come – that's why I went to represent her,' Brian retorted. 'As it so happens, she's in hospital. She had the baby early yesterday morning. It's a little girl.'

'Oh!' Adina was so stunned that for a moment she couldn't think of a word to say. It seemed bizarre that her niece should have been born on such a sad day, the day of her maternal grandmother's burial.

'Are they both all right?' she managed to ask eventually.

Unable to keep the smile from his face, Brian nodded. 'Fine an' dandy,' he assured her. 'An' the baby is a little cracker, even though I do say so meself.'

'Congratulations,' Adina said, as joy at the news of the baby's birth and grief at her mother's passing vied for first place in her heart. 'Will I be able to go to the hospital to see them?'

'I'm afraid not,' Brian told her regretfully. 'Only fathers are allowed to visit on the maternity ward, but I'll let you know as soon as they're home an' then you can come round an' see them both. You'll love the little 'un. She was eight pounds one ounce. That's a good weight for a first baby, me mam says.'

'I should imagine it is,' Adina agreed, although she really didn't know much about such things. 'I shall have to go now, but do give Ariel my love – and the baby, of course. What are you going to call her?'

'We ain't decided definitely yet, but when we do I'll let you know, eh? Oh, and Adina . . . I'm so sorry about your mam.'

She inclined her head before turning to make the short journey back to the shop. This was another day she would never forget.

A week later, Adina set off to visit her sister and her new niece. Brian had managed to get word to her via Mrs Haynes that they had come home from hospital the day before. Adina had spent hours over the previous

161

days sewing tiny little nightgowns from a flannelette sheet and had then smocked and embroidered them. She had been quite pleased with the end result as they were very pretty and she hoped that Ariel would like them.

Mrs Rowley welcomed her warmly when she tapped on the door and ushered her into a small parlour where Ariel was sitting with her feet propped up on a brown leatherette pouffe. Adina saw at a glance that the house was immaculately clean and tidy. Bright flowered curtains had replaced the dreary blackout ones, and a large bowl of sweet williams filled the air with their scent.

'My Henry fetched 'em for Ariel from the allotment,' the woman told her proudly as she saw Adina looking towards them. 'But I wish you'd have a word wi' this sister o' yours. Thinks she can run afore she can walk, so she does. I keep tellin' her she's got to keep her feet up for at least another week. Anyway, that's enough from me. I dare say you're dyin' to see your new niece, ain't yer? She's a lovely little thing, but then I'm bound to be biased. She is me first grandchild, after all. I'll leave yer to it now.' With that she disappeared through a door that led into the kitchen as Adina slowly approached a small wooden crib placed at Ariel's side.

'Oh Ariel, she's just *perfect*,' she gasped as she stared down at the tiny infant who was swaddled in a snow-white hand-knitted shawl.

'She is rather gorgeous, isn't she?' Ariel opened her arms and the two sisters hugged each other. Ariel was delighted with her new baby daughter but the joy of the birth had been marred by the death of their mother.

'How is Papa bearing up, Dina?' she asked as she stared into her sister's strained face.

'Oh, he seems to be coping.' Adina sighed. 'It seems so strange, though ... just the two of us. The house feels so empty and Papa is keeping the shop open from dawn until dusk now. I don't think he likes to be in the house too much at present but I suppose that's understandable.'

'Who would ever have thought all this would befall our family when we set out on the boat from Cologne that day, eh?' Ariel blinked back tears.

'Things could have been worse,' Adina answered quietly. 'If we had not left when we did, no doubt we would have faced the same fate as our Zayda and Bubba did in some awful camp. At least we are still alive, and now you have brought a new little life into the world. We should be grateful for that at least.'

They both stared down at the beautiful little girl. With her long eyelashes resting on her smooth pink cheeks and her tuft of golden brown hair she looked like a little angel.

'Have you decided what you're going to call her yet?'

'We have actually. We are going to call her Freda. It is the English version of Mama's name. Brian and I thought it would be a nice gesture. What do you think?'

'I think it's a lovely idea.'

At that moment the baby stirred and stretched her arms, and her mother immediately lifted her from the crib and placed her into her aunt's arms. 'Meet your Auntie Dina,' she smiled.

Adina's heart melted as she nuzzled the silky skin of the baby's neck and for the rest of the visit she refused to put her down.

'Please come again as soon as you can, Dina,' Ariel urged when Adina finally reluctantly rose to leave. 'Brian's mother is lovely, but I feel as if I'm being suffocated. She won't let me do a single thing except feed the baby.'

'And that is just how it should be,' Adina told her mock-sternly. 'You need to get your strength back before you do too much.'

Ariel kissed her as she bent down and told her, 'And thanks for the lovely nightgowns. I shall put one on her tonight.'

'You're very welcome.' Adina took her leave and slowly began to make her way home to Edmund Street, although she didn't relish the thought of going back there at all. It wasn't a happy house any more and she feared that it never would be again.

When Adina entered the shop, the bell above the door tinkled and her father looked up from the sweets he was carefully weighing into little brown triangular paper bags which he then secured with a twist.

'Ah, you are back,' he commented. 'I was beginning to wonder where you had got to. Have you been somewhere nice?'

Deciding that there would never be a better opportunity than now, Adina told him brazenly, 'Yes, I have actually. I have just been to meet your new granddaughter. She is quite beautiful and Ariel is going to call her Freda in memory of Mama.'

She watched a million emotions flit across his face as his hands became still, but then suddenly he filled yet another bag and told her brusquely, 'Mrs Benson called in earlier. She wondered how you were getting on with her alterations.'

Sighing, Adina walked past him into the little empty kitchen at the back of the house to start preparing their dinner.

Chapter Twenty-Nine

Although the war was over for the people of Europe it still raged on in Japan, and the newspapers reported daily on what was happening there. In August 1945 Churchill lost his seat in a Labour landslide and Clement Attlee was appointed as the new Prime Minister. It seemed that the people's regard for Winston Churchill as a war leader was now outweighed by their desire for social changes in peace time. Britain was facing austerity measures that were even fiercer than those of wartime, with food, petrol and tobacco imports severely reduced. There was no end in sight to the rationing, and Britain's reserves were all but exhausted.

Those who had fought for their country were slowly trickling back home, returning to their joyous families – but it soon became obvious that very few of them were unscarred by their experiences.

And then at last, at midnight on 15 August, the new Prime Minister announced the surrender of Japan – and another two-day holiday began, to celebrate what was to become known as VJ Day. King George and Queen Elizabeth travelled to Parliament in an open carriage, waving at the ecstatic crowds on the way as they were soaked by rain. Later the same day they made repeated appearances on the balcony of Buckingham Palace whilst the people rejoiced that at last they had no more enemies to fight. Once again, street parties, bonfires and flags appeared everywhere, but this time Ezra and Adina stayed indoors, too saddened at Freyde's death and the dreadful memories of VE Day to join in.

Now Britain could begin to count the human and economic cost of what Winston Churchill had referred to as 'its finest hour', and it soon became apparent that Britain was economically crippled. Thousands of homes had been flattened, and hundreds of thousands of soldiers had lost their lives whilst others, like Dovid, had lost their sanity. Now Britain would be forced to fight a battle of a different kind as her citizens tried to survive in the aftermath of the war.

It was now over three months since Karl had returned to Germany, but still Adina looked for his letter each day. It was more important than ever now that she heard from him, for the suspicion that had plagued her for weeks had now been confirmed. She was almost four months' pregnant.

She longed to confide in someone, but there was no one whom she wished to burden with her secret, even her own sister, and now as each day passed her terror increased. 'What am I going to do?' she asked herself over and over again, but she never came up with an answer. Her father must surely find out soon. Thankfully, Adina had always been slight of build so although her waistbands were becoming uncomfortably tight, only she was aware of her condition up to now.

She had considered running away – but where would she run to? And if she did and a letter from Karl arrived, she would not be here to read it.

And then one morning a solution was handed to her on a plate.

'Ah, Adina – I'm glad I've caught you. Could I have a quick word with you in my office before you start work?' Mrs Downes, the Headmistress, asked her cheerfully.

Adina followed the woman along the corridor with her heart in her mouth. Could she have somehow discovered that she was going to have a baby? And if she had, would she inform her father?

She slid into the office and closed the door quietly as the woman beamed at her.

'Adina,' she began, 'I know this might come as a surprise to you, but I have a proposition to put to you. The thing is, I have a dear friend who lives in London with her husband. She is a teacher too, and during the war they have had dozens of Jewish evacuee children at their school. Far, far more than we have had here. Anyway, I was talking to her on the phone the other day, and I happened to mention what a wonderful job you have done in trying to trace the children's families, which is where my proposition comes in.' She cleared her throat. 'My friend wondered if you would consider going to work at her school to do the same job there. It might mean you being away from home for approximately nine to twelve months, but I feel it would be a wonderful opportunity for you.'

When Adina blinked in surprise she hurried on, 'Of course, you would stay with my friends in their home and they would take very good care of you, so you can assure your father that there would be nothing for him to worry about. They would be able to pay you far more than I could too, so what do you think? Would you like some time to mull it over and decide?'

'Yes, I . . . I think I would,' Adina managed to stammer and she left the room in a daze. This could be the answer to all her prayers. Once in London she could wait for Karl to contact her without anyone here being aware that she was pregnant. She could ask Mrs Downes to forward to her any letters that arrived, and then once she had heard from Karl and told him of her plight he would hurry back and they could be married before the baby was born. At least that way she would not bring shame on her father. The thought of deceiving him now was terrifying, but anything was better than piling yet more heartache onto him. It would be bad enough facing his rage when he discovered that she had fallen in love with a German, but at least now a chance had been offered that might prevent him from finding out about the baby. With her mind racing she headed for the classroom but she thought it was going to be very hard to concentrate on anything today. She had a lot to think about now.

Two days later, after discussing the opportunity with her father, Adina made her decision. She felt very guilty at going and leaving him all alone, but to her surprise he seemed all for the idea.

'You will only remember the poverty-stricken part of London where we lived when we first came to England,' he told her. 'But this will be entirely different and you should grasp the opportunity to better yourself with both hands. Do not worry about me. I shall be fine and you can write to me often. It isn't as if you are going away for ever, is it?'

Adina's heart ached as she avoided his eyes. The truth of it was that once she set foot out of the door she *would* be leaving him for ever – but he could have no way of knowing that. This was her only way out.

Mrs Downes was delighted when she heard Adina's decision and promised to get in touch with her friends in London straight away.

'It will be such a weight off their minds,' she assured her. 'At present they are really struggling. Many of the Jewish children there are placed in orphanages, but it is imperative now that those who can return to their families do so. Of course, there are probably many who won't have families to return to, but at least a future can be planned for them once we know. I'm sure you won't regret this, my dear. Now off you go. I shall ring them and tell them of your decision immediately.'

Adina slowly rose from her seat and left the office as the Headmistress began to thumb through her address book. It was done; there was no going back now. She suddenly had the urge to visit Ariel. Once she left Nuneaton she might never see either her sister or her beautiful niece again. But then she would have Karl – and she knew that that would make up for everything.

One week later, Adina stood in the shop facing her father with tears in her eyes.

'Why don't you let me come to the station with you?' he asked for at least the tenth time in an hour.

'Because it is more important for you to stay here and keep the shop open.' Her eyes scanned his face, locking every little detail of his features away into her memory. Once she and Karl were married, she knew that her father would disown her, just as he had Ariel. He looked so old now, nothing like the vibrant man he had been when they had all first come to Nuneaton a mere six years ago, but then she supposed that it could not be otherwise. They had all gone through so much since then and the family had been torn apart. Now he would be all alone, and guilt was weighing heavily on her. The suitcase that stood on the floor beside the door of the shop was full of everything she owned, including the beautiful wedding gown that she hoped to be wearing soon, but it still contained pitifully little apart from the clothes that Adina had made for herself and a photo of the family taken during happier times.

That photo was all that she would have of them now, and she knew that it was her most valuable possession.

At that moment the taxi her father had ordered to take her to the station pulled up outside and he silently lifted her case and carried it out for her. Then whilst the driver stowed it safely away in the boot he placed his hands on his daughter's cheeks and gently kissed her.

'You take care now,' he told her. 'And be sure to write to me often.'

She nodded numbly. 'I will, Papa,' she promised chokily, and then he was ushering her into the car and she waved from the back window until the car turned a corner and he was lost from sight.

Adina had been to see Ariel the day before to say goodbye, and had confided in her about her relationship with Karl, although she had refrained from telling her about the baby. Ariel had been terrified for her, but after falling in love herself with Brian she did not condemn her. She of all people understood that love had the habit of striking you down when you least expected it.

'*Please* promise that you'll stay in touch,' she implored Adina when it was time for her sister to leave.

'Of course I will.' Adina had bent to kiss her baby niece with tears in her eyes and then she had hugged her sister for one last time and hurried blindly away. After all, who could know how long it might be before they saw each other again – or indeed if they ever would?

She was standing on the platform deep in thought when the train chugged into the station, and after yanking her suitcase aboard she sat down opposite an elderly couple who smiled at her kindly. Now she was regretting not letting her father accompany her to the station. At least that would have prolonged their parting by a few minutes. Although grief had changed him almost beyond recognition over the last months, she still loved him and was missing him already. But the family had been divided and now Ezra Schwartz would have to get used to living alone.

As the train pulled away, leaving great plumes of smoke in its wake, Adina took a final glance at the town that had become her home. She was remembering clearly the day she and the rest of the family had arrived there, so excited to be going to the new home that Ezra had found for them. They had all been so full of hope for the future then. Little had they known what life had in store for them.

'Going to visit family in London are you, dear?' the old lady sitting opposite suddenly asked and Adina pulled her thoughts sharply back to the present.

'Oh no. Actually, I'm going to work in London,' she replied quietly.

'I see.' The woman exchanged a disapproving glance with her husband before returning her attention to her book. She wondered sometimes what the world was coming to! A young girl like her, going off to live and work in London all alone. It made you wonder what the parents were thinking about, but then she supposed it was none of her business – just one more undesirable product of the war – and she pointedly ignored Adina for the rest of the journey, which could she have known it, suited the girl just fine.

By the time the train drew into Euston Station, Adina was feeling sick and tired, and she breathed a sigh of relief as the journey ended.

Mrs Downes had assured her that her friends, Mr and Mrs Montgomery, would be there to meet her but now Adina panicked as she wondered how they would ever find her. The concourse was teeming with people everywhere she looked, and she suddenly felt as if she was invisible as they streamed past without giving her so much as a glance. But then she consoled herself, she did have their address tucked safely into her pocket and if they didn't turn up she could always get a cab to where they lived. Camden Town couldn't be that far away, surely? One thing was for sure, there was no going back now so she stood and waited as patiently as she could.

Adina had stood in the concourse for almost half an hour when she saw a couple striding purposefully towards her. They appeared to be looking for someone and she held her breath as they approached.

As they drew abreast they hesitated and the man asked tentatively, 'Miss Schwartz?'

Adina nodded as she stared up at him. He was very tall with a mop of thick fair hair and he reminded her a little of Karl, which she supposed was a good start. She judged him to be at least six foot four and he had piercing blue eyes that crinkled at the corners when he smiled.

'That's a relief,' he chuckled. 'I'm sure we've done at least ten laps of the station.' As he spoke he took his wife's elbow and drew her forward. 'This is my wife, Felicity,' he introduced her and the woman smiled too now. In actual fact they looked a rather ill-matched couple, for she was very small and petite, not even reaching up to her husband's shoulders. Her brunette hair was cut into a becoming chin-length bob and she was elegantly dressed in a smart red coat and black patent shoes. She was carrying a matching black patent handbag and she held her hand out and shook Adina's warmly. 'Call me Fliss, everybody else does. Well, everyone but Theo's mother, that is, and she doesn't believe in shortening people's names. She lives with us,' she informed her with a smile. 'Or should I say we live with her – a fact that she never lets us forget. And this is Theodore, although he's known to most as Theo. What are we to call you?'

'My name is Adina, but my friends call me Dina,' the girl told her as she swallowed her nervousness. The couple seemed friendly enough, which was something to be grateful for, although they were much younger than she had expected them to be – somewhere in their mid-thirties, she judged.

'Right, well, let's get you home then, shall we? I hope you're not expecting too much. I'm afraid London has taken rather a battering during the war, what with all the doodlebugs and what have you. Still, I'm sure you'll be comfortable. Theo, take Dina's case, would you?' As her husband obediently did as he was told, Fliss linked her arm through Adina's and headed towards the exit.

'We'll take a cab, seeing as you have a case,' she told her. 'Although normally we would take a bus or walk.'

Adina's eyes stretched wide as she looked about at all the hustle and bustle. It seemed like a lifetime ago since she had lived in the city and she had forgotten how busy it was. Ruined buildings were everywhere and the streets looked dirty and uninviting. Still, she decided that now she was here she was going to make the most of it. After all, Karl could be in touch with her any day now. Theo loaded her case into the boot of a large black London cab and then as they all clambered inside he gave the driver the address and they shot off through the busy streets. Eventually, after a short ride they entered Camden Town.

The cab turned into Prince Regent Terrace, and drew up in front of number seven, a huge four-storey townhouse that had what appeared to be an enormous tarpaulin thrown across the roof. As she stepped onto the pavement and looked up towards it, Fliss followed her eyes and told her, 'I'm afraid a bomb took some of the roof off. We were lucky, though; some of the houses further along the street were completely flattened. At least we are still able to live in our home. We're waiting for the builders to come and repair it, but I fear we may have to wait for a long time. They are run off their feet at present, as you can imagine. So much of our great city was damaged during the bombing.'

Adina waited while Theo paid off the cab driver and took her suitcase from the boot, and turned her attention to the rest of the house. Steps led up to a large front door that looked in desperate need of a lick of paint. At the bottom of the steps, iron railings ran along the whole frontage, and yet more stone steps led down one side to what she assumed was a kitchen area. Somehow she had imagined the couple living in a much more impressive house, but then seeing as she had no intention of being there for very long, she wasn't overly concerned.

Now Theo took her elbow and led her up the steps where she waited while Fliss extracted a large metal key from her bag and hastily unlocked the door. Seconds later, Adina followed her into an enormous foyer and she stopped dead in her tracks, totally stunned by the interior. A parquet floor that had been polished until all the wonderful hues of the wood shone through stretched the entire length of the hallway, and from the centre arose a magnificent curved staircase that led up to a galleried

169

landing. The walls were covered in a lovely flock wallpaper in a soft shade of gold, and darker gold velvet curtains hung at the windows. A number of doors led off from the foyer, and whilst Theo disappeared upstairs with her case, Fliss held her hand out for Adina's hat and coat. She hung them on a heavy mahogany coat-stand and after hastily tidying her hair in a large gilt-framed mirror she took Adina down the long hallway, pausing in front of one of the doors. 'You must come and meet Theo's mother,' she said with a little wink. 'And don't worry; her bark is far worse than her bite, I assure you.'

They entered a large drawing room. Ornate settees on spindly legs were set out here and there; beside them stood small polished tables housing ornaments of various shapes and sizes that looked like precious antiques. A large fire was roaring within a marble Adam-style fireplace and suddenly Adina felt completely out of her depth. This room alone was surely bigger than the whole ground floor of the shop she had lived in with her family. However, it awakened memories of the Schwartz family residence in Cologne.

As Fliss walked further into the room Adina's eyes were drawn to a chair at the side of the fire where an elderly lady was sitting, studying her intently.

'Ah, Mother, this is the young lady I told you about who has come to help Theo and me locate some of the children's parents,' Fliss told her. 'She will be staying with us for quite some time.'

'Hmph!' The old woman leaned forward in her chair and peered at Adina more closely as the poor girl shifted uncomfortably from foot to foot. She had the feeling that the woman could see right into her soul.

'You're a Jewess, aren't you?' she demanded, as colour seeped into Adina's otherwise pale cheeks.

'I am Jewish, yes,' Adina replied as she held her head high and peered back at her attacker.

'Got a boyfriend, have you?'

Adina pointedly ignored the question. As far as she was concerned, she was here to do a job, and she intended to do that job to the best of her ability. Her private life, lowever, was nothing to do with anyone, least of all this overbearing old woman.

She was dressed in black from head to foot in an outfit that Adina felt would not have looked out of place in the last century, and her two gnarled hands were resting heavily on an ivory-topped walking stick. Her hair was steel-grey and pulled back into a tight bun on the back of her head. She was painfully thin and plain, her only adornment being the string of perfectly matched pearls that hung about her neck. She continued to stare at Adina, but when the girl continued to steadily hold her gaze, her face softened slightly and she looked entirely different.

'Girl can stick up for herself,' she commented to no one in particular. 'I like that. Can't abide wishy-washy people.' She cast a withering glance in her daughter-in-law's direction as she said it, and Fliss began to fiddle with the fringes of a chenille tablecloth that covered one of the tables.

'Come and sit down, girl,' the woman ordered, waving her cane towards the chair on the opposite side of the fire. 'And tell me your name and all about yourself.'

Adina did as she was told, folding her hands primly into her lap as she perched on the edge of the chair. 'My name is Adina Schwartz. My friends call me Dina and my family and I came here from Cologne at the beginning of the war.'

'Hm, and what was your father before he came to England?'

'My father was a banker,' Adina told her with a tilt of her chin. 'When we first arrived in London we lived in the East End for a while but then my father leased a small shop in the Midlands and we have lived there ever since.'

'And are the rest of your family still living in the Midlands?' the old woman pursued.

'S . . . some of them are,' Adina said reluctantly, not wishing to go too deeply into their personal affairs. 'My mother died recently, so my father is alone in the shop now.'

Thankfully, the door opened then and Theo came into the room. Sizing up the situation at a glance he waggled a finger at his mother. 'Now, Mother, you're not interrogating our guest, are you?' he scolded, although there was an amused twinkle in his eye. 'I don't want her turning tail and running for home before she has even had a chance to settle in.'

His mother glared at him but did not continue with her questioning, for which Adina was grateful.

Satisfied that she was behaving for now, Theo then informed them brightly, 'Mrs Leadbetter has told me that lunch is almost ready to be served. Shall we go into the dining room?' He looked pointedly at Adina as he told her, 'Mrs Leadbetter is our cook-cum-cleaner and she comes in daily. I really don't know what we would do without her.'

'She doesn't keep the house as I used to before these damn legs of mine went on strike,' his mother cut in scathingly. 'But then I've always said, if you want a job doing well you should do it yourself!'

Ignoring her comment, Theo held the door open and when Adina followed Fliss through it he then went to help his mother up from the chair.

'I can manage, I am not *completely* decrepit, you know,' she grumbled once he had got her into a standing position and she then barged past him as he shook his head with a wry smile.

Fliss opened another door further along the hall and Adina found herself in a beautiful dining room. A large mahogany table stood in the centre of it surrounded by twelve matching chairs, and thick curtains hung at the windows. A heavy matching sideboard took up almost the whole length of one wall and on it stood a number of highly polished silver tureens from which a delicious smell was emanating. Adina suddenly realised how hungry she was and sat down in the chair that Theo pulled out for her. Only one end of the table had been set, covered in a crisp white tablecloth, and Mrs Montgomery sat at the head of it with her son to the right of her whilst Fliss and Adina sat on her left. A portly, harassed-looking woman bustled in then and beamed at Adina before saying, 'Ah, so you got 'ere safely then, did you, luvvie? Miss Fliss said to be expectin' you.'

'Oh, shut up, Beattie, and serve the food,' the old woman snapped.

''Old your 'orses,' Beattie snapped back, obviously completely unafraid of her employer. 'I've only got the one pair of 'ands, you know, though I sometimes fink that two would come in 'andy, workin' for you.'

Adina had to purse her lips to stop herself from smiling as the woman began to transfer the steaming dishes to the table. Theo instantly began to lift the lids off to expose a perfectly roasted chicken and a variety of vegetables and roast potatoes.

'Not chicken *again*,' the old woman groaned. 'I'm sure I shall turn into a damn chicken and grow feathers at this rate.'

'Well, it was either chicken or nothing,' Beattie replied ungraciously. 'We are on rationin', you know, an' I was lucky to get that. Some people don't know when they're well off, it seems to me.'

'It looks delicious, Beattie,' Theo assured her quickly as he started to carve, and tutting indignantly the woman turned on her heel and stamped out of the room.

Adina wasn't quite sure where to look. She had found the whole episode rather embarrassing, not that it seemed to have bothered the housekeeper much. She was obviously used to these exchanges.

In no time at all her plate was piled high and the old woman said irritably, 'Well, get on with it then, girl. It won't bite you!'

Theo winked at her as Adina lifted her knife and fork and thankfully the old woman was silent then for a while as she tucked into her own meal with an appetite that would have done a woman half her age justice.

Soon after, Beattie staggered back into the room with a large home-made apple pie and a steaming jug of custard.

'I 'ope this will be to your ladyship's likin',' she quipped sarcastically and Adina held her breath. But the old woman simply glared at her as she pushed her empty plate away and wiped her mouth on a linen napkin.

'Perhaps it will be – *if* you've remembered to put enough sugar in,' she retorted.

In actual fact the pie was delicious and Adina left the table feeling as if she couldn't eat again for a month.

'I'll show you your room now,' Fliss offered as Theo helped his mother back into the drawing room.

Adina followed her up the magnificent staircase, admiring the pictures on the walls as she climbed. On the first landing, Fliss led her towards another staircase, telling her, 'We've put you up here out of earshot of Mother. She can be quite noisy at night if she wants something, which is why Theo and I sleep on the first floor with her.'

Adina got the distinct impression that Fliss was rather afraid of her mother-in-law, and she could quite see why.

On the second floor Fliss threw a door open and told her cheerily, 'This will be your room. There should be everything that you need but if we've forgotten anything, please tell us. We do want your stay with us to be comfortable.'

Adina was so taken aback at the room that for a moment she was struck dumb. It was enormous compared to the one she had had back in Nuneaton, and there was a panoramic view across the rooftops of London from the huge sash-cord window. At one time she had no doubt this room must have been the height of luxury, but now although it was spotlessly clean it looked a little shabby. The carpets on the floor were slightly faded, as were the curtains. There was an enormous wardrobe carved from solid oak on one wall and matching tables at either side of a great brass bed. A patchwork quilt that someone must have spent hours sewing was flung across it and two fat cushions rested against the shining brass headboard.

'It's really lovely,' Adina assured her hostess. 'I'm sure I shall be more than comfortable here. Thank you.'

'Right, then in that case I'll leave you to get unpacked,' Fliss told her with a smile. 'And I dare say a rest wouldn't come amiss either. Why don't you have a lie-down for a couple of hours? We can take you to see the school and meet the children tomorrow.'

When Fliss had gone, closing the door softly behind her, Adina crossed to the window and gazed out. She could see for miles, although it wasn't a pretty picture. Many homes were nothing more than piles of rubble now, and the sight made her feel sad. The war might well be over but there was still a long way to go and a lot of work to be done before the people of Britain could put it behind them.

Turning away, she lifted her case onto the bed and began to hang up her clothes, and as she lifted out the wedding dress she had so lovingly sewn, tears clogged her throat. *'Please come soon, Karl,'* she whispered to the empty room as she tucked it gently into the bottom of the wardrobe.

Eventually everything was unpacked to her satisfaction so she took a pad and pen from the bedside table and, sitting down in the chair in the bay window, she began to write a letter to Beryl, telling her of her new address. Her thoughts were full of the people she had left behind and she was feeling homesick already, but she was painfully aware that she would have to make the best of it. She had come too far to go back now.

Chapter Thirty

The following morning, after being presented with a hearty breakfast that she couldn't face, Adina accompanied Theo and Fliss to St Thomas's Primary, the school where they worked. It was just a few streets away and well within walking distance.

Thankfully the old woman had not put in an appearance, and when Adina commented on it, she was told that Mrs Montgomery was always served breakfast in bed. Adina stifled a grin at the thought of it and the banter that was bound to pass between Beattie and her employer.

The school was dismally rundown but luckily had missed being bombed. Many of the pupils were Londoners, but two classrooms had been set aside for the Jewish children who eyed her curiously when Theo introduced her.

'This is Miss Schwartz, children,' he informed them. 'And during the next few months she will be working closely with the Red Cross and the Salvation Army to try and trace your families in your home countries.'

Adina's heart ached as she was confronted with a sea of pale little faces. The more fortunate amongst them had been living with foster families, but the majority of them had spent the war closeted in North London orphanages. Theo had told her that the majority of the children were German Jews like herself, so now she addressed them in their native language. 'Good morning, children. How are you today?'

Instantly, many faces brightened and she knew that most of them had understood her. In fairness, after living in London for so long, they now had a grasp of basic English, but to have someone speak to them in their own tongue was a special treat.

Seeing the smiling faces, Theo left her to it and the rest of the day passed in a blur as Adina spoke to the children and liaised with the Red Cross and the Salvation Army, who were now constantly in and out of the school in their quest to trace the children's families.

When the bell rang later that afternoon it was Fliss who came to fetch her, and Adina was grateful as she wasn't sure that she would find her way home alone yet. All the streets looked similar, and she had visions of getting lost.

'So how did your first day go?' Fliss asked, as they walked along side by side.

'I think it went quite well,' Adina told her. 'The Red Cross are working hard but it's going to be awful for the children who have no parents left to go home to. What will happen to them?'

'I dare say the poor little mites will be transferred back to orphanages in their own country, or they'll stay here.'

Adina felt sad. A handful of the children had already wormed their way into her heart, and she hoped that their stories would have a happy ending. However deep down she feared that the majority of the children's families who had refused to flee their homes might well have been sent to Hitler's death camps.

Two of the little girls had clung to her skirts all day, and it was Rebekah and Esther that she thought of now. They had spoken so lovingly of the parents they had been torn away from, as had Cana, a little boy whose eyes had followed her about the classroom like a puppy's. All Adina really wanted was for Karl to arrive like a knight in shining armour and whisk her away to live happily ever after, but at least now after only one day in London she knew that she could fill her time purposefully until he came. The thought was strangely comforting.

'So, what would you like to do this evening?' Fliss asked now, pulling Adina's thoughts sharply back to the present.

'A walk would be nice,' Adina replied shyly. She had always been so sheltered living at home with her parents, and now she felt vulnerable and slightly out of her depth.

'In that case we'll go and have a stroll in Regent's Park.' Fliss slipped her arm through Adina's and they began to walk along past the ruins of what had no doubt once been magnificent buildings.

'It's sad to see the city like this, isn't it?' Fliss commented. 'Before the war London was a great tourist attraction, but there has been so much damage done. No doubt it will take years to return it to its former glory.'

Adina nodded in agreement as they entered the park through a pair of gates. Adina was totally enchanted: it was like a huge green oasis in the midst of so much carnage. They were now well into September and the leaves were beginning to turn to beautiful shades of russet and gold. Many had already fallen from the trees and they crunched underfoot as the two of them strolled along.

'I love it here,' Fliss sighed. 'Sometimes when Theo's mother becomes too overbearing I come here to escape for a while. I am a great disappointment to her,' she confided. 'She never misses an opportunity to tell me that Theo could have done so much better for himself.'

'Why?' Adina asked, baffled, and instantly wished that she hadn't. After all, she had barely settled in, so why should Fliss want to confide her personal life to her? From what she had seen of it, Theo and Fliss seemed happy enough, although she couldn't have failed to notice how his mother picked on Fliss at every opportunity.

'It's because I haven't given him a child,' Fliss told her with a catch in her voice. 'We've been married for nearly twelve years now but it's

175

just never happened, and his mother doesn't let me forget it for an instant.'

'Would you both have liked a child?' Adina suddenly felt guilty as she thought of the new life growing inside her.

'Oh yes, we would dearly love a family.' Fliss's voice held a wealth of sadness. 'We've thought of going to a doctor, but . . . Well, it's so embarrassing, isn't it? And if they did tests and we discovered that something was wrong with one of us, it would be awful.'

'Perhaps it will just happen one day when you least expect it to,' Adina said optimistically.

Fliss shook her head. 'I doubt that very much. My time is running out for having a baby now. I'm almost thirty-eight years old. It's rather old to have a first child, don't you think?'

'Well, lots of women I know back in Nuneaton were still having babies in their thirties,' Adina told her, hoping to raise her spirits. They had come to a bench and they sat down on it, enjoying the feel of the crisp September breeze blowing through their hair.

Fliss squeezed her hand affectionately, sensing the kindness in the girl. 'We'll just have to wait and see then, won't we? Theo is a great one for saying what will be will be, and we do still have each other, which is something to be grateful for. There are so many wives in London without their men coming home to them now. I just have to count my blessings.'

In the distance they could hear the sound of the traffic humming along and they sat for a while longer watching a small grey squirrel doing acrobatics in the trees above them. After a while Fliss rose. 'We ought to be thinking of getting back now. We have to face the old witch sometime.' She was smiling despite her harsh words as she told Adina, 'She's not so bad really, but Theo was an only child and I suppose she just wanted to fill the house with grandchildren.'

'That's still not an excuse for her to bully you,' Adina stated.

Fliss chuckled. 'Perhaps you're right. But I do think she's taken a shine to you.'

They moved towards the gates and were soon back at the house, where mouthwatering smells were coming from the direction of the kitchen.

Mrs Leadbetter had prepared them a large cottage pie and a selection of fresh vegetables to go with it, followed by a spicy bread pudding – and this evening even Mrs Montgomery didn't complain – although Adina noticed that she didn't compliment the woman on the meal either.

When they were all finished, Adina insisted on helping the friendly housekeeper with the clearing away and she got her first sight of the kitchen. She followed Mrs Leadbetter through a green baize door at the end of the hallway and then down some steps that led to the basement where the kitchen was situated. It was absolutely enormous and Adina stared about open-mouthed. A huge range stood against one wall with a row of gleaming copper pans suspended above it, and below the window, which looked up to the street above, was the most gigantic stone sink she had ever seen.

'Why, it's absolutely *huge*,' she declared.

Mrs Leadbetter chuckled. 'It certainly is, an' it takes some keepin' clean, I don't mind tellin' you. Not that I'm complainin'. A job is a job, the way I see it, and the Montgomerys are a nice couple. Not that I can say the same for that old harridan of a mother of his. So long as you stand up to her, she's fine. She certainly don't frighten me none. I give as good as I get, as you've probably noticed.'

Adina grinned as she carried the tray of dirty crockery and cutlery to the sink. The long wooden draining board had been scrubbed so much that the wood was almost white, and she realised that Mrs Leadbetter must work very hard indeed to keep the house so neat and tidy.

'Have you worked here for long?' she asked, as she watched the woman fill a great metal kettle and set it on the range to boil.

'Must be seven or eight years now.' The cook swiped a lock of hair that had come loose from the Kirby grips that held it back from her face. 'I come in every morning at half seven to do breakfast an' I leave each evenin' when I've done the washin'-up after dinner. 'Ceptin' for Sundays, that is. The young missus sees to the cookin' on that day.'

'Then why don't you get off early tonight and let me do it,' Adina offered.

'I wouldn't dream of it,' the woman sputtered indignantly. 'Though I wouldn't say no to you givin' me an 'and if you've a mind to.'

And so side by side they set to, and in no time at all the kitchen was gleaming again. Once Mrs Leadbetter had transferred all the clean crockery back onto the enormous pine dresser that stood along one wall she wiped her hands on her apron and stared about with a look of satisfaction on her face. It was apparent that she took a great pride in her work and Adina felt herself warming to her. Mrs Leadbetter had chatted the whole time and Adina learned that she had been born and bred in Camden Town and was extremely proud to be a North Londoner. She told Adina that she had been married to Bill, the love of her life, for twenty-two years until he had died suddenly of a heart attack before the war. She had three sons and two daughters who were all married and living away from home now. Two of her sons had been in the Army, but they were among the lucky ones and were on their way home now that the war was finally over. It made Adina think of Dovi and her heart broke afresh as she pictured him locked away in the asylum. It also made her think of Karl and how much she was missing him. But it couldn't be long now until he came back for her, she comforted herself as Mrs Leadbetter struggled into a coat that had seen better days.

'I'll be off now,' she said. 'Thanks for your 'elp, love. See you in the morning.' And with that she plonked a rather unbecoming hat across her grey hair and bustled off, leaving Adina to wonder what she should do next.

Deciding that this would be a good opportunity to post the letters she had written to her father and Beryl, Adina went to her room to fetch them. She put on her coat and then tapped softly on the door of the drawing room.

'Come in,' a voice invited, and when she stuck her head around the door she saw the old lady dozing in the chair by the fire and Theo and Fliss listening to the radio.

'Can you tell me where the nearest post box is, please?' she asked.

Theo smiled at her. 'Turn right out of the front door. Go to the end of the road and turn left, then right, and you'll come to it. But don't be out too late, will you? It's dark now and we wouldn't want you getting lost. Besides, there are some rather unsavoury characters about at the moment. Would you like me to come with you?'

'No. Thank you, but I'll be fine,' Adina assured him.

It was then that the old lady butted in. So much for her being asleep, Adina thought to herself.

'Famous last words. You're only a scrap of a girl,' she tutted. 'There are looters and all sorts out there. Think you'd be a match for them, do you?'

'I'm perfectly able to take care of myself, thank you,' Adina replied coolly, and with that she went on her way, leaving the old lady with an amused grin on her face.

Half an hour later when she returned, she was passing the drawing room when the woman shouted, 'Here, come in a moment, would you!'

Adina was sorely tempted to ignore her, but when she went into the room she saw that Theo and Fliss were no longer there. 'Was there something you wanted?' she asked.

'Well, of course there is, else I wouldn't have called you in, would I?' The old woman waved her walking stick towards the ceiling. 'Those pair have gone off to bed already. I ask you . . . at their age. Got no stamina, that's their trouble. Could you pour me a glass of sherry? It's over there on that table – look.'

As Adina followed her eyes she saw a crystal decanter full of a ruby-coloured liquid and some cut-glass goblets. She dutifully crossed to them and filled a glass, and as she was handing it to the woman, Mrs Montgomery asked, 'Don't suppose you'd care to join me, would you?'

'Thank you, but no. I don't drink, only on very special occasions.'

'Every day is a special occasion if you wake up in the morning,' the woman said mournfully. 'But then you young ones are all the same. You think you'll live for ever – and then one day you look in the mirror and you're old and good for nothing, and it's not much fun, I don't mind telling you.'

For the first time since meeting her, Adina felt a flicker of sympathy for the old woman and the thought came to her: *I could actually get to quite like her.* Only time would tell.

178

Chapter Thirty-One

During the first two weeks of her new life in London, Adina worked so hard during the day that she barely had time to think, but the nights were a different matter. It was then that a sense of loneliness and desperation for the position she was in almost overwhelmed her. Sometimes after school was over, she and Fliss would go for a long walk as Fliss pointed out places of interest to her. Much of London was one bomb-site after another, with ruins everywhere she looked. Builders were hard at work, but anyone could see that it was going to be a very long job. One night they strolled along the Embankment, but the River Thames was a disappointment. The stench from its muddy shores was nauseating, and as they stood there staring across at St Paul's Cathedral, a dead dog floated by, making Adina retch.

The nights were drawing in now as October fast approached, so the walks were becoming shorter as the women were tempted back to the roaring fire at home in Prince Regent Terrace.

Adina's life had settled into some sort of a routine surprisingly quickly. She would dine with the family and then, after helping Mrs Leadbetter, or Beattie as she insisted Adina should call her, clear away and wash up, she would then spend an hour or so reading poetry or snippets from the newspapers to Mrs Montgomery, who Adina had discovered had once loved to read. The old woman's failing eyesight made it difficult for her now, so Adina was only too happy to oblige her. At present they were working their way through the poems of Elizabeth Browning, and Adina found herself enjoying them almost as much as the old lady did. They had also done some of Shakespeare's *King Lear*, although Adina had found that rather more difficult.

Reading the newspaper had kept Adina abreast of world events in the aftermath of the war, and they had had a lengthy discussion earlier in the month when the Japanese forces in south-east Asia had formally surrendered to Lord Louis Mountbatten, the Supreme Allied Commander. It was then that an estimate of the British war casualties could be given. It was thought that a staggering 60,000 civilians had been killed during air raids and 86,000 badly injured; 420,000 members of the British armed forces had also been killed in action. Rationing was still strictly in force due to global shortages and no one knew how long it would take for everything to return to normal.

It was during these exchanges that the old lady would drop her haughty exterior and let Adina glimpse the more human side of her, although she continued to bully Fliss abysmally and never let her forget for a second that she had failed her by not giving her a grandchild. Luckily, Fliss let it slide over her head for most of the time. She was well-used to the old woman's tantrums by now, but just sometimes Adina detected a tear in her eye after one of these tirades, and she felt sorry for her.

Once the reading was out of the way, Adina would then have a leisurely soak in the indoor bathroom, which was luxury indeed after the tin one she had had to cart into the kitchen once a week back at home in Nuneaton. And then she would retire to her room to read and write letters.

Every day when they returned from the school Adina would check the tray in the hall, hoping to find a letter from Karl, but up to now she had only received one letter from Ariel who assured her that their father was fine. She had actually ventured into the shop to see him, with baby Freda in her pram, hoping that the sight of his first grandchild would allow her back into his life, but she told Adina that he had merely served her politely as he would any other customer and she had gone away feeling despondent.

Adina felt even worse after she read that. If her father would still not forgive Ariel, there was no way he would ever look at her again, once he discovered that she was pregnant by a German.

Her hand slipped to her stomach and tears stung her eyes as she thought of the baby growing there. Fliss had offered to let her go home for the weekend but Adina had made an excuse and told her that she had too much paperwork to catch up on, which wasn't really a lie. She was working very closely with the Red Cross, and that involved a lot of letter-writing. Sadly, only the day before they had received bad news about little Rebekah's family. It appeared that they had all been rounded up and taken to Auschwitz, which meant that they were very probably all dead. But the tracing of the families was only a part of Adina's job. Once it was confirmed that there was no chance of the children being reunited with their parents, she would then have to help decide what would happen to them. Many of the evacuees had been with foster families for almost the whole duration of the war and those families often kindly offered to keep them, but for the other children who were placed in orphanages the future was not so bright. It was all quite heartbreaking.

And now she had an added worry. Over the last two weeks her abdomen had swelled alarmingly, and she was having to fasten her skirts with a safety pin. She had bought herself two baggy oversized cardigans with her clothing coupons, but they would not disguise her condition for much longer and then she had no idea what would happen. No doubt Fliss and Theo would send her home in disgrace. If they didn't, she was certain that the old woman would, so all she could pray

180

for now was that Karl would turn up any day and whisk her and their unborn child away.

She was musing about her plight when a tap came on her bedroom door and Fliss stuck her head around it.

'Adina,' she said, 'Theo and I are going out to visit some friends of ours for a couple of hours. Mother has gone to bed. Will you be all right entertaining yourself, or would you like to come with us?'

'Oh, thank you, but I'll be absolutely fine,' Adina assured her. 'You get off and have a good time, and please don't worry about me. I was planning on an early night anyway.'

'If you're quite sure then.'

Minutes later, Adina heard the front door close and when she peeped from behind the curtain she saw Theo and Fliss climbing into a cab. It was an awful night, with the rain slamming against the windows and the wind howling from above. It was the first time she had ever had the house to herself and so, after tightening the belt of her dressing-gown, she decided to do a little exploring. She was well aware that there were two more floors above her and was curious to see what they were like.

On the landing she paused to make sure that there was no sound coming from the old lady's room below, but everything was as quiet as the grave. She moved along, cautiously opening doors and peeping into the empty rooms but there was little to be seen as most of the furniture inside them was covered in dust sheets – until she came to the last room, and what she found in there made her blink with surprise. It was a nursery, with everything a baby could possibly need arranged inside it. The walls had been painted in soft shades of blue, pink and lemon, and bright curtains hung at the window. A large wooden cot with a pretty white lacy pillow was positioned against one wall, and toys and teddy bears of various shapes and sizes were displayed on a number of shelves. There was a thick warm carpet on the floor and pretty pictures of Beatrix Potter characters displayed on the walls. As Adina ventured inside, her breath caught in her throat and she had to stifle a sob. Poor Fliss must have had this room made ready for the baby she had never borne.

Adina's heart flooded with sympathy for the woman as she thought how unfair life was. Here was she, unmarried and having a baby that had not been planned, when all Fliss wanted in the world was a child of her own and she was unable to have one. Crossing to a large white chest of drawers, Adina carefully opened one drawer and looked inside it. A pile of nappies was arranged on one side of it; a number of tiny nightdresses lovingly folded on the other.

The next drawer revealed a store of little bibs and Liberty Bodices, and Adina closed it, unable to look for a second longer. She suddenly felt very much as if she was intruding on a dream, and badly shaken, she hastily left the room after making sure that everything was exactly as she had found it.

Out on the landing she swiped away the tears from her cheeks and ventured towards the stairs that must lead to the top floor. Now that she had come this far, she reasoned that she might as well see the rest of the house.

The set of stairs that she was climbing now were uncarpeted, and her soft slippers sounded faintly on the bare wooden boards. High above her she could see the tarpaulin that had been secured to what was left of the roof flapping madly in the wind and she felt slightly nervous as she scurried along the landing. The rooms she peeped into up here had no wallpaper on the walls and bare wooden floorboards, and she guessed that in times gone by these would have been the servants' quarters. The rooms were little more than bare cells with no comfort whatsoever, and she tried to imagine the people who must once have slept in them. Another door led into what she discovered was an enormous attic with pieces of discarded furniture and large wooden packing cases strewn haphazardly about. The sound of the wind was deafening up here and it was bitterly cold, so after a very quick exploration Adina hurried back the way she had come, not stopping until she once more came to the landing which her room was on.

'Had a good look round, have you?' a voice asked sarcastically and Adina almost jumped out of her skin. She had been so busy thinking about the nursery that she hadn't noticed old Mrs Montgomery standing there outside her bedroom door.

'I er . . . yes. I went off exploring,' she said guiltily. 'I hope you don't mind?'

'Why should I?' The old lady shrugged. 'I haven't got any bodies hidden or anything to hide. Found the nursery, did you?'

Adina nodded as the old woman sighed. 'Theo did that for Fliss when they first got married. Trouble is, she never gave him anything to put in it.'

'It's very sad.' Adina said the first thing that popped into her head, feeling that some response was necessary. She suddenly wondered how the old lady had managed to get to her room unaided. She had had her suspicions for some time that in actual fact, old Mrs Montgomery could do a lot more than she admitted to – and now those suspicions were confirmed. She had certainly managed to get up here from the first floor without assistance, although she always told Theo that she could not manage the stairs unaided.

'I thought, seeing as those two are out of the way, it would be a good chance for us to have a little chat,' she now said. 'May I come into your room?'

'Of course,' Adina said immediately, wondering what it was she wanted to speak to her about.

Leaning heavily on her cane, the old woman came inside and sat down. She looked approvingly at the neat and tidy room before saying, 'So, is there something you wish to get off your chest?'

Adina flushed to the very roots of her hair. 'Such as what?' she managed to say eventually.

'You know very well what I'm talking about,' the old woman told her sternly. 'I'm on about this here.' She suddenly raised her cane without warning and gently prodded Adina in the stomach as the girl's mouth fell open in a horrified gape.

'I . . . I don't know what you are talking about,' she spluttered as she knocked the cane away indignantly.

'Do you not? Well, just look at those flying past your bedroom window then.'

Adina looked innocently towards the window, falling into the old woman's trap as she said, 'Look at what?'

'That row of purple pigs which just flew past – that's what! You know full well what I'm talking about, my girl. I wasn't born yesterday! You're pregnant, aren't you?'

Adina opened her mouth to deny it, but then she lowered her head in defeat.

'Yes, I am,' she said in a voice so quiet the old lady had to strain to hear it.

'Right, now we've established that, we can talk about it and see how I can help you. Sit down there where I can see you without having to strain my neck.'

As Adina meekly did as she was told, she asked, 'Why would you want to help me?'

'Let's just say that once upon a time, I found myself in the very same position.' The old woman's eyes grew misty as her mind wandered back in time. 'I was born and bred in Camden Town and my family were as poor as church mice,' she went on, and interested now, Adina raised her head and listened intently.

'I was the oldest of eight children and times were hard. I was in service before I was fourteen in a house not far from here, and every week when I got paid I used to go and give my wages to my mother. It was either that or the little ones didn't get to eat. My father was a heavy drinker, and half the money he earned as a furniture remover went straight over the bar of the Leighton pub in Kentish Town on his way home every Friday night. He and my mother had some right old ding-dongs, I don't mind telling you. Anyway, when I got to sixteen I met this sailor at a dance. He was Norwegian and just about the handsomest man I'd ever set eyes on.' She smiled ruefully at the memory. 'From then on, whenever he came to London he would take me out and treat me like a queen. And then one day I found out I was pregnant. I had to wait six weeks until he was back in London again, and when I told him he promised me he'd sort things out. He said he was going back home to make arrangements for me, and then we'd be married . . . That was the last I ever saw of him.'

Mrs Montgomery took a handkerchief from the pocket of her dress and blew her nose on it loudly. 'I was absolutely terrified of my father finding out. He was very strict with us, you see, and fond of using his belt. Anyway, one day my father was off work sick, and as I had just taken my wages round to my mother I offered to fetch his for him. My dear I'll never forget that day, for as long as I live. When I got to the yard where my father worked, his boss called me into his office. He'd always been very kind to the family and we were all fond of him. He always made sure that the children had a little gift for under the tree at Christmas, and when things were really tough he would slip my mother an extra shilling or two without my father knowing. Anyway, this day I'd been crying as I was starting to show and I knew that I couldn't hide my condition for much longer. I didn't know which way to turn and I was scared out of my wits.'

The old lady paused to look at Adina. 'You wouldn't think so now, but back then I was a bit of a head-turner. In fact, so much so that my father always told me it would be my downfall – and he wasn't far wrong. Anyway I went into the boss's office and straight away he saw that I'd been crying and he made me sit down while he brought me a cup of tea, bless him. Before I knew what I was doing I'd blurted every-thing out to him – he was so easy to talk to, you see? And that's when it happened: he'd lost his wife a couple of years before, and out of the blue he offered to marry me and bring up the child I was carrying as his own. He and his wife had never had any children, and he was keen to have an heir to inherit the business. Well, I don't mind telling you – you could have knocked me down with a feather! He was fifty-six years old and I was just sixteen, but what choice did I have? It was either that or be thrown out onto the streets when my father found out, and what would have happened to the baby then? So quick as a flash I agreed to it, and although I couldn't have known it then and I married him for all the wrong reasons, in time I grew to love the very bones of the man. He was the salt of the earth and he treated me like royalty. I shall never forget the look on his face the day Theodore was born, not for as long as I live. He looked as if I'd given him the greatest gift of all, which I suppose in a way I had. He and Theo had a wonderful relationship until the day William died, so there you have it. You're not the only one to wind up in the family way without a ring on your finger, and I'll warrant you won't be the last.' Old Mrs Montgomery heaved a sigh. 'The thing is now, what are we going to do about it? Who is the father? Will he stand by you?'

'Oh yes,' Adina assured her quickly. 'I'm waiting for him to come for me and then we'll be married.'

'Come for you?' the old woman asked, thinking the scenario sounded all too familiar.

'Well, the thing is, Karl had to go back to Germany to—'

'*Stop right there.*' The other woman held her hand up in horror. 'Are you telling me that *you*, a Jewish girl, are pregnant by a *German*?'

Slowly Adina began to tell her the whole story, and as it unfolded, Mrs Montgomery's eyes narrowed.

'Can't you see, girl?' she said harshly. 'He isn't coming back.'

'Oh yes he is!' Adina shot back, unable to face the alternative. 'Karl loves me, I *know* he does.'

The woman watched the different emotions flitting across the girl's face. After a time, she asked quietly, 'And what are you going to do if he doesn't come back?'

'I . . . I don't know.' Suddenly Adina was sobbing.

There is a solution to this mess, you know,' Mrs Montgomery said eventually, and when Adina raised tearstained eyes to look at her, she went on, 'You could give the baby to Theo and Fliss.'

When Adina leaped up and opened her mouth to protest, the woman silenced her with a glare. 'At least hear me out,' she said sternly. 'After my husband died I eventually sold the business. Theo wasn't quite old enough to take it over, and it fetched more money than I could ever spend in a lifetime. In two lifetimes, if it came to that. If you were to give the baby to my son and his wife, I would see that you had enough money to set you up for life.'

'You are asking me to *sell* my baby?' Adina breathed disbelievingly.

'Oh, don't be so melodramatic!' the old woman snapped. 'I'm offering you and the baby a solution, *that's* what I'm doing. The child would never want for anything, and you would be free to build a new life for yourself. What could *you* offer the child? Love doesn't put food on the table or clothes on your back, you know, and how will you manage?'

Adina's head wagged from side to side vehemently. 'This is *our* baby,' she declared. 'Mine and Karl's. And he *will* come for me. You just see if he doesn't!'

Shrugging, the old woman stood up and hobbled away. 'Yes, I'm afraid we *will* see,' she said softly as she closed the door behind her.

Adina stood there; her hands clenching and unclenching as she tried to deny what Mrs Montgomery had prophesied. Karl *would* come for her, she just knew it. It was the only hope she had left to cling on to.

Chapter Thirty-Two

The atmosphere in the house was somewhat strained for the next few days, although Adina thought that Mrs Montgomery had not told Theo and Fliss of her condition as neither of them had mentioned it.

As she and Fliss arrived home late one afternoon, her eyes instantly fell to the tray in the hall where Beattie put the mail, and she pounced on an envelope that was addressed to her. It was Beryl's handwriting – she would have recognised it anywhere even without the USA stamps.

'It's from my friend in America,' she told Fliss, her eyes shining. 'Would you mind very much if I went up to my room to read it before dinner?'

'Of course not,' Fliss told her indulgently. She had grown fond of Adina although she wished sometimes that she would go out a little more with people her own age. The way she saw it, the girl was too young to be stuck in with them every night, and it was nice to know that she had a friend, even if the friend was in America.

Adina shot away up the stairs and in no time at all she had ripped the letter open and was gleefully scanning the pages. Almost at once she sensed that this was the Beryl she knew writing to her, and not the one who had seemed to be choosing her words carefully since going to America. But in no time at all the smile died on her lips as she read on.

I thought I was coming out to live on some stud ranch like you see on the movies, with Tye's well-to-do parents. But in no time I realised that he had been lying to me. The baby and I are living in what amounts to little more than a ghetto. There is barely room to swing a cat around and the place is so damp and dirty I fear for Catherine's health. Tye's mother hates me and shouts at me and the baby all the time. Oh Adina, how could I have been such a fool? Tye is barely at home and when he does come back he smells of other women's perfume, and treats me like a skivvy. What am I to do? I feel I shall go mad, stuck here so far away from everyone I care about. I am so sorry to burden you with my troubles but I have no one else I can talk to and I feel so alone.

Adina read the letter right through twice and then slowly folded it and replaced it in the envelope. She hated to think of her friend being so unhappy, but what could she do about it? She had been diligently saving

186

her wages since coming to London for things that she would need for the baby, but even if she were to send Beryl every penny she possessed, she doubted that it would be enough to cover her fare home – if she could get a ticket, that was. She thought back to the suspicions she had had about Tyrone and wished that she had told Beryl about them at the time. But then commonsense took over and she knew that it would have made no difference, even if she had. Beryl had been blindly, madly in love, just as she was with Karl, and she would never have believed anything untoward that anyone said about him.

Sighing, she placed the letter in a drawer, and went down to join the family for dinner.

'You're very quiet this evening. Is everything all right?' Fliss asked as she loaded a succulent piece of lamb – from chops that Beattie had somehow managed to obtain – onto her fork. As usual Adina was merely toying with her meal, although Fliss wasn't overly concerned. She must be getting enough food, she reasoned, because she seemed to have put a little weight on.

'What . . . oh yes, thank you. Everything is fine,' Adina replied as she glanced at the old woman. Mrs Montgomery said nothing as she continued to eat. It was so nice to have something other than chicken or mince for dinner, and she intended to savour every single mouthful.

It was almost two hours later, when the kitchen was tidy again and Beattie had gone home after a hard day's work, that Adina joined the old woman in the drawing room.

'What would you like me to read to you this evening?' Adina asked, as her eyes scanned the bookcase.

Mrs Montgomery patted the seat at the side of her. 'Nothing for now, thank you dear, but I would like to talk to you.'

Reluctantly, Adina perched next to her as the old woman studied her solemn face. 'Have you thought any more about what we talked about?' she asked, and when Adina stiffened, she squeezed her hand. 'I know it isn't easy, my dear. But you mustn't just think of yourself. You must think of the baby. Whatever you decide to do, I think it is time we informed Theo and Fliss of your condition. You should see a doctor or a midwife to check that all is well with the child. You owe it that much, at least.'

When Adina sighed resignedly, Mrs Montgomery smiled with relief. 'Right, leave it to me,' she told her. 'I shall speak to them this very evening when you have gone to bed, and tomorrow, Fliss will arrange for you to see a doctor. A visit is long overdue already – and who knows what might happen to the baby if you don't go soon. Are you agreeable to that?'

Adina nodded. She could not go on trying to hide her condition for much longer, and in a way it would be a relief when the others knew. At least then she wouldn't have to keep lying to them.

Fliss and Theo took the news remarkably well. In fact, far better than Adina had dared to hope. True to Mrs Montgomery's word, Fliss made an appointment for Adina to see the doctor that very afternoon and after school she walked there with her to keep it.

The surgery was a dismal place with peeling paint and damp plaster on the walls, but the doctor was kindly enough as he examined Adina.

'I think the baby will come sometime early in February, but everything seems fine,' he assured her. 'I'm going to get the nurse to do a routine blood test before you leave and then I want to see you again in four weeks' time.'

Once back out on the pavement again, Fliss glanced at her, unable to keep the envy from her eyes.

'I wish it was me,' she said before she could stop herself, and then immediately blushed. 'I'm sorry,' she ended lamely.

'Don't be. In some ways I wish it was you too,' Adina told her as she fingered the band of steel hanging about her neck. It seemed pointless to wear it there now, she thought. Her father was not there to see it or question who had given it to her, so she slipped it off the chain and placed it onto the third finger of her left hand where it shone dully in the late-afternoon light. She still believed for the majority of the time that Karl *would* come for her, but sometimes now – just sometimes – she questioned what she would do if he didn't. Once the baby was born and she was no longer working, she would have no income and nowhere to live, and the thought was terrifying. What would happen to them both then? And so she clung ferociously to the belief that Karl had spoken the truth and that he really did intend to return. But it would have to be soon. There were less than three months to go until the baby was born – and what if he had decided to marry the fiancée he had left in his homeland instead? She pushed the thought away. Karl was an honourable man, she would have staked her life on it, and if he had decided to do that, he would have written and told her.

Over the next two weeks her waistline suddenly seemed to explode outwards. It was if the baby had sensed that he or she no longer had to hide and was taking full advantage of the fact.

'I feel like a duck,' she groaned to Fliss on their way to work one day. 'I'm not walking any more, I'm waddling.'

'All part of being pregnant, so I'm told,' Fliss said stoically. The night before she had sat on the settee with her hand on Adina's stomach as the baby kicked, and suddenly she couldn't wait for it to be born.

'Have you thought what you will do once the baby is born?' she asked now, and Adina flicked her hair over her shoulder as she replied, 'I shall be married to the baby's father by then. It can't be much longer until he comes for me.'

'But what will you do if he *doesn't* come?' Fliss probed gently, hating to hurt her but knowing that it could not be avoided. When Adina failed to answer her, she went on, 'Theo and I think you should stay with us after the birth, for a while at least, until you decide what to do.'

'I couldn't do that,' Adina retorted with what pride she could muster. 'I couldn't expect you and Theo to keep me *and* a baby, and it will be a little while until I can work again.'

'But we would like you to stay with us,' Fliss told her kindly. 'It would be lovely to have a baby in the house. Of course,' she rushed on as Adina turned to look at her steadily, 'we are well aware that it is *your* baby and we wouldn't want to interfere or anything. We just want to help. To be honest, at home there is a nursery all ready that you could use. We did it many years ago, hoping that we would have a child of our own to put in there one day, but sadly it never happened for us. So what do you say? Will you think of staying? If Karl isn't here by then,' she added hastily.

Adina refrained from telling her that she had already seen the nursery. Fliss's offer was like the answer to a prayer. And she would be able to pay her way once she got back to work – when she had found someone reliable with whom she could leave the baby.

'I'll think about it. And thanks for the very kind offer,' she said, and the subject was not mentioned again.

Over the next four weeks, Adina received another letter from Beryl and also one from her father and one from Ariel, but still nothing from Karl. It was almost the end of November by then and Christmas was fast approaching. Fliss had taken to going off on shopping jaunts each weekend and when she got home she would press baby clothes onto Adina. 'I wish we knew what it was,' she told her excitedly. 'Have you thought of any names yet?'

'No, I thought I would wait for Karl to get here,' Adina replied and Fliss's kind heart ached for her as she exchanged a worried glance with Theo. It was becoming more and more apparent to them that Karl was not going to come. He hadn't even written to Adina, but they didn't say that, of course. They had no wish to hurt her more than she was hurting already.

In mid-December Fliss insisted that Adina should stop working. Her hands and feet had swollen so much that she could not have taken Karl's ring off even if she had wanted to. She seemed to be tired all the time although thankfully the pregnancy was progressing with no complications. Fliss informed her that she was going to take a few months off work too to keep her eye on her, and Adina nodded silently, realising that there would be no point in arguing. Fliss was so excited about the baby it might have been her own she was expecting.

That weekend, Theo went out and came back with a Christmas tree that Fliss and Adina spent a pleasant couple of hours decorating whilst Mrs Montgomery looked on.

That evening, Theo and Fliss took Adina to the cinema and for two hours she was able to lose herself in the magic of *The Wizard of Oz*. She was totally entranced with the Wicked Witch, the Tin Man, Cowardly Lion and all the other wonderful characters in the film.

'Dorothy is a pretty name, isn't it?' Adina said musingly to Theo and Fliss as they walked home through the frosty streets that night.

'Yes, it is pretty,' Fliss agreed, glancing at her husband. Up until now, Adina had refused to even discuss names, adamant that it was something she and Karl should do together, but now Fliss wondered if Adina's hopes of him coming back to Britain in time for the birth were finally fading.

The pavements were like a skating rink and Fliss clung to Adina's arm, frightened that she might slip and hurt the unborn baby. She was looking forward to its arrival even more than Adina was, for the girl was in a deep depression for most of the time now and would stand gazing from the window longing for the sight of Karl striding along the street.

Theo had offered to find her a synagogue, where she could attend a weekly service, but Adina had declined. Sometimes she even doubted if there really was a God, after all that had happened in the world at large and to her own family in the last few years. She wondered about her father, all alone back in Nuneaton, and whether it was cold where Karl was. Was he thinking about her? Was he on his way to fetch her even now? Or had he forgotten all about her and married the girl he had been engaged to? As they passed beneath a streetlight his ring gleamed on her finger and she gulped to hold back the tears that were threatening to choke her.

Two more letters arrived for her in the days that followed, and she read them greedily. One was from Ariel, who informed her that the week before, during yet another visit to the shop, her father had spoken to her and even glanced into the pram and asked after the baby. Ariel felt as if it was a major step forward and hoped that this was the beginning of a reconciliation. The second was from her father, and as she read it the joy she had felt after reading Ariel's letter was snatched away. He wrote:

I deeply regret to inform you that your brother passed away on the nineteenth of December. He was found hanged in his cell at the asylum and we can now only pray that his soul is in Olam Haba. The hospital respected the wishes of our faith and he was buried in the grounds of the asylum within twenty-four hours, although it is sad that he could not have been buried in a Jewish cemetery. I am so sorry I could not get word to you sooner but I know you will pray with me that he has now finally found peace.

Adina gasped, and her hand flew to her throat. Poor Dovi. And what a terrible way to die. But then surely he was better off wherever he was now than being incarcerated in that awful place, being sedated until he was nothing more than a zombie.

Hot tears slid down her cheeks as she recalled happier times. She could see Dovi in her mind's eye, chasing her around the settee as her mother sternly told him to stop teasing her. She could feel him holding her hand as she timidly stepped into the lake in Cologne for her first swimming lesson. Now he was holding the back of her bicycle as she wobbled along, learning to balance. She could see his thick mane of hair and his laughing dark eyes as clearly as if he was in the room with her, and although her heart ached for the brother she had loved so much and lost, a part of her was relieved that his suffering was finally over.

Theo, Fliss and even Mrs Montgomery were very sympathetic when she told them of her brother's death, and spoiled her shamelessly, or at least they tried to but Adina would not allow it.

'I'm quite all right really,' she told Fliss when the latter brought yet another cup of tea up to her room. 'In a way, it's a blessing in disguise. The Dovi who came home from the war was not the same person who left us. Funnily enough, I think I did most of my grieving for him when he returned, because I knew I was never going to get back the brother I had lost.'

Fliss had asked Adina if she would like them all to wear black as a mark of respect, but Adina had assured them that she had no wish to spoil their Christmas and that they were to go on exactly as before. She knew that back in Nuneaton her father would wear a black armband for at least three months. She had written to tell him that she would not be returning home during the school's Christmas holiday because of the amount of work that needed doing, and that she hoped he would understand. She would try to manage a short trip home as soon as was possible. She still wasn't quite sure how she was going to do this, but for now she had more important things to worry about; she would cross that bridge when she came to it.

On Christmas morning Adina was overwhelmed when the family presented her with a number of beautifully wrapped gifts. There was a fine silk scarf in a beautiful shade of pale green from Mrs Montgomery, a manicure set in a lovely little leather wallet from Fliss and Theo that

Adina immediately announced was far too lovely to use, and a pair of warm hand-knitted gloves in bright red wool from Beattie. The latter was spending the day with her grown-up family and grandchildren, but she had prepared the Christmas dinner right down to the very last detail the day before, and now all Fliss and Adina had to do was pop the turkey into the oven and cook the vegetables.

Adina tried hard all morning to be cheerful as she had no wish to spoil their day, but sometimes it was hard as she thought of Dovi lying beneath the earth so far away from them all.

The Christmas dinner was like nothing she had ever experienced before. They pulled crackers and listened to Christmas carols on the wireless, and then when the main meal was over Fliss carried in the most enormous plum pudding that Adina had ever seen. When she sank her spoon into it she found a shiny silver sixpence and looked at Fliss bewildered.

The woman laughed as she told her, 'You've got the wish. Now close your eyes and wish for something you really want. Keep it a secret, mind.'

Adina did as she was bid, although none of them were in any doubt whatsoever what she would be wishing for. They all knew that she would be wishing for Karl to come for her, and being as fond of her as they had become, they too wished it might come true.

Chapter Thirty-Three

On the day after New Year's Day 1946, Adina woke to an eerie silence. Normally the distant hum of traffic woke her but today there was nothing but the soft sound of her own breathing. Struggling to the edge of the bed, she got up and crossed to the window, only to find that the ice on the inside of it had formed a lacelike pattern. She blew on it and rubbed at it with the sleeve of her nightgown, and once she had cleared a circle just big enough to look through, she peered out and caught her breath in wonder. The ugly sooty rooftops of Camden Town and the piles of rubble were gone, and instead she was staring at a bright new world. Overnight it had snowed, and everywhere was transformed.

Downstairs, she found Theo holding his head and sighing dramatically.

'Don't have any sympathy for him,' Fliss told her as she entered the dining room. 'He had far too much to drink at that party we went to last night. We all ended up in Trafalgar Square to welcome the New Year in, and His Lordship here can't even remember it.' There was an affectionate twinkle in her eye as she spoke.

'Serves him right then.' Old Mrs Montgomery was breakfasting downstairs for once. She dipped a bread and butter soldier into her second soft-boiled egg, mumbling, 'Self-inflicted wound.'

Fliss and Adina grinned at each other as Adina helped herself to a cup of coffee. She had completely lost her appetite over the last few days, though it was hardly surprising. The baby was so huge now she doubted if there was any room for food in there with it.

'Just try and eat a bit of toast or something,' Fliss implored her. 'You are eating for two, you know.'

'Huh! The size of this, I reckon I could be eating for half a dozen,' Adina grumbled as she patted her stomach, but she did attempt a slice of toast just to placate Fliss, who she knew meant well. The nursery was now ready and aired, and the numerous blankets, shawls and baby clothes up there were fit for a prince or princess.

Both Theo and Fliss had spent an awful lot of money on the baby already and Adina wondered how she was ever going to repay them. Thankfully, Mrs Montgomery had never again raised the matter of them adopting the child, and Adina was grateful for that because, had she done so, Adina would have had no choice but to leave. She loved the child even before it was born, because she knew that if Karl didn't return, it would be all she would ever have of him – not that she had completely given up hope. There was still time, she told herself daily. And there were still almost five weeks to go until the baby was due to be born. He would come . . . unless something had happened to him?

'And what do you think of the snow then?' Fliss asked as she placed a rasher of bacon and a fat sausage on her plate. Adina sometimes wondered where Beattie managed to get such treats, with food being in such short supply, but then the Montgomerys were hardly short of a bob or two and it seemed that nothing was impossible if you had money, except for a child of their own, that was.

Theo groaned as the smell of the food wafted towards him, and he staggered away from the table with his hand over his mouth, much to his wife's amusement. 'Serves him right. Now what was I saying? Oh yes, the weather. Theo and I thought we might go for a walk in Regent's Park after dinner. Would you like to come with us?'

When Adina hesitated she rushed on, 'I'm sure the fresh air will do you good, so long as you wrap up warmly. Oh, *do* say that you'll come.'

'All right then.' Adina had discovered some time ago that it was useless to argue with Fliss when she had her mind set on something, so she decided to give in gracefully. In actual fact the thought of a walk in the snow was quite appealing. And as the morning wore on she began to look forward to it. At eleven o'clock she went to her room for a lie-down as she often did nowadays, and her head had barely hit the pillow before she fell into a restless sleep. It was full of dreams of her family and Beryl and Karl, and when she woke up three-quarters of an hour later she was more drained than when she had lain down.

They had cold meat and pickle left over from New Year's Day for their lunch, and then Adina put her coat on and met Theo and Fliss in the hallway. Theo was feeling slightly better by then. 'Sorry about this morning. I'm afraid I was a bit the worse for wear,' he told Adina sheepishly.

Adina chuckled. 'Everyone has the right to let their hair down once in a while,' she told him. She had even more respect for Fliss and Theo now, since she had learned how wealthy they were. They had absolutely no need to earn a living, but chose to work at the school out of a genuine concern for the children there, which Adina felt was pretty remarkable.

Theo had pulled a large sledge out of the garden shed, and, placing it in the boot of his car, he drove to Hampstead Heath.

'There are bound to be some kids there who will like a go on this,' he told the women, and again Adina found herself thinking what a kind man he was.

The Heath was alive with families and dogs, all taking the air and enjoying the snow. The trees were bowing beneath the weight of the snow that had settled on them, and the lake near Kenwood House had

194

become a silver skating rink, where excited children skidded from one side to another.

''Ere, give us a go on yer sled, mate,' a little boy shouted, and whilst Adina and Fliss wiped the snow from the seat of a bench and sat down, Theo began to tow the boy along. A little further away was a sharp rise, and soon the children were forming queues to have a ride on the sled as Theo looked on indulgently.

'You know, Theo bought that sled years ago for the children that we thought we would have,' Fliss told Adina nostalgically. 'When we first got married we intended to fill the house with children – but it wasn't meant to be, was it? Life is a funny thing when you come to think about it and not always kind.'

Adina nodded in agreement as the child inside her began to wiggle about. She felt so guilty sometimes that she was the one having a child and not Fliss. She suddenly wondered for the first time who the baby would resemble. Would the child be dark-haired like herself or fair like his or her father? Would he or she have brown eyes or blue ones like Karl's? She stroked her stomach and fell silent as she dreamed of holding their child in her arms. It couldn't come quickly enough for her now. She was tired of waddling about and just wanted it to be over and done with.

Two hours later they set off for home, rosy-cheeked and pleasantly tired. Fliss had been right: Adina felt that the fresh air had done her good and hoped she would sleep well that night.

That evening, as she sat reading the newspaper to Mrs Montgomery, the old woman listened intently. It seemed that now the New Year was over there was going to be a massive number of properties built to house the people who had lost their homes during the war. Many of them were going to be temporary pre-fabricated houses in the cities that had been worst affected by the war, and in Hull alone it was estimated that 30,000 would be needed. The new homes had been nicknamed 'prefabs' and Mrs Montgomery sniffed as Adina read on.

'Prefabs indeed,' she scoffed. 'Why can't they just build *proper* houses?'

'Because it would cost too much and take too long to build them,' Theo cut in. 'Even the prefabs won't be ready for people to move into until 1948 or 1949.'

'Well, I'll just be grateful when we can railroad a builder who's prepared to mend our roof,' the old lady said with a toss of her chin, and they all laughed.

'Yes, but aren't we the lucky ones to still *have* our own home?' Theo said.

Adina supposed that they were lucky in a way. Herself in particular. They had taken her in and kept her with them through her darkest hour, and she would never forget that.

* * *

By mid-January the snow began to thaw and the roads and pavements became slushy underfoot. Fliss was like a mother hen, fussing over Adina.

'Now promise me you won't go out today,' she warned Adina each morning. 'It's so slippy and I don't want you falling and bringing the baby too soon.'

'I won't,' Adina would promise, although she was beginning to feel like a prisoner. She had barely ventured out of the house since the day they had taken the sled to the Heath, not that she could have walked very far now. She was tired all the time and more than a little irritable, not that anyone seemed to mind.

By the beginning of February, Adina prayed daily for the baby to put in an appearance. 'How much *longer* is it going to be?' she wailed to Mrs Simmons, the midwife who had come to check on her.

The woman chuckled. 'Babies have a habit of coming when they've a mind to and not before,' she said cheerfully, 'but it shouldn't be too long now. You're carrying very low, which is a sign the baby is getting into position ready to be born. Have you got your bags packed ready for the hospital?'

'Everything has been ready for the last two weeks,' Adina rejoined pettishly as she folded her arms over the huge mound that had used to be her flat stomach.

'Good – well, if nothing happens before, I shall see you at the same time next week.' The midwife snapped her little black bag shut. 'But at the first sign of anything beginning, make sure you get Theo or Fliss to take you to the hospital.'

Theo and Fliss had both tried to talk her into having a home birth but Adina had stood her ground. She felt that she would be safer at the Elizabeth Garrett Anderson Hospital, and so they had gone along with her wishes. She now watched glumly as Nurse Simmons left with a bright smile, and turned her attention back to the book she was trying to read. However, nothing seemed to hold her attention for long at present so she began to wander around the house, rubbing her back as she went.

That evening the baby became very still and Adina was relieved. She had had a dull ache in the pit of her back since teatime but decided that it was probably due to all the extra weight she was lugging around.

She had just had a nice leisurely soak in the bath and was in her bedroom drying her hair with a towel when there was a tap at the door.

It was Fliss: she seemed to be checking up on Adina all the time now. She stopped in her tracks as she stared at the lovely bridal gown that was spread out across the bed.

'What's this then?' She crossed to finger the heavy silk admiringly.

'I made it when I lived at home for when Karl and I get married,' Adina informed her, and then she chuckled. 'Not that I could squeeze into it now, but one day . . .'

'But I had no idea that you could sew like this,' Fliss gasped. 'It looks like something you would buy in Bond Street. It's haute couture.'

It *was* a beautiful gown – and Adina knew how lovely it looked on because Ariel had already worn it.

'I like to get it out and look at it from time to time,' she explained. 'It reminds me of Karl.'

Fliss gazed in awe at the dress. The skirt fell to the floor in shimmering folds; Adina had spent hours sewing tiny seed pearls all around the neckline, and Fliss thought it was one of the most stunning gowns she had ever seen.

'You'll wear it one day,' she assured Adina kindly. 'But come on now. It's time you were having a lie-down. We don't want you overdoing things.'

She helped Adina to refold the dress and transfer it back into the suitcase and then fussed over her as she turned the eiderdown back and plumped up the pillows. Once she was satisfied that Adina was comfortable she crossed to the door and waggled a finger at her. 'Now if you need anything during the night you just call, OK?'

Adina nodded as she settled back against the feather pillows. She hadn't been sleeping well for a while now as she was so enormous it was hard to get comfortable.

Something woke her during the early hours of the morning and she lay there disorientated for a moment trying to think what it was. And then she felt the damp sheet beneath her and gasped in horror. She had wet the bed! Something she had not done since she was a very little girl. Struggling to the edge of the mattress, she stood up and began to strip off the wet sheet. It was then that a sudden pain ripped through her. It was so sharp that it almost took her breath away, and her eyes widened in shock as it finally began to subside.

Could this be the baby coming? Deciding to be on the safe side, she put her dressing-gown on and lumbered down to the first floor where Theo and Fliss slept. She hated to disturb them but was so nervous that she did not want to be alone. After tapping softly at the bedroom door she heard sounds of movement from within and seconds later Fliss peeped out bleary-eyed and yawning.

'I . . . I think the baby may be coming,' Adina told her. Instantly Fliss was wide awake and, grinning from ear to ear, she flew back to the large double bed and shook Theo's arm.

'Theo, *wake up*,' she urged. 'Adina thinks she has gone into labour. We need you to get her to the hospital.'

The midwife had also discussed the possibility of having a home birth, but Adina had refused. Now she wasn't so sure and she told Fliss so as the latter helped her back to her room. Suddenly the thought of giving birth amongst strangers was terrifying and she wanted to stay with her friends.

'Well, I suppose I could always send Theo round to the midwife's house in Chalk Farm to ask her if she'd deliver the baby here,' Fliss said. 'Are you sure that's what you want?'

Adina nodded. The pains in her back were excruciating and she was very afraid now.

Theo was up and dressed within minutes and whilst he rushed off with his hair uncombed to try and locate the midwife, Fliss sat Adina in a chair at the side of the bed and deftly changed the sheets.

Half an hour later, Theo was back, panting as if the devil were on his heels.

'Nurse Simmons is on her way,' he informed a relieved Adina. 'She said she just had to get dressed and then she'd come on her bicycle. What would you like me to do now?'

Fliss looked more nervous than Adina as she chewed on her nails, but eventually she told him, 'Well, I don't know much about this sort of thing, never having given birth myself, but I believe we're going to need lots of clean towels and hot water. If you go and fetch the towels, Theo, I'll run down and get the water on the go.'

Without a word Theo turned on his heel and rushed off to do as he was told. Fliss then patted Adina's hand distractedly and hurried away down two flights to the kitchen to fill the kettle and any other utensils she could find. When she was satisfied that they were all heating up nicely she rushed into the hall where she could hear the doorbell ringing. It was Nurse Simmons.

'So how is Mother coming along?' she asked jovially.

Fliss wrung her hands. 'I have no idea. I've never done this sort of thing before,' she said in a small voice. 'But shouldn't you be getting upstairs to Adina? She's in a lot of pain.'

'Don't look so worried,' the nurse chuckled as she slipped her coat off. 'Nothing is going to happen in the next two minutes. First babies usually take their time. It could be hours yet. Now I'm going to need clean sheets, towels and as much hot water as you can supply me with.'

Fliss hurried away to grab an armful of sheets from the enormous walk-in linen cupboard as Nurse Simmons strode purposefully towards the stairs. By the time she delivered them to the nurse, the latter was bending over the bed and examining Adina, so Fliss hastily averted her eyes.

'That's fine,' the woman said encouragingly as she pulled Adina's nightdress back down.

Fliss scuttled away like a frightened rabbit to see if any of the water was boiling yet and almost bumped into Theo on the stairs. He looked nearly as terrified as she did.

'How is she?' he asked.

'Fine, I think. Did you take the towels in?'

'No.' He looked embarrassed. 'I didn't like to, so I left them on the landing outside her door.'

'Right, then you go and fill the big jug I've put ready in the kitchen with boiling water and bring it up here and I'll run back and take the towels in.'

Ten minutes later, the midwife had everything she needed. 'Why don't you two go back to bed now?' she suggested. 'I'll fetch you if anything happens.'

They shook their heads in unison, knowing they would never get back to sleep now with a new life about to come into the world.

'We'll be in the drawing room if you need us,' Fliss gulped, and grabbing Theo's elbow she hauled him away.

Upstairs, Nurse Simmons eyed the girl on the bed curiously. She was a pretty little thing and she wondered if she was related to Theo and Fliss. They certainly seemed very fond of her – but where was the husband? The girl was wearing a wedding band and she had already called out for someone called Karl, so the woman could only assume that she was married. Unless he had been killed in the war, that was, and she was a widow, otherwise he would have been here surely? So many babies she had delivered over the last few years had been born without their fathers ever seeing them. It was enough to break your heart.

Adina's back suddenly arched as a strong contraction gripped her and the nurse approached the bed, glancing at the clock on the bedside table. It was one forty-five and it looked as if it was going to be a very long night.

Chapter Thirty-Four

By eight-thirty the following morning, Fliss and Theo had been joined by Beattie and old Mrs Montgomery in the drawing room. Theo had paced the floor like a caged animal all through the night, glancing up towards the ceiling as if his thoughts could somehow hurry the birth along.

No one had wanted breakfast although Beattie had already made endless pots of tea since she had arrived.

Fliss looked as if she might burst into tears at any second and sat right on the edge of her seat, ready to fly upstairs should she be needed.

'For God's sake, Theo! Will you *please* sit down?' Mrs Montgomery said irritably. 'Anyone would think *you* were the expectant father, the way you're carryin' on! You'll wear a hole in the carpet at this rate.'

Theo was just about to do as he was told when a penetrating scream from above faintly reached them. Fliss became a shade paler still, if that was possible, as they all glanced at each other. And then the waiting continued until at last the door opened and a weary Nurse Simmons smiled at them as she wiped her hands on her apron.

'It's a little girl,' she told them. 'And mother and baby are both doing well. She's a bonny little thing, as I think you'll agree when you see her, and Mum did really well for her first baby. She's got some courage, that one. Now, who would like to go up first? I don't want her tired out, mind.'

'We will,' Theo and Fliss said together and hastily followed the midwife as she set off back up the stairs.

The sight that met their eyes when they entered Adina's bedroom took their breath away. The midwife had washed both mum and baby and changed the bed, and now Adina was settled back against her pillows with a wide smile on her face and a tiny bundle cuddled to her chest. Her face was so serene that it brought tears to Fliss's eyes and a rush of envy the like of which she had never experienced before. She knew then that she would have given the whole world to be in Adina's place.

They approached the bed as Adina pulled aside the snow-white shawl that Beattie had knitted as her gift to the baby, and they looked down on a mop of blonde hair. The child looked nothing like Adina and they could only assume that she took after her father. Her hair was so fair that it was almost white, and her eyes were the colour of bluebells. Her skin was like porcelain and Fliss was sure that she had never seen such a beautiful child in the whole of her life.

200

'Oh, Adina,' she breathed. 'She's *absolutely* lovely.'

'*Perfect* is the word,' Adina replied as she stared at her brand new daughter in awe. She felt as if she might burst with pride and could scarcely believe that this precious child was really hers.

Theo was temporarily lost for words and simply reached out to touch the tiny hand that curled over the edge of the shawl. His eyes were full of tears and he smiled at Adina, who seemed to understand the many emotions that were tearing through him. It had been much the same for her when the midwife had first shown the baby to her. She suddenly felt as if she had waited her whole life for this moment and knew that nothing else would ever compare with it.

'M . . . may I hold her?' Fliss asked, and somewhat reluctantly Adina put her tiny bundle into the woman's waiting arms.

'Oh *Theo*,' she murmured, as he put his arm about them both.

Adina experienced her first pang of alarm. They looked like a little family standing there, but this was *her* baby!

'Right, I suggest you get a nice hot cup of tea sent up for Mother now,' the midwife told the couple, breaking the spell. 'And hand the child back to Mum now, please. We don't want anything to interfere with mother and baby bonding.'

Adina sighed with relief as Fliss relinquished the baby back into her arms, then the couple left the room as the midwife began to tidy up and prepare to leave.

'I shall be back to see you later in the morning,' she told Adina. 'Meanwhile, make sure you do as I told you. I don't want you to even think of setting foot out of that bed. You need your rest now and there are enough people here to look after you. Do you hear me, young lady?'

'Yes, Nurse Simmons. And thank you so much,' Adina replied meekly.

With a final smile the midwife left the room and now for the first time since the birth Adina had her few special moments alone with her daughter.

'Hello, bubbeleh,' she whispered. 'I am your mummy and we are going to be *so* happy together. One day your daddy will come for us, but until then it will be just us two.'

Although she was feeling Karl's absence more than she could say, she somehow knew in that moment that the most important person in the whole world was now lying in her arms, and she swore softly to herself that nothing and no one would ever part them.

'So what are you going to call her then?' Fliss asked later that day as she placed a tray of food on Adina's lap.

'I thought I would call her Dorothy,' Adina replied.

Fliss clapped her hands with delight. 'That's lovely!' she cried. 'And we can call her little Dottie for short.'

Adina experienced a pang of resentment. Dorothy was *her* baby and *she* should decide if her name was to be shortened or not. But then she felt ashamed. Fliss and Theo had done so much for her; in fact, she didn't know how she would have managed without them. It was only natural that they should want to be involved. They obviously adored the child already. Theo had been out briefly and come back with the most enormous teddy bear that Adina had ever seen. She had no idea where he had managed to get it from but was sure it must have cost a fortune. He had not stopped beaming all day and was walking about looking like a cat that had got the cream.

The baby had barely whimpered and was so good that none of them knew she was there.

As yet, Mrs Montgomery had not seen her as Fliss had insisted that Adina should sleep. Adina wondered how she would react to the child. Would she resent the fact that the baby was hers and not her son's?

She found out early that evening when the old woman came into the room, leaning heavily on her son's arm. Adina had just fed the baby and now Dorothy was sleeping contentedly on her mother's chest with her long eyelashes curled on her cheeks.

'You can leave me now.' Mrs Montgomery flapped her hand dismissively at her son as she settled down into the bedside chair, and with a wink at Adina, Theo quietly slipped away.

'So, that's all the messy stuff out of the way then,' the old lady said abruptly.

'If you mean the birth – yes, it is,' Adina replied.

'So now what?'

'What do you mean?' Adina was beginning to feel apprehensive and it showed on her face as she held the child tighter to her.

'Well, what have you got to offer her? How will you provide for her? Don't you think she deserves a father?'

'She *has* a father,' Adina said steadily. 'And I'll manage somehow.'

'Huh! Easier said than done with the world the way it is at the moment,' Mrs Montgomery said shortly. 'The war may be over but it will be years before things are back to normal.'

Adina remained silent, determined not to get into an argument as the old woman peered closely at the baby.

'She's a pretty little thing, I'll give you that,' she muttered, 'but now let's talk sense, shall we? How about I make you a cash offer to go back home and leave the baby here with us?'

'I've already told you that I will not sell my baby,' Adina said shortly, but the old woman's expression never wavered.

'It would make sense,' she pointed out calmly. 'And I'm not talking pennies either. I'm talking about enough money to set you up for life. Think about it – you could go home and start anew with money in the bank. And you're still so young, you could have a *dozen* more babies if you wanted to, whereas Fliss's time is running out.'

'Please leave me!' Adina waved a trembling finger towards the door. 'I can't *believe* that you could be so callous. There isn't enough money in the whole world to buy this little girl.'

The old woman got unsteadily to her feet. 'You're all hormonal at the minute because you've just given birth, but we'll talk about it again in a few days, eh? You'll be thinking more sensibly then. That child could lead a charmed life if you agreed to Theo and Fliss adopting her. She would want for nothing, least of all love, whereas with you she'll know nothing but poverty – *and* she'll be branded a bastard.'

Tears were streaming down Adina's cheeks now but the old woman ignored her as she shambled from the room, leaving the door to swing wide open behind her.

'Don't worry, darling,' she whispered to the baby. 'Nothing and no one will ever take you away from me.'

The strain of the birth and all the excitement had taken its toll on her now, so she gently leaned over and tucked the baby into the crib that Theo had thoughtfully placed at the side of the bed and in no time at all she had fallen into a deep exhausted sleep.

It was some hours later when she woke to the sound of someone softly crooning. She knuckled the sleep from her eyes and when she turned her head she saw Fliss tenderly nursing the baby in the chair at the side of her.

'What are you doing?' she asked, as she saw the glass feeding-bottle in Fliss's hand.

Fliss started guiltily as she dragged her eyes away from the infant's sleeping face. 'Oh, sorry if I woke you,' she apologised. 'You looked so worn out that I didn't like to disturb you, and the baby was hungry so I made up a bottle.'

'But I intend to breastfeed her,' Adina protested weakly.

'You still can,' Fliss assured her. 'I checked with the nurse and she said that many babies need topping up with a bottle. And I'm sure you'll be wanting to get back to work soon, so it's best that she gets used to the bottle now, don't you think?'

'I suppose so,' Adina said uncertainly. The baby looked contented enough, she had to admit.

'Right then, I'll just change her and then I'll leave you in peace.' Fliss laid the baby carefully on the end of the bed before expertly folding a nappy.

'You look as if you know what you're doing,' Adina commented quietly.

Fliss chuckled. 'I've been practising for weeks,' she admitted. 'I thought if I could help out with her a little it would take some of the strain off you.' Within minutes she had changed and powdered the tiny bottom, then after planting a gentle kiss on the baby's soft cheek she reluctantly handed her back to her mother as she asked, 'Are you sure you wouldn't like me to sleep in the chair in here with you tonight? I could see to Dottie if she woke then, and you could get some rest.'

'I shall be perfectly fine, thank you,' Adina retorted, more sharply than she had intended to.

'Very well.' Fliss lifted the empty bottle and headed for the door. 'Goodnight then.'

'Goodnight.' Long after she had gone Adina sat staring at her daughter's perfect face as her mind worked overtime. Each time the baby opened her eyes Adina felt as if Karl was staring at her. The baby looked remarkably like him, the curve of her chin, the colour of her hair and eyes, even the dimples in her cheeks which were tiny replicas of his. Up until the baby's birth she had been able to think of no one but him. But everything had changed now. She had a daughter and suddenly Dorothy was the most important person in the world to her and she knew that she would have laid down her life for her if need be. Oh, how she wished that she had her own place where it could be just her and the baby. It unnerved her, seeing Fliss and Theo fuss over her, knowing how much they longed for a child of their own. And then there was Mrs Montgomery, who had made it more than plain that she was willing to set Adina up for life financially if she would only give the baby to her son and his wife, but Adina knew that she could never do that. There was not enough money in the whole world to make her part with her baby now that she had seen her and held her in her arms.

Sighing, she stared up at the ceiling. Fliss had been quite right about one thing at least. Soon she would have to go back to work to support herself and the child. She couldn't expect the Montgomerys to keep her for nothing indefinitely. They had done more than enough for her already and she would never forget that. It was just that now the thought of leaving the baby in someone else's care was terrifying.

She lay there for a long time fretting but at last her eyes fluttered shut again and she slept.

Much to the midwife's disgust, Adina was up and about again in three days.

'It's far too soon,' Nurse Simmons scolded. 'You should have stayed in bed for at least another couple of days.'

'I'm fine. And I need to get up so that I can go and register the baby's birth.'

'Oh, don't get worrying about that. I can go and do that for you,' Theo volunteered. It seemed that nothing was too much trouble for this kindly couple, to the point that Adina was beginning to feel vaguely uneasy about it.

But she merely smiled as she winded the baby over her shoulder. She had taken to being a mother like a duck to water and couldn't even begin to imagine what her life would be like without little Dottie now. She was such a good baby too, only crying when she wanted feeding or changing. Adina loved being a mother although she had been forced to be rather assertive with Fliss, who would have taken over the role completely if Adina had allowed it. Adina only had to move away from the crib and Fliss would be there, picking the baby up, insisting that she had wind or that she needed feeding. Mrs Montgomery watched all this without a word, although her expression clearly said what she thought.

The baby should have been Fliss's, as far as she was concerned, and she thought Adina was a fool to try and bring the child up on her own.

Theo fussed over the baby too when he was at home but he had gone back to work at the school now. Fliss had said she was going to have a little more time off to help with the baby, although Adina had told her that it really wasn't necessary, she could manage perfectly well. But Fliss wouldn't hear of it and so Adina had to bite her tongue and make the best of what was fast becoming a difficult situation.

Dottie was almost two weeks old when Adina came down the stairs with her in her arms one morning to find Beattie going through the post.

'Ah, there's one for you, luvvie,' she smiled, handing an envelope to Adina and cooing at the baby. Dottie already had everyone in the house eating out of her hand, except for Mrs Montgomery, that was. 'The old woman has already been and taken hers,' Beattie confided. 'It's amazing how she can get about when she wants to, ain't it?'

'Thank you.' Adina glanced at the envelope and saw that it was from Ariel.

'It's from your aunty,' she whispered into the child's soft downy hair. 'We'll have a read of it after you've had your breakfast, shall we?'

As the child stared up at her from trusting blue eyes, Adina's heart melted all over again. Dottie had lost the red-faced newborn look now and her mother thought she was even more beautiful, if that was possible.

Once the child was fed and changed, Adina settled her back into her crib where the baby instantly fell asleep. Tenderly tucking the blankets over her, Adina sat down to read Ariel's letter. She had hoped to catch Theo before he left for the school as it had occurred to her during the night that he hadn't given her Dottie's birth certificate yet, after kindly going to register the birth for her. Now she forgot all about it as she eagerly read Ariel's letter, but her contented mood changed as she read further down the page.

Ariel informed her that she was becoming seriously concerned about Ezra. He had lost a lot of weight and didn't seem to be his normal self at all. He had even allowed Ariel to go to the house and do a little cleaning for him, which she knew went totally against his independent nature.

She asked how much longer it would be before Adina could come home for a visit, as she felt that seeing her would cheer him up a little. Adina chewed her lip in consternation. Ariel had no idea about the baby, nor did her father, so how could she ever go home now? But then how could she ignore Ariel's request? If her father *was* really ill, she knew that she should go to him.

Crossing to the window, she stared thoughtfully down into the street below. She had believed that with the birth of the baby, all her troubles would be over – but in fact they were only just beginning. She had hoped that she would be married to Karl by now, but that hadn't happened. And now she was trapped between the devil and the deep blue sea. If she chose to ignore the letter she could make a life for herself and the baby and turn her back on her family for good. But would she be able to do that and live with herself? On the other hand, should she arrive back home with a new baby in tow, her father would turn his back on *her*. It was a dilemma that for now she had no idea how to resolve.

Chapter Thirty-Five

Everyone commented on how quiet Adina was at dinner that evening but she offered no explanation, simply excused herself and left the table early. She hurried upstairs to where Dottie was sleeping peacefully in her crib, looking like a little blonde-haired angel, but she had barely entered the room when there was a tap on the door and Fliss stuck her head round it.

'Can I come in?' she asked.

Adina sank into a chair as Fliss came to sit on the edge of the bed.

'So what's wrong then?' she asked bluntly. 'You haven't been yourself all day. Are you not feeling well?'

'I'm fine,' Adina assured her, and then suddenly to Fliss's dismay she burst into tears.

The older woman placed a comforting arm about her shoulders and remained silent until Adina's sobs subsided, then smoothing the hair from her forehead she said kindly, 'Why don't you tell me all about it, eh? They do say a problem shared is a problem halved.'

Adina blew her nose noisily on the handkerchief that Fliss had placed in her hand before blurting out, 'It's just *everything!*'

'So start at the beginning and we'll work through it.'

Adina gulped deeply before saying, 'I don't know what I'm going to do now. I thought Karl would be back and we would be married before Dottie was born, but that didn't happen. I would have staked my life that he loved me, so something must have happened to him or he would have been here. I don't know how I would have coped without you and Theo, but I can't put on you for ever. I already owe you both more than I can ever repay.' Only that afternoon, Theo had come home proudly pushing one of the latest coach-built prams from the Silver Cross factory. Adina herself had seen one in a secondhand shop that she had been intending to buy with her meagre savings, but once again Theo had beaten her to it, just as he had with everything else the baby had needed.

'And now,' she went on tremulously, 'my sister informs me in her letter that she is worried about our father. He hasn't been the same since our mother died but now she thinks that he may be genuinely ill and she wants me to go and see him.'

'So go and see him then,' Fliss said in a matter-of-fact voice.

'How *can* I?' Adina wailed. 'How can I just turn up with a baby? Our father is a wonderful man but he's very strict and he would never forgive me for having a baby out of wedlock – especially as the baby's father was a German. He turned his back on my sister for a long time because she married an Englishman, so what would he have to say about Karl? In his eyes, I would have committed the gravest sin imaginable.'

Fliss sat lost in thought for a few moments before suggesting, 'Why don't I look after Dottie for you whilst you visit him? You know she would be perfectly safe with me and she's used to the bottle now so she would be fine.'

Adina shuddered at the very idea, although she knew that what Fliss said was perfectly true. She would look after Dottie as if she was her own – but how could she bear to leave her baby, even for a few days?

'I don't think that is an option,' she said now. 'Dottie is *my* baby and it should be me who looks after her.'

'But you'll have to leave her with someone when you go back to work,' Fliss sensibly pointed out. 'And it's not as if you're leaving her for ever, is it? What harm could a few days do? And you'll feel so much better once you've seen your father. You said yourself that you felt terribly guilty about not going home to him during the Christmas holidays. Of course you had a reason not to then, but there's nothing to stop you now. He can have no idea that you've had a baby.'

'That's part of the problem.' Adina sighed glumly. 'Here I am, the mother of a beautiful baby girl, and none of my family even know about her. I can't keep her a secret for ever, can I? It looks as if I'm ashamed of her, and yet she is a blessing.'

'I'm afraid I can't help you there.' Fliss glanced at Dottie. 'What you decide to tell your family is entirely up to you, although I would strongly suggest that you leave things as they are. What they don't know cannot hurt them – but why don't you get an early night and sleep on it? And remember, if you do decide to go home for a visit, the offer to care for Dottie still stands.'

Long after Fliss had left the room Adina struggled with herself. Half of her wanted to just turn up at the shop in Edmund Street with her baby and bring it all out into the open. The other half trembled at the possible repercussions. It just seemed so sad to think that her father had another baby granddaughter that he did not even know about.

All night she tossed and turned, but by the time that dawn broke, she had made her decision. She would take Fliss up on her offer to care for Dottie and would go and see her father. If she did not, and something were to happen to him, she knew that she would never be able to forgive herself. But it would only be for a couple of days. She could not bear to be parted from Dottie for longer than that, so soon after her birth.

She told Fliss of her decision over breakfast the next morning, and Fliss nodded in approval, secretly thrilled at the thought of having Dottie all to herself for a while.

'I'll get Theo to call in and check the times of the trains from Euston this morning and you could perhaps go tomorrow?' she suggested, and so it was decided.

The next morning Adina packed a small case that Fliss had loaned her and kissed Dottie goodbye with tears in her eyes. She felt as if she was leaving her for ever rather than for just a short time.

Theo had promised to walk with her to the station and now there could be no more delaying the parting as Fliss ushered her towards the front door, the baby tucked comfortably in the crook of her arm.

'Now off you go and stop fretting,' she said sternly as Adina hovered on the top step. 'Dottie will be perfectly all right and we'll see you soon. Stay as long as you like.'

Adina managed a weak smile as she tripped down to the front gate, but all the way to the station she felt as if her heart was breaking, and she wondered how other young women in her position were ever able to give their babies up for adoption. She couldn't imagine her life without Dottie now.

At Euston she attracted more than a few admiring glances as she stood on the platform waiting for the train. Her belly was still quite wobbly, but she had borrowed a corset from Fliss and managed to squeeze back into an outfit she had worn before the pregnancy. Thankfully, no one but herself would know that, and Nurse Simmons had assured her that it would tighten up again in time. Her breasts were fuller too and she knew that she was going to have to express her milk regularly or she would be in pain. But today she had taken especial care over her appearance. She was wearing a straight blue skirt and a crisp green blouse topped by a rather becoming red coat and a small hat with a tiny veil attached to it that Fliss had insisted she should borrow.

'They look so much better on you than they do on me,' she had told her. 'And I want you going home looking smart. It wouldn't do for your father to think we had been neglecting you.'

When the train eventually chugged into the station Adina gracefully climbed aboard. She found an empty seat in a compartment and after putting her small case in the overhead luggage rack she settled into her seat and folded her gloved hands neatly into her lap. There was a middle-aged gentleman in a smart suit and a thick black overcoat sitting opposite her, and when Adina saw him watching her slyly she hastily averted her eyes and stared from the window. During the journey to Nuneaton he made a few attempts at conversation but when Adina merely answered him politely and returned her attention to the passing scenery he eventually gave up and did the crossword in his newspaper instead.

Later that morning, Adina stepped down from the train onto the platform at Trent Valley railway. station and took a deep breath. She had forgotten how clean the air was here after becoming used to the smog in London. Then, clutching the smart case that Fliss had also loaned her, she set off in the direction of the shop. It felt strange to be back in Nuneaton again, but then she supposed that was to be expected. So much had happened to her since she had last been there. She had left as a naïve young girl but she was returning as a young woman and a mother – not that her family could know that.

It was market day, and as she passed the stalls a thousand familiar smells and sounds assailed her, the tempting aroma of faggots and peas and steak and onion pie issuing from the pie stall, the smell of the cows enclosed in the pens as farmers heatedly bartered over the price of them. The loud squawking of the chickens as they scratched at the floor of their cages, indignant at their treatment. It was all just as she remembered it and yet it was strangely different now. She took a short cut through Riversley Park and her eyes smarted as she remembered the many stolen moments she and Karl had shared there. Then at last she was nearing the end of Edmund Street and as she turned the corner, the shop came into sight. Outside, a selection of fruit and vegetables were displayed in crates as usual, and even as she stood there the door opened and a customer exited carrying a large brown paper carrier bag with string handles.

Adina paused to compose herself, then with her head held high, she walked purposefully on and entered the shop. The bell above the door tinkled just as it always had, and when her father turned from arranging the sweet jars to see who had entered she struggled to stop the shock from showing on her face. He seemed to have shrunk to half his size and had lost so much weight that his clothes hung off him in loose folds. His face was ingrained with deep wrinkles that she was sure had not been there when she left, and he suddenly looked very old.

'Adina!' His voice was choked as he stared at the sophisticated-looking young woman standing before him. She had grown up all of a sudden and he felt a stab of pain as he realised that he had not been there to see it.

She placed her suitcase down on the floor and crossed to him and held him in her arms as her heart cried out at the injustice of it all.

'You look marvellous. London obviously suits you,' he told her when he eventually managed to untangle himself from her arms. 'But why did you not write and tell me that you were coming? I'm afraid it isn't too tidy in there.' He looked anxiously towards the door that led to the living quarters.

Adina smiled. 'Don't worry about that. I shall have it spic and span again in no time,' she assured him. 'I understand that you probably don't get too much time to do housework, with this place to run single-handed.'

'I do my best,' he muttered, then his face became hopeful as he asked, 'Are you home to stay? Is the job in London finished?'

'I'm afraid not. In fact, I think it will go on for at least another year or so,' she told him regretfully. 'But I will be here for a couple of days at least.'

Hiding his disappointment, he forced a smile. 'Then we shall have to make the best of every minute, shan't we? I shall shut up early tonight and you can tell me all about the exciting life you must lead in London.'

'It isn't exciting,' Adina told him truthfully. 'In fact, it is quite grim. The city was devastated by bombs and I think it will take many years of hard work before it is back to the way it was before the war.'

He nodded sadly but brightened again as he eyed her up and down. 'Well, you certainly seem to be thriving on it,' he declared. 'And so grown up; I scarcely recognised you when you first walked in. You are quite the young lady now.'

Adina lifted her case and strode past him. 'Right, I think I'll make us both a nice cup of tea before I unpack, shall I? And then perhaps I could take over the shop for a few hours before I prepare a meal for us whilst you have a lie-down. You look tired, Papa.'

He opened his mouth to say something but then promptly closed it again. How could he tell her that some days he had to force himself to get out of bed? That he missed Freyde and Ariel and Dovi more than he could say? Everything seemed so pointless now that the family were gone and all he could see stretching before him was a lonely old age. Admittedly he had seen a little more of Ariel lately, but his pride was such that he could not allow her fully back into his life again, although he secretly thought that his little granddaughter, Freda, was a beautiful child. She reminded him of Ariel at that age.

He watched his daughter disappear into the kitchen and pushed his sad thoughts to the back of his mind as the shop bell tinkled and another customer entered the shop.

As Adina looked about the room her mouth gaped open. It appeared as if a whirlwind had swept through it. There were dirty dishes everywhere and the hearth was full of cold ashes although the day was bitterly cold. She sighed as she took off her coat and hat. Her mother would have turned in her grave if she could have seen the way Ezra was living. Still, it was nothing that couldn't be put to rights so she rolled her sleeves up and set to with a vengeance. First of all she mashed a pot of tea and when it was brewed she carried a cup through to her father and hastily drank one herself. Then she filled the sink with hot water and set about the piles of washing-up.

Two hours later, the room was transformed back to the way her mother had once kept it. The floor was swept and mopped. She had taken the carpets outside and beaten them and there was a large fire roaring up the chimney. A shepherd's pie was cooking in the oven and she had even made a start on the upstairs which she had soon discovered, to her dismay, was little better than the downstairs.

She hastily stripped the dirty sheets from the beds and replaced them with clean ones, then she collected up all the dirty clothing that her father had slung haphazardly about his room. And now a large pile of laundry was placed at the side of the sink, but she decided she would not think of tackling that until the next day. The long journey and all the housework were beginning to catch up with her and she was already missing little Dottie so much that it hurt.

As promised, her father closed the shop early, or at least earlier than he usually did and they chatted about happier times as he tackled the meal she had cooked for him. He had grown used to snatching a bite here and there, and was no longer used to big meals although he did make a valiant attempt for her sake to eat some of it.

'That was delicious, bubbeleh,' he sighed as he sat back in his seat and rubbed his stomach contentedly.

Adina had to swallow quickly as the endearment he had always used to her slipped easily from his lips. She wanted to fall into his arms and tell him of all that had happened to her, but she knew that even loving her as he undoubtedly did, it would be the end of their relationship.

She was just putting away the clean dinner pots when the back door was flung open and Mrs Haynes breezed in with a broad smile on her face.

'So it were true then!' she cried with genuine delight. 'I heard as you were back an' I couldn't rest till I'd come round to see for meself. By, you look a fair treat, love. You've put a bit o' weight on an' you look all sort of . . . oh, I don't know – grown up.'

Adina laughed. 'Well, I am almost twenty-one now, Mrs Haynes. We all have to grow up sometime,' she quipped.

'Hmm, an' got a bit mouthy an' all, so you have,' the neighbour retaliated, but her eyes were twinkling. 'So are you 'ome for good then?'

'I'm afraid not. Just for a couple of days.' Adina filled the kettle and set it on to boil as her father settled down contentedly in the chair and stretched his feet out towards the fire. Mrs Haynes meantime sat down at the kitchen table. She was never one to say no if there was a cup of tea going and she wanted to hear about all Adina had been up to.

'Met any nice young men in the big smoke then, have you?' she teased as Adina warmed the teapot.

'I don't have time for young men,' the girl replied a little too shortly. 'I am there to work.'

'Oh, sorry luv, I wasn't meanin' no offence. But a lovely girl like you . . . why, I reckon you could 'ave your pick o' the chaps now. You've turned into a right little stunner an' no mistake.'

Adina's face softened as she poured milk into three mugs although it was already apparent that Ezra would not be wanting his. He was snoring softly and the two women exchanged an amused glance.

'My father,' Adina said, serious again now. 'How has he been?'

'Not so good, if I was to tell yer the truth,' Mrs Haynes whispered back. 'He misses you lot an' yer mam somethin' terrible, though he's a cussed old bugger an' he won't admit it. He has let Ariel call round a few times, which is a start I suppose, but he's so independent. I sometimes make him a dish of stew or a hotpot, but it takes him all his time to accept it. An' once I asked if he'd let me do a bit o' cleanin' fer him but he almost snapped me bloody 'ead off.'

They fell silent for a time as they sipped their tea then Mrs Haynes said softly, 'I was sorry to hear what happened to yer brother, love. I know what he did were wrong – especially what he did to our little Sarah – but she's over it now an' she brings us a lot o' happiness. I want yer to know I bear no grudges. It weren't really him that were bad. The war changed him an' he couldn't help it. It's a wicked sin, if yer were to ask me. But there, that's enough o' that talk, eh? Here's you only back for a while an' I'm depressin' yer.' She drained the rest of the tea left in her cup then standing, she patted Adina's arm affectionately.

'It'll do 'im good to have a bit o' company again,' she said, nodding towards Ezra. 'Happen it'll perk him up a bit, eh? An' now I'd best be off. Yer know what me old man is like if he don't get his last cup o' cocoa, an' Sarah an' our Freddie will be screamin' fer their supper. Goodnight love, sleep tight.'

Adina smiled as the woman left the room then hurried away to fetch a blanket, which she draped across her father's legs. He looked so worn out she didn't like to disturb him. Soon after, she made her own way to bed and as she slid between the cold sheets she shuddered. She had forgotten how cold it was in this room, or maybe she had grown used to the comforts she had back in London. She wondered what Dottie was doing now. Would Fliss have remembered to wind her after her last feed? Her heavy breasts ached as she thought of her.

Her thoughts then moved on to Karl, and a sense of utter despair swept through her. Strangely enough, she hadn't thought quite so much about him since giving birth to the baby, and more frightening still was the fact that, when she closed her eyes now and tried to picture him, the image of his face was blurred around the edges – until she looked at Dottie, that was, and then there he was, looking up at her again with those deep blue eyes that had always been able to turn her legs to jelly. And still she clung to the hope that one day he would come for her. What would happen to her and Dottie if he didn't? She knew without a doubt that she still loved him with all her heart, but as sleep claimed her it wasn't his face that she saw but her baby's, far away in London.

Chapter Thirty-Six

The next couple of days passed in a blur for Adina. The washing was all done, ironed and put away, and the house was shining like a new pin, so on the afternoon before she was due to go back to the Montgomerys she marched into the shop decked out in Fliss's posh coat and hat and told her father, 'I'm going to see Ariel. I'd like to see her and the baby before I return to London.'

He lowered his eyes but made no objection as she swept past him. Somehow he knew that the days when he could tell his daughter what to do were long gone. She was a young woman now and used to fending for herself.

Ariel was delighted to see her sister again and welcomed her with open arms. 'But you look so grown up!' she cried as she surveyed her, much as their father had done a couple of days earlier. A chubby bright-eyed girl was sitting in a playpen amongst a mountain of toys and teddies, and Adina beamed at the sight of her. Freda had been just a tiny baby the last time she had seen her, but now she had grown so much Adina would never have recognised her.

'She's a little terror now,' Ariel said as she looked down on her daughter. 'She's teethin' like mad an' keeps us up half the night,' she added, although her eyes were full of affection. 'Brian reckons we'll need matchsticks to keep our eyes open at this rate.'

Adina chuckled as she stroked her niece's shiny hair and was rewarded with a gappy smile.

'She's really beautiful,' she whispered, thinking of her own baby back in London. She had intended to tell Ariel all about her, but suddenly the words stuck in her throat and they spoke of other things instead.

'Everything is wonderful,' Ariel assured her sister. 'Although – well, to be honest it would be nice if Brian and I could get our own house. It's a little crowded here now Freda is getting bigger. The trouble is, Brian is struggling to get a regular job. He's willing to turn his hand to anything, but obviously he is quite restricted in what he can do now.'

Adina nodded sympathetically, wishing that there was something she could do to help.

'I'm sure something will turn up eventually,' she murmured as she lifted the baby from the playpen, then Ariel left them to get acquainted whilst she hurried away to fetch a clean nappy.

'How long are you staying for?' she asked sometime later as they sat laughing at little Freda's antics.

'I'm going back tomorrow. To be honest, I've already stayed for a day longer than I intended to,' Adina admitted. 'I'm so concerned about Papa. He just doesn't seem to be himself at all.'

'I agree, but I suppose it's hardly surprising, is it? Not when you consider all the knocks he's had over the last few years,' Ariel said sadly. 'I do go round there and do as much as he will let me, but he still tends to hold me at arm's length for most of the time, although he is speaking to me now, which is a step in the right direction.'

The rest of the afternoon was spent in talking about the work that Adina was doing in London, and Ariel's eyes grew misty as she heard all the sad stories about the poor children who no longer had families to go home to.

'And I hear that Beryl isn't very happy either,' Ariel said at one point. 'I bumped into her mother in the market a few weeks ago and she told me that Tye is giving her a hard time of it in America.'

'Yes, Beryl told me the same in one of her letters,' Adina agreed with a worried frown. 'I just wish I could afford to buy her an air ticket so that she could fly home.'

Ariel hesitated. There was something she had been longing to ask and now the question just slipped out. 'And what about Karl? Have you heard from him?'

'No . . . I never did,' Adina replied dully, averting her eyes, but not before Ariel saw the pain that briefly flared in them. She quickly changed the subject but she felt sorry for her sister, since she knew she had loved the man.

The time passed by so quickly as the two sisters caught up on all the gossip that Adina was amazed when she glanced at the clock and saw that it was almost four o'clock.

'Goodness me! Where has the time gone?' she exclaimed as she stood up and began to pull her coat on. 'Papa will think I've got lost. I shall have to be going or he'll have no dinner this evening.'

After Adina had kissed her niece, Ariel followed her to the door with tears in her eyes, not knowing how long it might be before they saw each other again. They hugged each other warmly then Adina hurried away through the darkening streets in the direction of the shop.

The following day, as Adina stood in the back room saying goodbye to her father, she felt as if she was being torn in two. She hated to leave him, since he looked so lonely and ill, and yet she could scarcely wait to get back to London and her baby.

'Now you be sure you take good care of yourself,' she scolded. 'And write to me often, do you hear me? Mrs Montgomery is talking about having a phone installed and at least we will be able to speak to each other then.'

He nodded numbly, missing her before she had even gone, not that his pride would have allowed him to tell her that. Instead, he kissed her warmly and bundled her towards the door. 'Go, bubbeleh,' he urged, 'otherwise you will miss your train.'

Adina turned and left without another word, but she cried silently all the way to the station and could not shake off the awful feeling that she was never going to see her papa again.

It was late afternoon and the light was fast fading by the time the train pulled into Euston after an uneventful journey. Outside the station, Adina stepped into the road and hailed a cab, something she had grown good at doing since coming to live there, and soon she was heading towards Camden Town.

Fliss had given her a key some weeks ago, so now she hurried up the steps, longing to see her baby again. Beattie was in the hall on her way to the dining room as she entered and she stopped with her hands full of gleaming silver cutlery.

'That were good timin', luvvie,' she chuckled. 'I were just settin' the table fer dinner. Had a good visit, did you?'

'Yes, thanks, Beattie.' Adina hung her hat and coat up then asked, 'Where is everyone?'

'The old dear is in the drawing room and the others are all up in the nursery.'

Adina frowned. 'What are they doing in there? Dorothy sleeps in my room with me.'

Beattie shrugged and looked decidedly uncomfortable. 'No use askin' me, luvvie,' she mumbled. 'Perhaps you'd be better askin' them.' With that she shuffled away as Adina strode towards the stairs.

At the end of the third-floor landing she could hear voices, and as she marched towards the nursery, anger flooded through her. She was grateful for all Fliss and Theo had done for her, and also for them caring for the baby, but she wasn't happy at all about the thought of Dorothy being in her own room yet, and intended to tell them so.

The door to the nursery was ajar and as she approached it she paused to listen.

'Who's a clever girl then?' she heard Fliss coo as she peeped through the door. Theo was holding the baby and Fliss was leaning over her with so much love shining in her eyes that the breath caught in Adina's throat. It struck her again that they looked like a family, and for no reason that she could explain she was suddenly frightened. Dorothy was *her* baby; they would have to understand that.

'Hello.' Her voice was cold as she stepped into the room and they both turned startled eyes towards her.

'Oh . . . Adina, we weren't sure when you would be back,' Fliss spluttered like a child that had been caught in the middle of a naughty act.

'Well, I *am* back now, so I'll take over, shall I?' Adina walked up to Theo and took the baby from him without a word as he and Fliss glanced at each other guiltily. Pure love coursed through her as she stared down at the perfect little face and she realised just how much she had missed her child.

'What is she doing in here?' she asked after a while and again the couple glanced at each other.

'Well, the thing is, she's sleeping through the night now, so we thought it was time to give you a proper rest.' It was all Fliss could think of to say.

'Actually, I *like* having her in my room,' Adina said acidly. 'And I don't think she is old enough to be sleeping on her own yet. I wouldn't hear her from my bedroom if she cried.'

'Oh, that's not a problem,' Fliss said a little too quickly. 'Theo and I have moved into the next room, so we could always come and fetch you if she needed you.'

'Wouldn't it have made more sense for *me* to move up here?' Adina said, ominously quietly.

'Not really. You need your rest and to tell you the truth, Mother was keeping us awake with her snoring, so we were actually quite happy to change rooms. I . . . I'm so sorry if we have upset you. That was never our intention.'

Fliss looked so close to tears that suddenly Adina's anger fled and she felt desperately guilty. These people had stood by her in her darkest hour and here she was being horrible to them – and all because she was feeling jealous.

'It's all right,' she sighed. 'I'm sure you meant well, but I really would like to keep her in my room with me for a while longer, if you don't mind.'

'Of course we don't mind.' Fliss took Theo's hand and led him from the room, leaving Adina feeling completely confused. Had she overreacted? She supposed she probably had, but she would worry about that later. For now she just wanted to cuddle her baby and catch up on all the time she had missed with her.

At dinner that evening Mrs Montgomery glared at her before saying, 'I hear you didn't like the idea of the baby being in the nursery then?'

Adina flushed but was determined to stand her ground. 'I appreciate the reasons why Theo and Fliss thought it might be a good idea,' she said, just as coolly. 'But I don't feel Dorothy is ready to be left on her own just yet.'

'Hmph! Well, she'll have to be on her own soon when you go back to work, won't she? When were you thinking of going back, by the way? And have you arranged for someone to look after her?'

'I've had some thoughts on that,' Fliss butted in. 'I was thinking that I could perhaps look after her for you. I'm not really needed at the school any more and at least you would know she was being well cared for.'

'There's no need for you to do that,' she assured her. 'I'm sure I can find someone reliable to look after her during working hours.'

'Oh, so you'd drag the poor little mite out in all weathers and leave her with a stranger, would you, rather than let her be here with someone she knows?' Mrs Montgomery growled.

'I . . . I didn't mean it to sound like that,' Adina defended herself. 'I just think it would be a shame for Fliss to have to give her job up. I know she enjoys working with the children and I'd hate her to lose a wage because of me.'

'My daughter-in-law has never *needed* to work,' Mrs Montgomery informed her pompously. 'Theo doesn't need to work either, if it comes to that. His father left them enough money to last two lifetimes.'

Not sure how she should answer, Adina fell silent. She did have to admit to herself that the idea made sense. Unlike them, she *did* need to work – and fairly soon, too. The money she had saved before the baby was born was dwindling alarmingly quickly, and she didn't want to become a burden to them. Each week she gave them a few pounds towards her keep, although Fliss always protested and told her that it really wasn't necessary. But it *was* necessary to Adina. She did have her pride.

Adina felt as if she had been backed into a corner and had no idea at all how she was going to get out of it.

Chapter Thirty-Seven

Adina returned to work when Dorothy was two months old. She hated leaving her but knew that there was no alternative if she was going to provide for them. After a lot of soul-searching she had reluctantly agreed to Fliss's offer; it did make sense, after all, and so now each morning Fliss waved her off with the baby snuggled contentedly in her arms. Adina was ashamed at the surge of jealousy she felt as she watched them each day but was helpless to do anything about it. She knew deep down that it was better for the baby to stay in her home environment with someone familiar who loved her, but she thought that Fliss was becoming too attached to Dorothy. In fact, sometimes she felt that Fliss was treating the baby as if she was her own.

Some days she would come home to find Dorothy dressed in yet another expensive outfit. that Fliss had bought for her, and her heart would sink. Adina wondered where she managed to find them, as clothing was still difficult to come by, but when she protested, Fliss would simply wave away her concerns.

'Oh, it wasn't that much,' she would say airily. 'Theo has contacts, so Dottie will never want for anything, and the colour really suits her, don't you think?'

Adina would nod glumly and sigh. Theo's contacts were no doubt something to do with the black market. It seemed that there were no shortages of anything for people who had money. Fliss treated the baby as if she was a little doll, and the worst part about it was that the baby seemed to enjoy all her attention. However, Adina had stood firm on one point and the baby was still sleeping in her room, which she supposed was something.

Spring was bearing down on them and at the weekends Adina would put the baby in her pram and take her for nice long walks, just the two of them. These were the times that she loved the best and she savoured every minute of every weekend. She would lift Dottie from her pram in Regent's Park, and after getting settled on a bench would point out the daffodils that were peeping through the earth and the fresh green buds on the trees as the child crowed with delight.

More than ever now she longed for a home of her own, but the possibility of that looked remote in the near future unless Karl returned to whisk them away. She would whisper in the baby's ear and tell her all about her daddy. 'One day he will come for us,' she would say. 'And then we'll all live together in a lovely house with a big garden where you can play to your heart's content. It will have a great big apple tree in it and Daddy will fit you a swing up.'

Dottie would stare at her as if she understood every word that her mother was saying, and Adina's heart would well up with love as she looked at the child, who meant the whole world to her. She still thought of Karl every single day and wondered what he would think of his beautiful daughter, but sometimes now, doubts would creep in. Why had he not come back for her as he had promised he would? Why had he not even written? The only possibility as far as she could see was that something must have happened to him, or perhaps he had married his fiancée, but as that possibility was far too painful to even contemplate, she went on forcing herself to believe that he would come . . . eventually.

It was one day in April that Theo came back from a shopping trip with a wide smile on his face, brandishing a bunch of bananas. 'Look what I found in Covent Garden!' he announced, as if he had discovered the Crown Jewels. 'Bananas! I haven't seen one since before the war. Things must be looking up.'

'They must,' his wife agreed. 'And it said in the newspaper today that the government are going to introduce free school meals for the children that need them and free bottles of milk.'

'About time too,' old Mrs Montgomery huffed. 'Some of the poor little mites that you see turning out for school haven't even got decent shoes on their feet. Not like that lucky little devil there.' She waved her walking stick in Dottie's direction and Adina felt colour flood into her cheeks. She had had a really bad day at school with Rebekah, the little Jewish girl whose parents had perished during the war. Sadly, the family who had cared for her during the war had decided that they could not take on the longterm responsibility of her, and the child was struggling to settle into the orphanage that she had been sent to.

'I have to sleep in a big room with seven other girls,' she had sobbed to Adina in stilted English. 'And they make fun of me because of the way I speak.' Adina had cuddled her and assured her that things would get better, but her heart was breaking for the child. And now here was Mrs Montgomery pointing out in a not too subtle way how lucky Adina was that they were all looking out for her and her daughter, which sadly she could not dispute. But she still could not see a way out of the position she found herself in. She had opened a savings account at the post office and after paying her board each week she saved every penny she could. But the flats in London were so expensive, as well as few and far between, and she knew that it would be ages before she could rent a place of her own, because then she would not only have to pay the rent but she would have to pay someone to look after Dottie too.

Seeing that the old woman's words had struck home, Fliss smiled at her kindly. 'Mother didn't mean that the way it sounded,' she reassured her as she cast a withering glance in her mother-in-law's direction. 'We all love having you and Dottie here, so don't give it another thought.'

The old woman tutted and swept past them on her way to the dining room as Adina made to take Dottie from Fliss who was holding her. She was intending to put her down for a nap whilst they all had dinner, but as she reached her arms out, Dottie cuddled into Fliss and started to cry. Adina felt as if someone had stabbed a knife into her heart but she merely lifted the child firmly and took the stairs two at a time.

Once the baby was settled in her cot, Adina sat down to have a think. Already Dottie had a strong bond with Fliss, but Adina had no idea what to do about it. Of course she was pleased that she could leave the baby in safe hands each day, but surely it should be *her* and not Fliss to whom the child held out her arms? Hot tears trickled down her cheeks as she watched Dottie sleeping peacefully, and she knew in that moment that somehow she would have to find them a place of their own to live in at the earliest opportunity.

In June that year, Adina received a letter from Ariel that she found quite worrying. In it, Ariel wrote that their father had taken to opening the shop for just four days a week. Alarm bells instantly rang in Adina's head. Her father had always been a very hard worker; even more so since he had been on his own. And yet in the letter she had received from her father just the week before, he had assured her that he was fine and had not mentioned the shop at all. Ariel went on to say that on one of her short visits he had agreed to go and see a doctor and she promised to keep her sister informed.

Adina briefly considered paying another visit to Nuneaton, but then decided against it. If she went it would have to be at the weekend, and that was the only opportunity she had to spend time with Dottie – unless Fliss whisked her off somewhere, that was – and that was becoming more and more of a regular thing. Dottie was now five months old and could have charmed the birds off the trees. She was a sweet-natured child and everyone who met her, instantly fell in love with her. Her blonde hair had grown and now framed her chubby cheeks with soft baby curls, and her eyes were as blue as the skies. Sometimes when Adina looked at her she found it hard to believe that anything so utterly perfect could have come out of her body. No, she thought now, I'll wait until I hear from Ariel again, and if Papa is no better then, I'll go and see him. It's far too soon to leave Dottie again.

Over the next two weeks, Fliss and Theo took Adina and Dottie out every weekend to show Adina the sights of London that she had not seen so far. In truth, Adina would have preferred to spend her time at home with the baby but she didn't like to hurt their feelings as they were obviously trying their hardest to make her feel a part of the family. The weather was stiflingly hot by then and Fliss had bought a pretty white Broderie Anglaise sunshade for Dottie's pram so that she wouldn't get burned. She had also bought her a much smaller pushchair that they could more easily lift on and off public transport when they embarked on their sightseeing tours. It was invariably she who ended up pushing it within minutes of them all leaving the house, but knowing how much the woman loved Dottie, Adina tried not to mind.

It was around about then that they also had a telephone installed. Mrs Montgomery hated it. 'Damn newfangled contraptions,' she would moan each time it rang. 'Don't know why we need a phone anyway!'

Adina couldn't have disagreed with her more, because now she was able to speak to Ariel on a regular basis. Her sister would ring as regularly as clockwork each Tuesday evening at seven o'clock, and somehow their chats made Adina feel less isolated from her remaining family.

On this particular Tuesday, Adina was pacing the hall as she waited for Ariel to ring when Fliss approached her.

'Here, let me take her off you,' she offered, and when Adina didn't immediately hand her over, she went on: 'She is due for a bottle any time now – and how are you going to explain a crying baby to your sister if she starts while you're on the phone?'

Seeing the sense in what she said, Adina quickly placed the baby in Fliss's arms just as the phone rang. Adina snatched it up but the smile on her face died away as Ariel gabbled, 'Adina, Papa is poorly. *Really* poorly, I think. He hasn't opened the shop for five days and Mrs Haynes says he hasn't even got dressed. She's seen the doctor go in to him a couple of times but when she asked him what was wrong, he refused to tell her. Brian has offered to keep the shop open for him today and Papa didn't refuse, which only goes to show how ill he must be feeling.'

Adina was reeling from shock. She couldn't imagine her father letting anyone outside the family behind his shop counter, let alone Ariel's husband.

'Do you want me to come home?' she asked.

'No – not at the moment. We'll keep a close eye on him and Brian is going in to open the shop up again tomorrow for him. But I promise to ring you if he gets any worse.'

They spent the next few moments chatting of other things then Adina placed the phone down with a heavy heart. Job or not, she would have gone like a shot knowing that her father was so unwell, but how could she go without Dottie? If he was really ill, her turning up out of the blue with an illegitimate granddaughter that he didn't know existed might make him even worse. And if she went home without Dottie, it might end up being for an indefinite period, and she couldn't bear to leave the baby for too long. It was a terrible decision to have to make, and she wrestled with her conscience for two whole days until Ariel rang again.

'I think you should come,' she said shortly.

Adina's heart sank. 'Why, what's happened?'

She heard Ariel stifle a sob at the other end of the phone and knew that she was going to hear bad news.

'Brian had been running the shop for Papa for the last couple of days,' she told her. 'And so I went round to do some cleaning for him. He told me nothing needed doing as usual, but this time I wouldn't take no for an answer. While I was there the doctor came so I went out into the yard to hang the washing out and give them some privacy, but I could still hear what was being said . . .'

'*And?*' Adina prompted her.

'Papa has a serious heart condition,' her sister informed her solemnly. 'The doctor would like him to go into hospital but you know how stubborn Papa can be. Adina . . . I'm frightened.'

'I shall be there as soon as I can tomorrow,' Adina told her without hesitation. She knew that she really had no choice now, but it seemed so unfair that her father should have developed a similar condition to their mother so soon after her passing.

Fliss was wonderful about it when Adina explained the predicament she was in.

'Of *course* you must go first thing in the morning,' she told her. 'And stay as long as you need to. You know Dottie will be perfectly all right here with me.'

Adina nodded glumly. She knew that only too well. In fact, Dottie sometimes seemed to prefer Fliss to her now.

'I shall go and fetch a suitcase for you right away,' Fliss rushed on. 'And I'll get Theo to ring and check the time of the first train to Nuneaton in the morning. He can take you to the station in the car.'

The new car that Theo had recently purchased was still a novelty. He had bought a rather grand Daimler and never tired of driving it. Adina imagined that it must have cost a small fortune, but then if the Montgomerys chose to waste their money on whims she supposed it was nothing to do with her.

She packed her case with enough clothes to last for a week, hoping that she would not need to be gone for longer than that, then she took Dottie to her room, determined to spend the last few hours quietly with her. Theo was taking Fliss to see a show in the West End, so for once she intended to make the most of having her baby all to herself. She stroked her hair and sang lullabies to her and wondered how she would manage to get through the next few days without her until finally the little girl fell asleep in her arms. And then as Adina stared down at her she fingered the band of steel on her finger and thought of Dottie's father and her heart ached afresh.

*   *   *

223

The next morning she was up bright and early, but she couldn't manage to eat any of the lovely breakfast that Beattie had prepared for her.

'I ain't happy about you goin' off with nuffink in your stomach,' the kindly woman scolded. 'You just be sure an' get yourself a sandwich or somethin' on the train, do you hear me?'

Adina nodded, knowing that she wouldn't be able to eat a thing until she had seen her father, and then Theo led her outside to the car after a tearful goodbye to Dottie.

In no time at all she was on the train where she stared impatiently out of the carriage window as it chugged towards Nuneaton. Once it pulled into the station, Adina dragged her case off the platform and set off at a trot for Edmund Street, although the suitcase seemed to get heavier with every step she took. By the time the shop came into sight she felt as if her arm was being pulled out of its socket but still she hurried on, concerned to see that the shop was shut. She was sure that Ariel had said Brian had been running it, but perhaps he had taken a lunch-break.

She flew up the entry as if there were wings on her feet as the expensive leather suitcase that Fliss had loaned her bounced off the walls, then at last she was through the yard and going into the kitchen. Straight away her eyes were drawn to Ariel who was sitting in her father's chair quietly crying into a large white handkerchief. Brian had been sitting at the kitchen table but he instantly stood up and after snatching up his crutch, he limped across and took the case from Adina.

'What's going on here?' Adina asked, as Ariel shot out of the chair and flung her arms about her sister.

'Oh Dina, I'm *so* glad you're here,' she sobbed.

Adina hugged her for a moment before holding her at arm's length and asking softly, 'Now calm down and tell me what's wrong. And where is Papa?'

Ariel took a deep shuddering breath. 'He . . . he's gone, Adina. During the night. Brian arrived this morning to open the shop and found him here in the chair. He had died in his sleep. The doctor thinks his heart just gave out.'

Adina reeled away from her as every vestige of colour drained out of her face. And yet deep down, she wasn't really surprised. She had not been able to shake off a terrible sense of foreboding ever since Ariel had phoned the evening before, and now she knew why. Brian hastily pulled out a chair and Adina sank down into it, still unable to utter a word. Now there was only herself and Ariel left, and it was a lot to take in.

'We've arranged the funeral for tomorrow,' Brain told her gravely. 'I hope that's all right? Your father is upstairs and I have washed him just as Ariel told me to, as I am the closest he had to a male relative now. We have also sat shiva for him throughout the night and written his name in the Book of the Dead.'

Adina nodded. She felt as if she was caught in the grip of a night-mare, and yet she knew inside that this was real. Her father was gone to join her mother and Dovi. And then at last they came, hot scalding tears that spurted from her eyes and threatened to choke her, and there was nothing more to be said as she and Ariel clung together.

The following day they found themselves once more in the Jewish section of Witton Cemetery, and Ezra was laid to rest next to Freyde his beloved wife. The funeral was a solemn affair attended only by themselves.

For days the sun had blazed down from a cloudless blue sky, but on the day of the funeral the heavens opened. Adina stood with her sister, tears and rain on her cheeks. She had not even had the chance to say a proper goodbye, and now she could only pray that if there really was an afterlife, her loved ones were finally reunited in paradise.

Chapter Thirty-Eight

That night, Ariel and Brian brought little Freda with them and spent the night with Adina in the shop. She could not face staying there on her own and when she begged them to stay, they were happy to oblige her.

'What shall we do with the shop now?' Ariel asked as they sat down to a meal that none of them really wanted. The whole place felt strangely empty as they stared around at their parents' familiar things. Adina could still clearly remember the day they had all arrived there and her father's many trips to the secondhand shops. She recalled him coming home with the chairs and the sideboard, and the way her mother had exclaimed with delight at sight of them before setting to and polishing them until she could see her face in them. Each and every piece in the room had little monetary value and yet they were all priceless.

'I don't know,' she told her sister as she poured herself another cup of tea and moved her uneaten meal away. 'There was a note from the landlord pushed through the door when we got back from the funeral to say that he'll be calling to see us in the morning.'

'Huh, he didn't waste much time, did he,' Brian said in disgust. 'I dare say he's worried he won't be getting his rent.' He then swallowed nervously before glancing towards the two sisters. He had been hoping to wait a while before putting the idea that had been growing in his mind to them, but now it seemed that he hadn't a moment to lose or the opportunity might be gone for ever. 'In actual fact I've been thinking about the shop,' he said quietly, and when his wife raised a questioning eyebrow he hurried on, 'Well, the thing is, I don't want to appear that I'm cashing in on your father's death, but I've really enjoyed working in it. It's something that I can do that isn't too physically demanding, and now that little Freda is here we need our own place to live. My parents have been wonderful, of course, but I thought . . . I mean, I wondered, how about Ariel and I take the shop on?'

'Us!' Ariel's eyes almost popped out of her head, but then the more she thought on his suggestion the more it made sense.

'If you were to ask me, I think it's a wonderful idea,' Adina said calmly. She knew how much Brian fretted about not being able to do some of the things that he had been able to before he was injured in the war. He desperately wanted to feel independent and provide for his family, and here was the ideal opportunity.

'Why don't we talk to the landlord about it tomorrow if you're serious?' Ariel suggested, and her husband's whole face lit up.

'You're on,' he said with a determined nod, and the women then rose and began to clear the table as he sat there with his head brimful of ideas.

The landlord, Mr Braithwaite, a tall gangly man with bushy eyebrows and a huge grey beard, actually thought that Brian's plan was a brilliant idea, and after discussing the rent they shook hands on it and the landlord left promising to return with the necessary paperwork the following day.

'I'm going to make this work, you just see if I don't,' Brian told his wife excitedly. 'I thought we could introduce some hardware,' he went on. 'You know – brushes and bowls and things like that. There's no one else sells them around here, so I think they'd do well.'

Adina slipped up to her room leaving the couple to their dreams and lay on her bed staring sightlessly off into space. It was strange to think that Ariel would be living in her old home again, but oddly fitting somehow – and she hoped that the little family would be happy there. At least some good would have come from their father's death, if it gave them a place of their own to live.

After lunch that day Adina went for a walk. She desperately needed some time to herself to put her thoughts into some sort of order and come to terms with her father's death. She found herself walking towards Stockingford and was soon approaching the gates of Astley Hall. Peering into the grounds, she felt a pang of sadness. The Nissen huts were almost empty. Many of the prisoners of war had been returned to their homelands, and now the grounds that had once rung with the sounds of men's chatter appeared to be little more than a ghost town.

As she stared at the deserted dwellings, it was hard to believe that almost ten thousand people had lived there throughout the duration of the war. She had no doubt that many of them would have returned home to find that their loved ones had perished, just as so many of the English had. She stood for a long while remembering the times she had come to these very gates to wait for Karl. The memories were so vivid that she almost expected him to walk up to her at any moment, enchanting her with the dimpled smile that Dottie had inherited. But he didn't come, and after a while she turned and retraced her steps with a heavy heart.

It was as she was heading back to the shop that an idea occurred to her. Perhaps it would be worth visiting the school where she had used to work? Karl had promised to send his letters to Mrs Downes, the Headmistress there, and who knew, she might just be in for a pleasant surprise if there was one there waiting for her that Mrs Downes hadn't yet had time to forward on to her.

Some time later she came away from the school with very mixed emotions. Mrs Downes, who was thrilled to see her and to hear how her friends the Montgomerys were, had informed her that yes, indeed a letter addressed to Adina from Germany *had* arrived at the school some weeks ago, but she had forwarded it on to the London address almost immediately. So why haven't I received it? Adina wondered, although she was thrilled to know that Karl *had* written. Perhaps it had been lost in the post? She consoled herself by thinking that even if this was the case, if Karl had written once he would surely write again, and she went on her way in a greatly heartened mood.

The next four days passed in a blur. Ariel and Brian were busily transporting their possessions from his parents' house to their new home, and Adina was happy to babysit for little Freda while the others excitedly rushed backwards and forwards in a friend's old van. They had precious little to bring apart from their clothes and their personal possessions, but it didn't really matter as they were inheriting the furniture that Adina's family had managed to amass.

Freda was a placid little soul and soon had her auntie wrapped around her little finger. Each time Adina cuddled her she missed her own child even more, and although she was willing to wait until Ariel and Brian had settled in, now that the funeral was over she was keen to get home to Dottie. Brian had signed all the necessary papers with the landlord and was busily adding stock of his choice to the shop, which his friend Paul was happy to fetch for him, much to Ariel's amusement.

'Do you know, Dina, I don't think I've ever seen Brian so happy,' she told her sister as the latter expertly changed her niece's nappy. 'This is just what he needed to give him some purpose in life again. He's been so frustrated since he came home from the war. Although, of course. I would rather it hadn't been at the expense of our father's death.'

'You mustn't think of it like that.' Adina tickled her niece's chubby arm as Ariel sat her up. 'Papa would have wanted you to be happy despite the fact that you had your differences in the past.'

'*Differences* is putting it rather mildly,' Ariel snorted. 'Papa always thought of me as the wayward one of the family, whereas you were his favourite. But then I'm glad we were on speaking terms again before he passed away.'

The young woman realised with a little pang of guilt that she had always been jealous of Adina. Her sister was the quiet, studious one who never answered back or disobeyed her parents, while she herself had rebelled, especially since coming to England, where she considered her father's strict religious beliefs were unnecessary. That was why it

228

had come as such a shock when Adina had confided that she was seeing a German prisoner of war.

Suddenly catching hold of Adina's hand, Ariel stared down at the band of steel on the third finger. 'You must still miss Karl very much,' she said. 'Do you think he will ever come back now?'

'I don't know,' Adina admitted as she lifted Freda and handed her a Farley's rusk.

Glancing furtively towards the door that led into the shop, where the two men were busily rearranging the stock, Ariel suddenly whispered, 'Can you keep a secret?'

Adina nodded.

'Good, then I'll tell you – and you'll be the first to know. The thing is I think I'm going to have another baby. But I don't want to tell Brian yet until I'm completely sure.' Her eyes were sparkling.

'Why, that's wonderful news,' Adina exclaimed, and then they suddenly became solemn as the same thought occurred to them both at the same time. It was the neverending circle of life: a birth and a death, just as it had been since time began.

More than ever now, Adina longed to tell Ariel about her own baby, but something held her back. Perhaps it was because she felt Ariel had enough to come to terms with at present, what with their father's death, a new baby on the way and starting up their own little business. But I will tell her soon, she promised herself. The next time I come to visit I shall bring Dottie with me and tell her everything. She then hurried over to the sink to fill the kettle. The men were long overdue a tea-break, and if she knew her brother-in-law at all, he would soon be shouting for one.

That evening, Adina strolled down to the phone box in Riversley Road and dialled the Montgomerys' number. She could hear the phone ringing in London and waited impatiently for Beattie or Fliss to pick it up. But after at least five minutes when no one had answered she pressed Button B to return her pennies and stepped out into the night with a frown on her face. She knew without a doubt that Mrs Montgomery would never answer the phone. She hated it with a vengeance and almost jumped out of her skin every time it rang. Beattie could well have gone home by now, but why hadn't Theo or Fliss answered it? It suddenly occurred to her that they might have been up in the nursery settling Dottie down for the night, and feeling slightly better, she set off back in the direction of the shop with a spring in her step. She had wanted to tell them that she would be home the next day. She was aching to hold Dottie again now, and as Ariel and Brian had now settled in, she could see no point in delaying going home any longer. But never mind; she would just turn up and surprise them.

*   *   *

229

The next morning, Ariel clung to her with tears in her eyes. 'You *will* come again soon, won't you?' she pleaded. 'You are all the family I have left now.'

Adina hugged her. 'That's not quite true,' she pointed out. 'You have Brian and Freda too.'

She then turned to Brian who was jiggling his daughter up and down on his one knee, and a pain pierced Adina's heart as she saw his trouser leg pinned up. The stump that was all that was left of his other leg was a reminder of how cruel the war had been to so many. Not that Brian complained. He was a cheerful chap, and Adina knew that he would look after his wife and his little family. She was leaving her sister in good hands.

'I er . . . I'll run you to the station if you like?' Paul now piped up as he flushed with embarrassment.

Ariel bit down on her lip to stop herself from grinning. Brian's friend had a crush on Adina; there was no doubt about it. He could hardly take his eyes off her, and stumbled about like a lovesick puppy whenever he got so much as a glimpse of her. Not that it came as any surprise to Ariel. Adina had developed into a very attractive young woman. Today she was wearing a pale blue cotton flowered dress that was cinched into her slim waist before billowing out into a flared skirt, and she wore her hair loose about her shoulders, which was very flattering. The funny thing was, Adina didn't seem to realise how attractive she was, which Ariel supposed was part of her charm.

'There's no need really,' Adina told him graciously. 'I don't want to put you to any trouble.'

But he almost fell over in his haste to snatch up her case. 'It *isn't* any trouble, really,' he gushed, careering out of the door. 'I'll wait for you outside while you say your goodbyes, but take as long as you like. I'll get you there in plenty of time to catch the train, I promise.'

Once he had disappeared from view, Ariel chuckled. 'I reckon you've got an admirer there,' she teased.

Ignoring the comment, Adina bent to kiss her niece's smooth cheek. She didn't want another man in her life, although Paul was a nice enough chap. Her heart still belonged to Karl and she knew that it always would.

'Now you be a good girl for your mummy and daddy,' she told Freda as the child cooed with delight and tried to grab the buttons on her dress. 'And you take care of yourself and don't get overdoing it,' she warned Brian.

'I will, and just remember, you're welcome here anytime,' he told her.

'Thank you. Now I'd better get going so this woman of yours can take that little scamp off you, so you can go and open your shop.'

Ariel followed her to the shop doorway where Mrs Haynes was also waiting to say goodbye with Sarah clutching her hand. It was wonderful to see the girl looking so well and happy again.

'Hurry up an' come home, luvvie,' their neighbour urged her as she planted a sloppy kiss on her cheek. 'I ain't none too happy about you bein' in London. My old man reckons it's a den o' vice down there.'

'Oh, don't you get worrying about me,' Adina replied with a smile. 'I'm a big girl now and well able to look after myself.'

'Hm, well, just make sure as you do,' Mrs Haynes retorted as she and Sarah waved.

Adina climbed into the front of the van with Paul, and then after one last kiss from her sister they were off. On the way to the station Paul was painfully quiet, not sure quite what to say now that he finally had her all to himself. Adina was glad of it; she had so many thoughts racing through her head that she was in no mood for conversation.

Once they arrived at Trent Valley railway station he carried her case onto the platform for her then stood there tonguetied as she smiled up at him.

'Thank you so much for the lift, Paul,' she said. 'And also for all the kindness you've shown to my sister and brother-in-law this week. I really don't know how they would have managed without you.' She stood on tiptoe and pecked him on the cheek, and colour immediately flooded into his face.

'I er . . . I'll be seein' you the next time you come visitin' then?' he said hopefully, and when she nodded he turned and hurried away, fingering his cheek where she had kissed him and vowing to himself that he wouldn't wash it for a week at least.

Once the train had pulled in and Adina had settled into a carriage, she stared from the window. She was full of so many emotions she didn't quite know which one to think about first. Overriding everything was deep sorrow at the loss of her father – and yet it was tinged with a bittersweet joy, for she hoped that he was with her mother and brother and was happy again now.

She was delighted for Brian and Ariel, who now had their own little shop to run, and she had the feeling that they would make a thriving business of it, for Brian was full of enthusiasm and determined to work hard. She grinned as she thought of what he would say when Ariel told him that they were to have a new addition to the family. She had no doubt that he would be delighted at the news – and so he should be, if the new baby turned out to be half as adorable as little Freda. And of course there had been the exciting news that Karl had written to her. The letter might even be waiting for her when she got home. And then her thoughts turned to Dottie and for the rest of the journey she struggled to control her impatience. She could hardly wait to see her and to hold her in her arms.

They were almost halfway to London when the sky suddenly became overcast and by the time the train pulled into Euston the rain was dancing off the slabs, leaving deep puddles all along the pavements.

231

Adina cursed softly. Her coat was packed right in the bottom of her case, and not wishing to delay seeing Dottie whilst she rummaged about for it, she splashed along eager to get home. These days, she knew the surrounding area like the back of her hand and took the short cuts home. Nevertheless, in no time at all she was drenched to the skin, but she didn't mind. She was almost there now and soon she would be holding her baby again.

By the time she arrived at the steps of the Montgomerys' huge terraced townhouse she knew she must resemble a drowned rat, but she bounced up the steps, dumped her suitcase on the ground and rang the bell with a wide smile on her face. While she waited for Beattie to answer she gazed up at the tarpaulin on the roof, which was still flapping wildly in the wind and rain. Good job Mrs Montgomery had finally found someone willing to come and fix it, she thought. She rang the bell again, and after another few minutes began to fumble in her bag for the key that Fliss had given her some time ago.

At last she found it, and swiping the rain from her face she inserted it in the lock and nearly fell into the hallway.

'*I'm home!*' she shouted, as she put her suitcase down on the hall floor where the water that ran off it instantly formed a puddle on the parquet tiles.

When no one answered, she headed for the drawing-room door. Mrs Montgomery would usually be in there at this time of day listening to the wireless, but today the room was deserted.

Next she headed to the kitchen. Beattie was sure to be downstairs preparing the evening meal – but once again she found an empty room. It was then she noticed that Dottie's big pram was gone from the hallway and her heart skipped a beat. Surely Fliss wouldn't have taken her out in this appalling weather?

She systematically peeped into each room that led off the long hallway, before kicking off her sodden shoes and mounting the stairs barefoot.

'*Hello?*' she called at the top of the first landing, and paused to listen for an answer but there was nothing but the sound of the tarpaulin flapping on the roof and the rain slamming against the windows.

She was beginning to feel vaguely uneasy now but forced herself to stay calm as she then took the stairs to the next floor. Everywhere was deserted and she couldn't understand it. Theo should have been home from school by now, and normally he and Fliss would be playing with Dottie in the nursery. That's where they must be, she reasoned to herself as she climbed towards the third floor, but as she opened the nursery door her heart sank. Not only was the room empty, but Dottie's cot had gone, and when she flew across the room and flung the wardrobe door open, Adina saw that all her clothes were missing too.

Now she hurried towards Fliss and Theo's room, and a quick glance into their wardrobes showed that all their clothes were gone too. She found the same thing in the old lady's room, and as she stared into the empty wardrobe in despair she felt as if her legs were going to collapse beneath her.

They had gone, but where? And why had they taken Dottie with them? Dottie was *her* baby, not theirs. But even as the thought sped through her mind, images of her baby holding out her arms to Fliss tortured her. Dottie absolutely adored her, and Theo too if it came to that. And then suddenly another thought occurred to her and she felt the tension in her body ease. Mrs Montgomery had recently found a builder who was prepared to come and mend the roof: perhaps they had moved to other accommodation whilst it was being repaired? Yes, that must be it – and no doubt they would have left a note for her somewhere telling her where she could join them. She systematically began to throw doors open, her eyes flitting along every surface for signs of a note but there was nothing upstairs apart from bare cupboards and drawers.

She flew down to the kitchen but there was nothing there either, so next she raced into the drawing room – and that was when she saw it. A bulky brown envelope addressed to her was propped up against a china figurine on one of the small tables. As she tore it open, a sheet of paper dropped out and she began to read it desperately.

Dear Adina,

As promised, you will find enclosed the deeds to the house; it has been signed over to you in the presence of my solicitor and is now in your name. I think it is very sensible of you to agree to Theo, Dorothy's father, bringing her up, and I assure you she will never want for anything, least of all love. Felicity loves the child as her own and as you already know, Theo adores her. Everything you now see belongs to you. My solicitor will also forward you a small sum of money once every four weeks for the next six months to ensure that you are able to meet all the bills until you find yourself a fulltime job. I have also left you a substantial amount to pay for the repairs to the roof. I hope you will be happy in the knowledge that we will give Dorothy the very best of everything; she deserves it. You can now put the past behind you and make a brand new start. There are not many girls of your age who own their home, so make the most of what you have been given.

I remain,

Yours sincerely,

Marjorie Montgomery

As the paper slid from her hand and fluttered to the floor, Adina gasped. What was the old lady talking about? The letter implied that Theo was Dorothy's father and that she had *agreed* to him and Fliss bringing her up. But Theo *wasn't* Dorothy's father and she had *never* agreed to Fliss and Theo taking her baby. There was nothing in the world that would ever have persuaded her to do so, so none of it made sense.

After a moment she withdrew an official-looking document from the envelope with shaking fingers and stared down at it in disbelief. These were the deeds to the house – and just as Mrs Montgomery had said, they were in her name. A copy of Dorothy's birth certicate was there too, and on it Theo was named as the father. Now too late, she understood why he had been reluctant to show it to her. There was also a substantial sum of money which she found amounted to two hundred pounds. She had never seen such a large amount of money all at once in her whole life before. And all this was hers now, but at what cost?

Part Four

A Place of Shelter

Chapter Thirty-Nine

That evening, Adina was so miserable that she couldn't seem to focus on anything. In Dottie's room she had found a teddy bear that had been left behind and she sat huddled in a chair hugging it to her as tears slid unchecked down her pale cheeks. They had taken her baby! She knew that somehow she would have to find her – but where would she start looking? To search for someone in London would be like looking for a needle in a haystack. The light slowly dimmed until eventually she was sitting in total darkness but she barely even noticed, until the sudden ringing of the telephone brought her springing from the chair. It had to be Fliss or Theo, she reasoned. Perhaps they were feeling guilty over what they had done and were ringing to tell her they were coming home.

'*Yes?*' she shouted breathlessly after snatching the receiver up – and then, just as she had hoped, Fliss's voice came to her.

'Hello, Adina. I was just checking that you were home and that you were all right.'

'Where are you?' Adina demanded.

Fliss sounded upset as she replied, 'You don't need to know that. All you need to know is that Dottie is safe and happy. She will have everything you ever dreamed of for her and I hope that in time you'll see this was for the best.'

'How *can* it be for the best?' Adina ranted, broken-hearted. 'Dottie is *my* baby, you know she is. You can't do this, I'll . . . I'll call the police!'

'If you did, they would soon see that Dottie is better off with us and where she should be,' Fliss told her gently. 'If they found us I would explain that Dottie was Theo's child – the result of a secret affair you'd had with him, and the letter that Mother left for you would substantiate that. I'd say that you felt her father and I could offer her a better life and so we gave you the house as a gesture of good will, and took over the care of her. When Theo registered her birth he named himself as the father on the birth certificate.'

'You've really thought of everything, haven't you?' Adina's voice was defeated. Who would ever believe her word against the Montgomerys'?

There was silence on the line for a moment until Fliss told her, 'I won't be in touch again, but rest assured that Dottie will be well taken care of. When you've had time to come to terms with this you'll see that it's for the best. Make the most of the start we have given you. Goodbye, Adina.'

'No . . . *don't go!*' Adina cried in a panic, but the only sound that reached her was the dull whirring of the empty line. Fliss had already gone.

She stumbled back to the drawing room and picked up the little teddy again. It had been one of Dottie's favourites, bought for her by Fliss, and when she held it to her face Adina could smell her baby on it: all Johnson's Baby Powder and Dottie's own sweet smell. But she was gone now, and as Adina stood there, she had the most awful premonition that she was never going to see her daughter again.

She cried herself to sleep on the sofa that night and woke in the early hours feeling stiff and sore. The morning light was just struggling beyond the lace curtains and she blinked and licked her dry lips before stumbling towards the kitchen, reasoning that a good strong cup of tea might make her feel a little better.

It was as she was sitting forlornly at the kitchen table that she heard a key in the lock of the front door and she hurried into the hall just in time to see Beattie step inside.

''Ello, luvvie,' the woman greeted her cheerfully. 'How did your dad's funeral go then?'

'Never mind about that for now. Where have they gone?' Adina asked desperately.

The woman stared at Adina in astonishment. 'Where've *who* gone?'

'All of them.' Adina spread her hands in despair. 'They've disappeared and taken my baby, Beattie. What am I going to do?'

Beattie scratched her head, feeling more bewildered by the second. 'Look, let's start again over a nice cup of tea,' she said as she headed towards the kitchen.

Adina followed her and watched as Beattie refilled the kettle and bustled about. In no time at all she had fresh cups in front of them and only then did she ask, 'Right, now why don't you start at the beginnin', eh?'

And so Adina told her how she had returned to the empty house to find that it had been signed over to her and her baby gone.

'But I thought you'd *agreed* to all this,' Beattie said when Adina had finished. 'Right since the nipper were born, old Mrs Montgomery told me that you'd 'ad 'er for the young Mr and Mrs, seein' that they couldn't 'ave a baby of their own an' that Theo were her dad. They left midweek but I thought you knew all about it.'

'Well, you thought wrong then,' Adina sobbed. It seemed that this had been planned for some time and she hadn't even realised what was going on. 'Do you *really* think I would sell my baby for bricks and mortar? What sort of a person do you think I am? And how *could* Theo be her father? I was already pregnant when I came here!' She suddenly wished that she had confided in Beattie about Karl now, but it was too late for regrets. The only people she had told were Fliss and Mrs Montgomery, and they had used this to their favour.

Deeply distressed and totally confused, Beattie patted her hand. 'I suppose all you can do is look on the bright side now,' she said, not quite knowing who to believe. Adina was certainly very convincing, but then the old lady had been too and she had seen firsthand how devoted the young Mr and Mrs were to the baby. 'At least you've got a nice 'ouse an' a roof over your 'ead now. An' let's face it, that little 'un will never want for nothing. Miss Fliss an' Mr Theo love her to bits.'

'I know that, but so do I,' Fliss sobbed. '*She's my daughter!* What am I going to do without her, Beattie?'

'It seems as if you don't 'ave much choice,' the woman told her wisely. 'What's done is done. It's doubtful you'll ever find them if they don't want to be found. They've got enough money behind them to be anywhere by now.'

'I'm still going to try,' Adina retorted with her chin in the air. 'And there's no time like the present, so if you'll excuse me I'm going to go and tidy myself up a bit and make a start. Theo's Daimler is very noticeable. If they're still hereabouts I'm bound to spot it if I search hard enough.'

She rose from the table, but as she made to leave the room, Beattie asked her, 'There's something I'd best ask you before you disappear. I'm sorry to bring it up now, what with all you've got on your plate, but what about me? What I mean is, will you still be wanting me to come in and clean for you?'

Adina shook her head. 'No. I'm really sorry, Beattie, but I have no intention of touching a penny of the money Mrs Montgomery left me except to pay the household bills until I find them, and I couldn't afford to pay you on what I earn at the school.'

The woman nodded. She had guessed what the answer would be but she would miss this job. Mrs Montgomery might have been a bit of an old tartar but Fliss and Theo had been lovely to work for. She simply didn't know what to make of it all.

Fetching a pad and pen from an enormous oak dresser that stood against one wall, she scribbled down an address, telling Adina, 'That's fair enough then. But if ever you should change your mind, this is where I live . . . Oh, and good luck, luvvie.'

'Thank you.' Adina gave her a quick hug and shot off up the stairs. Moments later she heard the front door shut and a terrible sense of loneliness engulfed her as she realised that for the very first time in her life, she was truly alone.

Adina returned to work three days later, but when she wasn't there she spent every spare minute scouring the streets of London, which was no mean feat. As soon as the school shut each afternoon she would target a different district, hoping to catch a sight of Theo's car, and she never returned home until she was so tired that she could barely put one foot in front of another or if it was just too dark to see anything. By the end of three weeks she had walked all around the streets of Bloomsbury, King's Cross, Fitzrovia, Paddington and Islington – with no success at all. Each night when she returned to the house she was so weary that all she was capable of doing was making herself a hasty sandwich and falling into bed.

Initially she had hoped that the staff at the school would know of Theo and Fliss's whereabouts, but they had not been able to help her. When Theo had handed in his notice, he simply told them that the family would be moving out of the area and had left no forwarding address. She had also visited the solicitor who had handled the transfer of the house into her name, but he had merely told her very politely that because of client confidentiality he was not allowed to divulge the whereabouts of the Montgomerys to anyone. Seeing the young woman's deep distress he had then softened a little and confided that, even though he couldn't have given her their address, in truth he didn't have it either. The Montgomerys had simply informed him that they would be in touch in the future if necessary.

In desperation, Adina had then phoned Mrs Downes at the school she had worked at in Nuneaton. But the bewildered headmistress had no idea of the Montgomerys' whereabouts either. And now the hopelessness of the situation Adina found herself in was finally coming home to her. London was such a vast place. It would take years to try and cover it on foot, and chances were that Theo and Fliss would have moved right away by now, to another part of the country, maybe – or even abroad.

The builders were due to come and start work on the roof the following week, and Adina knew that she would have to dip into the money that Mrs Montgomery had left her to pay them.

The next afternoon she came straight home after school and went immediately up to the empty nursery. And it was then that the futility of what she was doing really hit home. Theo, Fliss and her baby could really be gone for good. She just knew it now, and there was nothing she could do about it, although she knew that she would never give up looking for them, until her last breath.

The worst thing was that, deep inside, she knew that what Mrs Montgomery had said in her letter was true. Dottie *would* be better off with Theo and Fliss. They would give her everything that she herself could never have provided for her. She would go to a good school and wear the best clothes and have everything a little girl could ever dream of, whereas if she had kept her, the child would have been brought up without knowing her father, and Adina would have struggled to get her the bare necessities. Thoughts of Karl made her heart break afresh, and now she finally began to accept that she had really lost him too. The letter he had written her had never arrived. But if he had intended to come for her, he would have done so by now.

She began to walk around the house, really looking at it for the very first time. It was a fine house and at one time she would have marvelled at the thought of owning it, but now it brought her no joy. Her first instinct had been to hand the keys back to the solicitor and tell him that she wanted no part of it, but what good would that do? It wouldn't bring Dottie back and she would be homeless.

As she wandered back downstairs she noticed a letter lying on the door mat that she had missed when she first came in, and she saw that it was from Beryl. Taking it into the kitchen, she sat down and began to read it. Within a minute or so, she realised that her friend was in an even worse position than she was. She was desperately unhappy and worried about her baby's health. She told Adina that she rarely saw Tyrone, and when she did she had to beg him for enough money to buy even the barest essentials for her little one. His parents treated her as a skivvy and she sounded so desperate that Adina's heart ached for her.

Laying the letter aside, she made herself a cup of Camp Coffee, and as she sat at the table sipping it an idea suddenly occurred to her. Beryl could come here to live with her! The house was far too big for one person; she was rattling around in it like a pea in a pod and she had more than enough money to send some for Beryl to return to England.

The very same evening, she wrote to Beryl, enclosing a sum of money that was sufficient for her to return home. At least some good might come of the sorry mess she found herself in, Adina thought sadly, if she was able to get Beryl away from her tyrannical husband.

When she had finished, she rang Ariel. Her sister was the only close family that Adina had left now, and hearing her voice gave her a small measure of comfort.

She spent all her free time during the next ten days cleaning the house from top to bottom, but even though she kept herself busy Adina's thoughts were always with her baby. The pain of separation cut deep. She knew that the hurt would never truly go away, but still she convinced herself that she would find her somehow. At last she was satisfied that all was ready for Beryl's arrival. She had no idea if her friend would come by sea or air, or even when she would arrive – and so now she resumed her search.

With every day that passed, her spirits sank a little lower. Every time she so much as stepped out of the door she would instantly scan the streets for a sight of Theo's car but she never once saw it.

By the end of July 1946 she had lost a tremendous amount of weight, not that it mattered to her, for she no longer cared how she looked. All she wanted was to find her child.

And then one Saturday morning at the beginning of September, a knock sounded on the front door. It echoed through the house as she hurried to answer it, wondering who it could be. The builders had finished work on the roof now and she wasn't expecting anyone.

Inching the door open cautiously, she peered out to find a woman clutching a baby closely to her on the top step. 'Hello, may I help you?' she asked politely, and then as realisation dawned on her she gasped, '*Beryl!* You're here at last! I'm so sorry, I didn't recognise you for a moment. Come in, come in, I'm *so* pleased to see you.'

Snatching up a rather battered suitcase, Adina ushered her into the hallway where Beryl stood looking around her anxiously. The child in her arms was whimpering and Adina quickly took Beryl's elbow and led her down to the kitchen.

'You must be hungry and tired after your long journey,' she said sympathetically. 'And so must Catherine. Come with me I'll make you both a drink and something to eat.'

As Beryl went with her, her eyes flicked from side to side in awe. It had come as a great shock when she received the money from Adina to buy an air ticket home, but this house was an even bigger shock, and she wondered where the people were who owned it. Adina had told her in her letters that she was living with a family in London, but never in her wildest dreams had Beryl expected the place to be anything like this. Whoever owned it must be very rich indeed.

Up to now she had not uttered so much as a single word, and her silence continued as Adina led her into the biggest kitchen she had ever seen.

'Sit down and make yourself at home,' Adina told her, wondering what had happened to the girl she had used to know. Beryl's bleached blonde hair, which had used to be one of her most striking features, was now a dull mousy brown tied into the nape of her neck with a thin ribbon, and her eyes were empty and lacklustre.

When she placed Catherine onto a chair and slowly began to peel off the drab brown coat that she was wearing, Adina was shocked to see how much weight she had lost. She was so thin that she looked almost skeletal, and she was desperately pale, although there were the remains of a bruise all across one of her eyes that had now faded to a dirty yellowy colour, making her look slightly jaundiced.

Adina tried to sound cheerful as she bustled about refilling the kettle and fetching bread, cheese and butter from the pantry. And all the while the infant on the chair watched her from wary eyes as she clung to the sleeve of her mother's faded dress.

In no time at all Adina had made a bowl of bread and milk for the little girl and a plateful of cheese sandwiches for her mother. She then heated a large pan of milky cocoa. 'I had no idea how long it would take you to get here', she said. 'Did you fly or come by sea?'

'We flew,' Beryl informed her as she spooned the bread and milk into the child's mouth. 'It took hours and hours.' Adina knew that London

Airport had only recently been opened for civilian transport, and assumed that the long journey accounted for Beryl's exhaustion. 'We've come by bus and Underground from the airport. It wasn't easy with a baby and a suitcase to juggle, but at least we're here now. How are you, Adina?'

'I've been better, to be honest,' Adina pushed a mug of cocoa towards her and a beaker for the little girl. 'But I'll tell you all about that later. For now I just want to look at you. I can't believe that you're really here. I've missed you so much.'

And then suddenly they were in each other's arms and the tears on their cheeks mingled as the two friends each thought of all they had been through since they had last seen each other.

Chapter Forty

After Beryl had changed her baby's nappy and given her a warm wash and put her in her night-clothes, Adina took them up to the room she had prepared for them. There was a large double bed in there and Beryl instantly tucked the child down. The little one was asleep almost before her head had hit the pillow and as she jammed her thumb into her mouth Adina felt sorry for her. She looked so little and vulnerable.

'I could buy a cot for Catherine, if you like,' she whispered.

'No!' Beryl shot back, a little too quickly. 'She can sleep with me. She doesn't like to be on her own. She's quite a nervy child.'

'That's fine,' Adina assured her. 'And now that Catherine is settled, how about we go back downstairs and you can tell me all about what's been happening?'

Beryl glanced at her child one last time, hoping she wouldn't wake up and be scared, before quietly following Adina from the room. Soon they were installed in the drawing room where Beryl gazed about herself in awe.

'Blimey! This is quite some place, ain't it?' she whistled softly through her teeth, and just for a second Adina caught a glimpse of the light-hearted friend she remembered. 'Where are the folks that own it?' Beryl went on. 'Will they be home soon?'

'Unfortunately no, they won't, but I'll tell you all about that later.' Adina poured them both a small glass of sherry from Mrs Montgomery's crystal decanter. 'For now I want to hear all about you.'

Beryl spread her hands in a gesture of helplessness. 'Where do I start? It's been one disaster after another ever since the minute I left England. Most of the GI brides sailed out to join their husbands in America on the *Queen Mary* in February, as you probably know. I thought I was one of the lucky ones, being allowed to fly home with Tyrone immediately after we got married. He was an officer, you see, an' I'd kicked up such a stink that I think he had to pull a few strings. I wish to God I hadn't bothered now. Perhaps if I'd stayed back with the majority of the other brides he would have forgotten all about me. He'd certainly have been doing me a favour. In fact, I wish I'd never set eyes on him.'

She sipped at her drink as Adina stared at her sympathetically. Beryl looked as if she'd had the very soul sucked out of her. She had never seen her before without her make-up and was finding it difficult to believe that this was the same girl who had once befriended her back in

Nuneaton. Whenever she had thought of Beryl in the time they had been apart, she had always pictured her with the bright red lipstick and nail varnish that she had favoured. Beryl would never have dreamed of stepping outside the house without her 'war paint' on, as she had called it back then, but now she was devoid of any make-up whatsoever and she looked years older than she actually was.

'It was a shock, when we got to the States, I don't mind tellin' you,' Beryl continued. 'My in-laws' home was appalling, little more than a shack. It was in Texas, but in the back of beyond: nothing like the stud ranch he had conned me into believing. And what made it worse was the fact that from the second I set foot through the door, they made it clear that I wasn't welcome there. I hoped things would improve once Catherine arrived, but if anythin' that only made things worse. They moaned every time the poor little mite so much as whimpered. An' then Tye started to stay out at night, and when I complained, he'd thump me one.' Her hand rose self-consciously to her eye. 'I kept thinkin' that it would get better, but the trouble was, Catherine's always been a sickly baby – an' that got on his nerves an' all. He was forever tellin' me to shut her up. I had to beg for every penny he gave me, and after a time I suppose I just gave up. That's why the money you sent me came as such a godsend. I couldn't believe me luck, though it weren't easy to get away. I had to plan it all on the quiet an' then slip out with Catherine in the dead o' night so none of them would know I was goin'. If they'd found out about the money you sent they'd have taken it off me, see? An' then I'd have been stuck there for good.' Beryl held out her hands, to show Adina how they were still shaking. 'But how did you manage to raise that much, Dina? You must have a very good job.'

Adina took a deep breath: it was time to relay her story now.

'Do you remember Karl?' she asked. When Beryl nodded, the words began to spill out of her mouth. She held nothing back until eventually the whole sorry story was told. It was such a relief to have someone to confide in, and as she came to an end, Beryl's mouth gaped in amazement.

'Your mam, dad an' Dovi all dead, an' you had a baby!' she gasped incredulously.

Adina mopped at her eyes with a handkerchief as she nodded.

'An' now all this is yours?' Beryl gazed around in amazement.

'Only for now,' Adina gulped. 'I haven't touched a penny of the money the Montgomerys left me, apart from to send you some for your ticket and to pay for the roof repair and some bills. But when I find them and get Dottie back, I'll refund every penny, including the house. I don't want any of it if it costs me my baby.'

'Oh, Dina . . . An' here's me, feelin' sorry for meself. Why, I reckon you've had a worse time of it than I have, from what you've just told me. What does Ariel think of all this?'

'She never knew about the baby. No one did, only the Montgomerys,' Adina admitted.

'Hm, then that could make it difficult,' Beryl said quietly. 'It seems to me that even if you do manage to track them down, you're goin' to have a fight on your hands to get the baby back. It will be your word against theirs if it went to court an' they said that you'd given her to them for this place and an allowance.'

'But I *didn't*! I *wouldn't*!' Adina denied hotly.

'I know you wouldn't. Calm down,' Beryl urged. 'But no one else does, do they? Seems to me the Montgomerys have been very crafty, the way they've gone about this.'

'You don't think I'm going to get Dottie back, do you?'

Beryl opened her mouth to lie but then clamped it shut. 'I have to say it ain't lookin' likely,' she said. 'It seems to me they've stitched you up good an' proper, especially wi' that letter the old woman left for you. If you showed that to the police they'd laugh you out o' the station and think you were just regrettin' what you'd agreed.' She had never lied to Adina before and had no intentions of starting now. 'P'rhaps it might be better if you try to put everything behind you an' start afresh.'

'Could *you* do that if someone took Catherine off you?' Adina ground out indignantly.

'It wouldn't be easy, but if I were in your position, happen I'd have to. I'm so sorry for everything that's happened though. I can only imagine how awful it must be for you.'

A thin wail suddenly reached them from above and as Adina glanced towards the clock on the mantelpiece she was shocked to see that almost two hours had passed since Beryl had arrived. But then they had had so much to catch up on and talk about that the time had just flown by.

'That's Catherine,' Beryl said as she rose from her seat and hurried towards the door. 'I bet she'll be hungry again.'

'You go and fetch her down and I'll get us all something hot to eat,' Adina said as her friend disappeared through the door. And then she managed a weak smile. At least she wasn't totally alone any more.

By the end of the first week, Adina felt as if Beryl and Catherine had been there with her for ever. She would go off to work each day and arrive home to find the house sparkling and a meal prepared.

'I've got to do somethin' to keep meself busy, ain't I?' Beryl shrugged when Adina told her that there was really no need to wait on her. 'I shall have to think about findin' meself a job an' all soon. I can't expect you to keep the pair of us.'

'But I don't mind really,' Adina assured her.

Beryl shook her head. She had initially through of returning to live with her parents in Nuneaton. She knew that she would be welcome there, and that they would adore their little granddaughter, but with

Adina she felt that she had a measure of independence at least. She also hated the thought of leaving her. Adina seemed so alone. And so her mind was racing for most of the time as she tried to think of some sort of job she might do. Before she could do anything, she would have to find a childminder for Catherine, of course, and it was a daunting thought. She had never left her before.

Each night after dinner the two young women would bath Catherine and then once she was settled in Beryl's bed they would sit and chat. Already, Beryl was looking slightly better than when she had first arrived, although she seemed reluctant to leave the house, which Adina supposed was understandable. Adina would tell Beryl all about the children at the school each evening and Beryl would listen avidly. Sadly, Adina had discovered that Esther, one of her favourites, had also been orphaned and her heart ached for the child who had been placed in the same orphanage as Rebekah. Both of the little girls were struggling to come to terms with the fact that they would never see their parents again, and Adina wished that there was more that she could do for them. Every day, the Red Cross and the Salvation Army brought her horror stories of what had become of certain children's parents, and she felt so useless.

Strangely, since Beryl's arrival, Adina had almost abandoned her search for Dottie. She knew that her chances of ever tracing her were slight, as Beryl had pointed out, and now she was just taking one day at a time, although the longing to see her little girl never went away. It had helped, having Catherine there to coo over, and the toddler was finally accepting her. Adina had fetched the few remaining toys that the Montgomerys had left behind from Dottie's nursery and she loved playing with them with her little house guest, who would giggle with delight at all the attention that was being showered on her.

It was one evening when they had tucked Catherine into bed and were enjoying a cup of cocoa in the kitchen that Beryl tentatively broached an idea that had been playing on her mind for a few days. 'I've been thinkin' . . . this house is yours now to do as you please with, ain't it?'

Adina nodded over the rim of her mug. 'Yes, it is – why?'

'Well, the thing is, it's far too big just for us an' I need a job though I ain't too happy about the thought of leavin' Cathy with a stranger. So I thought, why don't I do a job that would mean I didn't have to leave the house?'

'What did you have in mind?' Adina asked.

'I was thinkin' of all them little ones where you work havin' to go into orphanages 'cos their parents have been killed or are missin', an' I thought, well, how about we have a few of them here? You know, start a little home for them. I know the people who took in evacuees got paid by the Welfare, so why shouldn't we do it?'

Adina stared off into space as she tossed the idea around in her mind.

247

A children's home! It was something that had never occurred to her, but the more she thought about it, the more the idea appealed to her. And what Beryl had suggested certainly made sense.

After a time she said, 'I'll have a chat to the Headmistress tomorrow and see what she thinks of your idea – if you're really sure it's something you'd like to do?'

'I am sure.' Beryl suddenly looked quite excited and once again it struck Adina just how much her friend had changed in the time they had been apart. Beryl had grown up, but then so had she – they had both had to, and now she felt ready for a challenge.

The very next day she approached Miss Wainwright as soon as she arrived at the school. The woman was actually glad of a chance to speak to Adina because she had been concerned about her for some time. The young woman still did her job efficiently, but all the sparkle seemed to have gone out of her and she didn't look at all well.

'How can I help you, my dear?' she asked, when they were both seated in her office.

'Well . . .' Adina took a deep breath and put the idea of her fostering the children to the woman, who listened carefully.

'You're rather young to be thinking of doing something quite so ambitious,' she said doubtfully. 'And won't it be too much for you? I mean, you already have your own baby to care for, don't you?'

If truth be told, Mrs Wainwright had thought it quite strange, the way the Montgomerys had left the school so quickly, leaving no forwarding address. She had always understood that Adina had lodged with them and Fliss had cared for the child once Adina had come back to work.

For a moment Adina was lost for words. What could she say? If she told the woman the truth, she would never take her word against the Montgomerys', so instead she said quietly, 'I lost the baby.' She wasn't really lying the way she saw it. She *had* lost Dottie.

Mrs Wainwright was shocked, but felt that this would explain so much. The poor girl. No wonder she had looked so ill! But she didn't ask any questions. It was obvious that Adina was struggling with her loss and she made a mental note to speak to the other members of staff to ensure that they never mentioned the baby again. Not that Adina had ever been very forthcoming about her private life. She had always been very polite, but kept herself very much to herself. Mrs Wainwright didn't even know what had happened to Adina's husband – if there had ever been one. He was no doubt one of the poor souls who had perished in the war. Adina certainly didn't seem the sort of girl to have a child out of wedlock.

Her thoughts were tugged sharply back to the present when Adina now told her, 'I assure you, Mrs Wainwright, age has nothing to do with it.' There was a determined note in her voice. 'I *love* working with

248

the children here, and you've seen firsthand that I have a good rapport with them. I really feel that this is something I could do successfully.'

Mrs Wainwright steepled her fingers and stared at her for a time. 'In that case let me have a word with the Home Finder at the Welfare Department,' she said eventually. 'I know the orphanages are full to overflowing, so let's take it from there, eh?'

When Adina smiled weakly, Mrs Wainwright thought how attractive she was. It seemed strange that a girl as young as Adina should be suggesting such a thing. But then most girls Adina's age had not given birth and lost a baby. Most young women were more interested in dressing up and going out to enjoy themselves. Furthermore, Adina could have had a string of admirers with her looks and temperament, but then nothing was straightforward any more. The war had seen to that.

She smiled at Adina kindly and dimissed her with a nod of the head and Adina floated away to her classroom with her head full of Beryl's brilliant idea.

The following weekend Beryl was due to catch the train to Nuneaton to visit her family after taking another small loan from Adina – on the strict understanding that it was only a loan.

'Are you quite sure you don't want to come with us?' she asked. 'You could go and see Ariel, Brian and Freda.'

But Adina shook her head. She was impatient now for the Home Finder from the Camden Welfare Department to come and see her as Mrs Wainwright had arranged, and she wanted to have the house looking as nice as it possibly could for her visit.

'No, you get off,' she encouraged with a smile. 'I shall be fine. I bet your parents are going to love meeting Cathy. In fact, I think you'll have a hard time of it, getting her away from them.'

'Oh, I'll be back, never you fear,' Beryl told her. 'I've had a taste of independence now, and even though it didn't work out with Tye as I'd hoped it would, I could never go back to livin' with Mum an' Dad again.' Her eyes settled affectionately on her little daughter. She was looking so much better already and was beginning to gain a little weight. Now Beryl was keen to start a job so she could feel that she was supporting them both without having to rely on Dina for handouts.

Adina helped them down to Euston with their case, young Cathy sitting in the secondhand pushchair she had bought as a gift for the child, then she stood on the platform and waved them off until the train disappeared from sight. And then the loneliness closed in again and she walked back up Eversholt Street on feet that felt like lead.

Chapter Forty-One

Adina stared at the two pinched faces sympathetically as she ushered the little girls into the drawing room ahead of Miss Higgins, the Home Finder from the Welfare Department. She never failed to be amused by the woman because she was so busy, and her hands were not still for a second. A small, stockily-built person, her piercingly bright blue eyes seemed to flit from one place to another constantly. Her hats were another source of amusement, and up to now Adina had never seen her in the same one twice. Today she was wearing a small straw affair heavily trimmed with feathers that floated off in all directions every time she turned her head. She tended to talk very fast too, as if she couldn't get her words out quickly enough, and sometimes Adina felt dizzy trying to keep up with her. But for all that she did seem to have a genuine concern about the children in her care and that endeared her to Adina.

The last few weeks had passed in a blur of assessments, but now at last Rebekah and Esther, the two little girls she had worked with at the school, were here to stay. Miss Higgins had just fetched them from the orphanage they had been staying in and they were staring around in awe, much as Adina once had when she had first arrived to stay with the Montgomerys.

It seemed such a long time ago, and so much had happened since then – but she wouldn't think about that for now. She wanted to make today a happy one for the girls. After all, this would be their home from now on.

They were each clutching a bag that contained all their worldly possessions; these were so pitifully small Adina's kind heart ached for them.

'Come along, girls,' Miss Higgins chanted in a singsong voice as she shooed them onto the settee. 'Aren't you lucky to be coming to live in such a beautiful house?'

The two little girls nodded in unison, keeping their eyes firmly fixed on Adina the whole time. They could hardly believe that they were really going to be staying here with her, and were terrified that Miss Higgins might change her mind at any minute and whisk them back to the cold, impersonal orphanage.

It was then that Beryl entered the room bearing a tray full of fairy cakes that she had baked that morning, and a large pot of tea. Cathy was toddling at her side, clinging shyly to her skirts.

'Hello, girls.' She smiled at them and they timidly smiled back. 'I'm Beryl an' this here is Cathy. We've been so lookin' forward to you comin'. I'm sure we're all goin' to get along just fine. Now, who wants to try one o' me cakes, eh? I ain't the best cook in the world, I have to admit, but I reckon they'll be edible. An' young Cathy here helped me stir the mixture.'

The two girls each dutifully took a cake and soon found that they were actually quite nice, if a little over-cooked.

Beryl then proceeded to pour the adults a cup of tea and beakers of milk for the children as Adina tackled the paperwork with Miss Higgins.

'That should just about do it,' the woman said a few minutes later as she tucked the forms safely into her bag and briskly drained the rest of her tea. 'And now I really ought to be getting along and leaving you two to settle in. Things to do, you know, but I'm sure you're both going to be fine here with Adina and Beryl. Goodbye for now, dears.' Straightening her hat, she stood up and trotted towards the door as the two girls watched her mutely. Neither of them knew quite what to make of her, although she seemed to be nice enough.

Adina saw her to the front door and shook her hand warmly. She knew that today, Miss Higgins was arranging for Cana, another little boy she had become very fond of at the school, to return to his family. Thankfully, he was one of her success stories, and after a lot of help from the Salvation Army she had discovered that his parents were still alive and desperate to have him home with them.

'Do give Cana my love and wish him good luck for me,' Adina told the woman, and then after watching her descend the outside steps, she returned to the drawing room. The two girls were still sitting as still as statues in exactly the same position as she had left them in, and sensing that they were feeling out of their depth she suggested kindly, 'Right, how about we go and show you both your rooms then, eh?'

'Rooms?' Rebekah squeaked nervously. 'W . . . won't we be sharing?'

'Of course not,' Beryl told her. 'You ain't in the orphanage now, love. You'll have your very own room here. An' it's a nice room an' all. You can see right over London from up there.'

The two girls lifted their bags and followed the young women upstairs, oohing and ahhing with delight at the first sight of the rooms Adina and Beryl had prepared for them. They were a world away from the cramped dormitories at the orphanage, and neither of them could quite believe their luck.

Rebekah's eyes filled with tears as she took in the polished wardrobe and the pretty patchwork eiderdown on the brass bed. It reminded her of the one she had once had on her own bed when she had lived at home in Berlin with her parents. But of course, she would never see her mother and father again now. Miss Wainwright had told her gently some time ago that they had both been sent to a concentration camp during the war, and had died there, along with her older brother Shimon.

Seeing her distress, Adina cuddled the thin body to her. 'Everything's going to be all right now,' she consoled her. 'We're all going to live here happily – just you wait and see.'

Beryl swallowed the lump that had formed in her throat as she hastily led Esther away to see her room. Poor little buggers, she thought. But they'll be fine now. Me an' Dina will see to that.

Both of the girls were now nine years old, although no one would ever have believed it as they were both remarkably scrawny and small for their age. Never mind, I'll soon put some fat on their bones, Beryl promised herself, and in that moment she just knew that the idea she had put to Adina some weeks ago was going to work. The Welfare was prepared to pay for the girls' keep, with a little left over which would enable both Dina and Beryl to earn a small wage each. She would no longer be dependent on her friend for everything, and it was a pleasing thought. The two young women had decided that for now, Dina would also continue to work at the school during the day, which would further help their income and more than pay for the household bills, and she would also continue with her sewing, which was fast turning into a very lucrative little sideline. As Beryl had quite rightly pointed out, she was more than capable of seeing to the running of the house, and she would be there to care for Cathy, so things should run smoothly, once the girls had settled in and they had got into some sort of a routine.

As it happened, the girls settled in surprisingly quickly and very soon they began to feel like a family. Little Cathy absolutely adored both Esther and Rebekah and constantly toddled about after them as if they were big sisters. Both Beryl and Adina were so busy that their own heartaches began to fade slightly, although they would never entirely go away. During the day when there were things to do, they had little time to think, but it was a different matter entirely when they went to bed each night. That was the time when Adina's longing for both her baby and Karl were strongest. She would lie in her lonely bed fingering the steel band on her finger as tears streamed down her cheeks and wonder where he was and what her baby was doing. Were they both happy? Did they ever think of her? She had no way of knowing so she just went on with her life as best she could. Both Rebekah and Esther had gone a long way to filling the gaping hole inside her heart, and now the house regularly rang with the sound of children's laughter. Adina had been busily sewing clothes for them almost since the day they had arrived, and now they looked well-dressed and far happier than she had dared to hope they might be.

Miss Higgins visited regularly during the first weeks of the girls arriving there. Secretly she had had reservations about two such young women taking orphans in, but from what she could see of it they were doing a remarkably good job, so soon she was happy to leave them to it – on the understanding that they would contact her, should she be needed.

Ariel and Brian brought little Freda to see them all shortly before Christmas, loaded down with gaily wrapped presents, and they were very impressed with the house and with what Beryl and Adina were attempting to do with the orphans. Adina had told them that the old lady with whom she had lodged when she first came to London had left it to her, and they assumed that Adina meant she had passed away and accepted what she said without question. Adina hated lying to them, but thought that the less they knew the better, and it was only a little white lie, after all.

When they arrived there was a fire roaring in the grate and a large Christmas tree standing in a bucket in the corner of the sitting room. It was Beryl who had insisted on having a traditional English Christmas and a tree, and Adina, Rebekah and Esther, who had now grown used to the English traditions, had been happy to go along with her wishes. They had all spent a very enjoyable afternoon decorating the tree with tinsel and baubles and homemade decorations. Now everywhere looked warm and cosy. When they had first arrived at the house Adina had offered to take the girls to the Belsize Square Synagogue, founded in 1939 by a group of refugees from Central Europe, so they could practise their faith if they so wished, but both girls had declined. They had been in England for almost four years now, since being evacuated from their own countries, and showed little interest in religion of any sort any more, which Adina supposed was understandable. Their faith was just a distant memory now like their parents, and her own beliefs seemed to have died with her father.

'Why, I can't believe that you really own all this! The old woman you worked for must have thought very highly of you,' Ariel had gasped when she had first arrived at the house, thinking how lucky her sister was. If she could only have known what the house had cost her, she might not have viewed it so kindly. She was now heavy with her second child and Adina was relieved to see that she looked happy and content.

'I think what you're doing with those two little girls is wonderful,' Ariel told her and Beryl one evening as they sat enjoying a last drink once the children were all tucked up warm and cosy in their beds. 'But when do you ever get any time to yourselves? Surely you should be out having fun. We'll never get you married off at this rate, Adina.'

'*I* have no intention of ever getting married,' Adina said tartly – and instantly felt guilty. 'I'm quite happy as I am,' she ended on a softer note.

'Me too,' Beryl said quietly.

Brian and Ariel exchanged a glance but decided that enough had been said on that subject so wisely turned the conversation to other things.

'The shop is doing really well,' Brian informed his sister-in-law as he rolled his brandy around in his glass. It was obvious that he was enjoying being his own boss and Adina knew how hard he was working from the snippets Ariel had told her.

'Have you closed it for now?'

He shook his head. 'Oh no, Paul is keeping it running whilst we visited you lot.' His eyes suddenly twinkled mischievously as he added, 'He was quite put out that he couldn't come with us. I think you've got an admirer there.'

Adina shrugged. 'Paul is a lovely chap but as we said, Beryl and I are quite happy as we are for now. I'm sure someone else will catch his eye before too long. He's far too nice to stay on his own.'

Ariel sighed contentedly as she stretched her feet out to the warmth of the fire. She was sorry that they could only stay for two days but knew that Brian wouldn't be happy to be away from the store for too long.

'So what would you like to do tomorrow?' Adina asked now, and before Brian could answer, her sister piped up, 'I'd like to go and see Buckingham Palace and Westminster Abbey too, if we have time.'

'That should be easy enough', Beryl said. 'The kids love sightseeing, though Cathy's getting to be a bit of a handful now. Still, I suppose that's to be expected, since she's coming up to the terrible twos!'

'It's all right for you. I shall have *two* little monsters rampaging about the place soon.' Ariel sighed dramatically though her eyes were smiling as she glanced at her husband and it gave Adina a warm glow inside. At least she didn't have to worry about her sister. Minutes later, Ariel gave a loud yawn and said, 'Ooh, sorry, I think the train journey must have caught up with me. Would you mind very much if I went to bed? I want to be raring to go tomorrow if we're going to see the sights.'

'Not at all,' they all assured her.

'I might come up with you.' Beryl stifled a yawn of her own. 'I've put hot-water bottles in all the beds so you should be comfy.' She dragged herself out of the chair and stretched before saying, ''Night all.'

When the others had gone, Adina stood up and began to tidy the room. She had been on the go nonstop since first thing that morning and quite fancied the thought of an early night herself, especially as Beryl had put a hot-water bottle in her bed. One thing she had soon discovered was that the bedrooms were freezing cold in the winter. Admittedly there were grates in each room, but it was hard enough to get coal to keep the kitchen stove and the drawing-room fire lit.

As she plumped up the cushions on the settee she could feel Brian's eyes on her. She turned to say something light-hearted, but the smile died on her face as he began to speak.

'So, now that we're finally on our own, how about we have a little chat,' he suggested.

'What about?' Adina lifted the empty glasses onto a tray, keeping her eyes averted from his.

'About all this.' He spread his hands, watching her steadily.

'I don't know what you mean.' Adina was feeling more uncomfortable by the second and longed for a chance to escape but wasn't quite sure how she could do that without appearing to be rude. 'I explained that the old lady I lived with left the house to me.'

'Yes, you did, and Ariel accepted your explanation – but it doesn't ring true to me.'

'Why not?' Adina said defensively.

Brian carefully placed his glass down and leaned forward in his chair. 'Because the way I understood it, you came here to stay with the old lady *and* her son and his wife. If anything happened to her, why would she leave the house to you instead of her family?'

For a moment Adina was dumbstruck as she tried to come up with another lie. Beryl was the only person in the world who knew why she had really inherited the house, and she was reluctant to tell Brian in case he told her sister. She knew how upset Ariel would be if she were to discover that she had a niece that she had never even known about.

'Well, she er . . .' Adina faltered and then suddenly she lowered her head.

'Come on, you can tell me.' Brian's voice was gentle as he saw the tears shimmering on her lashes.

'If I tell you, would you be prepared to keep it from Ariel?' she asked huskily.

'Yes, I would if I thought the truth would hurt her.'

She gazed at him for a moment, but then sensing that she could trust him she spilled out the whole sorry tale as he listened without interrupting. When she was done, he took a deep breath and placed his arm around her trembling shoulders.

'You poor love,' he muttered. 'I can't even begin to imagine what you have been through. You must have been to hell and back. I don't know how I'd cope if anyone took Freda away from me. And that damn lowlife that got you pregnant should be horse-whipped.'

'None of this is his fault,' Adina hiccuped through her tears. 'Karl didn't know that I was pregnant when he left, and he would have come back for me if he could have. I know it, he loved me.'

Brian had his own thoughts on that score, but tactfully kept them to himself. The way he saw it, Adina had gone through enough without him rubbing salt into the wounds.

'Ssh,' he soothed as he cradled her against his shoulder. 'Don't worry. I'll never breathe a word of what you've told me to Ariel. I don't believe in married couples having secrets from each other, but in this case I reckon me keeping just this one won't hurt.'

As Adina sagged against him and cried out all her pain, it occurred to her how lucky her sister was to have such a thoughtful husband, and it was comforting to know that she need never worry about Ariel again at least. Brian was a good man.

Chapter Forty-Two

The following day was one of the happiest that Adina had experienced for a long, long time. They all went on a sightseeing trip and enjoyed every single minute of it, arriving home that evening tired but happy.

'I just *loved* Trafalgar Square,' Ariel trilled as she and Beryl got the little ones ready for bed while Adina stayed downstairs preparing a meal for everyone. 'Feeding the pigeons there was such fun!'

Beryl smiled indulgently. The city had had much the same effect on her when she had first come to live here with Adina, but now she tended to take everything for granted and was sometimes even a little home-sick for Nuneaton where life was much slower and quieter. She had recently written to Tyrone asking him for a divorce. She had given him the address of a solicitor who would handle it for her as she had no wish to see him again, let alone give him her address. She was content for the first time in ages, and looking back now she wondered what she had ever seen in the GI, apart from his looks. Even now she could not deny that Tyrone was a handsome man.

'Do you miss your husband?' Ariel asked suddenly, as if she had somehow miraculously been able to read Beryl's thoughts.

'Not any more,' Beryl admitted, lifting Catherine out of the bath she was sharing with Freda. 'I'm sad that things didn't turn out as I'd hoped they would, but then things rarely do in life, do they? I suppose I fell in love with a dream. But then I did get Cathy out of it all, so I should be grateful for that.'

'Hm.' Ariel seemed to ponder on what she'd said for a while before asking, 'And what about Dina? Do you think she still misses Karl?'

Beryl thought carefully while pulling a clean vest over her daughter's head. 'I suppose she does, but I think she's come to terms with the fact that he's not coming back for her now. And let's face it – she's still only very young. I can't see someone as attractive as her havin' to be on her own for long if she didn't want to be, can you?'

'No – but what about Rebekah and Esther?' Ariel couldn't help but voice her concerns as she pulled out the plug and lifted Freda onto what was left of her lap. 'What would happen to them if Dina were to meet someone? She seems very fond of them and they obviously love her.'

Beryl chuckled as she slipped a nightdress over Cathy's sleepy head and gave her the rubber dummy to suck. 'I reckon whoever took to her would have to take to them an' all,' she replied. 'Dina is a very loyal person an' very committed to the girls, God bless 'em. They're lovely kids an' they've blossomed since they've been here. They wouldn't say boo to a goose when they first arrived, but we've brought 'em out of their shells. I can't see Dina turnin' her back on them for no bloke. But now if you'll excuse me I'm goin' to go an' tuck this one in before she falls asleep sittin' up.'

As she left the room, Ariel finished drying Freda and putting on her nappy and cosy nightie. She admired the two women for what they were doing for the orphans, but she couldn't help worrying about her sister. As far as she was concerned, Dina should be concentrating on getting married and having a family of her own, not taking in other people's children. But then saying that, her sister did seem happy, so she should be too. She determined that in the future she would try not to worry about her sister so much.

There were many tears the next morning as Brian and Ariel prepared to leave.

'I can't believe how quickly the time has passed,' Ariel wailed as she clung to her older sister. Dina was only twenty-two years old and yet she suddenly appeared to be much older, as if she had somehow grown up overnight. 'You *will* come and see us soon, won't you?'

Adina smiled at her sister. 'Of course I will, once the baby is born.' She ushered her towards the door. A taxi that Adina had ordered for them was standing outside and now she hugged her niece and planted a gentle kiss on her brother-in-law's cheek.

'Just remember, if ever you need us we're only at the end of the phone,' he murmured as they exchanged a meaningful glance.

'I know. Thanks, Brian. For everything. Look after them for me, won't you?'

'Always,' he told her with conviction and then everyone clustered around to wave goodbye as the little family trooped down the steps and clambered into the taxi.

The house felt strangely empty after they had left. Rebekah and Esther led Cathy away to play with them in the drawing room as Adina stared mournfully from the hall window into the road beyond.

'Come on, cheer up,' Beryl urged as she bent to retrieve a teddy bear Cathy had dropped on the hall floor. 'You'll be seeing them again before you know it.'

'I do know that, it's just that suddenly I feel so . . .' Adina looked so dejected that Beryl's heart ached for her. She had no need to ask what her friend was thinking about. She often found her up in the nursery staring around the empty room and knew that Adina missed her baby every single minute of every day. Even Rebekah, Esther and Cathy had not managed to completely fill the hole Dottie had left in Adina's heart, although they certainly kept her busy enough. In fact, what with her work at the school, looking after the girls and the sewing jobs she had taken on again, Beryl sometimes wondered how Adina managed to fit everything in.

'You know, you'll have to come to terms with what's happened soon,' she said quietly.

'I *have* come to terms with it,' Adina said indignantly.

Beryl shook her head. 'Oh no, you ain't – not from where I'm standin'. You'll eat yourself away at this rate. You know that wherever Dottie is she's being loved and cared for, so you should move on now too. I'm not sayin' you should forget all about her, but we've got a little family here that need you, Dina, an' the way I see it you can either let what's happened destroy you, or you can get on with your life and put it all behind you. I reckon you could if you tried hard enough. The Dina I've always known is a fighter – so what do you say?'

'I suppose you're right,' Adina mumbled. 'But it's so hard not knowing where she is or what she's doing.'

'I know.' Beryl patted her arm. 'Now how about we go an' have ourselves a nice strong cuppa before we set about puttin' this place to rights, eh? It looks as if the Jerries have dropped one o' them Doodlebugs in here.'

It was early on Christmas Eve morning 1946 when Adina was preparing the breakfast in the kitchen that she heard someone banging on the front door. Tightening the belt of her dressing-gown, she hurried into the hallway wondering who it could be, so early in the morning. Everyone else was still in bed having a lie-in and she wasn't expecting anyone.

When she opened the door she was confronted by a very harassed-looking Miss Higgins who was clutching the hand of a small boy with a tear-stained face.

'Oh, hello, dear,' Miss Higgins greeted her. 'I'm sorry to disturb you so early in the morning, but we have a bit of an emergency on and I was wondering if you could possibly help us out?'

'You'd better come in out of the cold.' Adina held the door wide and Miss Higgins swept in, dragging the little boy behind her.

'You sit down there and be a good boy whilst I just have a quick chat with Mrs Schwartz,' Miss Higgins told him as she deposited a rather battered-looking suitcase on the hall floor and gestured towards a chair.

The child did as he was told as Beryl appeared on the stairs knuckling the sleep from her eyes.

'Did I hear someone at the door?' she yawned – then as she spotted Miss Higgins she hurried down the steps towards them.

'Let's go into the drawing room,' Adina suggested as she flashed the child an encouraging smile.

Once they were all in the room she closed the door quietly behind them and instantly Miss Higgins burst out, 'The poor child. He's only four years old and his mother passed away last night. It seems his father was killed in the war and so he has no one now. The lady from the lodging house called us to ask us what she should do with him first thing this morning, and what with it being Christmas Eve . . . Well, I know this is terribly short notice and a great deal to ask, but do you think you could possibly take him? Just until we can sort him out a more permanent place.'

Before Adina could reply, Beryl piped up, 'Of course we'll take him, won't we, Dina? Poor little mite. I'm sure we can squeeze in another little 'un.'

Adina nodded. 'Yes, we can take him,' she agreed. 'What's his name?'

'It's Christopher. Christopher Bourne.' Miss Higgins looked so relieved that for a moment Adina feared she was going to kiss her. 'He's a good little chap according to the landlady at the house in College Street where he and his mum were staying, and it's tragic that he should lose his last remaining parent so close to Christmas. Not that there's ever a good time for that,' she added hastily. 'I'm sure he won't give you any trouble and I'll be in touch as soon as the holidays are over to decide what we're going to do with him. I shall have to enquire if any of the local orphanages have a place, unless some relative we don't know of comes forward. I don't think there's much chance of that happening though. The landlady couldn't recall anyone ever even visiting Christopher's mother. She went out quite a lot at night leaving Christopher in their room and tended to keep herself very much to herself, from what I could gather. Anyway, now that you've so kindly agreed to help me out, I must be on my way. I have a list of things to do as long as your arm before the office closes tonight. You can guarantee it's the same every Christmas.' Slinging her handbag over her arm she beamed at the two young women before marching purposefully towards the door. Once out in the hall again she looked down into Christopher's pinched, fearful little face.

'Now you're going to stay here over Christmas,' she told him with an encouraging smile. 'I'm sure you'll have a wonderful time and I'll be back to see you as soon as I can. Goodbye, dear.' And then she was gone, leaving Adina and Beryl staring at each other in amazement. Everything had happened so fast they had barely had time to take it all in.

By now the two older girls had crept downstairs and were peeping curiously at the new house-guest through the banisters.

'Come an' meet Christopher, girls,' Beryl encouraged when she spotted them. 'He's going to be staying with us over the holidays. That'll be nice, won't it?'

Rebekah and Esther smiled shyly as they came forward to meet him.

'You can play with my snakes and ladders game with me after break-fast, if you like,' Rebekah offered, and Adina felt a glow of pride sweep through her. The little girl had grown in confidence since coming to live

259

with them, and now with her long fair hair brushed and her blue eyes, shining she was becoming quite pretty.

Christopher managed a weak smile but remained stubbornly silent as Beryl caught hold of his hand and led him unresisting towards the kitchen.

'Come on, little 'un. Let's get you a bowl of nice creamy porridge, eh?'

'I'll go and fetch Cathy,' Adina told her and hurried away upstairs as the little party went off downstairs to the kitchen.

Half an hour later the two women exchanged glances as Christopher polished off his third bowl of porridge.

'Blimey O'Riley,' Beryl whispered. 'Anybody would think the child hadn't been fed for a month. I've never seen such a small nipper eat so much all in one go.'

Adina nodded in agreement as she filled his glass yet again with milk and placed two large pieces of hot buttered toast in front of him. There was something about the child that had struck a chord in her, and somehow she knew that she was going to like him even though as yet he had not uttered so much as a single word. He was very poorly dressed in a blazer that was at least two sizes two small for him, and his trousers were somewhere up above his skinny ankles. Christopher was quite tall for his age but skinny as a beanpole and he had a shock of curly dark hair that looked as if it hadn't been cut or washed for months. There was a spattering of freckles across his nose and dimples in his thin cheeks. But it was his eyes that were clearly his best feature, as far as Adina was concerned. They were a deep dark brown and heavily fringed. Now as she studied him she saw that they were full of unshed tears and she ached for the poor little chap.

'Why don't you take the children upstairs and help them all get dressed?' she suggested tactfully, and understanding exactly what she meant, Beryl lifted Cathy from her highchair and ushered them all quickly away.

Now that they were alone, Adina reached out to stroke Christopher's thin hand. 'It's going to be all right, I promise,' she said gently, and suddenly the tears he had so valiantly held back spurted out of him and in seconds she had him in her arms.

'That's it, sweetheart,' she soothed. 'Cry it all out. You'll feel better then.' And that is exactly what he did.

It was the first day after the New Year 1947 when Miss Higgins turned up on the doorstep again.

'I have good news,' she boomed, the second she skipped through the door. 'They have a place at Saint Paul's Orphanage and I can take our young man there straight away.'

'Oh no you can't,' Adina told her with steely determination. 'Christopher is staying right here with us, if you have no objections.'

'Wh . . . what? You mean you're willing to *keep* him?'

When Adina nodded she had the satisfaction of seeing Miss Higgins become still for the first time in their acquaintance.

'Well,' she finally managed to say, 'I must say I'm delighted to hear it, if you're really sure.' She glanced towards the drawing room, where she could hear the children playing, and lowering her voice, she said, 'It seems that the poor little chap has had a rough time of it, from things that have come to light. His mother was a . . . shall we say "a lady of the night"?'

'Perhaps that's the only way she had of keeping a roof over their heads after Christopher's father was killed in the war,' Adina said. Life had taught her not to judge.

'Yes, I dare say it was,' Miss Higgins sighed, then quickly became excited again as she asked, 'Are you really quite, quite sure that you'll manage another child here?'

'I could manage another two or three.' Adina told her without hesitation, and so it was that Christopher Bourne became a part of their little family.

Chapter Forty-Three

January 1947

Soon after Christmas the first snow began to fall and in no time at all England was experiencing the coldest winter it had known since 1880. Coal was piling up at the pits but many households and businesses were left without fuel because roads and trainlines were blocked by snow-drifts – some as high as twenty feet. Lack of coal had also curbed supplies of electricity and gas, and soon over four million workers had been laid off through power cuts. Blizzards stopped shipping in the Channel and kept the fishing fleets in port, further worsening the food shortages.

'Brr, it makes you wonder when it's goin' to end, don't it?' Beryl said one evening as they all sat around the wireless listening to the news. Alvar Lidell, the famous broadcaster, was saying that it looked as if the terrible storms they were experiencing were going to continue on into February.

'We should just think ourselves lucky I thought to get us a good supply of candles in before it got too bad,' Adina said. 'And at least we're better off than some. While you were out at the shops this morning I listened to the news and it said that the RAF are having to drop food supplies to stranded villages and livestock in Lincolnshire, Norfolk and Yorkshire.'

'Poor sods.' Beryl shivered. They were all wearing at least four layers of clothing, although the lack of electricity didn't seem to be worrying the children. They viewed it all as a big adventure and loved the flicker-ing candlelight.

Thankfully they still had at least a month's supply of food in the larder and it was quite nice not to have to go to school. Adina had taken Theo's sturdy wooden sledge out of the shed, and sometimes the two women took turns to drag it over to Primrose Hill, where the children built snowmen, skidded across the frozen lake or whizzed down the slopes on the sledge, whooping with joy.

All in all, both women were feeling more settled than they had been in a long time. There was never a dull moment with the children to keep them on their toes, and although Adina still missed Dottie and Karl, she found that she could move on now. It was as if she had found her vocation in life and she was growing to love the children in her care almost as if they were her own. The affection was returned tenfold and each of the children was blossoming, especially Christopher, much to Miss Higgins's delight.

Shortly after the New Year, Beryl had enrolled Cathy and Christopher in a Sunday school at the local church. In no time at all Rebekah and Esther begged to go too. When Beryl explained the predicament to the vicar, he assured her that children of all religions were welcome, and so the girls started to attend too. All the children looked forward to going each week, mainly because of the friendly young vicar who had recently been appointed there. Father Mick was about as far from a traditional vicar as anyone could have imagined. He rode about the potholed streets on a bicycle that looked as if it would have been more in place in a museum, and he was very attractive in an odd sort of way. He had long wavy dark hair that curled across his collar and blue eyes that always seemed to be smiling.

The children loved listening to the Bible stories that Father Mick and his female helpers would read to them. It was an excuse for Beryl to get out of the house too, so all in all Adina had decided it was no bad thing and encouraged it. She had had grave reservations at first about the two older girls going along. After all, they were Jewish: was it right that they attend a Christian church? But after their long stay in England and due to their circumstances, neither of the girls embraced their Jewish faith any more, so she bowed to their wishes and allowed them to go. She also discovered that it was quite nice to have the house to herself for a couple of hours each Sunday afternoon.

It was now early February and as usual Adina was enjoying a quiet Sunday afternoon with nothing but the wireless and newspaper for company when the phone in the hall rang. She sighed with exasperation. Beryl and the four children would be home soon and she had been making the most of the peace and quiet before getting their tea ready. Laying her paper aside she hurried into the hall to answer it. It was Brian on the end of the line and he sounded very excited.

'Ariel had another little girl in the early hours of this morning,' he whooped. 'She's a little beauty, Aunty Dina. Just wait until you see her! She was quite big too – eight pounds and nine ounces. We're going to call her Margaret.'

'Why, that's wonderful,' Adina told him with genuine pleasure. 'And are they both all right?'

'Mother and baby are doing well but Ariel is already saying she wants you to come and see her.'

'And I want to come,' Adina told him, 'though I doubt I'll manage it for a while with the weather as it is. Beryl was hoping to get back to Nuneaton to see her folks this weekend too, but she's had to cancel the trip for now. Half the train tracks are blocked with snow if the radio reports are anything to go by.'

'You're right there,' he agreed. 'But shall I tell her you'll come as soon as you can?'

'Definitely,' Adina assured him as a glow spread through her. She was looking forward to meeting her new niece already. 'In the meantime give them both a kiss from me and tell them I'll be there as soon as I can.'

She had no sooner put the phone down than the door opened and Beryl appeared with all the children in tow. They were covered in snow and Adina chuckled as she ran to close the door behind them to prevent the warm air from escaping.

'My goodness, you look like snowmen,' she laughed as she began to peel off damp little hats, scarves and mittens.

'We had a snowball fight on the way home,' Christopher informed her gleefully. 'I hit Esther in the face with onc an' she chased me all the way down the street.'

They stamped the snow from their Wellington boots onto the newspaper that Adina had put down, and once they'd pulled them off, Adina told them, 'There's a nice big pan of vegetable soup simmering on the stove downstairs to warm you all up.'

Once the children were seated and served, she quickly told Beryl of Brian's phone call.

'That's wonderful.' Beryl smiled. 'So you're an aunty again. You must be tickled pink.'

As Adina smiled back she noticed that Beryl's cheeks were glowing. Getting out into the fresh air must be suiting her, she thought. It was as they were all having a slice of homemade fruitcake that the doorbell rang and Adina went upstairs to answer it. Mrs Leadbetter was standing on the doorstep.

'*Beattie!*' Adina cried joyously. 'How *lovely* to see you! Come on in.'

Cursing and muttering, the large woman almost fell into the hall.

'Bloody weather,' she grumbled. 'I pick me time to pay a visit, don't I? I don't even know what made me venture out in this but I was sick of sitting at home with me basket of mending, and so snow or no snow I decided to brave the weather.' It was then that a peal of laughter floated up from the kitchen, and Beattie's eyebrows rose into her hairline. 'So where's all that noise comin' from then?' she asked in her usual forthright way as she unwound a thick scarf from her neck.

Adina chuckled. 'It's the children,' she told her. 'Oh Beattie, I have *so* much to tell you. Come into the drawing room and I'll explain what's been happening and then I'll take you down to meet them all.'

A very bemused Beattie followed her down the hallway, and after Adina had explained what had gone on since she had last seen her, Beattie looked even more bemused – although it was lovely to see Adina looking so much happier.

'Well, you could blow me down with a feather,' she admitted eventually. 'You certainly don't let the grass grow under your feet, do you, love, and good on you, that's what I say. But now tell me . . .' she became more serious now. 'Has there been any news of the Montgomerys?'

Adina slowly shook her head. 'Not a word, and truthfully I don't think there ever will be now. I've had to accept what's done is done, but I still miss my darling Dottie every single day.'

There was so much pain in her voice that Beattie's heart ached for her. The poor girl had gone through a lot, but at least it appeared that she was doing something useful with her life.

'Anyway, that's enough sad talk,' she said firmly now. 'Come on, take me downstairs an' let me meet your brood.'

And so Adina did, and Beattie's visit proved to be a huge success.

Later that evening, when the children were all tucked up snugly into bed, Beryl commented, 'I liked your friend, Beattie.'

'Yes, she's lovely, isn't she?' Adina agreed with a smile. 'Beattie took me under her wing right from the very first second I arrived here. To be honest, I didn't realise how much I had missed her until I saw her again today. She's promised to visit regularly now. I'm sure the children will like that.'

'That will be nice.' Looking vaguely uncomfortable, Beryl then coughed and said, 'I thought I might start going out on a Tuesday night, if you think you can manage the children. Would you mind very much?'

'Of course I wouldn't mind. It would do you good to get out a bit more.' Adina eyed her curiously. 'Were you thinking of going somewhere special?'

'Not *special*, exactly. But Father Mick needs someone to help out with the choir practice each week, so I volunteered.'

'Oh, I see.' Adina stifled a chuckle as colour seeped into Beryl's cheeks.

'Well, it's the least I can do, ain't it?' Beryl gabbled on. 'He's such a decent chap an' he does so much for the community. It don't hurt to lend a hand when you can, does it?'

Suddenly alarm bells began to ring in Adina's head. She'd had suspicions for some time that Beryl fancied Father Mick, but she was afraid for her. Beryl had already had one disastrous relationship and she could see no future for her as a vicar's wife even if Father Mick returned her feelings. Her friend was in the process of trying to get a divorce from Tyrone and Adina knew only too well that the Church would frown on him marrying a divorcée.

As if she had been able to read her thoughts Beryl told her, 'There ain't nothin' goin' on between us, if that's what you're thinkin'. Nothin' improper, anyway. I just think he's a genuinely nice bloke an' I want to help if I can.'

'I didn't say I thought anything *was* going on, did I?' Adina objected as Beryl rose from the easy chair and began to load their cocoa mugs onto a small tray.

'You didn't have to. I could see what you was thinkin',' Beryl retorted, and she then left the room in a huff leaving Adina to chew thoughtfully on her lip.

*   *   *

265

The big freeze finally ended in mid-March, but then the whole country suffered from floods as the thaw set in. Farming casualties included two million sheep and over half a million acres of ruined wheat, which added to the food shortages, but thankfully Adina continued to be able to feed the children adequately and life for them went on much as before.

Over the next two months both Beryl and Adina made separate trips back to Nuneaton to visit their families, although neither of them stayed away for more than two nights. They were totally committed to the children in their care now and delighted with the progress their charges were making, as was Miss Higgins, who descended on them early one morning as Beryl was getting the children ready for school.

'I know that what I'm about to request of you is an enormous lot to ask,' she twittered as she passed her capacious bag nervously from hand to hand. 'But do you think you could *possibly* help me out again? Just for four weeks this time,' she added hastily. 'You see, the thing is, I have a little boy who is going to be adopted by a wonderful couple in Cornwall, but he can't join them until the necessary paperwork is completed. So I wondered . . .'

'Of course we'll take him,' Adina butted in with a smile. And so it was that that very same evening, Jonathan landed on their doorstep. He was six years old and a real little chatterbox, and both women knew instantly that he would fit in.

It was early June by then and Beryl and Adina were tackling the over-grown garden at the back of the house so that the children could play out there.

'Trouble is, I don't know what's weeds an' what's flowers,' Beryl groaned as she pulled a clump of Michelmas daisies out by the roots.

Father Mick, who had very kindly dropped by to help, chuckled. 'I think you'll find they're flowers. Or they *were* flowers,' he said teasingly. 'Perhaps you should concentrate on cutting the grass down, Beryl.'

Beryl smiled at him and Adina's stomach dropped into her shoes as she saw the look that passed between them. As well as helping out with the choir each week and taking the children to Sunday school, Beryl was now also assisting the vicar with the youth club he had started. It had proved to be an enormous success with the local youngsters and Beryl seemed to be enjoying every minute of it. As yet, her solicitor had heard nothing from Tyrone, and Adina was becoming concerned that he might ignore Beryl's request for a divorce. He obviously didn't care about his daughter, or he would have been in touch.

The children were all running about in the long grass without a care in the world and as she watched them, Cathy suddenly ran to Father Mick and flung herself into his arms. He laughed as he tossed her into the air and as Beryl strolled over to join them Adina's heart sank even further. They looked so like a little family unit, but of course that could never be, so what was to become of them? Beryl had put a little weight

266

back on. She had also gone and had her hair trimmed into a very becoming bob that week, and now with her eyes shining she resembled the pretty girl that Adina had once known back in Nuneaton.

Beattie had rejoined the fold too now, since Beryl was finding the children's endless washing and ironing and the constant cleaning a little too much to handle on her own whilst Adina was at work or doing her sewing. Beattie had offered to come and help out and had swept back into the house like a ray of sunshine; the children had her wrapped around their little fingers in no time.

Twice since she had started working for them again, she had even babysat, and Adina and Beryl had been able to go to the West End to watch James Mason and Margaret Lockwood starring in *The Wicked Lady* and *The Man in Grey*.

'Don't you think James Mason looks a little like Father Mick?' Beryl whispered to Adina one evening as they each sat eating popcorn during the interval. They had gone to watch *The Odd Man Out*, and Beryl was almost drooling over the film star, much to Adina's amusement. Both the actor and the their favourite actress, Margaret Lockwood, had been voted the best film stars of that year and Adina had a sneaking suspicion that Beryl would have watched James Mason all day, if she could have done. When the lights dimmed they watched the second movie in silence and once it was done they set off for home.

'I wonder what the kids will think of their trip tomorrow,' Beryl said musingly.

'I've no doubt they'll love it.' They were all going on a bus trip organised by Father Mick to Southend, and since none of the children had ever been to the seaside before, as far as Adina knew, she had no doubt they were all in for a very enjoyable day. It was guaranteed that Beryl would be happy, if Father Mick was there. With every week that passed now, Beryl was reverting more and more to her former cheerful self – but what would happen if she grew *too* fond of the kindly vicar? Adina hated the thought of her friend having her heart broken again, but was powerless to do anything about it. Her thoughts turned to Karl once more as they strolled along in the balmy evening and she unconsciously fingered the band on her finger. She knew that she should really take it off and put it away, but somehow she couldn't bring herself to do so. It was all she had left of him now, and although he had hurt her deeply, she knew that she would never love anyone else. But then she did have the children now, and they were becoming her life.

The next day dawned bright and clear, much to Adina's relief, and it was all she could do to contain the children's excitement as she helped them all to dress. Even Esther, with her plain little face and mousy hair, looked pretty this morning as she chattered on about what she was planning to do once they got to Southend.

'I've saved up my pocket for three whole weeks so that I can get a bucket and spade when we get there,' she told Adina solemnly as the latter expertly plaited her hair.

'Well, it makes a change from you spending it all on books,' Adina chuckled. Esther was a bookworm, much as Adina had been when she was a child, and she would read anything and everything she could get her hands on. The children's personalities were beginning to develop now that they were in a stable environment, and sometimes Adina wondered at the difference between Esther and Rebekah. Esther was the quiet, studious one whilst Rebekah was turning into a very attractive girl who found fun in everything she tackled. Rebekah would never be a scholar and tended to wriggle out of going to school whenever she could, whereas Esther could not get enough of learning. Even so, Adina loved them both equally and only wanted what was best for them.

Jonathan and Christopher were hopping from foot to foot now in their excitement to be off, so it was a relief when Beryl appeared from the kitchen with an enormous picnic basket that she had prepared for them all. There were cheese and chutney, egg and cress, and meat-paste sandwiches, along with eight bags of Smith's crisps, a box of jam tarts that she had cooked the day before, a paper bag full of scones, and two large bottles of lemonade.

'This should keep the hungry little beggars goin',' she told Adina with a smile, and holding Cathy by her other arm, she asked, 'Are we all set then?'

'*Yes!*' the children chorused as they rampaged towards the front door, and so they set off.

On the coach home that evening, the children all dozed off, worn out after a most enjoyable day. They had paddled in the sea, run about on the beach, been on the donkeys, made sandcastles, and each had been treated to an ice-cream cone. As Adina looked at their sleepy faces a ripple of satisfaction slid through her. It was nice to see them all so happy, although she knew it was going to be a wrench when Jonathan left them. Not that she was going to have time to miss him for long. Miss Higgins had already approached her about taking another short-term placement when he left, and Adina had agreed to it immediately. She had discovered some time ago that the busier she was, the less time she had to fret about Dottie and Karl, and she was happy to be run off her feet.

Glancing ahead she saw Beryl and Father Mick chatting animatedly. They had barely left each other's sides all day and had been kept very busy organising games of rounders and cricket for the children on the beach. It couldn't have been a more perfect day if they had ordered it, and now Adina sat back in her seat, quietly content as she watched over her little family.

Chapter Forty-Four

On 20 November 1947 on a grey cold morning, an air of excitement hung in the air as Adina and Beryl got their young charges ready for a very special day out. Princess Elizabeth was due to marry her handsome fiancé today in Westminster Abbey, and they were all going to see as much of the proceedings as they could. The Princess's beau had been born into the Greek royal family and was known as Lieutenant Philip Mountbatten – the surname he had adopted from his maternal grandparents. But as from today, following his marriage to Elizabeth, he would be known as His Royal Highness, The Prince Philip, Duke of Edinburgh, a title that had been bestowed on him by his future father-in-law, King George VI. The whole country was excited about the forthcoming marriage, and for now the grim realities of postwar rationing were forgotten.

Rebekah was more excited than the others as, at ten years old, she thought it was wonderfully romantic and could hardly wait to see a real live Princess. Esther was happy to go along too, but in truth would much have preferred to stay at home with her head stuck in a book. Christopher was more interested in a day out than the wedding, and when Beryl teasingly asked him who he wanted to marry when he grew up, he wrinkled his nose in disgust.

'I'm not *ever* getting married,' he declared emphatically. 'Girls are *disgusting!*'

Beryl and Adina exchanged an amused glance and wondered if he would still be saying the same in a few years' time. Jonathan had long since left them to join his new adoptive family, but since then the two friends had cared for a further three children for a time, although at present they were back to their three longterm placements and little Cathy, with another little girl due to join them the following week.

Eventually they were ready to leave and they set off on the bus with a picnic hamper that Beattie had prepared for them. The roads from Buckingham Palace to Westminster Abbey had been closed and they found the whole area thronging with people hoping to catch a glimpse of the royal coach bearing the Princess to her wedding.

At last they stood amongst the crowds along the route as the state coach passed by, escorted by the Household Cavalry who were resplendent in scarlet tunics. The Princess, who looked enchanting in an ivory gown embroidered with flowers of beads and pearls, waved to them, her expression truly radiant, and Beryl and Rebekash sighed with delight at the romance of it all. Adina meanwhile was busily herding them all together again.

'Come on,' she urged. 'We need to get down the Mall so that we can see them at the Palace when they appear on the balcony after the wedding breakfast. If we don't get a move on we'll never find a place.'

The two women took the children's hands and led them in that direction, which was no mean feat as they struggled along shoulder-to-shoulder with all the other wellwishers. When the Princess and her new husband finally appeared, the crowd roared with appreciation and the children were caught up in the mood of it all. By the time they set off across St James's Park, to catch the bus home, they were all tired but happy.

'Didn't Princess Elizabeth look *beautiful*, and wasn't Prince Philip *handsome*?' Rebekah sighed dreamily as they climbed on the packed omnibus.

Adina smiled at her indulgently. Already, Rebekah dreamed of being married and having a family of her own when she grew up, whereas Esther was determined to become a doctor. The girls were as different as chalk from cheese, and yet for all that they got along splendidly, even if Esther did complain from time to time that Rebekah was soppy. Their lives had fallen into a comfortable routine now, and although Adina still missed Karl and her baby, she kept her feelings to herself and never mentioned them. She did her crying when she was alone, and to outward appearances she seemed content, which she was for most of the time.

It was late afternoon by the time they arrived back at the house, and Beryl hurried down into the kitchen to warm up a stew that she had made the day before, whilst Adina supervised the children, getting their hats and coats off and changing into their slippers. Once she had thrown some more coal onto the fire and they were comfortably settled in the drawing room, she joined Beryl in the kitchen to see what she could do to help. They had given Beattie the day off as she had been going to watch the wedding too with her sister who lived in Croydon, but Beryl seemed to have everything under control and the table was already neatly laid.

As Adina filled glasses full of milk for the children she asked conversationally, 'Are you off to the youth club with Father Mick this evening?'

Beryl nodded happily. 'Yes, I am, after I've got Cathy ready for bed. That is, if you don't mind watching them all? Phew! Me arms feel as if they're about to drop off after hoikin' Cathy about all day. She's gettin' to be a right weight now, ain't she?'

Adina warmed the teapot before pouring boiling water onto the tea leaves. She then placed the tea cosy on and left it to mash for a few minutes.

'She's doing marvellously,' she agreed. 'And of course I'll be fine with the children. I have a stack of paperwork to do from the school so I shall tackle that once I've got them all off to bed.'

'Thanks, Dina.' Beryl stirred the stew and once again Adina was struck by the difference in her friend since she had first returned home. She was dressed in one of the 'new look' frocks that Adina had sewn for her after Beryl had seen the style in a magazine. A new French designer called Christian Dior had recently burst onto the fashion scene and had introduced the latest trend of slightly longer skirts. Women were tired of the drab utility clothing they had been forced to wear during the war, and dresses like the one Beryl was wearing now were becoming very popular.

Beryl had been broken when she first returned to live with her, but now she was mended – and Adina was glad of that. As of yet, the relationship between Father Mick and Beryl seemed to have gone no further than friendship, and Adina could only hope that it would remain that way.

The meal was a light-hearted affair, with the children constantly talking about the wedding in between mouthfuls of beef stew and dumplings. As soon as it was over, Adina sent them back to the drawing room to do quiet activities such as board games, jigsaws or colouring in, while she and Beryl tackled the washing-up. And then once the kitchen was all shipshape again, Beryl darted off to get changed whilst Adina started to get the younger children ready for bed.

Not long after, Beryl floated down the stairs in her warm coat leaving a waft of Evening in Paris perfume in her wake. Adina had bought it for her for her birthday, and Beryl used it sparingly as she loved it.

'What do you think of this lipstick?' she asked as she eyed herself critically in the hall mirror and fastened her hat on. 'It's a new colour called Ruby Red. Do you think it's too bright?'

'Not at all. It is almost Christmas, isn't it?'

Reassured, Beryl gave her hat one last pat to make sure that it was firmly secured. 'Right, I'll just go and give Cathy a goodnight kiss before I go, and I'll see you later. Bye!'

At eight o'clock, when all the children had gone to bed, Adina settled down to tackle the pile of paperwork she had brought home from school.

Most of it involved the children whose parents she was still trying to trace, although she had done the majority of it now and she guessed that her work at the school would soon be over. It was no bad thing as far as she was concerned, as the Welfare Department were keeping her busy with children they had difficulty placing in long-term homes.

She began to open the various letters from the Salvation Army and the Red Cross, methodically noting which children they involved. It was a sad job, as she had discovered long ago. The majority of the people she was trying to trace had disappeared, leaving their children effectively orphaned.

Once Adina had confirmed this, it was then the job of the local Welfare Department to find them new homes, be it in an orphanage or with foster families.

She worked steadily on, but she was tired after the long day and the room was deliciously warm and cosy, with the fire burning brightly in the grate . . . In no time at all she was sound asleep with nothing but the ticking of the clock on the mantelpiece and the popping of the coals on the fire to be heard.

Something woke her, and as she blinked her eyes open she was aware that the fire had burned low and the temperature in the room had dropped considerably. After glancing at the clock she was shocked to see that it was gone eleven o'clock and she wondered if Beryl was home. Lifting the poker from the hearth, she gave the fire a good riddle then threw a little more coal on before hurrying away to the kitchen, intent on making herself a last hot drink before she went to bed.

The kitchen was in darkness, but when she clicked on the light she was confronted with Beryl, who was huddled at the table sobbing as if her heart was about to break.

'*Beryl*!' Adina was beside her in a moment. 'Whatever is the matter, love?'

When Beryl raised her head, Adina was shocked. The young woman's hat had slipped to one side and was now sitting at a rakish angle, and her lipstick was smeared. Mascara was streaked down her cheeks and her eyes were red-rimmed. Adina immediately thought the worst as panic flared inside her. 'Has someone attacked you on the way home?' she demanded.

Beryl shook her head miserably. 'N . . . no, it's nothing like that,' she managed to choke out as Adina drew out a chair and plonked herself down beside her.

'Then what is it?'

'It . . . it doesn't matter.'

'Of course it matters. Now tell me what's happened.'

For a moment she thought that Beryl was going to do just that, but then her friend suddenly rose from the table and headed towards the door.

'Where are you going?'

'To bed. I'll see you in the morning.' And before Adina could utter so much as another word, the door closed behind Beryl, leaving Adina to chew on her lip. She had never seen her friend so upset and had no idea what could have caused her to be so – but if Beryl wasn't prepared to talk to her, there was nothing she could do about it for now.

After turning off the lights she checked that the doors front and back were locked, then slowly made her way to bed.

* * *

272

The next morning at breakfast, Beryl's eyes were swollen and red and she was very quiet, but luckily the children didn't seem to notice it as she and Adina got them ready for school. When the meal was over they ushered them into the hall to get their shoes and coats on, and it was then that Beattie let herself in the front door with the key that Adina had supplied her with.

'Gawd luv us!' she exclaimed as she stopped dead in her tracks at the sight of Beryl's reddened eyes. 'Whatever's happened to you, pet?'

'Nothing,' Beryl said dully as she shrugged Christopher's arm into the sleeve of his coat. 'I'm fine.'

'Well, yer don't look fine,' Beattie retorted in her usual forthright way. 'You look bloomin' *awful*.'

'Thanks very much.' There was a hint of sarcasm in Beryl's voice as Adina and Beattie exchanged a worried glance.

Deciding that things had gone far enough, Adina now addressed Rebekah. 'Do you think you could drop Christopher off at his school on the way to yours for me?' she asked. 'There are a few things I need to see to and I thought I might go in to work a little late today.'

'Course I can.' Rebekah's chest puffed with importance as she took hold of Christopher's hand, much to his disgust.

''Ere,' he objected. 'I ain't a baby, you know. I can walk by meself.'

Adina herded the three squabbling children towards the door, and once they were gone she lifted Cathy and dumped her in Beattie's arms, saying, 'Could you take her into the kitchen for a while, please, Beattie? I need to speak to Beryl.'

Beattie nodded obligingly and pottered off in that direction as Adina took Beryl by the elbow and led her protesting towards the drawing room.

'Right,' she said firmly, once the door was closed behind them. 'Now you're going to tell me what the hell is going on because I'm not leaving this house until you do.'

Beryl's nostrils flared with indignation but then just as suddenly, her shoulders slumped and she sat down on the nearest chair. 'It's Father Mick,' she wept. 'I won't be seeing him again.'

'*What?*' Adina was shocked. She knew how much Beryl thought of him. 'But *why*? Has he hurt you in some way? If he has, I'll—'

'Of course he hasn't hurt me,' Beryl said, stopping her friend in mid-flow. 'At least, not how you're thinking, but . . . well, he kissed me last night.'

'Oh.' Adina deflated like a balloon although the news didn't really come as a shock. 'And is that such a bad thing?'

'It could have been, if I'd let him do what he suggested. He told me that he loved me and he was going to leave the Church so that we could be married when my divorce came through.'

'Then he really *must* love you.'

'Yes. I think we've both known how we feel about each other for some time now, but we also knew that the Church would frown on him marrying a divorcée. He *loves* what he does, Dina, and I couldn't let him make that sacrifice for me. He would never have been truly happy if he had been forced to leave his vocation. And so I told him it would be better if we were to end it now, before it had really begun. He'll get over it in time. But it's strange, isn't it? When I married Tyrone I was swept away by his looks and the kind of life he said he could offer me. Mick is as poor as a church mouse and yet I would willingly have gone to him even if it meant living on dry bread for the rest of my life. Love is a funny thing.'

'Don't I know it,' Dina agreed bitterly. 'Look at me. I would have staked my life that Karl loved me and would come back to me, but he didn't, did he? It seems that love can make fools of all of us.' Her eyes sparkling with tears, she leaned towards her friend and squeezed her hand affectionately as she told her, 'I'm so sorry. I guessed a long time ago how you felt about Father Mick and I feared this happening, for your sake.'

Beryl shrugged bravely. 'Well, I'll just have to get on with my life now and try to put this all behind me. I don't have much choice, do I?'

Adina hugged her friend and thought yet again how very wicked life could be.

Chapter Forty-Five

March 1948

'Come on you lot, or you'll be late for school,' Adina shouted. Instantly the children stampeded towards her and then chaos reigned for a time as they all tried to get their shoes and coats on at the same time. There were five children living in the house at present, the latest to join them being a small girl who had recently been orphaned. Annie was a bright little spark and had fitted into the household as if she had always been there, although she would not be staying with them longterm. Luckily, she had an aunt who lived in Manchester who was prepared to look after her and so Adina was caring for her until the aunt arrived to fetch her, which should be any day now. Adina knew that she would miss her when she left, but was getting used to saying goodbye to the many children she had cared for by now. Miss Higgins was still a regular visitor to the house and it was rare that they had an empty bedroom for long – Miss Higgins saw to that.

It was some months now since Beryl had make the decision to end her relationship with Father Mick, and Adina was painfully aware that the sparkle had gone out of her friend again. She would catch her at odd moments staring off into space and her heart would ache for her because she understood exactly how she was feeling. There were still days when she missed Karl so much it was almost like a physical pain, and she would find herself staring at little girls who looked to be about the same age as Dottie, filled with acute longing. But life had to go on and Adina was a fighter. She had taken on the role of getting the children to Sunday school each week as they all seemed to enjoy it and she had been saddened to see that Father Mick didn't seem to be quite the chirpy chap he had once been either.

'Off you go then. Be good, mind, and watch how you cross the roads.' Adina was only working afternoons at the school now and so Esther made sure that the younger children got to their school safely each morning before proceeding on to her own.

As she opened the door and the chattering children spilled down the steps, a the postman pushed through them and placed some letters in her hand.

'Thank you, Henry.' She smiled as he hefted his mail sack higher onto his shoulder and made for next door. She watched until the children were out of sight then glanced through the mail, noting an official-looking document addressed to Beryl. When she spotted a solicitor's address in the top corner she frowned. As far as she was aware, the only solicitor Beryl had had anything to do with was the one who was handling her divorce, and she wondered if he had finally got a reply from Tyrone. Not that it would make much difference to Beryl now, Adina thought sadly. Married or divorced, she knew that nothing could ever come of anything between Father Mick and her friend.

As she looked up, she saw Beryl descending the stairs with Cathy and she handed her the letter. 'It's from your solicitor,' she told her. 'I wonder if Tyrone has finally decided to give you a divorce?'

Beryl took it from her and she tore the envelope open.

'That's funny – Mr Barraclough says he wants to see me tomorrow morning at ten o'clock on a matter of some importance. What do you think that could be about?'

'I've no idea. But it won't be a problem. I can have Cathy while you keep your appointment – unless you want me to come with you, that is? In which case I'm sure Beattie wouldn't mind watching her for us.'

'I'll be fine going on my own,' Beryl assured her. 'I'm not going to get upset about anything he has to tell me about Tyrone. He's probably just being difficult and refusing to go ahead with the divorce because I left him.'

'Hm, I have an awful feeling you might be right.'

'Well, it doesn't really matter either way now, does it?' Beryl said, disheartened. 'I ain't planning on getting married again *ever*, so if Tyrone wants to play his little games he's welcome to. It'll be no skin off my nose now, though I would like to be shot of the bastard. I must admit I'm curious though.'

And then they went about their business as usual and neither of them gave the letter much more thought for the rest of the day.

The next morning, as soon as the children had left for school, Beryl came downstairs looking very smart in a black calf-length pencil skirt that Adina had made for her and a crisp white blouse.

'Eeh, you *do* look posh, luvvie,' Beattie said admiringly as she paused from polishing the hall table.

'Thanks.' Beryl blushed becomingly as she pulled her coat on. Now that it was time to keep the appointment she was suddenly feeling apprehensive about what it might entail.

'I shan't be long,' she promised Adina as she stroked Cathy's shining hair, and then she was gone and Adina hurried upstairs to make the beds whilst Beattie kept an eye on the little girl who was happily playing with a doll's house.

When Beryl came back an hour and a half later, Adina was shocked to see how ghastly she looked.

'My God, you're as white as a sheet,' she gasped as she pressed her friend down onto a hall chair. 'Whatever did the solicitor say? Has Tyrone refused to give you a divorce?'

'N . . . no,' Beryl told her unsteadily. 'He can't. He's dead, you see. Apparently he was killed about three months ago in a car accident, but the solicitor has only just found out about it.' She shook her head in disbelief. 'He was a bad 'un, but I would never have wished this on him. I just can't take it in. He was only twenty-seven years old.'

Beattie rushed away to put the kettle on, convinced that a cup of tea was the cure for all ills. Beryl certainly looked like she could do with one. Beattie needed one herself, and that was a fact – and she hadn't even known the bloke!

'Oh, Beryl.' Adina was so shocked she scarcely knew what to say. 'I'm so sorry. What will happen now?'

'Nothing. I get a copy of his death certificate and that's that.'

She stood up and took her coat off just as Cathy came hurtling towards her. Meanwhile, Adina's mind was working overtime. The significance of this obviously hadn't dawned on Beryl yet, but it had to Adina. Beryl was now a widow, and whilst the Church would have frowned on Father Mick marrying a divorcée, they certainly wouldn't object to him marrying a widow. If he still wanted to, that was. But she wouldn't mention the fact for now, of course; it would have seemed too disrespectful somehow when Beryl had just learned of her husband's death. She needed some time to come to terms with it first and Adina was prepared to wait for the right moment to point it out to her.

The right moment actually presented itself far more quickly than she had thought it would when she accompanied the children to Sunday school the following Sunday afternoon. It was a blustery day as Adina led them into the church hall, where she saw Father Mick standing at the window staring vacantly out across the churchyard. He looked so sad that it tore at her heart as she approached him. Every week he would look up expectantly when she entered, hoping to see Beryl, and then he would try to mask his disappointment with a smile.

'Oh, we're the first here, are we?' she said cheerfully as she ushered the children into their seats. 'We must be a little early.'

'What? Oh . . . yes, you are.' Looking at her more closely, he then asked quietly, 'How is Beryl?' It was obvious he was missing her, so keeping her voice light Adina seized her opportunity.

'Actually, she's having a bit of a tough time of it at present,' she said casually as she peeled her woollen mittens off.

When he raised an eyebrow she went on, 'Her solicitor informed her a few days ago that her husband in America had died in a car crash, so she's a widow now.'

He instantly looked concerned as he said, 'How awful! How has she taken it?'

'Well, as you know they were estranged and Beryl is no hypocrite, so I'd be a liar to say that she was heartbroken. But even so, Tyrone was the father of her child so she wouldn't have wished for this to happen to him. She admits that she was swept away with the romance of dating a GI when she met him, along with hundreds of other young women during the war who are now seeking divorces. I was only reading in the newspaper recently that divorces reached a record-breaking peak last year. It's very sad, isn't it? But then she is still young enough to meet someone else. Beryl is such a warm-hearted person that I can't see her being on her own for long unless she wishes to be, and now she can start again with a clean slate so to speak.'

She watched with satisfaction as a million emotions swept across the young vicar's face. Obviously he was feeling sorry for Beryl but she wondered if he had realised the full implications of what she had told him. Without spelling out what Tyrone's death meant to him and Beryl, all she could do now was wait and see what happened.

It was mid-April when there was a knock on the door one Tuesday evening and Adina hurried away to answer it. Beryl was listening to the radio in the drawing room and all the children were in bed. Adina had been about to go up for a bath after a long afternoon at the school. Her work there was coming to a close now and she knew that she would miss it, but she had done what she had started out to do and felt a measure of satisfaction. Some of the children she had worked with had been returned to their families, but the majority of them had been placed in orphanages or in foster homes. She was thinking of them now as she walked along the hallway, but when she opened the door to find Father Mick standing on the doorstep, all other thoughts were chased from her mind.

'Good evening,' he said.

'Good evening,' Adina looked at him questioningly. He looked so embarrassed that she couldn't help but feel sorry for him.

'I er . . . I was wondering if Beryl was in and if I might have a word with her?'

'Yes, of course.' As Adina held the door wide for him to step into the hallway she felt a little flutter of excitement. 'She's in there.' She pointed towards the drawing-room door before saying apologetically. 'You don't mind showing yourself in, do you? I was just going to pop upstairs for a bath.'

'No, of course not.'

She watched him stride purposefully towards the drawing room as she headed for the stairs, and unconsciously crossed her fingers. Beryl was due for some good luck, Adina thought, and all she could do now was hope that Father Mick would be the beginning of it.

*   *   *

278

An hour later she stood indecisively at the top of the stairs debating whether or not she should disturb her friend and her visitor or get an early night. She was now wrapped in her comfy old candlewick dressing-gown and feeling refreshed and relaxed after a nice long soak in the bath. She leaned over the banisters but all she could hear was the dull murmur of voices so she crept away to her room. No doubt Beryl would tell her all about the visit first thing in the morning, so for now she decided she would leave them to it although she was bursting with curiosity.

The next morning, when Adina entered the kitchen she found Beryl humming happily as she stirred a large pan of porridge on the stove.

'Ah, good morning,' she chirped happily. 'There's fresh tea in the pot if you'd like to pour yourself one. You can pour one out for me too while you're at it, if you wouldn't mind.'

Adina grinned as she lifted the tea cosy from the pot. 'Somebody sounds happy this morning. It wouldn't have anything to do with a certain young man's visit last night, would it?'

Beryl blushed becomingly as she added brown sugar to the porridge. 'It was lovely to see Mick,' she admitted. 'He came to offer his condolences about Tyrone's death. He said he didn't like to come too soon in case it looked disrespectful, but he's talked me into taking the children to Sunday school again.'

'I'm very pleased to hear it. That means I'll get Sunday afternoons off again,' Adina said. She had the strangest feeling that her wedding dress might just be put to good use again before too much longer . . .

Chapter Forty-Six

August 1949

'Aw, do I *have* to wear this?' Christopher groaned as he yanked at his bow tie.

'Yes, you do, young man. You want to look nice for Beryl's wedding, don't you?' Adina stifled a grin as she patted his hair into place and held him at arm's length for inspection. 'Right, now I want you to promise me you'll keep tidy while I go up and give the girls a hand with getting into their bridesmaids' dresses. And then I have to help Beryl get dressed, so just behave, do you hear me?' Although her voice was stern there was a twinkle in her eye as Christopher nodded miserably. He couldn't see why there had to be all this fuss and palaver over a wedding anyway. Adina had promised to take him to a football match at Wembley Stadium next week, and to his mind that was much more worthy of excitement.

Adina hurried away, and once she was happy that Cathy, Esther and Rebekah were ready, she went to help Beryl get into her wedding dress. It was the one that Ariel had once worn and now it would be worn again, which made Adina very happy. Beryl had left her wedding dress behind in Texas when she had fled from Tyrone's tyranny, and anyway it would have been an ill omen for her to wear the same dress for her second marriage. Although Adina's dress was made from the same parachute silk, it was of a completely different design, since Adina had originally made it for herself.

Beryl twirled in front of the cheval mirror in her room, while Adina lifted a filmy veil from a large cardboard box. In actual fact, Beryl had been intent on wearing a plain two-piece costume. 'After all, it *is* my second time,' she had told her, but Adina was having none of it.

'You're still a bride, and you'll *look* like a bride if I have anything to do with it,' she'd insisted. 'And it's not as if I'm ever going to wear it now, is it?'

Beryl's eyes had filled with tears at that remark. 'Aw, don't get sayin' that,' she'd protested. 'You'll find someone some day, and it will probably be when you're least expecting it.'

Adina shook her head solemnly. 'No, I won't get married now. What I felt for Karl was a once-in-a-lifetime love and if I can't have him I won't settle for second-best. Anyway, I'm quite happy with my little crew here, and now that I've finished working at the school I'll have all the time in the world.'

Now as Beryl sat at her dressing-table and Adina fastened her veil on, Beryl asked, 'Are you quite sure that you're going to manage here on your own?'

They had had this conversation at least a dozen times before and Adina sighed. When Mick had proposed to Beryl, the latter had felt torn between her love for him and her loyalty to Adina and the children. After all, as she had pointed out, it had been *her* idea in the first place for them to foster the children, and now here she was considering clearing off and leaving Adina to it. Added to that was the fact that she too loved Rebekah, Esther and Christopher, and she knew that she would miss them. But as Adina had equally firmly pointed out, they had been just what she had needed at the time to give her life some purpose, and she didn't regret a thing.

Still, Beryl had dithered. 'But I'm going to miss them *so* much,' she had whispered with tears in her eyes. And so they had come to an arrangement. She and Mick would have the children for the whole day once per week whenever Adina needed a break. As for money, she earned enough by caring for the children and her sewing to be able to live quite comfortably now. In fact, she had even managed to replace some of the money that Mrs Montgomery had left her, and now it was safely put aside for a rainy day.

'I won't be on my own, will I?' Adina answered Beryl now. 'I've still got Beattie coming in to help and there'll be two less to run around after, once you and Cathy have gone.'

'You cheeky bugger,' Beryl giggled and then clamped her hand over her mouth guiltily. 'Oops, I can't go sayin' things like that now I'm about to be a vicar's wife, can I?'

'I don't think Mick would mind what you said,' Adina said wryly. 'He loves you to bits and in his eyes you can do no wrong. I just hope he'll make you happy, that's all.'

'Oh, he will,' Beryl replied dreamily, and then becoming serious, she peeped at Adina in the mirror saying, 'Life's a funny thing ain't it? Nothin' ever seems to turn out as we imagined it would, but somehow I know I'm goin' to be happy with Mick.'

Adina's throat clogged with tears, and at the sound of the doorbell ringing she raced towards the bedroom door, glad of a chance to escape. The florist was standing on the front step with an enormous box, and after thanking her Adina carried it carefully upstairs and into Beryl's room.

'I got you a little surprise, I hope you don't mind.' Lifting a garland of cream and red roses from the box, she fastened it onto the top of Beryl's veil. 'There, that just finishes it off nicely.' She beamed with satisfaction as Beryl's mouth dropped open, then hurried back to the box to fetch a matching bouquet.

'Oh Dina, you shouldn't have! You've gone to so much trouble already,' Beryl choked.

'It was my pleasure. And there are some smaller posies for the girls here too and a buttonhole for Christopher. We can't have him feeling left out, can we? Now I must get downstairs and see if Beattie has everything under control. She's been baking for days, bless her. I'll see you at the church. Good luck, not that you'll be needing it.'

She skipped away before Beryl could say another word just as the car arrived that would take Adina, the bridesmaids and Beryl's mother to the church. Mr and Mrs Tait had arrived the day before and were delighted that their daughter was about to marry a vicar. Mrs Tait had chipped in the night before and helped them rearrange all the furniture in readiness for the wedding breakfast that would take place there following the church service. Now as Adina descended the stairs she found them both in the hallway looking as smart as a new pin. Mrs Tait was sporting a new hat that exactly matched the peacock-blue two-piece costume she was wearing, and even Mr Tait was dressed in a smart navy-blue suit and tie today.

'So come on then,' he grinned. 'When do I get to 'ave a peep at me lovely daughter?'

'Just as soon as I get this lot out to the car.' Smiling widely, Adina ushered the children and Mrs Tait outside, and soon they were heading for the church in their kindly neighbour's car that had been lavishly trimmed with ribbons.

'Ooh, everythin' is just *so* lovely,' Mrs Tait chuckled delightedly as she balanced her new handbag on her lap. 'Can't believe we're doin' this again. Second time lucky for our lass, eh?'

Adina had made herself a smart New Look navy-blue costume with a long skirt and padded shoulders, teaming it with a little white hat and bag. The only extravagance had been the flowers – but then Adina believed they were worth every penny. After all, how could a bride not have flowers?

The church bells were ringing when the car dropped them off at St Chad's, Father Mick's church. It was filled to capacity as many of his parishioners had turned out to wish the young vicar and his wife-to-be well. It seemed natural that he would want to be married in his own parish, although another vicar would be officiating at the ceremony. As soon as they all got out, the car headed back to fetch Beryl and her father, and as Adina clutched Cathy's hand, she got her first glimpse of the bridegroom. Mick was standing just inside the church doorway with his brother, who was going to be his best man. He was looking very smart in a new black suit, sporting a carnation in his buttonhole, and he was positively glowing with happiness. A little pang of envy flamed through Adina as she briefly pictured Karl standing there, but she quickly stifled it. Beryl deserved to be happy and Adina had a feeling that after today, she would be.

* * *

When the bride entered the church some minutes later, a hush fell over the congregation as she floated down the aisle on the arm of her father. But it was clear that Beryl had eyes for no one but the handsome man waiting for her at the altar, and from then on there might have been no one else present as they solemnly recited their vows. And then at last the vicar declared them to be man and wife and a great cheer went up as the bridegroom kissed his bride. After signing the register the beaming couple left the church in a hail of confetti and rose petals, before heading back to the house where Beattie had prepared them a buffet fit for a king. Adina had no idea where Beattie had managed to get everything from with food rationing still in operation, but when she asked her, Beattie just tapped the side of her nose and said, 'Ask me no questions an' I'll tell you no lies.'

There were homemade sausage rolls and Twiglets, which Christopher declared 'disgusting'. There were also plates of sandwiches of several varieties, and Beattie had managed to get a whole ham from somewhere, although Adina didn't touch that. It was strange, she thought, that she had somehow along the way forsaken her religion, yet she still couldn't bring herself to eat anything to do with a pig. Beattie had also made a large number of cakes, jellies and blancmanges that the children polished off in minutes. She had even managed to rustle together the ingredients for a wedding cake, which she had iced and which took pride of place in the middle of the table.

It was a wonderfully happy party but eventually the taxi arrived that would take the newlyweds away. They were catching the train to Eastbourne for a three-day honeymoon before moving into the small vicarage beside St Chad's. Whilst they were gone Cathy would be returning to Nuneaton with her doting grandparents, where Beryl had no doubt she would be spoiled rotten.

'Now you make her do as she's told,' Beryl told her mother as she planted a last kiss on the little girl's soft hair. 'She's a right little tearaway if you don't keep her in check.'

'Oh, get off wi' you. She's a little angel,' her mother laughingly objected and then they all waved until the taxi was out of sight, with the tin cans they had tied to the back bumper rattling along the road behind it, before trooping back inside.

'Right, I'd better go and get our bags packed now if we're to catch the train back to Nuneaton.' Mrs Tait dabbed at her eyes with a little lace handkerchief. 'I just hope everything turns out well for our Beryl this time after what happened with that Tyrone.'

'I don't think you need have any worries on that score,' Adina reassured her. 'Beryl and Mick were made for each other.'

'Well, they might have been, but I still can't imagine our Beryl as a vicar's wife.' Mrs Tait tittered. 'An' when I think what a handful she were when she were younger an' all.'

'Yes, but she's done a lot of growing up since then, so stop worrying. Here, give Cathy to me and I'll keep her occupied while you pack your case.'

Mr Tait, meanwhile, was headed for the drawing room. 'I reckon I might help meself to another glass of ale while I wait for the missus,' he said jovially. 'No sense in seein' it go to waste, is there?'

Adina grinned as he hared off, only to be caught by Beattie, who was busily loading dirty pots onto an enormous tray, and asked to help.

Once the Taits had departed with Cathy, Dina set to and helped Beattie with the clearing up whilst the girls and Christopher went upstairs to play in their rooms. It was gone seven o'clock that evening before the two women managed to get the house back to any semblance of order, and Beattie looked worn out.

'Why don't you go and sit down, and I'll put the kettle on?' Adina suggested. 'I think you've overdone it this week, what with all the cooking you've done and all the excitement of today.'

'Hm, trouble is I still think I'm twenty-one in me head,' Beattie chuckled. 'It's just my old bones that remind me that I ain't. Still, it was worth it to see Beryl lookin' so happy, wasn't it? I don't reckon I've ever seen a happier bride. Now you go up and get the kids washed an' changed into their nightclothes an' I'll make us both a nice cuppa an' we'll have some of that leftover cake. Come through to the kitchen when you're ready, eh?'

When Beattie had finally departed for home, barely able to put one foot in front of the other, and the children were all in bed, Adina collapsed onto the couch and kicked her shoes off with a grateful sigh.

Beryl had been moving her clothes and Cathy's to the vicarage over the last week and now it suddenly sank in that her friend was gone for good. Loneliness closed around Adina like a shroud. It would be just her and the children from now on, and whilst she loved the little ones she knew that she was going to miss Beryl dreadfully.

Feeling suddenly restless, she gazed around as if she was looking at the house for the very first time. She had never changed a single thing in it since Fliss and Theo had left it, but now she felt the urge to put her own stamp on the place and make it her own. She had never been too keen on the flowered wallpaper in there and decided that she would get some nice striped paper and redecorate it. She could perhaps tackle the hall then. She had never papered a wall in her life before but decided that now was the time to learn. She would need something to fill her hours while the children were at school. And one thing she had discovered over the last couple of years was that she was capable of being totally independent, which was just as well, for she realised with a little start that the children in her care were all she had now apart from her sister, and she was far away in Nuneaton with her

284

own family. It was a daunting thought, but Adina was determined to survive.

Slowly climbing the stairs she looked at the wedding dress that Beryl had carefully laid across her bed when she had gone upstairs to get changed into her going-away suit. Now as she tenderly fingered the parachute silk, a tear slid down her cheek. The dress she had once made so lovingly for herself had been worn by both Ariel and Beryl now, but she knew that she would never wear it, and as she carefully wrapped it up, her dreams finally crumbled into ashes.

Part Five

A Promise Kept

Chapter Forty-Seven

December 1970

'So will that be all right then?' The anxious social worker gazed at Adina over the rim of her china cup. 'I know it's frighteningly short notice, two weeks before Christmas, and I'm not pretending that Emily is the easiest girl in the world to handle. But her current carers are adamant that they won't keep her for another single day and I really don't know who else to approach. You have such a good record with teenagers.'

'It will be perfectly all right,' Dina told her calmly. 'I have a bedroom all prepared as Mary left last week, so you may bring Emily here as soon as you like.'

'Ah, Mary,' the woman smiled. 'You did such an excellent job with that girl. She was a right little handful when she first came to you. I feared that you would never manage her, but you turned her around. How did her wedding go? I hear you organised everything for her, right down to her wedding dress.'

'Oh, I didn't buy it,' Adina told her. 'It was one I made many years ago, and over the years I've restyled it so often for different girls I've cared for that I wonder how the material stands up to it. Still, at the end of the day she looked beautiful, and that's all that matters, isn't it? But then I suppose all brides do. They seem to have a sort of glow about them, don't they? And I think Simon will be good for her. He's such a lovely, hard-working young man and just the sort of person Mary needs to keep her in line, so all's well that ends well with that one. I just wish I could have had that sort of success story with all of them, but one thing I've learned over the years is that some are beyond help, more's the pity.'

She smiled at the social worker, thinking what an attractive young woman she was. She was dressed in a pair of bell-bottom trousers and a bright gypsy blouse heavily embroidered with ric-rac braiding and laced up the front. She had taken the place of Miss Higgins, who had retired two years earlier, and although Dina knew that Claire Sutton must be at least in her mid-twenties, with her long straight hair spilling about her shoulders she appeared to be much younger. Adina was now forty-six years old but no one would have guessed it. She still had a flawless unlined complexion and her hair was still dark, if not quite as vibrant as it had once been. Over the years she had cared for almost fifty children, some for just a short time, others for years, and she was now well respected by the local Social Services Department, although single carers were still frowned upon for the majority of the time.

She still had a great affection for Rebekah, Esther and Christopher, the first children she had cared for, although they had long since flown the nest. Rebekah had married a handsome young builder at just eighteen whilst Esther had spurned marriage and had trained as a nurse before going on to become a very successful doctor. Christopher had also done well for himself and now had his own thriving veterinary practice in Battersea, but they all kept in touch, and Adina was very proud of all of them. They had once taken the place of the little girl she had lost and she knew that she would always have a soft spot for those three.

Now, Claire Sutton glanced at the watch on her wrist and gasped. 'Crikey, I'd better get off. Will it be all right if I drop Emily off to you later this afternoon?'

'Of course.' Adina placed her cup and saucer down and followed the young woman to the door. 'Goodbye, dear. I'll see you later.' Once she had closed the door on her guest she looked about with satisfaction. The house was almost unrecognisable now to how it had been when she had first lived there, and over the years she had changed the décor and the furniture in each room to her own taste.

The clock on the hall table chimed one just then so she hurried down into the kitchen to put the kettle on. Beryl would be round to see her shortly just as she did each week, and Adina was looking forward to a cosy chat. Over the years since her marriage to Father Mick, Beryl had given birth to four more children and was now the mother of two girls and three boys whom she doted on almost as much as their father. Thankfully she had settled to life as a vicar's wife as if she had been born to it and seemed thoroughly happy with her lot. At times there had been a shortage of money but never love, and she still adored her husband as much as she had on the day they had married.

She arrived spot on time at one-thirty and plonked herself down at the kitchen table as Adina poured them both a cup of tea and pushed a plateful of sandwiches towards her.

'So how's tricks?' she asked amiably as she helped herself to a corned-beef one.

'Fine. I have another placement coming later this afternoon and I'm also interviewing a new help in about an hour or so. I do miss Beattie since she retired, I have to admit, although she certainly seems to be enjoying herself. She's off shopping with her sister most days.'

'And have you been to the doctor's yet?' Beryl asked sternly. Adina had lost a lot of weight just lately and she was concerned about her.

'No,' Adina admitted. 'I haven't had the time, to be honest, but don't look so worried. I will go as soon as I get the chance. And I'm sure it's nothing serious. I probably just need a good tonic.'

'Hmph, you do too much, that's the trouble.' Beryl bit into her sandwich. 'What with running round after the children and all the sewing jobs you do, you're running your blood to water.'

'Ooh, hark at the pot calling the kettle black,' Adina laughed. 'And what have you got lined up for the rest of today?'

'Well, when I leave here I've got to go to the church hall and get the stalls organised ready for a jumble sale we're having on Saturday, an' then . . .'

Her voice trailed away as she saw Adina's raised eyebrows and she quickly changed the subject.

'So who's this person you have applyin' for a job then?'

Adina shrugged. 'I don't know that much about her, to be honest,' she admitted. 'Although her references are good. She's twenty-four years old and is studying to become a nurse, so she needs a part-time job.'

'Will she be living in if she's suitable?' Beryl was now on her third sandwich and wolfing them down like there was no tomorrow as she hadn't had time for any breakfast and had just realised how hungry she was.

'She's quite welcome to stay if she wishes to. I've certainly got more than enough room now that I only have one placement and another one coming later today. I thought we might be able to come to some sort of an arrangement if she was agreeable, where she could have her room for free for helping out a certain number of hours per week. It gives me more time to get on with my sewing jobs if I have someone to assist with the housework.'

'Let's just hope she's better than the last one then, the idle little devil,' Beryl muttered. 'She wouldn't have known what cleanin' were if it had come up an' slapped her in the face. From what I could make of it, *you* ended up cleanin' up after *her* an' then she just ups an' leaves without a by your leave, takin' the contents of your purse with her. I'm tellin' you, good reliable help is hard to find nowadays. I reckon they broke the mould when they made old Beattie, bless her. Now *she* was a worker, if ever there was one . . .'

Adina nodded in agreement and they then went on to chat about Beryl's brood until it was time for her to leave.

At exactly three o'clock the doorbell rang and Adina quickly checked her hair in the hall mirror, straightening the row of pearls she was wearing over a powder-blue twinset before opening the door.

A very attractive young woman was standing on the top step. She was smartly dressed and had long thick fair hair which shimmered down her back, and a heart-shaped face. When she smiled Adina noticed the dimple in her cheek. She was wearing the minimum of make-up and Adina was impressed by her natural beauty.

'Do come in,' she invited, crossing her fingers that this girl would turn out to be better than the last one. 'Would you like a cup of tea?'

291

'No, thank you.' Adina noticed that she spoke beautifully. She was obviously from a good family, if the way she spoke and held herself was anything to go by.

'Won't you come into the drawing room?'

The girl followed her, her eyes settling on the Christmas tree standing next to the television set, which was one of Adina's more recent purchases. She had started to celebrate Christmas each year for all the children who passed through her door, and now actually enjoyed the festival herself.

'Do sit down.'

The girl gracefully did as she was told and once Adina was seated opposite her she asked, 'So how did you hear about the job?'

'I saw it advertised in the shop window at the bottom of the street,' the girl replied, and holding her hand out she told her, 'My name is Amelia Forbes but my friends call me Melly.'

Adina shook her hand, warming instantly to the girl. She had such a nice personality and such a ready smile that it would have been hard not to.

'Adina Schwartz,' she introduced herself. 'And now, tell me a little about yourself.'

The girl's face momentarily clouded. 'I'm doing my SRN Course at St Bart's Hospital. I'm in my final year now and am engaged to be married to a junior doctor. At present I'm living in the nurses' quarters, but it isn't ideal there, to be honest. Rather cramped, if you know what I mean. So I thought if I could get a part-time job and be able to live in, I would be much happier. Richard and I are getting married next August, so I could only do the job until then. I hope to be qualified by that time and then Richard and I are going to live in Devon to be closer to his family.'

'I see.' Dina appreciated the girl's honesty. 'And what about *your* family?'

The girl's face clouded. 'My mother passed away last year, so apart from Richard I have no one now,' she told her.

'I'm sorry.' Without thinking, Adina reached out to squeeze her hand sympathetically. There was something about the girl that she had instantly taken to, so she went on, 'Shall I tell you what hours I'd need you to work and what that work would entail?'

'Yes, please.' The girl nodded eagerly.

'Well, I'm a foster mother so I usually have at least two young people staying here at a time. And I also run my own sewing business, dressmaking and alterations, et cetera. So as you would expect I'm usually quite busy, which is where you would come in. I usually employ someone part-time to help out with general cleaning and washing and ironing. Twenty hours a week should do it, and for that I could offer you a very small wage and a room.'

'That sounds perfect,' the girl said. 'Would you need me to work set hours?'

'Not at all,' Adina assured her. 'I'd be quite happy for you to do the jobs around your work hours at the hospital to suit yourself, as long as they all got done.' She smiled ruefully before admitting, 'I'm afraid the last two girls I've employed haven't worked out very well at all for different reasons, so how about we do it on a trial period? Say for a month? And then we can both decide if we're happy with the arrangement.'

Melly held her hand out. 'It sounds fine to me. I could do a couple of hours each evening and then fit the rest of the hours in on my days off. When would it be suitable for me to move in?'

'Perhaps I ought to show you your room first to make sure you're happy with it,' Adina suggested and the girl rose and followed her, looking about curiously as they climbed the stairs.

Adina led her to the room that had once been hers when she had first come to stay with the Montgomerys. 'Why, it's wonderful compared to what I'm used to in the nurses' home.' Melly smiled widely and Adina felt herself relax.

'In that case, you can move in as soon as you like,' she told her. 'I'm in the middle of a rather large job at the moment. I'm working on a wedding dress and four bridesmaids' dresses which have to be finished by the end of the month, so the sooner you can move in the better.' The girl was so easy to talk to that Adina felt sure they were going to get along. 'I'll show you the rest of the house now.' She moved towards the door and once again the girl stared about keenly as Adina showed her from room to room.

They ended up down in the kitchen, which like the rest of the house Adina had modernised over the years, and again the girl enthused about it.

'Now how about that cup of tea before you go?' Adina suggested, and taking a seat at the table the girl nodded.

'That would be lovely, thank you.'

Once they each had a drink in front of them Adina asked, 'Have you no other relatives at all?'

The girl shook her head. 'I'm afraid not. My grandfather died before I was born and my grandmother shortly after. I don't remember her, to be honest. Mummy and Daddy lived in Exeter where Daddy had his own business, but sadly he went bankrupt shortly after the war and he died when I was nine. Since then it's been just Mummy and me.'

'You must miss her,' Adina said softly and the girl nodded tearfully. 'I miss both of them. They were the best parents any girl could ever have wished for. But at least I have Richard now. I'm sure you'll like him if you ever get to meet him.'

'I'm sure I shall,' Adina said kindly as she stared into the girl's eyes.

They were the colour of bluebells and that, combined with her shining blonde hair and her easygoing nature, made her very attractive indeed. Adina almost felt as if she had known her for years instead of just for a few minutes.

When they had finished their drinks, Adina saw her to the front door where they once again shook hands.

'Until tomorrow then,' Adina said, and the girl beamed before tripping off down the steps. It was there that she paused to ask, 'What should I call you? I didn't think to ask.'

Adina grinned. 'Dina will be just fine.'

'Bye then,' Amelia said as she set off down the street, and Adina closed the door with a warm glow in the pit of her stomach. Somehow she had a good feeling about this girl.

Chapter Forty-Eight

Within days of her moving in, Adina wondered how she had ever managed without Melly, as she preferred to be known. The girl was great fun and had a wonderful sense of humour, plus she certainly wasn't afraid of hard work although Adina sometimes worried that she was doing too much. She would go to classes two days a week and then spend two days on the wards. Then in the evenings and on her three days off she would set to and tackle the list of jobs Adina had given her to do without a quibble. The week before, the house had been bulging at the seams when Ariel, Brian and their brood had descended on them to deliver their Christmas presents and stayed for a few days. But Melly had taken it all in her stride and dealt with the extra work uncomplainingly.

'She's such a lovely girl and *so* hardworking,' Ariel had said one day when Melly had set off for the hospital. 'I'm so pleased you've managed to find someone reliable to help out at last.'

'She's a little gem,' Adina agreed. 'And I have to admit she's wonderful company too. Nothing is ever too much trouble for her. I'm just sorry that I shall lose her next year when she marries her fiancé. They're moving down to Devon because they can't afford to buy a place in London.'

'Couldn't they stay here with you?' Ariel suggested.

'The thought had crossed my mind. But I think I'll wait until a little nearer to the time to suggest it. There's a lot can happen between now and then.'

'Mm, I suppose you're right.' Becoming solemn, Ariel then asked, 'Are you feeling all right, Dina? You look awfully pale and I'm sure you've lost even more weight since the last time I saw you.'

'Oh, don't *you* start,' Adina groaned. 'I have enough with Beryl nagging me to go to the doctor's all the time.'

'Well, just make sure that you do then, or you'll have the pair of us nagging you. I'm just glad that you have Melly here to help out now, which is more than can be said for that latest placement you've taken on. Now she's going to be trouble with a capital T from what I've seen of her, so just watch out.'

As Ariel said, Emily Sutton, Adina's latest placement, was another matter entirely. Emily was fourteen years old but as Melly whispered one day, she seemed to have a chip as big as a house brick on her shoulder. Admittedly, the girl had arrived in care having come from a very dysfunctional family, but instead of trying to make the best of things she constantly complained. She also took to staying out late after a very short time of being there; a fact which caused Adina no end of bother.

'*Nine o'clock* is your time in, miss,' she said sternly at eleven o'clock one night when Emily rolled in looking suspiciously as if she had been drinking.

Emily tossed her long mousy hair across her shoulder and sneered, 'An' since when have *you* been me keeper?'

'Since the minute you set foot through my door,' Adina rejoined.

Emily glared at her rebelliously. 'An' what are you goin' to do about it?'

'There's not much I can do,' Adina admitted. 'Apart from to tell you that if you don't obey the house rules you can move to another foster home. And those include putting that cigarette out right *now*. If you must smoke you can do it outdoors.'

The girl made a great show of grinding it out. She was dressed most unsuitably considering the bitterly cold temperatures outside, in hot pants, and her short jacket was open to display a low-cut top that left little to the imagination. Her face was plastered in so much make-up she looked almost clownish, and Adina felt a surge of temper ripple through her veins.

'I suggest you get yourself off to bed now,' she told her. 'You have school tomorrow.'

'That's if I decide to go!' the girl shot back, and with that she turned and stamped out of the room.

Adina sighed as Melly glanced up from the assignment she was working on to ask, 'Would you like me to make you a cup of cocoa?' She had remained tactfully silent while Emily was there, but now she was concerned to see that Adina looked somewhat stressed.

'That would be lovely, dear.' Adina rubbed her eyes wearily. She had spent the greatest part of the day sewing in the downstairs study that she had converted into a sewing room, and now she was so tired that she could barely keep her eyes open.

Melly was back in minutes balancing two steaming mugs and a plateful of biscuits on a tray.

'Oh lovely, thank you.' Adina lifted one of the mugs and sipped at it gratefully. 'You know, I think I might be getting too old for this fostering lark,' she commented. 'I can actually earn a very good living with my dressmaking now, so I'm not sure why I still bother to do it.'

'You do it because you are good with most of the children you care for,' Melly said admiringly. 'Look at what a fine job you've done with young Lucy. From what you've told me she wasn't much better behaved than Emily when she first arrived here, and now here she is about to fly the nest and become independent.'

Adina smiled. In actual fact, Melly was right, Lucy, her other place-ment, had been quite a handful when she first came, but she had managed to turn herself around and in March she would be leaving to work as a Red Coat at one of the many Butlins holiday camps that were springing up around the country.

Lucy had turned out to be a lovely girl once she realised that the whole world wasn't against her, and Adina was inordinately proud of her. Lucy had always wanted to work with children and Adina had an idea that she would love her new job. She would be another success story to add to her list, although she was realistic enough to admit that she hadn't succeeded with all the children she had cared for. Some of them had gone beyond help by the time they came to her, and were determined to go their own ways – and Adina had been forced to accept that fact early on in her fostering career.

Now, as her thoughts turned to other things, she asked cautiously, 'What are you and Richard planning on doing for Christmas? Will you be going to visit his folks in Devon?'

'Unfortunately not. Richard is on duty in Casualty on Christmas evening. Still, it could have been worse. At least I'll be able to be with him during the day.'

'Then why don't you invite him here for dinner?' Adina suggested. 'It will be frightfully expensive if you dine out on Christmas Day. The restaurants charge an extortionate amount and he'd be more than welcome to come and join us. I think it's about time I met him.'

'Really?' Melly beamed prettily. 'Why, that would be wonderful. Thank you. I'll ask him tomorrow, although I'm sure he'll snap your hand off. We're saving really hard for our wedding at present so every penny counts. As soon as Christmas is over I shall have to start scouting around the jumble sales for something to wear for the wedding. There's no way I could afford to pay the prices of the dresses in the shops around here.'

'Hmm, well, I just may be able to help you out there,' Adina told her as she eyed her up and down appraisingly. 'Come with me.'

Melly followed her upstairs without a word and once they were in Adina's bedroom she went to the wardrobe and lifted out the large card-board box in which she kept her wedding dress. After carefully lifting it from the layers of brown paper and tissue it was wrapped in, she shook it out and Melly's hand flew to her mouth.

'Why, it's absolutely beautiful!' she gasped as she fingered the silky material. 'But I couldn't possibly wear this. Was it your wedding gown?'

'I made it for myself many years ago,' Adina said softly, 'but I never got to wear it – although many others have. I've altered it and washed it so many times that I wonder how it manages to stay looking so fresh. But I don't want you to feel under any pressure to wear it. You mustn't say you like it just to spare my feelings if it's not your style.'

'Oh, but it *is*. I think it's lovely,' Melly said dreamily. 'Would you mind very much if I tried it on?'

'Of course not.'

Adina looked on with amusement as Melly stripped off to her underwear there and then; she then lifted the dress over the girl's head and began to do up the little row of buttons up the back as Melly held the skirt out and posed in front of the mirror.

'Oh, it's just a like fairytale gown,' she said delightedly. 'Are you really sure you wouldn't mind me wearing it? I'd feel like a princess in this.'

'I'd love you to wear it, but now will you just keep absolutely still while I have a good look at it on you. I think I might need to take it in just a little around the waist.' She slipped away to her sewing room and returned minutes later with a box of pins.

'Now hold still while I pin it,' she ordered and the girl obligingly did as she was told as she admired herself in the mirror.

Emily finally disappeared two days before Christmas although Adina wasn't really surprised. She had an idea that the girl would have returned to her alcoholic mother but there was little she could do about it other than to report her disappearance to the Social Services and the police. She was saddened that she hadn't been able to get through to the girl, but also determined that she wasn't going to let it ruin Christmas for the rest of them.

She had invited Beryl, Mick and their brood, but as she had expected they had had to decline the invitation because Christmas was one of their busiest times. Adina had also invited Beattie for Christmas dinner, but the woman had already had an invite from one of her numerous grandchildren, which Adina felt was just as it should be. Christmas was a time for families, after all. And so this year she would be cooking the Christmas dinner herself, and as she rushed about the shops getting the last-minute bits and pieces, she found herself looking forward to it.

At last everything was done and now she decided to give the house a final tidy-up. It was Christmas Eve and she was feeling happier than she had been for some time.

Melly was working at the hospital today and Lucy had gone to spend Christmas with her grandparents in Leeds, so it would be just Melly, Richard and herself there for Christmas dinner. She went about her chores merrily humming, but occasionally she had to stop and press her clenched fist into the pain in her side. It had been getting progressively worse over the last few weeks and now she reluctantly promised herself that she would go and see the doctor after Christmas. Beryl had certainly been nagging her long enough to do it. In the drawing room she found a pile of Melly's assignments laid neatly on the table, and as she was going upstairs anyway, she decided that she would put them into her room for her. She had never been in there since the day the girl had arrived as she had no wish to invade her privacy, but she was sure that Melly wouldn't mind.

When she opened the door, the room was just as she had expected it to be. The curtains were drawn and the bed was neatly made with not a single thing out of place. Crossing to a small table standing in the deep bay window, Adina placed the paperwork on it – but then as she turned to leave, her eyes were drawn to a small photograph in a silver frame standing on the bedside table. Trembling, she slowly approached it, and as she lifted it, found herself staring down into two familiar faces. It was a photograph of Fliss and Theo, obviously taken some years ago. *But why would Melly have a photo of them?* she asked herself, and as the answer suddenly screamed at her, she dropped heavily onto the bed. Could *they* be the people Melly had known as Mummy and Daddy? If they were, it meant that Melly was . . . *her daughter* – little Dottie, the child they had stolen from her so long ago.

Suddenly everything began to fall into place. The blonde hair and eyes the colour of bluebells. The dimple in her cheek – all so like Karl's, her father's. It was incredible and yet how else could it be explained?

Without really thinking what she was doing she began to open drawers and soon she found a photo album. It was full of Fliss and Theo happily holding a baby girl. *Her baby girl* – there was no mistaking her. The last glimpse she had had of Dottie's face was carved into Adina's memory for all time, and even now, after all these years, she would have recognised her amongst a million baby photos. As she turned the pages there was Melly at different stages of her life. On one page she was a toddler; old Mrs Montgomery was in the background of that one too, and now there could be no mistake. Melly had said that her grandmother had died whilst she was still quite young, which tied in with the photographs.

And then there was one of her on her first day at school, proudly showing off her new satchel. One of her on a bike and another of her opening her Christmas presents. As Adina slowly turned the pages she saw her daughter at various stages of her life growing up before her very eyes and her throat clogged with tears. No wonder she had felt so drawn to her the first time she had met her – but *why* had she never realised who she was before? The signs had all been there but somehow Adina had missed them. And now what was she to do about it? Her first instinct was to pour her heart out to Melly and tell her everything the second she set foot through the door, but she knew that she must think this through first. She mustn't let her heart rule her head. Carefully replacing the album exactly where she had found it, she crept from the room, her heart bursting with joy. Somehow, after all these long years, she had found her daughter again. Perhaps there was a God, after all?

* * *

When she heard Melly enter the hall that evening it was all she could do not to rush out and hug her, but she forced herself to be calm and greeted her as she always did.

'Brrr, it's freezing out there. I wouldn't be surprised if we didn't have snow,' Melly laughed as she kicked her boots off. Her cheeks were glowing with the cold and suddenly Adina found herself staring at a female version of Karl.

'Come down to the kitchen. I've got a pan of chicken soup on. That will warm you up,' she said, trying to act as normally as possible.

Melly hung her coat and scarf on the hall-stand and, blowing into her hands, she followed her downstairs.

'Richard will be here for twelve o'clock tomorrow. Is that all right?' Before Adina could reply, she went on excitedly, 'He's *so* looking forward to meeting you. I've told him how good you've been to me.'

'Rubbish. It's you that is good to me. You've been such a great help since you arrived,' Adina denied.

'I'm sure you're both going to get on,' Melly rushed on. 'Once you've met him you'll see why I love him so much.'

'I dare say I shall,' Adina said as she ladled the aromatic chicken soup into a bowl. 'Now get this down you, and then you can go and have a nice hot bath.'

'You sounded just like Mummy then,' Melly chuckled and Adina felt as if someone was plunging a knife into her heart, but she said nothing. She had never heard Melly say so much as one single bad word against Fliss or Theo, and she knew that she would have to feel her way very carefully before making a decision about what she should do. Even so, as she looked across at the girl, a surge of love powered through her. Her daughter was somehow miraculously back where she belonged – and for now that was enough.

Chapter Forty-Nine

The Christmas Day that Adina spent with Melly and her fiancé was as near to perfect as it could be. Richard Wilson, Melly's fiancé, was a lovely young man, tall dark and handsome, and the love that passed between them each time they glanced at each other was so touching to see that it brought a lump to Adina's throat. She couldn't have chosen a more wonderful young man for her daughter if she had set out to do it, and she somehow knew that Richard would cherish her.

The Christmas dinner was delicious. She had cooked a huge turkey which Melly declared would feed them for days, and served it with all the trimmings. There were crispy roast potatoes and juicy roast parsnips, brussel sprouts and carrots, and so many other dishes to choose from that Richard scratched his head, wondering just how much he could eat. They pulled Christmas crackers and wore paper hats, and the house rang with laughter as they read out silly jokes. Following the main course, Adina served a huge Christmas pudding that she had had soaking in brandy for weeks, and once Richard had polished off his second helping he leaned back in his seat and rubbed his stomach uncomfortably.

'Aw, I shan't be able to eat again for at least a week,' he groaned.

'Serves yourself right for making such a pig of yourself,' Melly giggled as she poked him in the ribs, and he caught her hand and squeezed it tenderly.

'Right now, how about you two go up into the drawing room and watch a film on the television?' Adina suggested. Melly and Richard had noticed that she had done little more than pick at her dinner but tactfully refrained from saying anything until the meal was over.

'Certainly not, we're going to help you clear away,' Melly said, and then, 'but you've hardly eaten enough to keep a sparrow alive.' She started to gather the dirty dishes together. 'No wonder you're so thin.'

'Rubbish,' Dina retorted. 'And you can leave those things for now. We'll tackle them later. Come on, let's go and have a sherry.'

'Hmm, if you put it that way, why not?' Melly grinned. It was Christmas Day, after all. They all happily trooped off into the drawing room and the young lovers were soon comfortably settled on the new leather-look sofa with generous glasses of sherry in their hand.

'Ah, you can't beat old Bing Crosby,' Melly sighed contentedly after watching *White Christmas* for at least the fourth time in as many years.

'Daddy always said Christmas wouldn't be Christmas without a Bing Crosby film on the television.'

Adina felt a surge of jealousy as she heard Melly talking so affectionately about Theo, but she remained silent. It still hurt her to think of the time she had missed with her daughter – a time that she could never recover – but she intended to make the most of every second now.

They spent a pleasant afternoon watching TV and nibbling chocolates, and then Richard shocked them all at teatime when he polished off two dishes full of Beattie's delicious strawberry trifle and two mince pies. Although she had retired, Beattie still called round regularly to make Adina the odd treat, and she had made these the day before she set off to spend Christmas with her family.

'I thought you weren't going to eat again for at least a week?' Melly teased.

'I'm just filling a hole.' Looking at Adina, he winked cheekily. 'It's a good job I don't live with you, Miss Schwartz. I'd be as fat as a pig in no time.'

'I'm just glad that you've enjoyed it,' Adina replied with a wide smile, and with that she helped herself to another small glass of sherry and settled further down into her seat with a contented sigh.

When it was time for Richard to go to the hospital, Adina was sorry to see him leave. She and the handsome young man had hit it off right away and she hoped that she would see him again.

'Now don't be a stranger,' she told him as she showed him to the door with Melly. 'Call in whenever you like.'

'I will, Miss Schwartz, and thank you for a wonderful day. I can't remember when I last had such a lovely meal. You are almost as good a cook as my mum is,' he, teased, then planted a kiss on her cheek. She blushed furiously as she told him, 'Call me Dina, please. Everyone else does.' She then slipped away to leave the lovers to have a moment to themselves. It had been a truly enjoyable day, and now that she had her daughter back under her roof, she had an idea that there would be many more to come.

Beryl called in to see her two days after New Year's Day. 'So what's put the smile on your face then?' she asked plonking herself down at the kitchen table. She loved being a vicar's wife and it never failed to amaze Adina how happy she always seemed, even though she was usually run off her feet organising one thing or another.

'Oh, I suppose I've still got the Christmas feeling on me,' Dina told her vaguely.

'Good, I'm pleased to hear it. But have you made an appointment with the doctor yet?'

'I have, as a matter of fact.' Adina grinned at her friend's surprised expression as she loaded some ginger biscuits onto a plate. 'I'm going to see him in the morning, as it happens.'

'And about time too. If you get any thinner you'll slip through a gap in the pavement.'

Ignoring her friend's jibe, Adina glanced at the clock. 'Lucy should be back from her grandparents' soon,' she commented, 'Melly is taking her to Oxford Street later on to get her a pair of those platform shoes that are becoming so popular.'

'Can't see how the youngsters walk in 'em meself.' Beryl shook her head.

'Well, you didn't used to say that when you were a teenager and you tottered around in heels,' Adina pointed out.

Beryl grinned wryly. 'No, I dare say I didn't. I think I must be getting old.' They were chatting about what they had both been up to over Christmas when Melly suddenly entered the room and smiled at them.

'Is Lucy back yet?' she asked pleasantly.

'I'm expecting her any minute now.' Adina reached for another cup as Melly joined them and in no time at all she was telling Beryl all about the wonderful wedding dress that Adina was lending to her for her wedding day.

'In actual fact I know the dress quite well,' Beryl told her with a grin. 'You see, I got to wear it on my wedding day when I married Mick.' She did not mention the marriage to Tyrone.

'You *did?*' Melly's eyes popped. 'Why, how wonderful!'

'Hm, I'm surprised you want to wear it though. Isn't it a bit outdated now?'

'Not at all. It's got an antique style to it which I like,' Melly declared. 'Dina did offer to restyle it for me, but I love it just as it is. She's letting me wear her veil too.'

'Well, I've no doubt you'll look stunning. With your face and figure you couldn't do otherwise.'

The slamming of the front door interrupted the conversation and Lucy breezed downstairs, her cheeks pink, and instantly began to tell them about the wonderful Christmas she had just spent with her grandmother, until Beryl reluctantly rose and stopped her midflow.

'Sorry all, but I have to be off,' she told them as she pulled her coat on. 'Mick and I are delivering some groceries to the old folks this afternoon.'

Adina followed her to the door where Beryl paused to whisper, 'I must say, Melly is a truly lovely girl, isn't she?'

'Oh, she's an absolute sweetheart.' Adina felt her chest swell with pride and once again she was tempted to tell her friend the truth, but now was not the time. One day soon I'll tell her, she promised herself.

She had no sooner let Beryl out into the cold foggy day when the two girls erupted up out of the kitchen. 'We're off to the sales now and we wondered if you'd like to come with us,' Melly said.

The offer was tempting, but: 'I don't really think you'd want me tagging along,' Adina said.

'We wouldn't have asked if we didn't want you to come,' Melly told her. 'Oh, *please* come. We intend to have a bit of fun. I'm back at college tomorrow and I want to make the best of my last day off.'

Adina wavered. The thought of spending the afternoon with her daughter was so tempting.

'All right. But only if you're both quite sure you don't mind being seen out with an oldie.'

'You'll *never* be an oldie,' Melly said as she headed towards the stairs. 'I think you're quite beautiful, if you must know. Now let's all go and get ready and we'll meet back here in ten minutes.'

Once again, Adina chewed on her lip as her daughter disappeared. Time and time again she had been tempted to tell her the truth about her parentage, but each time she thought the time seemed right, the words had lodged in her throat. She realised that when she did tell her it would come as a great shock to Melly, or Dottie as she still tended to think of her. It was more than obvious that Fliss and Theo had adored her and she them, which didn't help somehow. Would Melly feel resentful when Adina revealed that she was her real mother? That she had been born out of wedlock and that her true father wasn't even aware of her existence? Or would she even believe her, if it came to that? Fliss and Theo had done a remarkable job of making the girl believe that she was theirs, even down to changing all their names and taking on new identities when they had moved away. Adina had spent a long time pondering on how they might have done this, but then she had realised that at the time they had kidnapped Dottie they had been very wealthy people and money could buy anything, even false identities.

Admittedly to outsiders, Adina appeared respectable, since she had a lovely home and she had done well for herself, but the stigma of being an unmarried mother still remained. Sighing heavily, she hurried away to get ready. There was no point in worrying about it now; she was just going to go and enjoy being in her daughter's company.

They had a wonderful afternoon and Dina could not remember a time when she had enjoyed herself so much, although she did begin to tire as the day wore on. Melly and Lucy seemed to have boundless energy as they rushed from shop to shop in Oxford Street and Carnaby Street, and then on to Biba's in Kensington High Street. Lucy managed to find a pair of platform shoes that made her look at least two inches taller, and Melly treated herself to a brightly coloured tank top that was hugely reduced in the sales. She also fell in love with a maxi-skirt but decided against being extravagant as she and Richard were saving so hard for their wedding.

Dina waited until the two girls had drifted away to look at another sale rail before hastily buying it for for her anyway. She could see that Melly had fallen in love with it and knew that it would suit her, although she thought that Melly was so beautiful she would have looked lovely in a paper bag. Sometimes when she looked at her she could hardly believe that she had given birth to someone so perfect: if only Karl could have seen her. She knew that he would have loved her too. As always when she thought of him she would unconsciously finger the steel band on her finger and the little ache in her heart that had never truly gone away would eat away at her all over again. He had been the love of her life, and although she had had several would-be suitors over the years, none of them had managed to measure up to him, even though he had broken her heart. She had once said that if she couldn't marry Karl, she would marry no one – and she had been true to her word.

When they eventually caught a bus home, they were all in a light-hearted mood.

'I might wear my new top tonight,' Melly said as they turned the corner at Marble Arch. 'Richard is taking me out for a curry. I'll have to dig something out of my wardrobe that will go with it.'

Once back at the house, Melly told them, 'I'm going to shoot off and get a bath so that I'm ready in plenty of time. Is that all right? Is there anything you need me to do first?'

'Not at all,' Adina assured her. 'But here, take this with you.'

'What is it?' Melly took the bag curiously and when she peeped inside she beamed with delight. 'It's the skirt I liked . . . but why did you buy it?'

'Because you liked it,' Adina said matter-of-factly, handing Lucy a similar bag containing a jumper she had admired. 'I can treat you both if I want to, can't I?'

Without warning Melly suddenly flung her arms about her and gave her a big hug, and Adina's heart skipped a beat. She had dreamed of holding her daughter for so many years and now she finally was.

Her throat was full as she finally disentangled the girl's arms from her waist and pointed at the stairs. 'Go on then, go and get ready. You don't want to be late for Richard, do you?'

Melly skipped away as Adina turned to hug Lucy so that no one would see the tears that had sprung to her eyes.

It was a few days later when Beryl called around unexpectedly one morning to find Adina sobbing uncontrollably in the sewing room. She had had a key to the door for some time in case of emergencies, and she stood in the doorway astounded.

'Why, love, whatever is the matter?' She flew across the room and placed her arm about Adina's heaving shoulders.

'Oh Beryl, everything is such a mess,' her friend sobbed. 'It's Melly.'

'Why, what's she done?' Beryl's eyebrows rose into her hairline. 'She seems such a lovely girl. I never dreamed she'd give you a moment's trouble.'

'She hasn't,' Adina managed to choke out. 'It's quite the opposite. She's an angel and I love her so much it hurts.' Pulling herself together with an effort, she blew her nose noisily. 'The thing is . . . Melly is my daughter. She is my baby Dorothy, who Fliss and Theo stole when they left me the house. I found out quite by chance one day just before Christmas when I went to put some papers away for her in her room. She has a photo of them at the side of her bed and she talks about them all the time. They are both dead now but she obviously loved them dearly. She had no idea at all that she wasn't really their daughter.'

'*What?* Why, this is incredible! And you mean to tell me that you haven't told her yet?'

'No, I haven't – and I'm not going to,' Dina told her.

Beryl's eyes bulged. 'But why? Surely she has a right to know what they did to you, and who her real mother is.' Beryl was indignant now, which was apparent from the way she was bristling.

'I did fully intend to tell her when the time was right,' Adina sniffed. 'But then we were talking last night and she made a confession. She told me that she hadn't really applied for the job here just by chance. When Fliss passed away, Melly found papers with this address on it from years ago amongst her things. She guessed that Fliss and Theo must have lived here at one time and so when she saw the job advertised she thought it would be nice to live here for a while as they had. She thinks that I bought the house off them.'

Beryl scratched her head in consternation. 'So surely that's all the more reason for you to tell her what they did to you. And to her, for that matter.'

'What would be the point in shattering her memories of them?' Adina said. 'What they did was wrong, but they obviously gave her a far better life than I ever could have. And I have her back in my life, for now at least. The last thing I want to do is hurt her.'

Beryl removed her arm from Adina's shoulders and straightened, worrying about how thin her friend had become. She felt as if she was all skin and bone but she would address that issue at another time.

'So what is she doing, working for a living?' she questioned. 'From what you told me, I thought the Montgomerys were rolling in money.'

'They were, but apparently Theo invested it all in a business and he went bankrupt in the 1950s.'

Beryl's head wagged from side to side. 'Well, I'll be blowed,' she muttered. 'It's strange how things turn out, ain't it?'

306

'I suppose it is, but at least I've found her again and now I just want to enjoy the time I have with her.'

'That's your decision, but I have to say you're a lot nobler than me. If I was in your shoes I'd tell her the truth like a shot and shame the devil, though I can understand you don't want to hurt her.'

'*Hurt her!*' Adina exclaimed. 'It would turn her whole world upside down and I love her too much to do that. Things are best left as they are. I was just feeling sorry for what might have been when you walked in, that's all.'

'Well, I have to say, now that you've told me I can see the resemblance to Karl. She's his double, ain't she?'

Adina nodded ruefully. 'Yes, she is. Sometimes when I look into her eyes it's almost like looking into his again.'

'You still love him after all this time, don't you?' Beryl whispered sympathetically.

'Yes, I do. I've never stopped. But at least I have Melly back now and I want you to promise that you'll leave me to deal with this in my own way and not interfere. You are the only person I've told. Will you do that for me, Beryl?'

'Of course I will,' Beryl said sadly. 'You should know by now that I'd never do anything to hurt you. God knows, you've done enough for me over the years. Though I have to say I don't agree with your decision not to tell her. But that's up to you and I'll go along with it.'

'Thank you,' Adina said, and the two friends held hands as they sat there each lost in their own thoughts.

Chapter Fifty

It was early in May as Adina and Melly were breakfasting together that Melly suddenly said, 'I suppose you won't be needing me now that Lucy's gone and you've decided not to take any more children.'

Adina had noticed how quiet Melly had been since Lucy had left a month before to start her new job as a Red Coat at Butlin's, but this was the last thing she had expected.

'Of course I still need you,' she said quickly. 'Whatever made you think that I didn't?'

Melly looked around the neat and tidy kitchen. 'Now that there is just you and me here, there's hardly anything to do. We both clear up after ourselves, so all I'm doing really is a bit of dusting and some washing and ironing.'

'That's right – and while you're doing that I have the chance to get on with my sewing, which is what I would rather be doing,' Adina pointed out. When Melly still looked doubtful she rushed on, 'I really like having someone here with me. It's lonely by myself after being used to having the house full of children, so let's hear no more about you leaving, do you hear me? Oh, and by the way, I picked a brochure up from the florist's yesterday, so tonight when you get in from Bart's we'll choose what flowers you'd like for the wedding. Did you have anything particular in mind?'

'I do love roses,' Melly admitted, instantly brighter again. 'Though they might be a little expensive, mightn't they?'

'Don't you get worrying about that. I shall be seeing to the flowers.' When Melly opened her mouth to object, Adina held her hand up. 'It's no use arguing. I insist, the flowers will be my treat, so eat your breakfast and get yourself off to work otherwise you'll have Sister O'Flanagan after you.'

'Actually, I've been meaning to talk to you about the wedding,' Melly said shyly. 'Richard and I thought it might be nice if we got married in London. In fact, we were hoping that Father Mick might be able to marry us.'

Adina looked astounded and she hurried on, 'I know I've left it a little late to book the church, but as I said to Richard, I'm more at home here now than anywhere else. So would you mind very much if I got married from here?'

'I'd absolutely *love* it,' Adina said with a radiant smile. 'But aren't Richard's folks put out that you don't want to get married in Devon?'

'Not at all. They understand that our work and our friends are here, and Richard has already spoken to them about it. They said that it's our day and they're quite happy to travel here for the wedding.'

'In that case I'll speak to Beryl and Mick straight away,' Adina told her. 'And I'm sure there won't be a problem.'

'That's settled then.' Melly then obediently gobbled down a slice of toast and rising from her seat, she planted a kiss on Adina's thin cheek before heading for the door. 'I'll see you this evening. Have a good day and don't get working too hard. You look worn out.'

'I'm fine,' Adina told her with a smile, but as soon as Melly had left the room she became solemn and fingered her cheek where her daughter had kissed her. Every single day since the girl had arrived she had thanked God for her, and now she would have the pleasure of seeing her go to her wedding from her rightful home. It was more than she could have hoped for.

The wedding was now just six weeks away and Melly was a bag of nerves. Adina almost had to force her to eat. Father Mick would be marrying them in St Chad's Church, just as Melly had requested, and afterwards they would be having a small reception back at the house before leaving for their honeymoon.

'Have you asked her yet whether she and Richard would want to live here?' Beryl asked Adina one day during their ritual coffee morning.

'No, to be honest I thought better of it,' Adina muttered vaguely.

Beryl frowned. 'How come? You obviously dote on the girl. I would have thought you'd do anything to keep her close by.'

'She has her own life to lead and I don't want to appear as if I am interfering. I count myself lucky that I'll be seeing her get married.'

Beryl was still puzzled, but decided enough had been said on the subject. As she stared at her friend she couldn't help but notice the way she had changed over the years since she had first known her. When they had first met, Adina had been the typical obedient Jewish daughter. Shy and timid; a girl who wouldn't say boo to a goose. Then she had become the abandoned pregnant girl when Karl left her. She had gone all through the heartbreak of losing her parents after seeing the brother she adored slowly go insane before hanging himself. And then she had come to London where the Montgomerys had tricked her and kidnapped her daughter. When Beryl had first arrived back from the States, rescued by this same friend, Adina had been at an all-time low and yet somehow she had found an inner strength and had managed to survive. She had been a foster mum to countless children and built up a thriving dressmaking business. And now here she was at forty-seven years old, an elegant sophisticated woman who was entirely self-sufficient. Beryl was quietly proud of her although she didn't say so. Adina wasn't one for fuss and palaver and would simply have told her she was being silly.

An hour later, when Beryl left, Adina went into the sewing room to work on the veil that she was making for Melly. The other one was past its best now, and although Melly had insisted she was happy to wear it, Adina was determined she should have a new one. She had already sewn over 300 minute sequins on it by hand and was just about to add a few more when the doorbell rang.

Cursing beneath her breath, she laid the filmy netting down and hurried down into the hall where she quickly checked her sleek chignon in the mirror before opening the door.

A smartly dressed middle-aged man was standing on the step and she smiled at him politely before asking, 'May I help you?'

He simply stood there staring at her as she began to feel perplexed. His hair had obviously been fair when he was younger but now it was a salt and pepper colour; he had strikingly blue eyes and towered above her.

She stared back for a moment and then as recognition dawned, her hand flew to her mouth and she had to clutch the door handle for support.

'Karl . . . is it really you?'

He nodded as his eyes filled with tears. 'Yes, it's me, Adina. May I come in?'

She hesitated just for a fraction of a second before holding the door wide and he stepped past her into the hallway. They stared at each other, not knowing what to say until she asked weakly, 'Would you like a cup of tea?'

'That would be very nice. Thank you.'

He followed her down into the kitchen where she gestured towards a chair. 'Won't you sit down?'

They were acting like two strangers. All her life Adina had dreamed of this moment – and now that it had come she didn't know how to cope with it.

A heavy silence lay between them as she bustled about making them tea, and then it was poured and she had no choice but to sit down opposite him.

'H . . . have you been in England for long?' she asked politely, saying the first thing that popped into her head. He was still very attractive and her heart was beating so fast she was afraid he would hear it.

'For almost three weeks.' He took the cup and saucer she held out to him, 'I visited the shop in Nuneaton and Ariel graciously gave me your address. She and Brian have a fine family. And the shop is also thriving, by what they told me.'

'Yes, they have done very well for themselves and I am very proud

310

of them,' Adina said. 'Brian bought the shop from the landlord some years ago. But you must have found everything very different from when you were here before.'

'The new decimal currency is the strangest thing to get used to,' he admitted. 'I struggled with your pounds shillings and pence during the war but I find this currency even more difficult. But it seems that you have done well for yourself too. Ariel speaks very highly of you.' He glanced around the room as he spoke, and it was all Adina could do not to shout at him, *Why did you leave me? Didn't you know how much I loved you?* But the words stayed trapped inside. She was proud and would never admit to him just how much he had hurt her, even though the sound of his voice could still set her pulses racing. She suddenly became aware that he was staring at the band of steel on her finger that he had given her so many years ago and she flushed.

'I've done all right, I suppose,' she said noncommittally. 'And yourself?' She knew that there was a sharp edge to her voice but didn't seem able to control it as all the hurt he had caused her rose to the surface again.

He hung his head in shame and suddenly said, 'I'm *so* sorry for what I did to you, Adina. I know that I owe you an explanation.'

'You owe me absolutely nothing.' Her voice was as cold as ice and yet inside she was crying.

'But yes . . . yes, I do. I told you when I left that I would come back for you, and you must believe me when I tell you that I fully intended to do that. I *swear* it. I loved you, Adina, and I have never been able to forget you.'

Adina shrugged. 'It was all a long time ago now,' she said.

'Please . . . may I explain?'

'If you wish to, although I really cannot see what difference it could make now. We both made new lives for ourselves. I just assumed that when you returned home you realised that you still loved your fiancée and married her.'

'I did marry her,' he said, and a knife sliced through her heart. 'But not for the reasons you think.' He took a deep breath before continuing, 'When I first met you I thought you were the most beautiful girl I had ever set eyes on. Even so, I had no intention of beginning a relationship with you. A German and a Jew? We were just about the worst combination there could have been back then and we both knew it. Added to that, as I told you before I went away, I was already engaged to be married. But I couldn't help falling in love with you. It just happened and there was nothing I could do about it. I came from a very good family and my parents chose my bride for me and arranged the marriage when I was still quite young. But after meeting you I knew that I couldn't go through with marrying Marlena. So I went back to Bremen intending to end my relationship and to return to you – but nothing was the same.'

She saw the stark pain on his face as he remembered but he forced himself to go on. 'I had already had word that my grandparents had been killed and that my parents had fled. But nothing could have prepared me for what I found. Most of Bremen had been flattened, including my parents' farm, and Marlena's parents' home was gone too, so I had no idea where any of them might be, or even if they were still alive.'

Despite her mixed emotions at seeing Karl again Adina felt a pang of sympathy for him. It was as if he was finally shifting a great weight from his shoulders as he blundered on.

'I immediately began to make enquiries of the few people left there, and after some weeks I was directed to a small town just outside Bremen. It was there that I found Marlena and my mother living in what amounted to little more than a hovel. My father was dead. He had been injured during a raid and on the same night Marlena's parents had also been killed. She had then managed to get my mother and father away, and had nursed my father until he died.' Karl took a deep breath before going on. 'My mother was almost unrecognisable. Her mind was completely unhinged and Marlena was now nursing her too, day and night with no respite. Oh Adina, how could I leave them both after all they had gone through? I would have been heartless, so I had to make a decision – and as much as I loved you, I felt I had no choice but to stay and take care of them both. I wrote to you and told you what had happened, and prayed that you would understand, and shortly after-wards, Marlena and I were married in a quiet ceremony.'

Karl stopped once more, to take a sip of tea before continuing.

'We were unhappy together right from the start, and totally unsuited. Even so we had two children, a girl and a boy. I knew within a very short time that she was as unhappy with me as I was with her, but neither of us quite knew what to do about it. And then my mother died. It was a blessing, if I am to be honest. After that, Marlena and I only stayed together for the sake of the children. I was racked with guilt. You were the woman I wanted to spend the rest of my life with, but I felt loyalty and responsibility for the little ones. I promised myself that when they were a little older I would tell Marlena the truth about you and try to find you again. But then before that could happen, my wife was diag-nosed with a terminal illness; a muscle-wasting disease that would get progressively worse. I felt as if my hands were tied. I wanted to come back for you, but how could I leave her like that? And my darling chil-dren were still young and they needed me. And so I stayed and it was terrible to watch her waste away before my very eyes until eventually she died. It was a blessed release for her. After that the years just seemed to fly by. My daughter married shortly after Christmas and my son is running the family business for me, and at last I felt that I was able to come and make my peace with you. If you will allow me to, that is.'

Adina was reeling with shock at what he had told her and yet outwardly she appeared to be quite calm. Over the years she had become an expert at concealing her true feelings. And she knew that he had told the truth about writing to her because Mrs Downes had once told her that she had forwarded on a letter with a German postmark. Now she wondered again what might have happened to it. She had certainly never received it.

Slowly her shock and anger seeped away, to be replaced by sadness.

'I never received your letter,' she told him.

'Ah, that explains why you never wrote back.' He ran a hand through his hair. 'In the one I sent you I begged you to write back and tell me that you understood. When you did not reply, I assumed you had met someone else and married them.'

'Well, I did make a new life for myself,' she told him as their eyes locked. 'And as you can see, I am very comfortable.'

'But you never married?'

She shook her head. 'I had no wish to. I have fostered dozens of children over the years and I have a very lucrative dressmaking business that keeps me more than busy.'

'But surely you sometimes yearned for a child of your own?'

She swallowed hard as she thought of Melly, but simply murmured, 'There is more to life than just getting married and having babies.' She briefly wondered what he would say if she were to tell him that she had a child, *his child*, but thought better of it. If she couldn't tell Melly, then how could she tell him?

As if thoughts of her had conjured her up from thin air, Melly suddenly ran down the stairs and breezed in with a wide smile on her face, only to stop abruptly as she saw that Adina had a visitor.

'Oh, I'm so sorry,' she apologised as she turned to leave. 'I didn't realise you had a guest.'

'It's quite all right, you don't have to go.' Adina held a hand out to her. 'This is Karl. He and I were er . . . friends, a long time ago during the war. He's visiting England and thought he would look me up.'

Melly flashed him a friendly smile as she went to shake his hand, and as Adina looked at the two of them a lump formed in her throat and threatened to choke her. Melly was like a female version of her father, could she only have known it. Her hair was exactly the same colour as his had once been, and so were his eyes. Even the dimple in her cheek was in exactly the same place as his. And here they all were together at last, a family, but only she was aware of it.

'I am very pleased to meet you,' Karl said formally as he shook her hand.

Melly smiled at him again before heading back the way she had come. 'It was lovely to meet you too. But I'll make myself scarce for a while now. I have an assignment to work on and I'm sure you two must have a lot of catching up to do.'

As soon as the door had closed on her, Karl looked at Adina with that look she remembered so well, which seemed to see right into her very soul.

'What a charming girl,' he remarked. 'Is she one of your foster children?'

'No, Melly lodges with me,' Adina informed him. 'She is getting married in August and then she will be moving away with her fiancé who is a junior doctor at Saint Bart's Hospital.'

'And what will you do then?'

'The same as I have always done.' The haughty look was back on her face again now. 'I shall get on with my life.'

'Do you have any more young people here?'

'No, I have decided to retire from that career now.'

'Then won't you be lonely? From what I have seen of it, this is an extremely large house for you to rattle around in all on your own.'

'But that isn't your concern.' The second the words had left her lips she wished that she could take them back as hurt washed across his face. She wanted to throw herself into his arms and tell him that she still loved him, that she understood why he had stayed away, but it was too late for that now, and as confusion overwhelmed her she suddenly wished that he would leave.

Rising from her seat she told him steadily, 'I'm so sorry but I am quite busy at present working on an outfit that must be finished by the weekend.'

'Of course; how thoughtless of me.' He rose so abruptly that he almost overturned his chair, and then as he strode toward the door he paused to ask, 'Do you think you can ever forgive me, Adina?'

She stared back at him, the words stuck in her throat, until he asked, 'Would you allow me to take you out? To the theatre or perhaps for a meal?'

'I suppose so,' she said uncertainly, and suddenly she saw a glimpse of the young man she had carried around in her heart all these years when his face broke into a smile.

'How about this evening? I am staying in a hotel in central London – perhaps I could take you for a meal? There is a very nice restaurant not far from there.'

'Very well,' she said softly.

'Wonderful, then I shall pick you up at . . . shall we say seven o'clock?'

At the front door he paused again as if there was something else he wanted to say, but the moment passed and he smiled before running down the steps and striding away.

Once she had closed the door Adina leaned heavily against it as Melly exploded out of the drawing room where she had been trying to concentrate on her assignment.

'Oh, what a *handsome* man!' she said with a cheeky twinkle in her eye. 'And you've agreed to go out with him.' She looked slightly guilty then, before giggling, 'I couldn't help but overhear. Was he once your boyfriend?'

'I suppose he was,' Adina replied uncomfortably. 'But that was a very long time ago now.'

'Well, he obviously still likes you,' Melly trilled. 'Now, what are you going to wear? Let's think. Hm, that blue velvet dress you made to wear over Christmas would be perfect. It really suits you and it's so elegant.'

'Now don't go getting carried away,' Adina scolded as her heart started to settle into a steadier rhythm. 'I'm hardly a young girl going out on her first date.'

'Even so, you want to look your best. It's so exciting to think he's looked you up after all this time. He must have cared about you a great deal. I've never known you to go out with anyone since I've been living here, so he must have been special to you too.'

'Now that's quite enough of all this romantic nonsense.' Adina put her hands on her hips. 'If you keep carrying on like this I shall change my mind and decide not to go.'

'Sorry,' Melly muttered humbly. 'I'll get back to work and stop interfering, shall I?'

'I think that would be a very good idea,' Adina agreed as Melly turned to go back to her studies. Once she was gone Adina slowly made her way to her bedroom where she stared distractedly into the mirror. She saw a middle-aged woman staring back at her. Admittedly, her face was relatively unlined and there was only the tiniest hint of grey at her temples. She had kept her youthful figure too, running around after all the children she had cared for, but even so the girl that Karl must have remembered all these years was long gone. As she thought back to the things he had told her, it was like the pieces of a jigsaw puzzle falling into place at last. If only the letter he had sent her had arrived! At least then she would have known why he hadn't come back for her. But now at last she did know, and it went a long way to easing her heartache. He had loved her, after all, but circumstances had kept them apart. Even so, it was too late now for a reunion. Nothing could ever come of his returning to find her, and it broke her heart afresh.

315

Chapter Fifty-One

Karl had been back in Adina's life for almost six weeks now and Beryl was thrilled about it.

'He's obviously still smitten with you, so why don't you put the poor bloke out of his misery an' tell him you still love him?' She had just finished helping Adina carry the wedding dress that Melly would be wearing the following day upstairs to her room after having its final press.

'Oh, don't *you* start,' Adina groaned as she hung it on Melly's wardrobe door. 'I have enough with Melly keeping on at me.'

'And so she should.' Beryl huffed indignantly. 'It ain't never too late to grab at happiness, you know, and you're hardly in your dotage. Surely you can forgive him now you know why he didn't come back for you? The poor devil's hands were tied.'

'I understand that, but now Karl is merely a friend,' Adina rejoined stubbornly as she stroked the shimmering folds of silk. 'I'm a little long in the tooth now for a happy ending, don't you think?'

'No, I don't. But anyway I ain't got time to stand here arguing with you now. I've got to be off. All I'll say before I go is, you should have a little more compassion for him. It ain't like he ever stopped loving you, is it? He was just in an awful position where he couldn't do anything about it. He would have had to be a right heel to leave his girlfriend when she was carin' for his mother.'

'I understand that,' Adina repeated primly. 'Now go, will you, and leave me to get ready. We're going to see a show tonight.'

Beryl chuckled as she barged out of the door shouting, 'It's all right for some, bein' wined an' dined. Make the most of it, gel.' And then she was gone, and when Adina heard the front door slam a second later, she sank down onto the edge of Melly's bed and stared off into space.

Since Karl had come back into her life they had enjoyed numerous outings together. He had also spent a lot of time at the house and had bought her so many flowers that now the downstairs was beginning to look like a florist's shop. He and Melly had hit it off right from the start, so much so that the week before, she had shyly asked him if he would mind giving her away when she got married. Adina had found it strangely fitting that it would be her father walking her down the aisle, even if neither of them were aware of the fact.

Up until now Karl had acted like a perfect gentleman and had done no more than give Adina a chaste kiss on the cheek when he delivered her home to her door. But Adina could sense that he was hoping for more and it saddened her to know that it was not going to happen. It was too late now. Sighing, she rose and went to her room where she would have a short nap before getting ready to meet Karl that evening.

The day of the wedding dawned bright and clear, and once again the house was alive with activity. Richard's parents had travelled up from Devon and were staying in a local hotel although Adina had invited them for dinner the evening before. They had all had a wonderful time, and once Richard's parents had left to return to their hotel Melly had hustled Richard towards the door. 'Go on, you – I don't want to see you again now until we are in the church tomorrow. It's bad luck,' she had scolded him.

As Adina watched him kiss her tenderly her eyes had filled with tears and she had turned so quickly that she had almost collided with Karl, who had come into the hall to say goodbye.

'They make a wonderful couple, don't they?' His hands settled gently on her shoulders and Adina nodded dumbly. More than anything in the world she wanted to tell him the truth but the words stayed locked deep inside, never to be uttered. The way she saw it, she owed Melly and Karl that much at least.

And now Melly was ready for church, dressed in the gown that Adina had once made for herself, and Adina was sure that she was the most beautiful bride she had ever seen.

'You look truly stunning,' she told her emotionally. 'But I have one more thing for you that I think will finish your outfit off.' She lifted a box and took out a sparkling tiara made of crystals. They caught the light flooding through the window and sent rainbows of colours spiralling about the room.

'Oh, Dina!' Melly's hand shot to her mouth. 'You really shouldn't have. You've done so much for me already.'

Adina fastened the tiara onto the filmy veil she had spent so many hours sewing.

'I wanted to,' she told her. 'And all I ask of you is that you will keep it in your family and one day, if you are blessed with a daughter, you will let her wear it too and tell her about me.'

Melly flung her arms about her and kissed her soundly, setting Adina's heart racing. 'I won't have to tell her about you!' she cried. 'She will know you and you will be there at her wedding. You're still a young woman, you know. Anyone would think you were going to die tomorrow.'

'Well, you never know. But let's not talk of sad things today. Now where are your flowers? I think I ought to be off to the church and leave you in Karl's care. Goodbye, my dear.'

'Dina . . .

Adina paused at the door to look back at her.

'Thank you . . . for everything,' Melly said softly. 'You've been as good to me as my own mother. I do love you, Dina.'

'And I love you too.' Adina dabbed at her eyes with a handkerchief before hurrying downstairs to Karl, who was pacing up and down in the hallway.

'The bride will be down in a minute,' she told him, as she picked up her bag and made for the door. 'The car should be here for you in five minutes so I'll see you in the church. Goodbye for now.'

Karl grinned as she hurried away down the steps. She looked little older than the girl he had once fallen in love with, in her new lilac outfit and dainty hat, and it was all he could do to stop himself from chasing after her and telling her so, but for now he had another duty to perform and so he turned and waited patiently for the blushing bride to join him.

The wedding was a joyous occasion and everything went perfectly, much to Adina's relief. Karl looked so proud as he walked Melly down the aisle, but from the second Melly reached her husband-to-be, standing in front of the altar, she had eyes for no one else, which Adina knew was just as it should have been. The whole affair was bittersweet for her. It seemed fitting that Melly's true father was walking her down the aisle in the dress that Adina had once made so long ago to marry him in.

It was much later in the day, when the party was in full swing at the house that Karl managed to catch Adina alone in the kitchen. She had just come down to fetch another bottle of wine for the guests, and when she turned around he was right behind her.

'I have to say it's been a wonderful day,' he said softly. 'And now that I've managed to get you alone, there is something that I have been meaning to ask you.' He gently removed the bottle from her and placed it on the table, then took her two hands in his and gazed deep into her eyes.

'I know that you have a lot to forgive me for.' When she opened her mouth to protest he rushed on, 'But I hope that now you know why I did not come back for you, you will find it in your heart to understand.'

'Of course I forgive you, but please don't go any—'

'Adina,' he interrupted, 'I am going to ask you something that I should have asked long ago. You are the only woman I have ever truly loved, so will you do me the very great honour of becoming my wife?'

Her eyes mirrored her heartache as she slowly shook her head.

'No, Karl. Thank you for asking me, but the answer is no.'

'But why not? We are still young enough to have a life together. Don't you love me?'

Taking a deep breath, she forced herself to say, 'No, Karl, I'm afraid

318

I don't – not any more. I view you as a friend now. A very dear friend, but I don't wish to marry you. I'm so sorry.'

'I don't understand.' He looked so bewildered that her heart went out to him as she disentangled her fingers from his.

'You must understand I've made a new life for myself now,' she told him gently. 'And truthfully, I am happy with it as it is and I have no wish to change it.'

'I see.' He looked stricken. 'And is there nothing that I can say that will make you change your mind?'

'Absolutely nothing. I'm pleased that you came to find me. You have laid a lot of ghosts to rest. But now I think it is time you returned to your own country. You have children there who need you.'

He rose to his full height, looking so handsome that she had to clench her fists to stop herself from crying out.

'In that case I shall go and say my goodbyes and then leave. But if ever you need me or you change your mind, will you get in touch? You have my address.'

And suddenly they were strangers again as he turned slowly and walked towards the kitchen door, where he paused to say, 'Goodbye, my love.' And then he was gone.

Beryl walked in some minutes later with a frown on her face. 'Karl has left,' she said bluntly. 'He went a bit suddenly, didn't he? Have you two had words? He had a face as long as a fiddle on him.'

'He asked me to marry him and I turned him down,' Adina muttered.

'You did *what*?' Beryl was outraged. 'Have you lost your mind, gel?' She closed the kitchen door behind her before saying, 'Why in the name of God did you do that? You've loved him all these years and now you turn him down! It just don't make any sense.'

'It makes perfect sense. I love him too much to marry him, you see?' Adina took her friend's hand and said quietly, 'You have been the best friend I have ever had, and so I think it's time that I told you the truth – but you *must* promise first that what I am about to tell you remains just between you and me?'

Beryl nodded reluctantly. She had an awful feeling that she wasn't going to like what she was about to hear.

The friends sat down together side by side just as they had so many times before over the years, and once Adina had composed herself she said, 'I can't marry Karl. You see, I found out just after Christmas that I have cancer and it is inoperable. The doctors gave me six to twelve months so I am already living on borrowed time.'

'Oh no!' Beryl's eyes filled with tears.

'So you see, that is why I didn't want Melly to know who I really was or for her to come and stay here after she was married. I want her to remember me as I am now. And Karl, well, he has already nursed one wife until she died. I don't want to put him through that again. It's

319

far better that he thinks I don't love him any more. Can you understand now?'

'Yes, I think I can, but it's so unfair,' Beryl cried as a tear slid down her cheek.

'No, it isn't,' Adina smiled. 'Don't you see? Everything came out right in the end. The man I love didn't leave me because he didn't want me. And I got my daughter back, even if it was only for a precious short time, against all the odds. I might have lost her when she was little but over the years, and thanks to your brilliant idea, I've been a mum to countless children. I have already seen a solicitor, and when I die this house will be Melly's. I hope she will come back here to live with Richard then, and some day my granchildren may be brought up here. I really couldn't ask for more. And now I have told you, shall we go back and join the party? I want to make the most of every minute of today.'

Beryl squeezed her hand as she rose from her seat, and not for the first time thought what a truly remarkable, selfless woman Adina was.

Now, sliding the band of steel from the third finger of her left hand, Adina pressed it into her friend's palm, 'I want you to give this to Melly when I am gone,' she told her. 'Over the years it has been my most precious possession. Will you do that for me?'

'Of course I will,' Beryl told her chokily. And then arm-in-arm they went to rejoin the party.

It was late that evening, when Beryl sat in the tiny vicarage enjoying a cup of cocoa with her husband, that Mick asked, 'Are you all right, love? You've been very quiet since we got home.'

Beryl wrestled with her conscience. She had promised Adina that she would keep the secret she had entrusted her with, but she felt as if she would burst if she didn't share it with Mick.

'Adina told me something awful today,' she admitted tentatively. 'And she made me promise that I wouldn't tell anyone. But the thing is . . . Well, I feel that she's about to make a grave mistake an' I really need your advice.'

'I see,' he said. It was obviously something very serious. 'If you're breaking your promise because you feel that it would be in her best interests, I'm sure that she'd forgive you.'

Beryl nodded as she thought on what he'd said for a moment and then suddenly it all spurted out. By the time she had finished the sorry tale she was crying softly and Mick slid his arm across her shoulders.

'That's just awful,' he muttered. He had become very fond of Adina over the years.

'Yes, it is,' Beryl sobbed. 'But what's even more awful is that once again she's putting everyone else's feelings before her own. Karl loves her, that's plain to see, so why can't she just tell him the truth and let him make his own mind up about whether or not he wants to spend what time she has left with her? What should I do, Mick?'

'It's difficult.' He stared off into space for a while as he gave it some thought before asking, 'Do you know where Karl is staying?'

She nodded vigorously.

'Then I think in this case you could be forgiven for paying him a little visit and having a quiet word in his ear.'

Beryl blinked through her tears. 'But what if he's already left?'

Mick patted her hand comfortingly. 'I think there's very little chance of that. He'll have to book a flight home so I think if you paid him a visit first thing in the morning, you'd be in plenty of time to catch him.'

'And do you really think I'd be doing the right thing?' Beryl set a lot of store on Mick's advice. He was a man of the cloth, after all.

He nodded. 'In this case, yes I do. She deserves better than to die alone. Adina is a good woman.' Comforted, Beryl settled back against his shoulder and suddenly the morning couldn't come quickly enough.

Bright and early the next day, Beryl waltzed into the hotel in Bloomsbury where Karl had moved to in order to be closer to where Adina lived.

'I'd like to speak to Mr Karl Stolzenbach, please,' she told the man at Reception.

'I'll just ring his room and check that he's available for you, madam,' the man replied. He tapped a number into his phone, told Karl that he had a visitor, a Mrs Beryl Norris. He listened and then told her, 'Mr Stolzenbach says to go straight up, madam. He is on Room 86 on the second floor.'

'Thank you.' Beryl took a deep breath before clutching her handbag tightly to her and heading for the lift. Minutes later she stood hesitantly outside Karl's room, then drawing herself up to her full height, she tapped on the door.

It opened almost instantly. 'Ah, Beryl,' Karl said courteously. Do come in.'

Beryl unbuttoned her coat and placed her bag on the floor before settling into a chair and staring at him solemnly.

'I know what happened yesterday,' she said straight out. 'And I also know why Adina sent you away.'

'She sent me away because she does not love me any more,' he said bitterly. 'Not that I can blame her. She must hate me for the way I treated her all those years ago, but I swear to you, Beryl, I went home to circum-stances I could not easily turn my back on – but I never stopped loving her.'

'And *she* never stopped loving you,' Beryl said bluntly. 'Why else would she have worn your ring all these years?' She swiped her hand across her forehead and went on, 'I've come here to tell you something. Now listen to me . . .'

Long before she had finished, tears were rolling unchecked down Karl's cheeks. But she had only told him what she felt he needed to know; she had not breathed a word about Melly being his daughter. That could only come from Adina, if and when she wished to tell him. And if he decided to stay, that was.

'I can hardly believe it,' he muttered brokenly. 'She would have sent me away and faced the end alone.'

'Only because she felt that you'd been through enough, having to nurse your wife until she died,' Beryl pointed out. Then rising, she buttoned her coat again and lifted her bag before heading for the door. 'I've done what I came to do,' she told him quietly. 'It's up to you now, but I thought you deserved to know.'

He took her hand and squeezed it. 'Thank you, Beryl. You are indeed a true friend.'

She snorted nervously. 'Yes, well . . . Let's just hope that Adina thinks so too. The ball is in your court now, Karl. Goodbye.'

She hurried away as he stood there with his mind racing. A long time ago he had let Adina down badly, but now at last he had a chance to make it up to her – if she would allow him to.

Epilogue

'Karl . . .'

'Yes, mein Liebling?' Karl kissed Adina's feverishly hot fingers and leaned closer over the bed where she lay with her dark hair fanned out across the pillow like a halo.

'I . . . I have something I must tell you.'

He smiled at her adoringly. They had been married by special licence four and half months before at Camden Town Hall. Ariel and Brian and their family had travelled down from the Midlands to be there and Karl's children had flown in from Germany. Delighted to see their father so happy, the pair had been more than willing to give the couple their blessing. Beattie had attended too, sniffing all through the service into an enormous white handkerchief, along with Rebekah and Esther, and of course Melly and Richard, who had now both finished their training and were happily settled in Devon.

Adina had looked absolutely stunning in the wedding gown she had made so many years ago, although it was vastly different now. She had shortened it to calf length and wore it with a natty little hat, insisting that she was far too old for a long dress and veil now. Karl looked dapper in a new dark suit that he had bought especially for the occasion.

For the first three months of their marriage they had been deliriously happy, both only too well aware that they must make every second count. During that time they had packed in more laughter and love than many married couples shared in a whole lifetime. But for the last six weeks Adina had slowly deteriorated and Karl knew now that the end was near, and he wondered how he would bear it.

Now he looked towards one of the two nurses he had employed to care for Adina round the clock and asked, 'Would you mind giving us a moment alone?'

'Of course not. I'll be down in the kitchen if you need me,' she replied pleasantly.

Once the door had closed behind her he turned back to Adina and said softly, 'What is it you wish to tell me then, that is so important?'

She stared up at him for a moment with her eyes full of the love she felt for him, before turning away and saying in a small voice, 'I have kept a secret from you, Karl. I never intended to tell you, but now I feel that you have a right to know. I've had a lot of time to think, lying here, and I believe I now know why I never received the letter you sent to me when you returned home after the war. I know it was forwarded on from Mrs Downes at the school in Nuneaton because she told me so. But I believe that old Mrs Montgomery intercepted it when it arrived here.'

'But why would she do such a thing?'

Adina sighed. 'She had a good reason not to want you to return for me, but all will be revealed in the letter I have written for you. It's in the bedside drawer here, but I want you to promise that you won't read it until I have gone.'

He began to speak, but she raised a gentle finger to his lips and silenced him. 'Shush now. You will understand when you read the letter, and if you will only make this one last promise to me, I shall die content. What you choose to do once you have read it is up to you, but I pray that you will forgive me for not telling you my secret sooner.'

'Of course I will promise. But there is nothing I could not forgive you for, my darling,' he muttered brokenly, and then he gathered her into his arms until eventually Melly entered the room bearing a laden tea tray. She had travelled from Devon to be with them three days ago when Karl had phoned to tell her that Adina had taken a turn for the worse, and she had been like a ray of sunshine in the house ever since. Nothing was too much trouble for her. Adina had fretted about the fact that Melly had had to leave Richard in Devon, but the girl had laughed away her concerns.

'Oh, Richard will be fine,' she'd assured her. 'It will make him appreciate me all the more when I get home, if he has to fend for himself for a while.' And so Adina lay back, content to know that even if it was only for a short time, she had her husband and daughter under the same roof.

She would watch them and feel a warm glow of satisfaction as she noted how alike they were in temperament as well as in nature. She had recently contacted her solicitor, who had then visited her, and she had made some slight changes to her Will. The house would still go to Melly, but on the understanding that Karl would be allowed to stay there whenever he wished. She supposed that once she was gone he would divide his time between London and Germany, and she needed to know that she had provided accommodation for him should this be the case. She had also left instructions on how she wished her funeral to be conducted, even down to the choice of music, hoping that it would take some of the stress of having to arrange it all from Karl. And now all she needed to do was have a final chat with Beryl – and the chance for that came later that afternoon when her friend called in for what had become, over the last weeks, her daily visit.

Knowing how close the two women were, everyone discreetly disappeared when she arrived, and gave them some space, and when Beryl left after almost an hour, she was crying. She had the strongest premonition that she would never see Adina alive again.

The following morning, Karl, who had fallen asleep in the chair at the side of his wife's bed, felt a slight pressure on his fingers.

'Will you come and lie with me?' she whispered.

'Nothing would give me greater pleasure,' he assured her as he inched his large frame onto the bed, being careful not to hurt her. She was so fragile now.

He slipped his arm gently around her and she snuggled up to him contentedly. 'Do you know something Karl? I never dreamed I could be this happy.'

He smiled as they held each other and fell asleep together – and when he awoke, Adina Stolzenbach had gone to what he hoped was a better place.

Melly was inconsolable, as were Beattie and Beryl, and Ariel too, of course. But Karl felt strangely calm. His love for Adina had been such that he knew she would never be gone from him completely.

It was much later that evening, when his wife's body had been taken away by the undertaker, that he remembered about the letter. The house was quiet now and so he went upstairs and opened the bedside drawer and took the letter back downstairs to read. For a while he stared at her familiar handwriting on the envelope, and then he opened it and began to read.

My dearest love,

It is time to tell you of the secret I have kept from you all these years. When you returned to Germany I discovered that I was carrying our child.

She went on to tell him of all that had happened, and as the story unfolded, a sense of elation swept through him, although his heart broke afresh for everything his beloved Adina must have suffered. Now at last he understood why he had always felt such an affinity with Melly. She was his daughter, his firstborn child.

Whether or not you decide to tell Melly when you know the truth will be up to you, but if you do tell her please do not let her know that she was stolen from me. I have long since forgiven Fliss and Theo for what they did. They were wonderful parents to Melly and I know that she loved them devotedly. It would be too cruel to destroy the memories she has of them now and I trust you to give her an explanation of why I allowed them to keep her. You could perhaps tell her that I allowed them to adopt her because I knew that she would have a better life? But do please make sure that she knows how very much I loved her, and that I never stopped loving her; that on the day she walked back into my life she made me the proudest woman on earth. I know I can trust you to do this for me and you will find the right words when the time is right.

Remember me with fondness, my darling. You made me the happiest woman on earth and I wouldn't have traded a moment of our time together for a king's ransom.

I am waiting just beyond the door and one day it will open once more and we shall be together again for all time.

Your loving wife,

Adina xxxx

Karl screwed his eyes tightly shut as a terrible pain of anguish and loss stabbed at his heart, but then his mood lifted as he began to think of Melly. Adina would live on through their daughter.

Adina Stolzenbach was buried in Bushey Jewish Cemetery, according to her wishes. The same people who had assembled for her wedding were present at her funeral and it was a sombre affair, for all who had known her had come to love and respect her.

'I can still remember the very first day she ever set foot in the house when she was little more than a lass,' Beattie sobbed. 'But the girl had spirit and look what she became. She was an example to us all.'

Back at the house in Prince Regent Terrace, Beattie had laid on a funeral tea for anyone who wished to attend. When everyone had finally left, only Melly and Karl remained.

'I have something that Adina wished you to have,' he told her quietly now, and when he held out the shining steel band that he had made for Adina all those long years ago, Melly recognised it instantly.

Beryl had given it back to Adina just before she and Karl got married, for Adina had insisted that no other ring, not even one made of solid platinum, could ever take its place.

'B . . . but that's Adina's wedding ring!' Melly stuttered. 'She always wore it and I couldn't quite understand why she didn't have a new one when you and she got married?'

'Ah well, there is a story behind this band of steel, my little one. And now it is time I told it to you. Come . . .'

Then placing his arm protectively about his daughter, Karl sat her down and began to speak. Adina had left him the most precious legacy of all.